MURDER
IN MAYFAIR

BOOKS BY VERITY BRIGHT

MURDER
IN MAYFAIR

VERITY BRIGHT

bookouture

Published by Bookouture in 2024

An imprint of Storyfire Ltd.
Carmelite House
50 Victoria Embankment
London EC4Y 0DZ

www.bookouture.com

ISBN: 978-1-83525-569-8
eBook ISBN: 978-1-83525-566-7

'He who tells a lie is not sensible of how great a task he undertakes; for he must be forced to invent twenty more to maintain that one.'

∼ Alexander Pope

1

Surely not, Ellie? We've only been at this exhibit a few minutes!

Lady Eleanor Swift tried to temper her independent spirit and listen more enthusiastically to the young man gesturing at the head of the crowd.

'Onwards, ladies and gentlemen! We are not yet halfway through our tour of the fifty-six colonies, dominions and protectorates represented in magnificent splendour at this first ever British Empire Exhibition held here in Wembley, only ten miles from the centre of London itself!' Sporting an eye-catching red, white and blue striped blazer, her ardent guide waved at the small group in front of him to gain their full attention. Eleanor winced in sympathy.

There must be at least a hundred thousand people here, Ellie. The noise is deafening. No wonder he's having trouble being heard.

She dragged her bright, green-eyed gaze away from the vast, ornate Burmese temple she'd been admiring. Like all the pavilions and palaces, it had been built solely for the occasion. Its exquisite architecture set in sculptured gardens seeming so incongruous against the sooty sprawl of Wembley, which lay just beyond the immense exhibition site.

Awe-inspiring though the building was with its forty-foot pyramid-shaped central roof, she really wanted to leave her tour and over-zealous guide and meet the native Burmese exhibitors inside the temple. To chat about their lives, their families, and their dreams back in their homeland. She felt a frisson of discomfort at the thought of them, along with all the other 'exhibitors' in the pavilions, having been dragged halfway across the world. And all so she and every other visitor could gawp at them in an apparently authentic diorama of 'everyday life' back in their homeland. Everyday life which, the exhibition literature and guides repeatedly informed the visitors, had been vastly improved by becoming part of the great British Empire. Indeed, the brochure she carried stated one of the exhibition's main aims was to 'foster a closer friendship among the peoples of the British Commonwealth of Nations'. She wondered, a little cynically, from what she had seen so far, if treating them as exhibits in a zoo was really the best way to achieve that?

'This way. Please keep up,' the guide hollered from halfway across the wide tarmacadamed causeway, urgently waving his parasol emblazoned with flags. Once she'd dodged the river of other sightseers to reach the group, he held his arms out.

'In stepping across this, one of many purpose-built pedestrian streets on the exhibition site, miraculously, we will be transported six thousand miles from Burma to West Africa!'

A moment later, he swept his arm around the tall sandstone walls and huddle of straw-topped huts. Pointing at the ring of black-skinned men in vibrant orange robes bent over the baskets they were weaving in their laps, he held up three fingers on his other hand. 'Three minutes here to witness life in a typical African Gold Coast setting and then we are off to India!'

Eleanor's fiery-red curls swung out from her sage-velvet cloche hat as she shook her head. All eyes except hers jerked right at the trumpeting roar of elephants herding past on the other side of the arch in the walled enclosure. Thankful for the distraction, she sidled further to the back of their tour group. It was time to sneak away and finally talk to the exhibitors on her own.

Before she could, a policeman passed by, reminding her how much she was missing her fiancé's company. Also a policeman, a detective chief inspector, he was forever caught up in matters far too serious to grant him a free afternoon to idle away with her. Although, ironically, he was somewhere at the exhibition at that moment. She shook herself. *Snap out of it, Ellie. Hugh is only here because King George and other royal and foreign dignitaries are attending the opening days. It's an honour he's been appointed to head up police security. Poor chap's already apologised enough for having no hope of being free to meet up for even a snatched sip of coffee.*

'If we might move on now?'

A ring of thin-lipped expressions met her gaze.

'Oh, do please continue,' she said to her group. 'I shall catch you up in a jiffy... possibly.'

The guide's eyes widened in panic. 'But, madam, er, miss, supposing you don't find us? The exhibition site covers two hundred and sixteen acres and is a maze of enormous buildings. The Palace of Engineering occupies thirteen acres alone. And the stadium can accommodate one hundred and twenty-five thousand people at a time. I mean, imagine what might happen!'

'Let's think.' She pulled a thoughtful face, then held a finger up. 'I know! I would simply make my own way around all the palaces, pavilions, and stands. And I'd still arrive at the Palace of Industry before nightfall, where my butler will be waiting with a raft of sniffy admonishments about my lateness in keeping our rendezvous, no doubt. Which, incidentally, will make his day all the better,' she added with a quiet smile of affection.

'But,' the young man's lips flapped disappointedly, 'travel experiences of the most exquisite, and extraordinary kind, await on this tour. Without a guide, you'll miss so many of the instructive lessons available in each exhibit.'

'Perhaps,' she said, fighting a frown. 'Or perhaps I'll decide for myself if what I am seeing is accurate. "Authentic everyday life" indeed!' she muttered to herself.

Her guide shook his head. 'Travel is only valuable when—'

'When you follow your heart and see first-hand a country's traditional ways of living.' She regarded him quizzically. 'University graduate?'

'Almost.' He patted his chest, then shrugged. 'Well, next year isn't so far away, really.'

'No. Travelled much during the holidays, have you?'

'Oh, extensively, for sure. Scotland and Wales twice each, you know. As well as England's south coast.'

She bit her tongue, ever thankful for her own numerous years of travelling the world under her own steam. 'Then, I wish you the opportunity to journey further afield so you can see even a snippet more of the world in all its genuine wonder.'

He raised his eyebrows. 'But I am. That's why I took this temporary job here as a guide.' He pointed at the cluster of huts. 'I had no idea what the Gold Coast and its inhabitants look like. Or what they do all day long. Now I do.'

'Mmm. When I was there some years ago, a great deal of the country had been developing strongly for many decades. Particularly in medical advancements. And their foreign trade has been thriving for centuries. This' – she waved at the huts – 'may still be typical in rural areas, but it's quite different in the towns and cities.'

His jaw fell. 'Goodness!'

She nodded with a genial smile. 'And now, once you've told

me your name, I shall skip off to explore here by myself. No slight on your marvellous efforts.'

'My name?' He tugged on his blazer cuffs. 'Percy Hedges.'

'Thank you, Percy. My first stop will be the tour booking office. To tell them what a splendid and exemplary guide you've been.'

'Really? Oh, thanks!' Looking relieved, he pointed eagerly across at the opposite archway. 'The office is left, then right past Bermuda, then East Africa and Nigeria. You'll see it after crossing the railway bridge, just before the Ceylon Pavilion, miss. Next to the Mackintosh's Toffee kiosk. They built the railway purely for the exhibition, you know.'

'Yes, I do.' To his evident surprise, she shook his hand. 'You'd best hurry on to India with the rest of your party, with my apologies for keeping everyone waiting.'

As the guide and his group were swept away by the tide of humanity, she stepped under the arch he'd pointed out. Immediately, her brow furrowed. Had he said left or right?

'Dash it! Why do I never listen properly to directions?' she grumbled aloud. Plumping for right, she strode on determinedly.

The next enclosure, however, wasn't listed as the Bermuda Pavilion. Nor did it seem grand enough to represent an admittedly small archipelago of islands, but ones which her endlessly knowledgeable butler had told her were strategically important for the British Empire. The only sign read, 'Sorry. Closed until further notice'. She peered through a gap in the tall wooden doors set in pale-cream brick walls, only to realise they were, in fact, locked gates. An expanse of sandy earth, peppered with barrels and precariously high stacks of hay bales, ran down to a half-completed, two-storey, colonial-style building. A scattering of creamy-coated goats mooched amongst it all.

Mystified, she retraced her steps to the archway of the Gold Coast Pavilion and turned left instead. Along the way, it was impossible not to stop and gaze in wonder at the magnificent buildings built especially for each of the countries represented. Bermuda's was undoubtedly the smallest she'd seen so far. Yet it was still the size of an eight-bedroomed house. East Africa's vast pavilion was a dramatic white-walled enclosure flanked by towers four storeys high. But there was something captivatingly special about Nigeria's monumental pink-sandstone-walled pavilion which made her heart skip at the atmosphere of mystique and romance it exuded.

She stopped, realising she was trying to take in too much, too quickly. She reminded herself she was staying at the Ritz for the night, so tomorrow she could take all the time in the world to wander at will. Happier, she hurried on, still looking for the tour office.

Twenty minutes later, her duty was done, her honest praise over young Percy's merits as the epitome of a British Empire tour guide delivered. Now free to please herself, she paused to enjoy the sight of fine-tailored suits and fur-trimmed ladies' coats streaming by. And rubbing shoulders with them, mismatched working-class jackets, flat caps and neatly patched Sunday-best dresses. Evidently, the minimal ticket price of one shilling and sixpence had been effective in encouraging everyone to visit and be awed by the magnificence and far-reach of the Empire.

This reminded her of the other reason she had come. A few years ago, her beloved uncle, on dying, had bequeathed her not only his country estate in the rolling English countryside, but also the most loyal and dedicated team of staff. Headed up, of course, by her butler, Clifford. He had been her uncle's stead-fast batman in the army, long-serving butler in civil life, and staunch confidante in his personal one, despite their class differ-ence. Recently Clifford had announced that an annuity her uncle had invested in, to secure funds for refurbishing Henley Hall, had matured. And she had only one genuine wish for how the money should be spent. Which accounted for her plea to Clifford that the ladies had the day off to accompany him and her to the exhibition, before returning on the evening train.

She glanced at her watch. She still had ages before they had arranged to meet.

'Ceylon or Hong Kong first?' she mused aloud, able to see the start of both pavilions from where she was standing. 'Hong Kong it is!'

'There's a surprise!' a familiar voice intoned from behind.

'Clifford!' She spun around to take in her ever impeccably black-suited butler, looking as distinguished as ever in his matching wool overcoat and bowler hat. 'We're not due to meet for ages yet.'

'Indeed. Not for some time hence, my lady.'

'Ha! So, even with me misplacing the map I realise you secreted in my pocket, all your respectful ribbing yesterday about my hopeless timekeeping was a waste of hot air.'

'Perhaps.' He slid the commemorative toffee tin and the large sheaf of promotional literature he was holding under one arm to hold up his pocket watch. 'However, bravo.'

'For what? Staying out of trouble, I suppose you mean, you terror?'

He shook his head, eyes bright with amusement. 'For managing to remain with the tour party I booked for you until almost the halfway point. Were I a betting man...' He left that hanging.

'Very droll.' She wagged a finger at him. 'You're going to have to up your wily ruses, you know.'

'Challenge accepted.' He whipped out his slim pocketbook and added a note.

'Lady Swift?' a taut female voice called. 'Oh, apologies, I must be mistaken.'

'No, it's me.' Eleanor spun around enquiringly. 'How lovely to see you again,' she said with extra gusto, recognising the unmistakable beauty and flawless elegance of the coiffured blonde dressed in a fur-trimmed wrap. The woman's name, however, eluded her. She discreetly flapped a mystified hand for help.

'Lady Philomena Chadwick,' her butler murmured without visibly moving his lips.

'What a coincidence to bump into each other somewhere so crowded,' Eleanor rolled on seamlessly. 'How are you, Lady Chadwick?'

'Well enough, thank you.'

The woman's manicured fingertips fiddled with the mink stole around her neck while she looked anywhere but at Eleanor. Having been the one to accost her, strangely, Lady Chadwick now seemed to have nothing to say.

Her awkward manner struck Eleanor as odd. If she hadn't wanted to chat, why hail her? She smiled, trying to put her at her ease. 'There's far too much to see, isn't there? I'm going to savour a couple more of its delights and then take a few minutes to have tea with my staff.'

'With your... well, really...' Lady Chadwick shook her head. 'You are just as I remembered, Lady Swift.'

Unsure if that was a positive statement or not, Eleanor waited with a polite smile to find out.

'Yes, quite the unorthodox member of high society.' Lady Chadwick's eyes scanned Eleanor's fiery-red curls, then flitted away as if afraid to be caught looking.

Still none the wiser, Eleanor shrugged. 'Is everything alright, Lady Chadwick?'

She hesitated, then sighed. 'Oh dear, not as I'd like. Though I shouldn't confess such to you. We've only met once at a charity luncheon.'

'That doesn't mean you shouldn't reach out,' Eleanor said encouragingly, her natural empathy surfacing. 'If you need a little... help, perhaps?'

Lady Chadwick blinked rapidly. 'Are you staying here for a while? In London, I mean?'

'I'm staying at the Ritz tonight, yes, so I can come back to enjoy the rest of the exhibition tomorrow.'

'Oh, then, I...' Lady Chadwick glanced away. 'I don't suppose you'd have a small window of time to meet for tea together tomorrow at all, would you?'

The true answer was a resounding no. Eleanor had planned way more for the following day than she could fit in already. 'Yes, of course,' she heard herself say without hesitation. 'Shall we have tea at the Ritz? Say half past five?'

'How marvellous!' The quietly determined Lady Chadwick Eleanor remembered meeting several months back seemed to have returned in a blink. 'Until then, Lady Swift. Good day.' With a flick of her fur-trimmed wrap, she stepped away into the crowds beyond the tea terrace, leaving Eleanor staring after her.

'What was that all about?' she muttered to Clifford. 'She seemed rather, well, troubled, is the first word which springs to mind. Which is why I agreed to meet her. We'll see less of the exhibition tomorrow now. Apologies, I may just have slightly railroaded your no-doubt meticulously worked out schedule.'

He shook his head. 'From previous experience, such an occurrence was entirely anticipated, my lady. Now, shall we then to Hong Kong's much talked of pavilion?'

'What a treat!' she said with genuine joy. 'You're going to accompany me?'

'If the lady wishes. I have not arranged to rendezvous with the remaining contingent of your staff for a while yet.'

'Yes, of course... wait a minute.' She folded her arms. 'Tell me you're not meeting them before we all get together so that you can pour a bucket of iced water on the list of suggestions I asked each of them, and you, to prepare?'

'I am not, my lady.'

She frowned, unconvinced. 'But only because the bucket would ruin the perfect line of your suit!'

He looked back at her impassively.

'Clifford,' she said pleadingly. 'I love Henley Hall just the way Uncle Byron left it to me. With all his wonderful and eccentric spirit imbued in every room. The only changes I will countenance making are those which make life easier for you and the ladies. You all work far too hard, purely on my account.'

'Too gracious, my lady.' He gestured forwards.

She flapped a hand for him to walk alongside her for once. 'Anyway, how did you know I'd choose Hong Kong before Ceylon? Ah! Because I never visited Hong Kong sailing with my parents as a child, nor on my solo travels later, I suppose?'

'On the contrary.' His eyes twinkled mischievously. 'Where else might my mistress be found scurrying to?'

She hid a smile. 'I don't "scurry", Clifford. I'm a titled lady, remember?'

He nodded mischievously. 'So it has been rumoured. However, Hong Kong would naturally win, being the only country's pavilion to include a restaurant!'

2

An hour later, Eleanor was far from done enthusing over the exotic wonders of Hong Kong's extraordinary exhibition area. And its mouth-watering restaurant fayre. Still, she followed her butler out, the rare chance to enjoy some downtime with all her staff proving an even stronger pull.

'What a fantastic experience that was, Clifford,' she enthused. 'I never imagined stepping under that stunning green-roofed entrance would propel us into such a bewitching stage-set of Hong Kong's magical architecture. All those exquisite scrolling wood screens on the walls and carved reliefs on the doors throughout. And all shipped here especially for the exhibition!' She nudged his elbow, making the intricately plaited bamboo basket now hanging on his forearm swing. 'You should definitely have relaxed your precious rule about not eating in front of your mistress. Everything I tried was sublime. And fancy them thinking to recreate two dozen shops from the actual main street in Hong Kong, as well as those four incredible display halls.'

'Fancy indeed, my lady,' he said drily. He made a show of peering into the bamboo basket at the myriad wrapped craft items she hadn't been able to resist buying. 'It was almost as if the vendors had been informed ahead of our arrival of a certain lady's predilection for shopping.' He tutted good-naturedly. 'And for spoiling her band of aproned elves. Whom, I thought we agreed, I would briefly meet on my own first?'

'Did we?' she said innocently. 'Anyway, don't think I haven't spotted that commemorative tin of toffees you've now secreted at the bottom of the basket. They're for the ladies to enjoy, aren't they, you closet softie?'

He said nothing, gesturing instead across the two hundred foot long artificial lake. 'Shall we? Assuming the ladies have actually made their way past the numerous distractions to the Palace of Industry's entrance, of course.'

As they crossed the stone footbridge over the eastern end of the lake, she paused. The sight of the two elephants she'd heard earlier now splashing in the shallow water brought an unexpected wash of fond memories from her previously adventurous life in South Africa. The one before her short-lived and disastrous marriage, that was. She laughed at the keepers calling hopelessly as they ran after their lumbering charges.

'Elephants are impossibly stubborn, you know, Clifford. Like butlers, I've learned.'

He scanned her face. 'The lure of adventure hasn't lost its lustre, perhaps?'

'Umm... I'm sure it has,' she said, unable to drag her gaze from the elephants.

'But not entirely, I fear,' her sharp hearing heard him murmur.

A few minutes later, despite the relentless hubbub of sightseers, Eleanor caught the sound of her ladies' raucous giggling before she could see them. Evidently, however, her fiery-red curls gave them the advantage at the last minute.

'Lawks, 'tis her ladyship and Mr Clifford, girls!' her cook's strident voice warned.

Clifford fixed the four women with a chiding look as they scurried into line to curtsey at Eleanor's arrival. She smiled between them, ever grateful such a wide range of ages, experience and personalities could work so well together. In truth, she knew a substantial part of it was due to Clifford's firm but fair hand in running his domain, the impeccably tight ship that was Henley Hall below stairs. Something he deserved all the medals of the Empire for, she thought. Along with her young maids, Polly and Lizzie, even her motherly, soft grey-haired housekeeper, Mrs Butters, was often led astray by her middle-aged cook's irrepressible sense of mischief. Much to Eleanor's quiet delight.

'Hello, ladies,' she said with a smile. 'What do you think of the exhibition so far?'

'Oh, my stars.' Mrs Butters pressed her hands to her navy-blue coat front. 'We'll none of us sleep for forever thinking back over all these treats our eyes have been feasting on, m'lady.'

'And the fancy buildings too, Butters,' her cook muttered with a saucy glint in her eye.

'Ahem, Mrs Trotman,' Clifford said firmly.

She smiled innocently. 'I only meant as well as all the wonderful products and new inventions on display, Mr Clifford.' Her words were rather undermined as she gawped after four strapping Canadian mounted policemen on chestnut thoroughbreds, resplendent in their unmissable red jackets.

Clifford sniffed pointedly. 'Her ladyship has graciously decided to join our earlier arranged rendezvous.'

She pretended to whisper behind her hand. 'Actually, ladies, Clifford has graciously not made too much fuss about me slithering along uninvited.'

Mrs Butters flustered forward with a quiet chuckle. 'The lady of the house can't ever have need of an invitation. But fancy wanting to spend extra time with the likes of us, m'lady.'

Mrs Trotman nodded. 'Specially after saying as you wanted

to hear the opinions of us aprons over ideas for new things as would be useful for Henley Hall!' She pulled a thick pad of paper from her coat pocket and waved it eagerly, which made Clifford's brows flinch, Eleanor noted.

'I absolutely do.' She threw her butler a consoling look. 'From each of you. Though there might be some restraints that our resident household accounts expert will need to guide us on. But hopefully, not too many.'

All eyes swivelled pleadingly to Clifford who stroked his chin. 'Hmm, five ladies let loose on the idea of shopping? How could that possibly work within budgetary restraints...' He lightened his tone at their crestfallen faces. 'Rest assured, getting to grips with all the "newfangleds" as I believe you call them, Polly, will be the most arduous task, I'm sure. Doubtless, her ladyship might be persuaded to attend the demonstration ceremony when you have?'

She laughed. 'Absolutely! It would save me slithering along uninvited. Again!'

Realising that her butler was trying to catch her eye, she groaned. 'Let me guess, we're running out of time?'

He waved his pocket watch. 'Only if you wish to enjoy the hot-air balloon experience booked for thirty-five minutes hence?'

'Ooh, I definitely do. But we haven't even looked at the ladies' list of ideas yet.'

'And a good job, too.' He held up a placating hand at the collective gasp from all five women. 'Because, given its importance, perhaps it is better postponed until sufficient time can be properly lavished upon it?'

She nodded vehemently.

He closed his pocket watch. 'Which means we just have time for you to enjoy a tea and cake session. Disgracefully, with your wayward band of elves, no doubt.'

In a trice, Eleanor found herself seated outside one of the

bustling tea room terraces. Knowing better than to beckon her ladies forward to sit before they had been given Clifford's permission, she busied herself getting settled.

A flurry of gruff shouts caught her attention. She flinched as an ebony-skinned boy of perhaps eleven or twelve shot out of the crowd and dashed towards her, his expression fearful. Hot on his heels, a sinewy man in a colourful robe stumbled after him in backless sandals, barking words she couldn't understand. His intention, however, seemed painfully clear. She quickly rose and stepped forward, recoiling a moment later at the force of the impact. The boy caught her eye gratefully as he darted on to be swallowed up by the crowds.

'Oops, how clumsy of us both,' she said innocently.

The man's only reply was a curt jerk of his gaunt chin below his unsettling amber-eyed glare. After scanning around for the boy, he turned and slouched away back the way he'd come.

Clifford raised an eyebrow, but said nothing. She shrugged.

'He looked as if he was going to give him a thrashing when he caught him.'

'Which the lad may well deserve, my lady, unless you can testify otherwise?'

She bit her lip. 'No, in truth, I don't know what he might have done to anger that man. But he was only young.'

'And from the Gold Coast too, perchance? If the colours of the gentleman's robe are any guide to his nationality?' He placed the tray down. 'My lady, the ways of other nations are theirs alone to decree. A tenet I know you hold staunchly.'

Feeling abashed, she sat back down. He turned and gave a barely there flick of one gloved finger, which prompted an excited flurry among the ladies as they hurried to take their places. Except the ever-wide-eyed young Polly, who needed a coaxing tug from Mrs Trotman. 'Park your skirts, my girl. 'Tis alright, Mr Clifford has said so.'

He raised a hand as Eleanor's housekeeper reached towards the tea things. 'Thank you, Mrs Butters, but her ladyship was quite clear in her instructions that you four be released from your duties today. I shall play mother, therefore.' He peered sideways at Eleanor. 'On this singular occasion.'

'Oh, what a pity, Butters.' Mrs Trotman nudged her friend. 'After we spent so long admiring all those new designs of floral aprons with a clever crossover front. We should have picked one out for Mr Clifford. How would that have been, sir?'

He shuddered. 'As heartily unwelcome as it would be undignified, Mrs Trotman.'

Eleanor tried to stifle her chuckle at the image of her ever-impeccably attired butler bedecked in a flowery housecoat, but was too caught up in her ladies' infectious laughter.

'Five against one, I see, my lady,' he murmured good-naturedly as he placed a slice of Victoria sponge cake on her plate using two forks as impromptu silver tongs. 'Again!'

'It's your own fault for being such a good sport,' she whispered back. 'And talking of singular occasions, might you break your most precious rule and take a seat and at least a sip of tea too?' She beamed around the table as he perched reluctantly on the edge of the chair beside her. 'Now, tell me, Mrs Butters, what was everyone's favourite thing you've seen so far?'

'Well, m'lady,' her housekeeper said as Clifford topped up Eleanor's tea. 'Polly, she loved everything. And Lizzie loved the beautiful, castle-like buildings. They remind her of home back in Scotland. And Trotters—'

Clifford held up a hand. 'I think we'll skip Mrs Trotman's favourite thing, which I'm sure will be too indecorous for the ears of her ladyship.'

Eleanor's cook tried to look indignant. 'Actually, Mr Clifford, 'tis the butter statue of the Prince of Wales.' She pointed at the maids. 'We couldn't drag these two young'uns away for forever gawping at it.'

'We weren't much better, mind,' Eleanor's housekeeper said, as the four of them started giggling uncontrollably. 'Who'd have thought it?'

Eleanor looked at Clifford in confusion. 'I must have misheard?'

He shook his head, lips twitching. 'I can assure you not, my lady. The Canadian authorities have indeed included such in their pavilion. To showcase their remarkable new refrigeration system, it seems.'

'And his highness is even dressed in his smart buttoned jacket and boots,' Mrs Trotman managed through her laughter.

'And leaning on an enormous horse!' Polly gasped, holding her sides.

Along with her ladies, Eleanor's shoulders shook with the force of her laughter. 'A statue of Prince Edward, Clifford? And... and his horse? Made entirely out of...'

'Butter. Yes, my lady.' Even Clifford's usually implacable composure threatened to falter.

'Ow, that hurts. It's too funny,' Eleanor finally managed.

'Indeed. Perhaps, however, we should restrain our mirth before we are requested to leave.' He discreetly indicated several heads that had turned their way. 'Now, might we hasten to the main event so you may step into the balloon with some hint of ladylike decorum? Rather than hare disgracefully through the exhibition ground after it to scale its trailing rope into the basket like a monkey?'

She laughed. 'I'm sure you're not supposed to compare your mistress to a monkey! Although,' she added ruefully, 'I've been compared to worse.'

'Why ever could that be?' her butler muttered mischievously as they set off.

3

Hastening anywhere with the swarming masses attending the exhibition was no easy task, however.

'We need to divert off the grand Kingsway Parade, which serves as the main north–south artery to the open-air stadium, my lady.'

She nodded in agreement. 'We're going nowhere here. There must be a less crowded way to get to the balloon launch site?'

'There is. I think. We'll just have to risk fewer visitors using Commonwealth Way and then Pacific Slope.'

He waved for Eleanor's already panting ladies to catch up. Even her longer than average legs, however, were struggling to keep pace with his extended stride.

She shook her head. 'Clifford, the poor things look exhausted. I could sprint on ahead if—'

'Or, you could not!' he interrupted with a sniff. 'If you will excuse the suggestion. This exhibition is intended as a celebration of the Empire's grandeur, not a showcase for a certain lady's distressing ability to hurl decorum to the bottom of the lake.'

'Spoilsport,' she teased through her shortened breaths. 'Especially after all my years in South Africa, I could probably coax one of the elephants to rescue me from the watery depths. Purely to save your impeccable butlering togs from a soaking, of course.' She pointed across a small park area with a striking gold-topped bandstand at its centre. 'Look, the two of them are still having an absolute ball in there.'

'Having marauded uncaptured almost the entire lake's length,' he tutted over the elephants' continual trumpeting, then called over his shoulder, 'Not far now, ladies. Quick steps, please.'

Five minutes later, Eleanor couldn't deny she was secretly pleased Clifford had insisted they and the ladies stuck together. Arriving as one made the spectacle so much more magical as she rounded the last corner, emerging near the red carpet lined with gold posts. Threading her way through the crowd of onlookers, she stared up at the vast rainbow-striped hot-air balloon which had been obscured by the huge pavilion buildings until now. The sporadic bursts of the flaming burner caused the silk outer shell to shimmer in the afternoon sun above the circular open stage, which was painted as a map of the world, the British Empire picked out in eye-catching pink-red.

Dwarfed as it bobbed just off the ground, the balloon's woven basket was adorned with silk flags of the Empire's dominions fringed with voluptuous, matching tassels. Even the four thick restraining ropes at each corner, being valiantly wrestled by teams of three stocky men in bright waistcoats, were coloured red, white and blue. As was the criss-cross net which enveloped the balloon's canopy to run down to the corners of the basket's wide top rim. She stared in awe and turned to her butler.

'Clifford? Be honest. What's your real reason for mutinying and not coming up with me? You love this sort of thing.'

His lips pursed. '"Abstaining", my lady. If you will forgive the correction. "Mutinying" is the province of undisciplined and unprincipled crews of the high seas.' He hesitated. 'If you really must know, his lordship would likely have bowed out of accompanying you just as much as I.' He lowered his voice. 'The two of us barely survived a most... harrowing escape in such a balloon some decades ago. Having, ahem, needed to render our pilot unconscious at significant altitude.'

'On one of Uncle Byron's mysterious adventures?' she breathed, desperate to know more.

He nodded with a shudder. 'Though the memory of that one haunts like only yesterday, I will admit.'

'Say no more,' she said quickly. 'But apologies for unwittingly raking it up.'

'Just a short delay before launch, good folks!' a ruddy-faced man called through a brass loudhailer. He was dressed in pilot's goggles, thick leather gloves and a cumbersome ankle-length fawn coat. 'A slight adjustment to the burner is needed, but ticket holders can join me in the meantime.'

She hurried forward, politely declining any help from the grinning assistant. Bypassing the gold-painted footstool, she slid lithely over the side and into the basket. The creaking of the ropes as they took up the strain reminded her of being aboard her parents' sailing boat, her home until their disappearance when she was nine. The flutter of the silk flags reminded her of the whisper of the sails at night as the yacht slipped across exotic moonlit seas to another dawn of wondrous delight. For a moment, she had a child-like urge to cut the ropes and sail away like a picture-book princess.

Her reverie was interrupted by the other passengers boarding. Now, sandwiched in at close quarters with five smart-suited men and two plump ladies in lavishly trimmed pink and apricot coats respectively, the atmosphere became charged with a mixture of excitement and apprehension. One of the ladies sported a mink stole which reminded her of her odd meeting with Lady Chadwick.

What was *that all about, Ellie?*

But then the pilot's words dismissed all thought of Lady Chadwick from her mind.

'Up we go, ladies and gentlemen! Hold on at all times.' He caught Eleanor's eye and chuckled. 'And no dancing, please. We're a spectacle enough already, you know!'

The burner roared fiercely as he signalled to the men holding the ropes to let go. The basket flexed with a plaintive groan, swayed alarmingly, and then rose with unexpected speed, leaving below a sea of open-mouthed onlookers.

'Mind the shackle on the drag rope swinging at the back there,' the pilot called, staring up into the balloon's canopy. 'It's one hundred and ten feet long. Weighs just short of forty pounds. Normally it would be coiled into the sling bag on the rear in case we needed to lose height quickly. But here at the exhibition, we won't be going too high. Nor leaving this grassed area. The drag rope is paid out to the ground so the anchormen can hang on to the end, ten feet between them. That way, our balloon will only travel in a wide circle to give you a three-hundred-and-sixty degree bird's-eye view of the wonder that is the Empire Exhibition!'

Spotting Clifford's unmissable commanding frame between her four ladies, now already fifty or more feet below, she waved her hat. As it sailed out of her hand she winced, imagining her butler's dismayed tutting. Which given the peculiar hush at their altitude, she felt she would probably hear. Despite the relentlessly surging mass of people below, up in the basket, only the creak of wicker and swoosh of wind through the balloon swirled around them. And the fierce roar of the burner when the pilot turned it up.

'Just look at the India Pavilion from up here. Magnificent!' one woman called to the others.

This prompted the rest of the passengers to herd across and cram together to see the spectacle. Except Eleanor, who automatically pressed herself the other way to counter the lurch of the basket. Her slender form, however, had little impact.

'Good grief, folks!' the pilot shouted, flapping a gloved hand wildly. 'You can't all stand in the same corner!'

Eleanor nodded. 'How about two of us take a side each and call out the sights? We'll turn in a circle anyway, so no one will miss anything.'

'Spiffing idea,' said one man who was looking a tad green around the gills. Evidently a desk-bound life and impromptu air travel were unhappy bedfellows, she thought sympathetically.

Soon everyone was evenly distributed in the basket again, much to the pilot's relief.

She stared down over the array of sculpted towers, castellations and palatial façades.

'It's like the most exquisite model village, isn't it?' Eleanor called to the others. 'I feel as if I'm Gulliver having arrived in Lilliput. I can see Malaya and Sarawak's beautiful pavilions.'

'We've got British Guiana and Malta,' one man croaked, pulling on his necktie like a man with stage fright. Beside him, his companion tutted. 'Ceylon and South Africa, actually!'

'We've got Australia, I believe,' one woman called. 'So captivating.'

'I say, should they be doing that?' the queasy-looking man muttered in a worried tone.

Eleanor frowned. 'Who? And what?'

'The elephants. They're rampaging!'

Eleanor risked leaning over the side to look. 'They're just having a water fight,' she called reassuringly. 'A rather forceful one, mind,' she added as a large swathe of onlookers below fled the arcs of water the elephants were now squirting in every direction. 'They'll calm down when they're ready.'

'But not before they've destroyed the exhibition! Look, they're charging out of the lake!'

Eleanor couldn't actually deny that, but was comforted knowing Clifford would be looking after her ladies.

Her comfort was short-lived, however, as one elephant headed directly for the area under the balloon, pursued by its trumpeting mate. The men holding the balloon's anchor rope dropped it and scarpered in every direction.

'Folks!' their pilot yelled. 'We're about to go on an unscheduled flight!'

The balloon shot upwards and drifted away from the launch site on the stiffening breeze.

Unhelpfully, the panic in the pilot's voice seemed to have infected most of Eleanor's fellow passengers, who were futilely shouting over the side for help, or arguing with each other. His efforts to calm them were hampered by his own, rather foolish admission she thought, that he had little control over the untethered balloon's path!

But hopefully, Ellie, not insufficient skill to land safely.

Below, the elephants had come to a stop and were busy wrenching the flower garlands from the carefully prepared displays along the main thoroughfare. She bobbed down instinctively when the basket momentarily plummeted thirty feet before swinging wildly back up as the burner roared like a dragon, lighting up the increasing worry on their pilot's face. She recoiled as the queasy man leaned over the side, making a horrible noise. The two women clutched their scarves over their mouths. Almost immediately, she felt their wicker chariot dive again, even lower this time. As it rose, the passengers rounded on the pilot.

'Can't you fly this wretched thing properly?' the larger of the two women said scathingly.

'Never mind that!' the pilot shouted back angrily. 'You'll

throw us all out if you crowd around me! Stay spread out in the basket and stay calm, for Pete's sake! We'll land when we can.'

'Don't speak to my wife like that!' the man nearest her growled.

'Please! Everyone!' Eleanor called soothingly. 'We'll be fine if we do as the pilot asks, I'm sure. Now, try and enjoy the view. We're flying over—'

'Drifting dangerously close over!'

'Flying a little low over,' she said firmly, trying to hide her grimace as the basket sailed uncomfortably near to the pink sandstone turrets of the Nigeria Pavilion. 'The wonderful African display area.'

It's really rather a magical bonus, this unexpected flight, Ellie. If only the others would stop panicking and enjoy it, too.

The woman who seemed to have made herself spokeswoman for the other passengers rounded on the pilot again. 'I demand you set us down immediately!'

He glowered at her. 'Where, exactly? On top of one of the pavilion roofs? Or perhaps on the main thoroughfare? We'd only kill or injure a dozen or so people, I reckon. No, we'll just have to keep going until we find somewhere safe to land.'

Eleanor winced as the passengers erupted into renewed panic, the other woman fainting on the spot.

Oh dear, Ellie.

'Has anyone any smelling salts?' she called. 'If not, pat her hands repeatedly and fan her face with your hats, gentlemen.'

The woman being taken care of, she craned over the side again, scouring the ground, hoping to help the pilot find a suitable landing place. A moment later, she spotted the village of straw-topped huts which supposedly depicted the true Gold Coast. And then the closed-up display area she had mistakenly arrived at instead of Bermuda.

That expanse of sandy earth, Ellie. It's perfect. It even has stacks of hay bales, which would at least soften a crash landing.

She turned to holler to the pilot, but a flash of movement behind one haystack caught her eye.

Dash it, Ellie! We can't land on the poor goats that were mooching about before.

She frowned, craning her neck further out. It hadn't been a goat she'd seen. In fact, there were no animals in the compound now at all.

The basket tipped as it dropped, causing more panic among her fellow passengers as they herded to the other side. Ignoring them, she stayed where she was. Directly below, two suited men were facing each other behind a haystack. She felt her shoulders stiffen. Something in their equally aggressive stances signalled trouble. The man on the left was holding something up in one hand, his other hidden by the hay bales, but his box-square face seemed grimly set. She squinted, but it was too far away to see what he was holding.

Then she saw the flash of a gun barrel thrust forward by the other man. Before she could cry out, the balloon's burner burst into life. Both men glanced up and then back down, the man on the left instantly falling to the dirt like a lifeless stone.

'No!' Her cry was drowned out by the roar from the burner. As the balloon drifted onwards, she closed her eyes, the image of the gunman's pockmarked cheek imprinted on her mind.

'We have to land!' Eleanor cried, pointing over the basket's side to emphasise the urgency.

The pilot wrenched his attention away from the other passengers who were still shouting stridently. 'Listen, lady. Don't you go hysterical on me too!'

'But you don't understand,' she cried more forcefully, spinning back around to track the movements of the gunman. 'Oh, no! We've drifted too far already!' She hauled the thick drag rope aside to scour the ground below better. 'You must land. Now!'

The pilot shook his head. 'No can do. There's a problem with the burner, so just calm down!'

'Calm down?' she said through gritted teeth. 'A man has just been shot! He must need urgent medical attention.'

Assuming he's still alive, Ellie. Or the gunman doesn't finish him off.

The pilot wasn't listening, as the other passengers had crowded around him again, the men shouting about the burner, the woman shrieking. Her brow knitted. None of them had reacted when the man fell, so they couldn't have seen what she had. And the noise of the gun firing must have been masked by the sound of the burners for those in the balloon, and by the elephants for those on the ground. She opened her mouth to shout again, but quickly closed it. The pilot obviously couldn't land and the passengers were panicked enough as it was. She stared over the side, struggling to keep her bearings on the fatal walled enclosure as the balloon drifted ever further away.

Seeing everyone spread out around the basket again at the pilot's urging, she stepped forward and tapped him on the arm.

'How long will it take to fix the burner?'

He shrugged. 'Can't say. One of the valves is stuck open, so it's filling the balloon's canopy with hot air faster than I can let it out through the vent.'

'Then estimate how long!'

'Twenty minutes,' he said grudgingly. 'Maybe more. And plenty longer if you don't back off and let me work on it!'

That's too long, Ellie.

Her gaze fell on the trailing end of the drag rope following in the balloon's wake. She watched it slinking up and over the domed tops of the display buildings and myriad kiosks as the balloon continued to rise and dip erratically.

That's it, Ellie! It's the only chance of helping the shot man.

'Pilot?' she called, staring ahead at the red and gold flat roofs approaching. 'Prepare to compensate for the weight loss of one passenger.'

'What the deuce?' he hollered back. 'I've no parachutes to hand out!'

'We're way too low for one anyway, I think. What height are we now?'

'Seventy feet or slightly less. But—'

'No time.' She was already wrenching at a long length of rope that secured the decorative flags along the basket's sides. Hearing her father's voice in her thoughts, her fingers threw together the body bowline harness he'd insisted she memorise as a child on their yacht. Looping the longest end around the drag rope in front of her, she added a tight figure of eight knot at chest level. Giving it a tug, she nodded.

Hopefully, that should stop you hurtling to the ground, Ellie.

She pointed at the pilot. 'How tall would you say the top of the red Mackintosh Toffee stands are? The ones with the steps up to the roof made from other toffee tins? Quickly.'

He frowned. 'Thirty to thirty-five feet. But it's positive madness if you're thinking...'

She shook her head vehemently. 'No, it's not. I have to get down there fast.'

She realised the other passengers were listening to the exchange open-mouthed.

Seeming to accept the inevitable, the pilot waved his gloved hand at her. 'I can buy you possibly ten feet by jamming the valve to make us drop that far. But only for a moment or so. More than that and we risk it exploding.'

'Perfect. And once on the ground, I'll try and hang on to the rope's end long enough to get some stout men to bring the balloon to a stop.' She spun around. 'Now, everyone, trust our pilot. Do as he says and you'll be fine.'

'But will you be, my lady?' she heard Clifford's concerned voice in her head. Ignoring it and the collective gasp from the passengers, she eased herself onto the rim of the basket, legs dangling outside.

'Good luck, madam!' one man called.

She nodded, confident at least that learning to descend the mast safely on her parents' yacht would stand her in good stead. She took a deep breath, having no time to lament the lack of a solid mast to tension the rope swinging in her hands.

'Pilot, get ready. In five, four, three...' She swung her legs out just enough to grasp the drag rope between her knees. Then flicked out her right ankle to loop the rope around it and up over her laces. With a determined stamp, she jammed her left boot on top of the other, locking the rope against her first boot. Inching more of herself over the edge of the basket, she tested the lock by lifting her weight off the basket altogether by her arms. It held, holding her fast on the spot. 'Pilot! Two... one!'

As she left the safety of the basket, she heard a muffled shriek and the sound of a body falling to the floor behind her. Undaunted, she thanked her butler's suggestion she wear her gloves against the cooler air up high.

Easing the downward pressure of her left foot to release the lock just enough, she let the rope flow slowly through her hands. The figure of eight loop attaching her impromptu harness, however, made for jerky progress, but she'd anticipated that. And the need to pause at intervals as the rope swung wildly. Looking down again, she buried the unsettling thought that she was still dangling close to sixty feet or so above the ground on nothing more than a swaying rope.

After she had descended a little more than her own height, she felt the unnerving sensation of dropping sharply.

The pilot must have jammed the valve as promised, Ellie.

The sure sign her impromptu landing stage was not far off.

She released the lock of her boot even more to increase the speed she dropped, doing her best to control how quickly she now spun around the rope as she lost height. The Mackintosh Toffee kiosk looked to be about half a minute away if the balloon continued on its present course. The distance to the ground, she hastily guessed, was still around fifty feet, leaving her another fifteen to twenty feet of rope to descend to match the height of the Mackintosh kiosk roof. She knew if she climbed down too low, she would be dragged into the side of the kiosk. Too little and she'd miss the roof altogether.

She released the lock of her boot a little more, dropping twice her height near enough before jamming her foot brake on with all her force.

It was only then she tuned into the cries of the people

below. Evidently the sight of her swinging along under the balloon had replaced their panic over the marauding elephants, who, it seemed, might even have been restrained.

Focus, Ellie! Nearly there... any second now.

She felt her heart falter as she released her foot brake altogether. Her boots smacked down with a judder onto the roof of the main kiosk. Immediately, she started running, alleviating the jolt from landing but still hanging on to the drag rope as she leaped off the roof and onto the first of the toffeetin steps.

Staying on her feet, however, was harder than she'd anticipated. Hastily paying out more rope through the figure of eight loop bought her just enough free movement to run down the seven steps.

Leaping the four or five feet from the last one to the ground, she felt a sharp, jarring pain up her shin. The drag rope jerked suddenly, knocking her onto all fours on the paved causeway. Stumbling up, she shouted to the crowd who had parted in shock.

'Grab the end of this rope! And rein in that runaway balloon!'

A dozen men of all classes rushed forward as one.

'Problem with the burner. Pilot can't land,' she explained as the tarred end of the drag rope slapped her chin on slipping out of the figure of eight knot she'd improvised. The men grabbed it, automatically spacing themselves out as they were dragged forwards, heels dug in.

They've got it, Ellie. The balloon's fine.

'Which way is the Gold Coast display?' she cried to the crowd that had gathered around her again.

'Start by turning right after the Hong Kong Pavilion!' a voice shouted back.

She sprinted in the direction pointed, weaving her way through the throng as best she could, keeping one eye out for any exhibition policemen. But she'd spotted none by the time she'd passed Hong Kong's fairy tale entrance.

She jerked to a stop, willing her brain to conjure up the route she'd taken earlier through the exhibition's bewildering maze.

'Follow your intuition, Ellie,' she muttered aloud, darting off right.

'Well fancy one country not even bothering to turn up and leaving its pavilion closed like that. Disgraceful show,' a haughty male voice said a few moments later. Spinning back around, she caught the man's arm.

'Sorry, but where is it? The closed display area. Quick!'

'Straight ahead, then left,' the man said, shaking her off with a disparaging sniff. 'But there's nothing to see.'

'Find a policeman. Urgently,' she said firmly. 'And send him there immediately.'

'For why, pray tell?'

'Just do it!' she called over her shoulder.

The tall wooden gates set in pale-cream brick walls stared back sullenly. She pounded on them.

'Open up! Anybody inside?'

No one stirred.

Fearing she had taken too long already, she scoured the tall walls. The only way in was to scramble up the ornate corner bricks, protruding just enough for her to get a foothold on. With waning energy, she reached the top, then used one of the stacks of hay bales she'd seen earlier to safely reach the ground on the other side.

As she ran across the loose dirt, she registered movement out of the corner of her eye. Whirling around, she spotted the angry amber-eyed man from the Gold Coast disappearing through a low gate on the other side of the enclosure. For a moment, she hesitated, then her nurse's training kicked in.

The injured man has to be your priority, Ellie.

She set off again towards where she'd seen him fall, hoping
he was only injured. Though a sickening feeling in the pit of her
stomach told her it was likely otherwise. But on reaching the
haystacks and quickly scouring the area, she stopped, looking
around in confusion.

'What on earth?' she muttered to herself.

'Quite!' a voice replied sharply.

'Got you!' she cried, spinning around, arms thrust up in a
defensive pose. 'Ah, Clifford! Goodness. You frightened the
wits out of me.'

The concern in his harried expression only deepened. 'Not
possible, my lady. Since there can be no doubt my mistress left
every last screed of those in the hot-air balloon when she leaped
out. As my heart so nearly did.'

'I can explain.'

'My lady, there can be no reasoning for what possessed—'

She held up a firm hand. 'Not now. Save your tellings-off for
later. Because you need to help me find a shot man. And the
one who pulled the trigger.'

There was no missing the quiet groan which uncharacteris-
tically escaped his lips. 'Please, tell me this is merely the adverse
effects of shock from your reckless rope descent?'

'I wish I could. But I saw it happen, Clifford. From up in
the balloon. And somewhere just here, where we're standing.'
She looked around and then at his arched brow.

He's right, Ellie. There's no body, injured, dead or otherwise!

5

The policeman tipped back his blue helmet decorated with a silver shield and scratched his head, his terrier-like face unmoved by Eleanor's pleas.

'I'll say it again, miss. The "closed" sign on them gates is clearer than any argument you got up your pretty coat sleeves.' He leaned in, eyes narrowed. 'Especially to an obviously educated lady such as yourself.'

'Titled,' Clifford said pointedly. 'A *titled* lady, Constable.'

The policeman hesitated, then shook himself. 'Nonetheless, orders is orders. And them's what I'm going to follow to the letter. That there sign, miss, says you have no business being in here. Nor' – he held up an officious finger – 'has your title, I hasten to add.'

'Oh, Constable, for heaven's sake!' she huffed. 'Listen to the words I'm saying, will you? I saw a man shot in this very compound. Not fifteen minutes ago.'

He fixed her with a stern look. 'I can't see no body.' He swept a dismissive uniformed arm around the empty area. 'Only a *busybody* with no business being here!'

'Ahem!' Clifford cleared his throat sternly. 'The incongruousness of the lady's story with the rather contrary evidence before you notwithstanding, Constable, I will thank you to remember who you are talking to.'

'And I'll thank you to take your interfering trunk back outside, sir. Pronto. And with the lady alongside you.'

It took all her remaining self-restraint not to reach out, grab the policeman's collar and shake him. 'Constable, why on earth did you hurry along to this particular compound a few minutes ago?'

'On account of a gentleman making a complaint he was accosted by a hysterical female what hassled him to send for a policeman.'

Clifford peered sideways at her. '"Accosted", my lady?'

'I did not, and I am not hysterical.' She gritted her teeth. 'I am reporting a crime. A murder! Or at least an attempted one.'

'Not possible,' the policeman sniped. '"There will be no breaches of the law for the duration of the exhibition." Them's our orders. Not one misdemeanour. What. So. Ever. So, whatever your female fantasy game is, it needs be played well away from here.'

Her fists balled at his pointed dismissal of her report, mostly, she seethed, because she was a woman! 'Fine. As you wish. Then to save you any further trouble, I shall call him.' She beckoned to Clifford and made as if to head for the gates, one of which was now open.

The policeman stepped in front of her. 'He who?'

'Chief Inspector Seldon.'

'But that's...' He faltered at her slow nodding.

'Exactly.'

She took the time to catch her breath and calm down while the constable was gone to scour the area around the hay bales again. But even Clifford, who was bent over his haunches to better peer through his pince-nez, just kept repeatedly shaking his head.

'Nothing to corroborate your tale, my lady.'

'It is not a tale!' she huffed. 'I thought you of all people...' She tailed off, cursing her frustration as he rose, busying himself aligning the already perfectly straight seams of his gloves. 'Oh, Clifford, I'm sorry. I didn't intend to snap at you. It's just that I'm absolutely certain of what I saw.'

'Even from such a height in the balloon?'

'Y-e-s. Why wouldn't I be?' Her impatience bubbled up again. 'I mean, what other explanation could there be?'

'I dread to imagine,' a deep voice rumbled near her ear. She turned to see the most dashingly handsome man who never failed to release a cloud of butterflies in her stomach. Chief Inspector Seldon, her fiancé, and head of security for the Empire Exhibition, looked divine in his customary dark-charcoal suit. He smiled fleetingly, then whispered, 'Sorry in advance, Eleanor. Whatever this is about, I'll have to keep it professional.'

'I understand, Hugh... I mean, Chief Inspector.' Her eyes darted to the policeman hurrying up beside him.

'That's her!' he said, pointing his truncheon. 'Only I'm sorrier than I know how to say for wasting your valuable time, sir.'

'You don't say.' Seldon glanced at Eleanor with a hint of amusement in his deep-brown eyes. The ones beset by dark half-moons, she noted with concern. Feeling bad for having placed him in an awkward position, she reassured herself she'd done the right thing, given the gravity of what she'd witnessed.

'I saw a man shot, Chief Inspector,' she said earnestly.

'What!' Seldon blanched, his hands reaching out towards hers before he wrenched them back down. 'Are you, umm... alright?'

'No, she definitely isn't!' the constable jumped in before she could answer. 'Nothing she's said has made one ounce of sense, sir.'

Seldon rounded on his subordinate, which Eleanor had never seen him do before, his extra height making the officer shrink back. 'Regardless, why in blazes didn't you say what had been reported to you on the way here, man?'

'Because it can't be right! The lady is insisting she saw it happen right there, sir.' He jabbed his truncheon towards the dirt. 'You show me where the body is? Or the blood? Not so much as a drop!'

'Umm, Lady Swift,' Seldon said in a soothing manner. 'You say a man was shot? Fatally so, you think. But what were you doing in here? This part of the exhibition is closed, as it clearly states on the gates.'

'I know. But I wasn't in here when it happened.'

'Thank heavens,' he murmured, then raised his voice. 'Then where were you, please?'

'In a hot-air balloon, but—' She broke off at his pained look, not missing the glance that had passed between him and Clifford.

'Constable,' Seldon said. 'For thoroughness, search the area over by the far side. Now.'

Left alone, he let out a long breath. 'Eleanor, please tell me the gossip of a lady leaping out of a runaway balloon wasn't you?'

She tutted. 'Now, Hugh, that would have been reckless.'

'Your middle name, as I recall all too well,' he said gravely. 'Clifford?'

Her butler stepped forward. 'In her ladyship's extremely limited defence, Chief Inspector, she did use a rope to reach the ground.'

She gasped. 'That's hardly taking my side, you traitor!' She turned to Seldon. 'Hugh, I only did it to try and save a man's life.'

His horrified gaze seemed to take in the harness still tied

around her front for the first time. 'By putting your own in danger? Again!'

She shrugged. 'I did waste— I mean, spend a full minute making a safety line.'

He groaned and raked a hand through his chestnut curls. 'Eleanor, please just tell me what you believe you saw?' He glared at Clifford. 'But actually, you'll have to wait until I've charged your butler with inexcusable dereliction of duty first!'

Clifford's impassive expression didn't flinch. 'As you wish, Chief Inspector.'

'Oh, leave him alone, Hugh,' Eleanor said. 'For a likely glorious few minutes in the poor fellow's day, he wasn't stuck with me. He wasn't in the balloon, you see, because... well, for good reason.'

'Good reason!' Seldon gruffed. 'Which clearly I have no right to know. And despite being your fiancé, I'm still entirely reliant on your butler to try and keep your infernal impulsiveness in check. Tremendous!'

She smiled placatingly. 'Feel better?'

He nodded ruefully. 'Blast it, you two. Can we just get this over with? Because if I'm going to have the truly special treat of any unexpected time with you, Eleanor, I really can't bear it to be taken up with talk of murder.' He sighed despondently. 'As always.'

She opened her mouth to refute his statement, but then shrugged. He was right. Murder had been the reason they had first met several years before. And the unnerving reason they had rubbed each other up the wrong way from then on. Somehow, throughout it all, however, they had fallen hopelessly in love.

'Well,' she said with a sigh, 'you once had the audacity to say I attract dead bodies like aged spinsters attract moth-eared cats.'

'Not "the audacity", Eleanor. The "honesty". Because, bizarrely, it's true.'

She smiled at Clifford nodding, but then her face clouded over.

'Look, Hugh, I'm so worried about that poor man. The one I leaped... climbed down from the balloon to try and help.'

Seldon's expression softened. 'Have I ever told you that you are—'

'Impossible? Yes. In fact, I rather fancy Clifford has created one of those meticulous charts of his to record just how many times you have.'

'I was actually going to say the most tirelessly selfless, irresistibly caring, brave yet exasperating creature I have ever met. But "impossible" is reasonable shorthand. Now.' He held up his notebook to halt her protest. 'Start at the beginning.'

Having recalled every detail of the scene she could remember, her brow furrowed. 'But before you ask, Hugh, no, I can't begin to explain how or why there is no sign of any of it ever having taken place. To the point I can't actually blame your constable chap for maybe thinking my mind was a marble short of the full set.'

Clifford's lips twitched. 'Just the one short, my lady?'

Seldon grimaced. 'I'm glad you didn't hear what he said while on the way back here! I thought I was coming to deal with a confirmed lunatic.'

She hesitated. 'Honestly, I can't say at this moment that I don't feel like one. But I know what I saw. Right down to the fact that a chap from the Gold Coast was in here when I broke in.'

'Broke in!' Seldon clapped his hands over his ears. 'Eleanor, please stop telling me things I can't hear. I'm a policeman!'

'And the finest there is. Which is—'

'Step right this way, gentlemen!' The three of them turned at the constable's voice.

Eleanor's eyes widened. 'Hugh, that's him! The chap from the Gold Coast in the bright-coloured robe. Not the tall fellow with epaulettes and the embroidered hat. This is better. He can tell you...' She tailed off at Seldon's sigh. 'What is it?' she whispered.

'Not good. Not good at all,' he muttered. 'Please, for once, Eleanor, do as I ask and stay here.'

With no further explanation, he strode forward and joined the two men being ushered into the enclosure by the constable.

She cocked her head, trying to catch a whiff of the conversation. In doing so, her eye was caught by something glinting in the dust. She bent and scooped it up.

Looks like a broken silver clasp from a piece of jewellery, Ellie. Perhaps a bracelet, or necklace?

At the sound of raised voices, she slipped it into her pocket without thinking and concentrated on what was going on a few yards away.

'Yes, Ambassador, I do see. No, it wouldn't do at all, sir,' she heard Seldon say.

She winced, whispering, 'Ambassador, Clifford? Of where?'

'Whomever country's exhibition area this was to have been, I would conjecture,' he whispered back.

At that moment, the man from the Gold Coast she had thwarted from chasing after the young boy pointed forcefully at her, while unleashing an even more forceful stream of words she couldn't understand.

'Ha!' The ambassador scowled at her and then turned back to Seldon, arms folded. 'I trust I have made myself clear, Inspector?' he barked in a gravelled voice.

Seldon nodded respectfully. 'Abundantly so, yes, your Excellency. I'll sort things out. Please be assured of that.'

'Really? I will wait and see for myself!' the ambassador growled, wafting him away towards Eleanor.

'Golly, Hugh, he's no fun, is he?' she whispered as he reached her.

'It's not his job to be, Eleanor,' he muttered. 'Nor mine. Mine is to do precisely as he says. He is a very high-ranking official in his country and Whitehall have laid out my orders very clearly.' He rubbed his hands over his lean cheeks. 'But I'll have to apologise to you later. Because I could really do with your help in making this look like you're cowing to authority.'

'Of course, Chief Inspector,' she said more loudly, then lowered her voice again. 'Making what look like it?'

'My sending you off with a very strong caution. And' – he closed his eyes at her gasp – 'please, Eleanor, no fuss. The ambassador has threatened to make a formal complaint if his full instructions are not followed to the letter. He believes this... incident is just another attempt to embarrass his country, you see? And given the debacle he came to see for himself.' He looked around the empty enclosure. 'Honestly, I can understand why he would think that.'

Eleanor bit her tongue. Given the displays she'd seen at the exhibition so far purporting to be 'an authentic diorama of local life', she wondered if he'd have been even more disgusted or embarrassed *had* his country taken part.

'I shan't ask what's happened with that, Hugh. I can tell by the stress in your sleep-deprived face, it's been hell already.'

He let out a deep breath in relief. 'Thank you, Eleanor. Now, you just need to leave quietly. And if you could pull off a bit of contriteness too, it would save a lot of—'

'Hugh? You're not telling me everything, are you?'

He squared his shoulders and waved a commanding hand for the benefit of those watching, she realised, given how troubled his eyes looked. 'The ambassador has made clear there can be no further investigation into what you've reported.'

She had to fight to keep her gaze on Seldon's face. 'But, Hugh,' she whispered. 'I saw a man shot!'

He lowered his voice. 'I don't doubt it for a second. Blast it, you've proved too many times to be the shrewdest, sharpest-eyed woman ever born. But perhaps they were... play-acting? And' – he waved an arm around the enclosure – 'even if the ambassador felt otherwise about your claim, what could I actually investigate?'

'It's not a claim, Hugh,' she said with feeling. Her thoughts flew back to the balloon. 'At least, I swear what I reported is exactly what it looked like.' She caught Clifford glancing at her. 'But even my ever-loyal butler has a doubt, I fear?'

He bowed from the shoulders. 'My lady, only based on the incontrovertible lack of evidence. Plus the distorted perspective the significant height of the balloon would have given you. Not to mention the disorientating effect of the other passengers' panic at being adrift. Thus, another interpretation of what you witnessed seems to be warranted.' At her silence, he added, 'And you admitted to failing to hear the actual shot. But I stand to be corrected, of course.'

She looked between the two most unquestionably intelligent and rational-minded men she knew. The two people she trusted implicitly. Both of whom were in complete agreement that she had seen something, but not quite what she'd imagined. She sighed.

'Alright, chaps. I can concede to logic and cogent argument.' She managed a wan smile for Seldon. 'And authority. On this occasion anyway, I'll leave quietly.'

As she left the enclosure with Clifford and joined the throng in the main thoroughfare, she shook her head slowly, her brows knitted.

So what exactly did you see, Ellie?

6

Eleanor looked up and frowned. 'It's no good tutting and shaking your head, Clifford. Whatever terrible faux pas you're scolding me for, I'm afraid I've missed it.'

He nodded, gesturing over the commemorative tea towel map of the exhibition now covering the bamboo basket hanging on his wrist. 'Precisely, as with the magnificent Malaya and New Zealand Pavilions we toured for a full hour, my lady. To say nothing of our odyssey through the exquisite works displayed in the Palace of Arts. All of which you have comprehensively "missed", sadly.'

'Dash it! You're right.' She bit her lip. 'Well, instead of enduring any more of my witless company, you'd better toddle off alone and indulge your insatiable appetite for engineering and scientific tedium.'

'And forgo more character assassination?' he said drily.

'Oh, I didn't mean that the way it came out, Clifford. Any more than I've meant to be a wet blanket since we left Hugh. I've just got stuck in constantly questioning myself about what I saw from the balloon.' She held her hands out. 'I am sorry. Honestly, I wish I could start today all over again.'

He shook his head. 'In the words of the eminent Nobel Prize laureate and literary champion of the British Empire, "Never look backwards or you'll fall down the stairs."'

She laughed. 'Oscar Wilde?'

'Emphatically not! He was many things, but a flag waver for the Empire...' He grimaced. 'I was quoting the author and poet, Rudyard Kipling. Born in India, his notable works include many observations of his own experiences in the colonies and dominions of the Empire. In fact, the gentleman had the recent honour of being invited to name the fifteen miles of roads running through this very exhibition site.'

'An honour indeed. Then if you really insist on not leaving me for a while, how about India next?'

'Mmm. To squander the untold delights of the India Pavilion while the lady's thoughts are so unsettled would be a great shame. For both of us. Your late uncle and India had a special connection, as you know.'

She nodded, the familiar lump filling her throat whenever she thought of her beloved uncle. 'What then?'

His lips quirked. 'After the powers that be invested twelve million of our country's diligently earned pounds in this once-in-a-lifetime experience, I'm sure we'll find something suitably unsuitable.'

A few minutes later they arrived at a dance hall, one more thing she never imagined she'd find at the exhibition. And then she heard Mrs Trotman's breathless voice from inside.

'Ooh, Butters, I told you we'd get a good eyeful and no mistake!'

'Lawks, though!' Mrs Butters hissed back as she emerged. 'It's Mr Clifford! We're in trouble now.'

'No, you're not,' Eleanor called, hurrying over to meet her four ladies, quietly delighting in their universally rosy cheeks, from dancing she assumed. 'The day is for each of us to do whatever captures our imagination.' She beamed along their line as they curtseyed. 'And Clifford was adamant he wanted to enjoy the next thing on his list with all of us together. Fancy that!'

Her cook and housekeeper giggled, looking unconvinced, but her younger maid stared at her butler. 'With the likes of us, Mr Clifford? Really?'

He rolled his eyes good-naturedly at Eleanor's innocent look. 'Evidently, yes, Polly. Now, the ultimate marvel of design awaits. Shall we, ladies?'

After a short stroll, they came to what looked like a train platform. But the train in front of her was such as she had never seen.

'Leap, ladies, leap!' Clifford called.

They all hastily stepped aboard one of the diminutive open-sided rail carriages slowly rumbling past the packed platform. Men and women in workaday jackets, smart coats and fascinators alike were throwing themselves on and off with childlike glee rarely seen in public. Clifford's lips twitched.

'It seems, my lady, that the "Never-Stop Railway" has clearly achieved its ambitious brief to be an innovative and exhilarating novelty no one can resist riding around the exhibition site on.'

'So, it really never stops?' Eleanor asked again once they were all settled in a handy six-seater compartment.

Perched rigidly beside her with the basket placed between them, Clifford's eyes twinkled. 'I believe the clue is in the name, my lady. Propulsion is by means of a continuous screw mechanism in place of the usual static track. The screws' coils are more tightly spaced at stations to slow the carriages. And more widely spaced in between' – he held up a gloved finger as the exhibition buildings began passing much quicker – 'to facilitate greater speed.'

'Hold on tight then, my girl.' Mrs Butters pulled Polly closer to her side.

Wincing at the young maid's squeals, Clifford removed the tea towel on top of the basket, Eleanor clapping her hands in delight as he did.

'A picnic! You wizard!'

With five bottles of lemonade and Union Jack printed straws distributed, he handed several waxed paper parcels to Mrs Butters to unwrap. 'Your list of suggestions then for Henley Hall, ladies? Assuming your pads are not too soggy to read, of course?'

'Thank the stars, no, Mr Clifford,' Mrs Trotman said emphatically. 'Who'd have thought those elephants would have reached us with all their squirtings, mind.'

Eleanor's brow furrowed. 'But you were all by the balloon launch site, I thought?'

'We was that, m'lady. But Mr Clifford herded us all off to chase after your hat when you waved it so hard you dropped it.'

'Fortunately,' he murmured to her, 'your rope-scaling antics were therefore not observed by the rest of your staff.'

'Only sorry, but one of them elephants trampled your beautiful hat, m'lady,' Lizzie said.

Eleanor couldn't help laughing. 'Then I'll have to shop for a new tam o'*elephanter* to replace it!'

Once the ladies' giggles had subsided, Mrs Butters handed Eleanor their list. She read aloud, tapping Clifford's page for him to add each item. 'For the kitchen, hot plate for pancakes, clever boil-itself electric kettle and likewise, a tea-making clock!'

'The last item is hardly necessary, Mrs Trotman,' Clifford said sniffily.

Eleanor tutted. 'But anything clock-related fascinates you.' She waved her lemonade, pointing out he hadn't bought one for himself. 'And the only thing you ever really indulge in is a much-deserved cup of tea. So why aren't you keen?'

'I merely thought the timekeeping element superfluous.

Unless the lady of the house now intends to adhere to Henley Hall's meal and refreshment schedule in a timely manner?'

She laughed. 'I'll try.'

'Then tea-making clock willingly added, my lady.'

Eleanor read on. 'Copper parrots, worms and tails. What on earth?'

'For Trotters' homebrew distillery, m'lady,' Mrs Butters whispered conspiratorially.

Her friend nodded proudly. 'I've a bucket load of new recipes. For starters, guelder rose brandy, marrow gin and quince liqueur, m'lady.'

Eleanor winced. 'Well, they sound only marginally lethal. Now, let's add all those to the list, Clifford. If the budget will stand it, of course?'

'Considerably more so than our heads the morning after sampling, my lady.'

The ladies nudged each other, failing to hide more giggles.

Eleanor frowned. 'Why are "food mixer" and "refrigerator" crossed out?'

'On account of Trotters refusing to move with modern times, m'lady,' Mrs Butters said, glancing at her friend.

Mrs Trotman tutted. 'I've got arms to mix, haven't I? And apart from a few really hot days a year, the cool larder and cellar do a good enough job already.'

'Moving on then, if you're sure,' Eleanor said. 'For the laundry, an electric iron and an Everitt clothes press.'

'Excellent suggestions, Mrs Butters,' Clifford said. 'However, you have missed out the most important items of all.'

'I have?' Eleanor's housekeeper stared at the other women, receiving only puzzled looks in reply. 'What'd they be?'

'A centrifugal spinner and a condensing boiler for the new drying room.'

At their collective gasp, he nodded.

'What a wonderful idea!' Eleanor cheered. 'To save you ladies struggling on wash days in winter.'

Mrs Trotman threw her butler a cheeky glance. 'To spare Mr Clifford's blushes most, I'd wager though, m'lady. He goes ever so pale at a face full of us women's underfrillies hanging on the line!'

'Ahem!'

Eleanor hid a smile. 'Now, I think it's someone else's turn. Lizzie?'

Taking the pad, her Scottish maid read out slowly. 'Clever bed-warming blanket for her ladyship's room. It's electric! Ach, they felt so toasty to touch, m'lady. You'll ne'er want to get up in time for breakfast.'

'And the change therein?' Clifford murmured, catching Eleanor's eye.

'Brilliant idea, Lizzie,' she said, with a toss of her red curls. 'Most of all because it will save Polly struggling to hurry the warming pans upstairs every night.'

'Speaking of whom. Your ideas, Polly?' Clifford said.

'I thought her ladyship might like that... that magical hair drying machine we saw, Mr Clifford,' the young maid said shyly, not looking at the pad.

'Ah, of the electric variety, also. Perfect. Since I understand such an apparatus can save a full twenty minutes in getting ready.' His eyes twinkled again. 'A Lady Swift's twenty minutes at that.'

'Being an hour and a half, you mean!' Eleanor mock huffed. 'What else, Polly?'

'A new set of noses for Victor the vacuum, your ladyship.'

'She means nozzles,' Mrs Butters clucked as she pinched the young maid's cheek affectionately. 'But that's not the end, is it, my girl? Go on, ask Mr Clifford.'

At his nod, she stared at her shoes. 'Beg pardon for askin',

Mr Clifford, sir, but when her ladyship and you have decided the newfangleds as to be bought, might we be allowed to... to...'

'To schedule a party in the kitchen for naming them, Polly?' Clifford said kindly. 'I'm sure we could extend an invitation to her ladyship, too, to save her needing to otherwise slither along uninvited.'

'Again!' Eleanor finished for him with a laugh which set the other women off too. 'I eagerly accept the invitation, thank you. And well done for a perfect suggestion, Polly. We had great fun voting on names before.'

The list rolled on; brighter, long-lasting light bulbs and a vast range of new cleaning products were all voted for. Along with new mattresses which Clifford agreed would save days of trying to dry the current ones come spring-cleaning time.

Eleanor's suggestion of a gramophone for the shared staff sitting room was met with open mouths from the ladies. She nodded. 'And a selection of records for everyone, please.' She tapped his page again. 'Oh, and I heard someone earlier raving about those electric heaters. We'll get a few in, for each of your rooms.'

'As you wish, my lady.' He made some further notes, then pulled a weighty tome from the basket. She leaned over to read the title.

'*Design in Modern Life and Industry.*'

He nodded. 'For the new heating system as well as improvements to the drainage and sanitation I would propose. Including modern decorative, ahem, porcelain ware for guest bathrooms. Together, most essentially, with a new generator to cope with the greatly increased draw of power this long list of suggested purchases will demand.'

She clapped her hands. 'Excellent! But what about Joseph? My wonderful gardener can't be left out.'

'Indeed not.' Clifford reached into the basket again. 'Hence this promotional booklet on the merits of the remarkable Ransomes lawnmower. With optional seat attachment, balanced above an ingenious roller. Thus it cuts as it rolls and spares the gardener his pedestrian labours.'

'He's a stickler for the old ways, but we'll nag Muddy Boots into letting you treat his worn bones, m'lady,' Mrs Butters said.

Clifford gestured at Polly, whose head was lolling against Lizzie's shoulder, her eyes drooping. 'Ladies, as you have a two-hour return train journey, perhaps we should leap off now as we leaped on?'

On the mainline platform, Eleanor smiled as Clifford repeatedly ran over the connections and timings for the ladies' train home. Once he'd finished, she waved them off reluctantly.

'See you all tomorrow evening, ladies!'

'By which time,' Clifford said as they walked away, 'I hope a good night's sleep and meeting Lady Chadwick tomorrow will have sufficiently restored your spirits, my lady?'

She shrugged. 'Honestly, I can't promise that. One, because Lady Chadwick's manner was so peculiar that I'm not looking forward to meeting her again. And two, because earlier today if I didn't see a man shot, if not killed, then I don't know what I *did* see.' She felt a frisson run down her spine as if someone was watching her. She spun around. 'Clifford, look, it's him again!'

The man from the Gold Coast was crossing the road behind them. Walking next to him was a man dressed in a cheap suit that had seen better days. He had a hard-nosed face that Eleanor thought reflected too much belligerence to warm to. His drooping bottom lip also added the air of a permanent pout. She just caught him curtly utter the words to the man from the Gold Coast. 'Later tonight. And be on time for a change, will you?' before the pair vanished into the constant flow of people.

Her shoulders stiffened at the sight of a young boy holding hands with his mother and father only yards away.

Clifford sighed. 'I would suggest we pay a discreet visit to the Gold Coast display area to see your young boy is safe and well, but you promised Chief Inspector Seldon to keep away from there. And I fear any more excitement today will finish off even my mistress' near-indomitable fortitude!'

7

By the following afternoon, keeping her promise to her fiancé and remaining well away from the fatal closed enclosure at the exhibition had worn thin. Nevertheless, she was loath to leave the area entirely, still troubled as she was by the events she'd looked down on in horror from the balloon. Fortunately, she'd promised to meet Lady Chadwick and staying in London even a while longer, rather than returning home, felt marginally less like betraying her conscience.

As she descended the grand central staircase at the Ritz, she waved at her butler, who was just turning away from the reception desk. He hesitated for a moment, then glided across the deep-pile rose carpet in the circular vestibule. Lips pursed, he slid in behind the dramatic display of tall ivory lilies beside her.

'My lady, at the Ritz, one should never be seen consorting with one's staff. Most particularly, not in the grand foyer!'

'I'm not "consorting". I'm hobnobbing.' She smiled impishly. 'Now, stop huffing and tell me if I pass your exacting standards for a titled lady. Am I suitably attired for the famed Palm Court? But you need to know before you reply, it's my best effort.'

She twirled the velvet ribbon cuffs of her sage silk tea dress, swinging the fine pleats of its drop-waisted skirt to swish low at her calves. With the delicate embroidery of the bodice echoed in her matching jacket, meeting at the soft scoop of the neckline nestled demurely against her collarbones, she hoped it was sufficiently elegant.

Evidently, all her long-winded indecision in her suite upstairs had been worth it as Clifford nodded approvingly.

'Most assuredly, my lady. However, I must apologise for having significantly overstepped. Most notably, in regard to the household accounts.'

Mystified, she shrugged. 'But you're always the most fearsome terrier when it comes to them?'

'Too gracious, I think,' he murmured. 'What I meant was, after the strain of keeping away from a certain... area at the exhibition today, I imagined you would be somewhat fatigued. Especially given the additional stress of needing to maintain decorum for the duration of an entire formal tea. Therefore, I have presumed that rather than suffer the two-hour train journey home this evening...'

Her breath caught. 'You mean?'

'Yes, my lady.' He lowered his voice further. 'The lure of your house pyjamas and squabbling with your butler, extremely discreetly, I stress, in the confines of your private suite's sitting room, can prevail tonight.'

'So you were booking us in for another night, not checking us out!'

He bowed. 'Indeed. Now' – he consulted his pocket watch – 'it is time to elegantly hasten. After all, even "fashionably late" does actually have a limit.'

Despite not wishing to be rude and keep Lady Chadwick waiting, Eleanor found it impossible to hurry down the luxurious claret and magnolia carpeted grand gallery. Richly tasselled gold and cream swagged drapes adorned the floor-to-ceiling mirrored panels, while inset burgundy velvet settees were intimately lit by muted table lamps on marquetry occasional tables. Spaced strategically along the gallery, glass cabinets on elegantly turned legs were filled with opulent jewellery and objets d'art available to purchase if one's wallet was sufficiently deep.

She paused on reaching the thirty-foot columns that framed the entrance to the indoor arboretum of the Ritz's Palm Court. A captivating gold-leaf fresco of urns, acanthus leaves and lavish scrolls adorned the coffered ceiling inside, elaborate rosettes highlighting the cinquefoil at either end of the intricate leaded glass central panel. Potted palms were dotted around, reflected in the full-length mirrors, while across the marble floor, a fountain topped by a twenty-foot gold figurine filled the main alcove. Immaculate ivory linen-dressed tables accompanied by Louis XVI medallion backed chairs occupied the central area of the room, while music from a string quartet floated in the air.

A waiter in a red waistcoat and ebony suit tails so crisp her own butler would be proud welcomed her like royalty. He led her to a table under the canopy of a palm where a pale-apricot silk-suited Lady Chadwick was drumming the tablecloth with a perfectly manicured set of nails.

'Lady Swift.' The blonde coiffured beauty managed to smile and frown at the same time. 'I had begun to worry you'd changed your mind.'

'Never, where a delectable tea is surely involved,' Eleanor said honestly, settling into the opposite seat. Thinking that might have sounded impolite, she added, 'Please forgive me if I'm a little late. And the real treat is to catch up with you. After all, we barely had a chance to become acquainted at the charity luncheon months back.'

'Yet you left quite the impression on me, which is why I am relieved you've come. Now, we need to choose,' Lady Chadwick said, already perusing the gold-embossed menu beside her place setting.

Confused by what sort of impression it was she'd left, Eleanor settled for a smile and followed her companion's lead in studying what was on offer. Unexpectedly, it was a list of teas. Flipping it over, she was disappointed not to see a list of accompanying sandwiches and cakes.

The waiter reappeared at that moment. 'Your favoured usual, Lady Chadwick?' he said in a clipped tone.

'Yes. Lady Swift?'

'Ah... I think I'll...' Her eye caught the line at the bottom of the list. 'Leave that to the Ritz's marvellous tea sommelier. Who better to know what will pair best with today's seasonal nibbles?'

Fortunately, this was met with a bow of approval. 'Madam is obviously a connoisseur of tea taking.'

Secretly hoping that might ensure a more generously filled tiered stand of whatever food was presented, she waved a gracious hand in reply.

With the waiter gone, Eleanor wasted no time. 'How have you enjoyed the exhibition, Lady Chadwick?'

'Exhibition? Oh, of the Empire? I... I haven't visited it much. Just the once, and rather briefly. So busy at the moment, you know.'

Eleanor tried to keep from frowning.

Why, Ellie, would anyone profess to being too busy to enjoy the spectacle of a lifetime, yet be so keen to idle away an hour drinking tea with someone she barely knew?

'How lucky then that you spotted me in the brief time that you were there.'

Lady Chadwick fiddled with the lace edging of a handkerchief just visible at her jacket cuff. 'Yes. Lucky indeed...'

Before Eleanor could ask what exactly her companion had

requested to see her about, the waiter returned with a silver wheeled trolley and the reverent ceremony of taking tea began. He placed the finest of bone china cups and saucers on the table, followed by two teapots. They were accompanied by every conceivable silverware accoutrement including sugar tongs, spoon bowls, filigree petit four servers and a press for the lemon slices in the shape of a chirping bird. Then, placing one gloved hand behind his back, he produced a bottle of champagne with a flourish. Only after two flutes of golden bubbles had been poured just so, did he set down a three-tiered silver stand. Artfully arranged with a tempting array of crustless sandwiches and petit fours, confusingly, the second layer was empty. Eleanor shot the waiter a questioning look. Lady Chadwick, however, merely waved him off and flicked her Ritz monogrammed napkin across her lap.

'You were saying?' Eleanor coaxed.

Lady Chadwick's hand faltered as she reached for a cucumber sandwich. 'It's a rather delicate matter.'

'Ah,' Eleanor said softly, reaching for one herself. Taking a bite and a sip of her floral-scented amber tea, she looked at her companion afresh. The confident society lady was nowhere to be seen. The woman's features looked positively haunted. She smiled, trying to put her at ease. 'This sandwich is delicious. I believe the Ritz make their own special bread for it. And the tea is equally sublime. Mine is rose congou. And such a treat. I remember it vividly from my cycling travels in the far east of China.'

Lady Chadwick looked up. 'Exactly! But that's only part of the reason.'

'For...?' Eleanor said, fighting to keep her confusion off her face again. She used the sugar tongs to select an exquisite-looking egg and watercress sandwich for each of them.

Lady Chadwick hesitated. 'For asking you to—'

She was interrupted by the waiter returning with a plate of

oven-fresh scones, which he slid into the empty tier of the cake stand.

'Plain and fruit varieties. With clotted cream and strawberry preserve.'

'Wonderful,' Eleanor said, hoping he wouldn't return for a while.

As he left, she turned back to her table companion and patted her hand. 'Now, you were saying?'

Lady Chadwick bit her lip. 'I'm... I'm in something of a bind, you see.' She blinked repeatedly, as if trying to maintain her composure. 'A fearful one, actually. There's been a theft. My pearl necklace!'

Nothing could have been further from what had been shooting through Eleanor's thoughts. 'Your necklace was stolen?'

Lady Chadwick nodded glumly. 'It's terribly valuable. It has thirty-seven pearls in two strings. All of them are natural pearls, not those horrible cultured ones! Which is why I need your help, Lady Swift. Oh please, say you will?'

'Umm, well. I'd love to, of course. But how? In fact, firstly, why do you think I can?'

'Because you've done all manner of things we women aren't supposed to, including travelling the world alone! And I remember hearing among my circle,' she leaned across the table and whispered, 'that you once disguised yourself as a man! And on another occasion, recovered a stolen diamond!'

It was actually a black opal, but Eleanor felt it churlish to correct her. 'Er, yes. I may have. But surely, you just need to call the police?'

'I can't! It's my husband, you see.' Lady Chadwick's cup clattered on its saucer. 'He's a high-up member of the civil service. Always working on something frightfully hush-hush. He cannot risk the neighbours spreading gossip over the police being involved in our affairs.' She tapped the table forcefully.

'Besides, I suspect one of my staff is responsible.' She reached for a chocolate and raspberry tartlet. 'I simply have to get it back. Before my husband returns from his business trip. But let's not dwell on that,' she ended hurriedly.

Ah, Ellie! So her husband knows nothing about the theft.

'How and where was your necklace stolen, Lady Chadwick?'

'From my house on Park Lane. The night before last. I had a... a little soirée. To which I wore my necklace, naturally. But in the morning' – Lady Chadwick closed her eyes – 'it was gone.'

Eleanor selected a pistachio macaron. 'Then why suspect someone on your staff, particularly? Why not a guest?'

Lady Chadwick stared at her in horror. 'A guest! Lady Swift, surely you cannot imagine I would know, let alone invite to my house, the sort of person who would *steal*? Especially from their host!'

Eleanor shrugged. 'Then maybe it was an intruder?'

Lady Chadwick shook her head firmly. 'There was no sign. Of a break-in, I mean.' She dropped her half-finished cup of tea back on the saucer again, her shoulders slumped. 'Oh, goodness! Do you see why I came to you? I'm far from au fait with such unpleasantness.' Her fingers gripped her napkin against her stomach.

'I can see that,' Eleanor said gently, feeling all the more concerned for a fellow female in distress. 'Try a hazelnut florentine, or a champagne truffle, and take a breath. Then maybe you'll feel up to telling me the rest.'

Looking a little restored after nibbling for a minute, Lady Chadwick managed a wan smile. 'I can't remember if I said some other things went missing a few weeks ago?'

Eleanor shook her head.

'Well, that's why I know it has to be one... one of the staff. Because on that occasion, there were no guests in the house. And, again, there was no sign of a break-in.' She waved a dismissive hand. 'But I don't care about those trinkets. I just must have my pearl necklace back. It's worth more than all my other jewellery put together!' She paled. 'I have to have it back before I go mad!'

'Think calm thoughts. And sip your tea,' Eleanor said hurriedly. If she was going to have a hysterical female on her hands, she needed her butler's help. 'Have you interviewed your staff about it, then?'

'Naturally. But, of course, they… they denied it. Do say you'll take the position, Lady Swift? Please?'

Eleanor refocused on her companion's face, now filled with pleading anticipation. 'Sorry. What position?'

'As I said… oh goodness, I'm sure I said… about the governess?' Lady Chadwick's eyes widened. 'Maybe I am losing my mind. Oh dear.'

'I probably missed you saying it,' Eleanor lied sympathetically. 'Is she the one you suspect, then?'

'Certainly not. We haven't a governess at present, you see. That's why you can pretend to take her place. Oh, only temporarily, of course. Now, I'll make things as easy as possible—'

'Wait!' Eleanor swallowed hard. 'Me? Pretend to be a governess? Why, I haven't even children of my own.' Somehow, that admission made her heart falter. 'Not, umm, yet, anyway.'

Lady Chadwick waved her objections aside. 'No matter. The children won't know. And the rest of the staff will think nothing unusual about a temporary replacement. It will give you the chance to mingle and question them discreetly.'

Eleanor opened her mouth to politely, but firmly, decline. Instead, she caught a look of desperation and panic in her companion's eyes.

'I really have no one else to turn to, Lady Swift.'

'Alright. I'll do my best,' Eleanor heard herself say.

Lady Chadwick's face lit up. 'My saviour! I don't know how to thank you.'

Before Eleanor had a chance to add any caveats to her agreement, her companion checked her watch. 'Goodness, time has run away with us. Please forgive me, but I simply have to be somewhere else.' She fumbled in her handbag and then held out a card. 'My address. Until tomorrow then?'

'Yes. No. I also have some business to see to first,' Eleanor said quickly, unable to shake the feeling that she hadn't quite been told everything. 'The day after tomorrow might work.'

'Oh, but of course,' Lady Chadwick said contritely. 'Let me send my carriage here for you tomorrow. To be entirely at your disposal to ferry you wherever you need. And then we can say the day after that for sure?' She looked at Eleanor hopefully.

'Deal.'

After a flurry of hurried thank yous, Eleanor found herself alone with the last remaining petit four, feeling a tad bemused. She shook her head at the choux pastry.

'Clifford is going to lose every ounce of starch from his collar about my agreeing.' Imitating her butler's voice, she picked it up. 'My lady, it is categorically beyond the realms of decorum for a titled lady to pretend to be a governess!'

8

Eleanor ached to be somewhere else. Regent's Park would normally have enchanted her with the tall trees' shadows on either side of the three mile long circuit drawing out in the setting sun. But today the horse's leisurely pace was torture. Her fingers rapped faster on the deep-buttoned leather seating of Lady Chadwick's carriage.

'Clifford, have you been deliberately finding new reasons why I should want to boil your head?'

Perched stiffly on the seat opposite, her butler's lips quirked. 'Perhaps, in answer, it might help to know that Henry VIII created this park as a royal hunting ground in the 1530s?'

'No, it would not. What would help is to know why you're here?' Secretly delighted he had unexpectedly reappeared at the Ritz that afternoon, his evasive replies, however, were testing her limited patience. As much as Lady Chadwick had done the previous day. But that wasn't why she wished she were elsewhere.

She reached into the pocket of her holly velvet coat and pulled out the note she'd found slipped under the door of her suite on rising just in time for the hotel's final breakfast sitting.

'Written in your own meticulous hand, Clifford, this clearly states you had left last night for Henley Hall after I retired. And that you would arrange for my things to be sent back up by train. There's even a sniffy postscript, "Please give my heartfelt farewell to decorum!"' She threw her head back against the seat at his nod. 'I'm so confused. The moment I said I'd agreed to help Lady Chadwick, you made hasty excuses and flounced off. The next thing I knew was this.' She waved the note. 'And then, two hours ago, you turn up at my hotel door out of nowhere!'

He folded his hands in his lap and tutted. 'If I might remind my lady that, as a butler, I do not "flounce".' He reached inside his jacket and handed her a new notebook. 'For your investigation into the theft of Lady Chadwick's pearl necklace.'

She traced her finger over the shimmering green and blue of its silken cover. 'Thank you. It's beautiful!'

He nodded. 'My pleasure. For the record, my farewell to decorum was meant in anticipation of the inelegant mountain of breakfast which would likely be laid waste to in my absence. And as to any suggestion I would abandon my mistress while she fulfils her promise to Lady Chadwick—'

'Oh, Clifford! I understand now.' She leaned forward eagerly. 'You'll stay on at the Ritz where we can meet until I've discovered—'

'Categorically not,' he said firmly.

She closed her eyes and groaned. 'Explain?'

'Certainly. The moment I settle the hotel's bill tomorrow morning and see you into this very carriage bound for Lady Chadwick's Park Lane address, I shall take up alternative lodgings. Lodgings far more appropriate for a mere butler.'

She opened her eyes. 'So you *are* staying up in London while I investigate? Wonderful! But dash it! You deserve so much more than a miserly cell-like boarding room in some dubious part of the capital. Which, for yourself, is all you would countenance, I know.'

'Perhaps. However, given that there is still over half an hour before your rendezvous with a certain chief inspector—'

'Wait! What rend—' Her arms folded in irritation. 'I only said I fancied a trip to the Empire Exhibition tonight to see the architecture of the pavilions under the magic of the night sky. It's one more aspect of the exhibition that might not be quite authentic, I confess, but it is rather magnificent! And how did you know I'd rung Hugh asking if I could meet him to have just one more look at the enclosure where... Well, anyway, if he telephoned you while you were at Henley Hall to get you to dissuade me, I'd say that's too rich for words!'

He shook his head. 'No telephone call received, my lady. Nor any request for dissuasion. I may, however, have telephoned the gentleman myself and enquired if you had asked to visit the scene you... witnessed from the balloon.' He raised his hand as she opened her mouth. 'My lady, as your butler, I was aware that only this course of action would satisfy your troubled conscience.' His tone softened. 'And bravo for managing to stay away from the exhibition all day without any restraining influence.'

She laughed. 'It nearly killed me, you know. I've been aching to be there for hours!'

'No doubt. Perhaps until we are, to distract your thoughts, we might discuss what you learned over tea at the Ritz regarding the theft of Lady Chadwick's necklace?'

She nodded. 'Great idea! But first, thank you for being so supportive.' Leaning forward, she recounted the conversation.

'... and then over our third pastry, a delectable layered nut cream finger with gold iced topping, Lady Chadwick insisted again she's convinced it was a member of staff who stole her necklace.' She tapped her chin thoughtfully. 'Or it might have been over the sublime chocolate almond sponges?'

Clifford raised a brow. 'Mmm. I fear I may have learned more about the comestibles consumed during your conversation than the actual substance of the discourse itself. However, putting aside the distressing conundrum of whether the accusation was made during the mille-feuille, or the hazelnut financier among the petit fours selection' – his lips twitched – 'it seems Lady Chadwick, in London street parlance, believes it to be an "inside job".'

She nodded. 'I shan't ask how you know such slang terms, Mr Scallywag. The question is, how did they open the safe? Lady Chadwick insisted the necklace was always kept in there and apparently only her husband knew the combination.'

Clifford frowned. 'How then did Lady Chadwick come to be wearing—'

'I thought the same thing. I haven't managed to ask her that yet.'

'Unless, forgive the presumption, Lady Chadwick...'

She sighed. 'I know. I'll say it for you. Unless she is lying about one, or both, of those things.'

'Indeed. It is certainly unlikely in the extreme that any of the staff would have been entrusted with the combination. Or that they would possess the light-fingered skill to open the safe without.'

'Ha!' she crowed. 'Hoisted by your own petard! You can't only be a "mere butler", as you constantly insist, because, otherwise, Uncle Byron would never have entrusted you with the combination to the Henley Hall safe!' She halted his protestation with a flap of her hand. 'Even though he was well aware your dubious light-fingered skills would open it in a blink.'

'Ahem!' He adjusted his perfectly aligned tie. 'Moving on, the thief might have had an accomplice among the staff, perhaps?'

She pondered that briefly. 'If the thief was a guest at the soirée, possibly. But you should have heard Lady Chadwick's indignation when I suggested that!'

'Hmm, it seems your... new employer,' he said with a sniff,

'needs to answer a raft more questions before any headway can be made.' He glanced out of the carriage. 'Now, we are almost at the exhibition's south-west entrance.' He glanced out again. 'Where you likely agreed to meet Chief Inspector Seldon?'

She nodded, dumbfounded by his wizardry. Until, that was, her gaze focused on the rear view of a tall, broad-shouldered figure in a familiar blue wool overcoat. He was scanning the tide of pedestrians spilling in and out of the train station entrance opposite.

Not waiting for Clifford to help her out, she tumbled through the door.

'Hugh! I mean, Chief...'

She clapped her hand over her mouth as her fiancé spun around, finger pressed to his lips. He cleared the space between them in three long strides.

'Blast it, Eleanor! You agreed to be discreet,' he whispered fiercely.

'I'm so sorry, Hugh. I thought that was only inside the actual exhibition site itself?'

His troubled brown eyes roved over her face, settling on her lips with a quiet sigh. 'I wish it was that simple. I didn't want to mention it on that wretched telephone apparatus because everything I say to you comes out wrong. The truth is my job and future in the police force are on the line if we're caught. And then I'll never be able to marry you in the next hundred years.'

'Hugh!' she gasped. 'I never would have asked if—'

'I know,' he said softly. 'But neither would your conscience ever rest without one last chance to be certain.'

'My lady, perhaps your scarf might assist the gentleman?' Clifford said, wrapping his own smart grey one up around his chin like a muffler.

Confused, she unwound hers from her neck and held it out to Seldon. He shook his head with a quiet smile. 'Clifford means to hide your irresistibly beautiful, but very noticeable fiery-red curls, Eleanor. Not my mop! Hello, by the way. I didn't expect you to come by carriage.'

She shrugged, thinking this was no time to explain what she had got herself into with Lady Chadwick.

'And, Clifford, thank goodness you're here,' Seldon continued.

Her butler leaned forward conspiratorially. 'Regrettably, sir, my attempt to escape was thwarted.'

Seldon's lean cheeks rose with amusement. 'Bad luck. Definitely run faster next time.'

Always delighted to see her two favourite men sharing a joke, even if good-humouredly at her expense, she hid a smile.

'It's nice to see you haven't lost your humour. Or your sanity, Hugh. Even without me being a nuisance tonight, all this pressure must be a hideous nightmare for you.' Her brow furrowed. 'But do feel free to refute the "nuisance" part of my observation.'

'Couldn't. Too dishonest for a policeman.' He smiled at her mock huff, but sobered quickly as his hand slid inside his coat. 'This mad risk is only possible at all tonight because there's a special ceremonial display in the stadium and all visiting dignitaries and their guests will be there. Including our irascible ambassador. But because of that, security is tighter than ever and the entire site is closed to visitors unless they have one of these.' He slipped two gold-lettered tickets into Clifford's waiting gloved hand.

Eleanor tugged anxiously on his coat sleeve. 'Hugh, even a half-witted policeman on the gate won't see me as a highfalutin official.' She caught her butler turn away, his lips quirking.

'No, my love,' Seldon whispered tenderly, brushing his hand all too briefly over hers. 'They'll see you as the bewitching princess I do. Now, let's move.'

9

Arriving at the tall wooden gates of the closed enclosure, Eleanor was breathless with trepidation. But on sneaking inside, she felt her stomach knot. Exactly as it had when she'd gazed down in horror from the balloon.

'Eleanor? Did you hear me?' She caught the urgency in Seldon's tone and shook her head apologetically in reply.

'Fifteen minutes is the best I can offer,' he hissed.

'Thank you, Hugh. That's so much more than you should have done.'

His emphatic nod felt like a stab to her guilt-ridden heart. 'By the way, Eleanor, I checked with all the mortuaries in the area. And the missing persons' lists too.'

'And?'

'Nothing. No deaths by gunshot wound registered since Friday morning. And no additions to missing persons.' He pursed his lips. 'Either this is one devil of a cover-up or...' He looked away. 'Fifteen minutes. I'll be back then. Now, I have to be seen where I should never have left.'

In a blur of his long, efficient strides, he vanished through the gate, closing it behind him.

'My lady.' Clifford appeared at her side. 'What do you wish me to do?'

Far from the comfort his measured tone usually gave her, it twisted the knife on her growing doubt. They had investigated too many murders together for him to even have asked her that. Clearly, like her fiancé, he too felt she'd been mistaken in what she saw.

Which, in truth, would be a good thing, Ellie.

She stood and tilted her head up, imagining the balloon flying overhead and her looking down. But it was hopeless. The sky was a featureless dark blanket, lit only by the stadium lights reflecting off the clouds. She couldn't even be sure which way she'd been facing.

'Clifford, quick. Please use your infallible skills to sketch this enclosure and everything in it as if you were looking down on it from above.'

'As you wish.' In a smooth flow of crisply inked strokes, the map took shape. Halfway through, he broke off to briskly walk around the hay bales and the front porch of the unfinished pavilion on the far side of the enclosure. A few minutes later and the sketch was complete. Shining his pocket torch on it, he held it out for her. Rather than taking it, she stepped slowly around the page with her fingers, jerking to a stop three quarters of the way.

'There!' She jabbed at the paper. 'Where exactly is that?'

He led her to the spot but, maddeningly, the loose ground by the two stacks of hay bales and wooden barrels showed no sign of a skirmish. Let alone a bloody one. Nor did it bear any marks of a body having been dragged away. Despite this, her insides twisting all the harder, she nodded.

'It happened just here, Clifford,' she said grimly. 'The men were behind this stack of hay. I can picture them clearly now.' She stepped past him, sweeping the torch he had given her slowly over the earth.

'Dash it! It looks like the loose earth here has been raked over,' she muttered on reaching the end of the haystack. 'No footprints I can find. Not even mine.'

'But there is an indent over here from the weight of a heavy barrel,' Clifford said thoughtfully, beckoning her to where he rested on his haunches. 'See here. A slight indented mark. It seems our mystery man's raking missed this.' He measured it with his gloved hand. 'Twelve and a half inches long and curved exactly like part of the base of this barrel.'

'Which proves it was moved!'

'Suggests,' he countered, rocking the barrel backwards a little. 'Interestingly, it is empty and thus, even being of oak, weighs only a hundred pounds or thereabouts. Considerably less than even a slender man of modest stature. Thus, the two men you described would have left footprints if an empty barrel could have left this mark on being shunted aside in a fight. Or by the flight of a murderer.'

She sighed, her initial hopes dashed. 'We'd better go and wait near the gate for Hugh. I can't bear that he's risked so much for me.'

But her butler clearly wasn't listening.

'The rope!' he murmured.

'That's no good, Clifford,' she said soberly. 'The balloon's drag rope definitely didn't leave a mark. We were drifting too high up at that point.'

'Not the drag rope, my lady.'

Mystified, she followed him as he strode back to the tower of hay bales. '*This* rope.' Whipping off his glove, he pointed to the frayed end of one of the ropes holding the haybales together. It was hanging down just below his chest level. He then pointed at the other end, equally frayed, lying on the floor.

'Nibbled by one of the goats that were ambling in here before?'

'Possibly, but...' He shone the torch into the bale, then dug his hand into the hay. 'The unfortunate creature – aha! Got it! – would now be dead!'

As they reached the enclosure's gates, a shadowy form slipped in.

'Thank goodness you're ready,' Seldon whispered. 'Eleanor, I know I said fifteen minutes, and it's only ten now but—'

'Hugh. We—'

'I can't. I'm sorry, but I've just heard a party of workmen have been sent here to assess how quickly they can finish what they were told to stop building, blast it!'

'Then you need to make sure they don't disturb the rest of the area.'

He groaned. 'Eleanor, please, I tried to help you settle your thoughts. You can't come again. Even though you haven't found anything.'

'You're right, I haven't,' she said, nodding. 'But Clifford has.'

Seldon frowned as Clifford gestured for him to open his palm and then dropped a small, cylindrical item in it.

'One bullet, chief inspector. You will find the spot it came from marked by an "X" on this sketch of the enclosure.'

'Goodnight, Hugh,' she whispered, unable to stop her lips reaching up to his.

10

On the top step of Lady Chadwick's imposing five-storey red-brick townhouse, Eleanor chided herself for hesitating.

A promise is a promise, Ellie.

After finding the bullet at the enclosure, anything other than waiting at the Ritz for news from Seldon seemed frivolous. But her suite was no longer hers. Clifford had checked her out and promptly delivered her into Lady Chadwick's carriage, where the coachman had driven her to Chadwick House, Park Lane.

She glanced at her one modest suitcase, packed with what, she had no idea. Somehow in the short period Clifford had been at Henley Hall, her housekeeper had used her sewing skills in time for his return to London. The result was the pewter-grey dress with a high-necked collar that she was now wearing, and which fitted her slender frame perfectly. With the matching lace net keeping her usually rebellious curls in a neat fan at her neck, Clifford had mischievously noted she at least looked the epitome of a respectable governess. Inside, however, her forthcoming charade was making her feel anything but.

'Here goes,' she murmured as her finger depressed the bell button.

After a few moments, the ebony front door opened slowly, breaking the one ribbon of sunshine cast by the polished letter box.

'Yes?' The leathery complexion and saggy jowls of the face gazing back at her seemed incongruous with the smart butler's suit and testily tight knot of the black tie below it. The oil slicking his hair sideways over his pate meant, as he jerked his chin questioningly at her, it stayed stubbornly still.

'Ah, good morning,' she said genially. 'I'm the new governess.'

He looked her over frostily. She estimated him to be either side of fifty. 'The *temporary* governess. From an agency, one can only assume?'

Her smile stiffened. 'I am here on Lady Chadwick's instructions,' she said more firmly.

'Are you sure?' he snipped. 'Since this is the front door. The staff door is at the *rear* of the property.'

Dash it, Ellie! Your first blunder.

'Withers!' a female voice called from somewhere inside the entrance. 'That's quite enough! I will be in my drawing room.'

'Yes, my lady,' the butler said over his shoulder. He took half a step back to let Eleanor across the threshold.

Inside, her immediate impression was one of restrained sophistication. The black and white diamond tiles drew the eye down the elegant expanse of the hallway to the central staircase, which wound up to a galleried landing. Muted oyster- and salmon-hued drapes adorned the windows, while an ornate Queen Anne chaise longue in ivory silk dominated the alcove. It was all terribly refined, but nowhere was there any suggestion that children lived in the house.

'You appear to have forgotten something, Miss...?'

She spun around. 'An introduction, perhaps? A little remiss

of me, of course. I'm Miss Smith. And I heard a moment ago, you are Withers. Delighted to meet you.'

'*Mister* Withers.' He marched back out and returned with her suitcase, which he slid under the onyx telephone table with the end of his black shoe. 'Follow me.'

She tried to memorise the layout along the lengthy hallway, determined to start working out how the thief could have moved through the house unseen the night of Lady Chadwick's soirée. But at the brisk speed Withers was leading her, she managed little more than counting the number of doors she was herded past. Clearly, Lady Chadwick liked to receive her guests deep in the heart of the house. Assuming it had one, she mused. If only some of the impersonal watercolour landscapes hanging on the walls had been replaced by a few family photographs, it might have felt more like a home.

Withers stopped at the end of the hallway and opened a narrow door. An equally narrow, worn flight of stairs dog-legged up out of view. They also ran down to wherever the heady odours of boiling greens, vinegar, and methylated spirits were fighting it out below. The dark mustard-painted walls of the stairwell added a suggestion of more mustiness, which left her feeling she had stepped into a long-soured pot of the condiment itself.

'The staff stairs, Miss Smith.'

'Thank you, Mr Withers. I'm learning lots already.'

He climbed on ahead of her without replying and pulled open another narrow door on another landing.

'The second floor,' he announced. 'Where Lady Chad-wick's drawing room is located. Not that a revisit there would be necessary for a temporary governess after this interview.'

She settled for a nod in reply, thinking how ironic it was that she was the only one who would interview anyone. And starting that very afternoon. Not looking forward to trying to extract anything from Withers, however, she made a mental note to get it over with as soon as possible.

'And which other rooms are on this floor?'

'None you will require!' he said coldly.

The sumptuous scene beyond the door he held open a minute later made her blink. Surely this wasn't the same house? As she stepped from the staff stairway into the room, she felt as if she had been transported back to the Ritz. Vanilla and gold silk curtains dressed the windows, and matching cushions dotted the polished mahogany furniture. A restrained sprinkle of marble statues graced the airy floor-to-ceiling windowed space. She glanced towards the worn, narrow, mustard staircase. Even given the seemingly universally held view over the necessary divide between the upper classes and their staff, the difference felt vast.

'There you are, finally,' Lady Chadwick said in an impatient tone.

Eleanor refrained from curtseying. Governesses were staff, true, but most were of genteel breeding and respectable backgrounds. Just women caught in straitened circumstances. All too often caused by faultlessly failing to find, or keep, a husband to provide for them, she thought sadly. She stood straighter.

'Good morning, Lady Chadwick.'

'That will be all, Withers,' she said dismissively. 'Miss Smith can pour our tea while I check her references and experience. I do not wish to be disturbed.'

'Very well, my lady.' The door closed behind him with a loud click.

Lady Chadwick turned to Eleanor. 'I'm so sorry, Lady Swift. But I needed to keep up appearances with Withers there. Now, thank goodness you've come.' She pointed her towards a wooden chair while settling into the deep-cushioned cream settee adjacent. She pulled a handkerchief from her dress cuff and wound it around her fingers. 'Do please excuse me if I seem a little... terse. The strain of all this is simply intolerable.'

'I'm sure,' Eleanor said, feeling a wash of sympathy. She was only playing the part of a woman caught in a less than favourable situation. It seemed the woman opposite her, now wringing her hands, genuinely was.

Lady Chadwick waved weakly at the waiting tea tray. 'We shall have to keep up appearances, you understand?'

Eleanor nodded. 'I do, so I shall play along as necessary. Although at this moment, we're alone.'

Lady Chadwick shook her head vehemently. 'When one has staff, one is never alone!'

Eleanor nodded. 'You're right. All of this charade will be for nothing if anyone discovers why I'm really here. But that is why I need to get started immediately.' She shuffled forward, pouring two cups of the insipid yellow liquid without ceremony, too eager to unleash the questions burning on her tongue.

Lady Chadwick, however, was shaking her head again. 'You can't start today! The children will be back soon. You'll need to be taken to your room. And then be shown the schoolroom. Likewise the children's sleeping arrangements.' She tapped her chin thoughtfully with her long, slender fingers. 'I'm sure I mentioned we don't keep a nanny any longer?'

Eleanor hid a frown. For a smart household like this, she'd have expected a nanny to be employed.

'So,' Lady Chadwick continued, 'preparing them for bed and settling the darlings off to sleep will naturally be necessary. To deflect any suspicions about you, of course,' she added quickly.

'I shall do my best,' Eleanor said resignedly. 'Especially where the children are concerned. And I'm genuinely looking forward to meeting them. However, we can seize the time you're supposed to be interviewing me right now to gain a better picture of what happened the night of the theft.'

Lady Chadwick nodded slowly over the rim of her teacup.

'Good. Firstly then, you said you had a soirée. How many guests were there?'

Lady Chadwick hesitated. 'Not many. Maybe a dozen at most.'

'And you were wearing your pearl necklace, yes?' At the other woman's nod, she continued. 'What I'm wondering is, how did the thief have the opportunity to steal it?'

Lady Chadwick glanced away. 'You see, the whole problem arose part-way through the evening. As hostess, I couldn't leave my guests for too long, could I? Just imagine how that would have looked! Terrible! And unforgivably so.' Lady Chadwick took a sip of tea. Eleanor watched her carefully, but her hostess kept her eyes down. 'But it was scratching my neck constantly by then. My necklace, that is. Which is... why I did it.'

'What did you do?'

'Hastened to my bedroom to take it off.'

Eleanor stirred more sugar into her tea in a desperate attempt to make it taste something. 'Did any of your guests know why you had slipped away?'

Lady Chadwick turned her cup on its saucer. 'Yes. I was talking to a... a colleague of my husband when the irritation became too much.'

'Ah! Maybe this man is familiar to you and therefore would know the layout of the house well?'

Lady Chadwick shot her a shocked look. '"Familiar?" Indeed! I mean, he and my husband are colleagues. They work on the same very important, and very hush-hush projects, though they are in different departments. But there is nothing improper!'

Eleanor held a hand up. 'I'm sorry. I'm just trying to build a picture of the evening. Now, were any of your other guests aware of the difficulty with your necklace, do you think?'

Lady Chadwick rearranged her dress and the colour in her cheeks faded. 'Not that I know of.'

'But this, er, colleague could have mentioned it to one or more of them?'

Lady Chadwick gasped. 'What if he did? You can't possibly be suggesting that any of my guests might be guilty? Everyone is, well, one doesn't like to use such terms, but moneyed. As well as respectable. It was obviously,' she lowered her voice further, 'one of the staff, as I said before.'

Eleanor bit her lip. It wasn't the time or place to stand up for domestic workers everywhere. And besides, she needed to keep an open mind about anyone in the house on the evening in question. Pursuing the guest list at this point, however, was obviously pointless. She topped up their teas to give her time to think.

'Which of your staff knew your necklace was not in the safe that evening?'

Lady Chadwick thought for a moment. 'All of them. They would have seen me wearing it. But only my maid knew I'd taken it off in my room. Although she could have mentioned it to any of the other staff. The whole lot of them are always gossiping.'

'Interesting. I'd like to speak to your maid first then. Today.'

'You can't. It's Grace's half afternoon off. She won't be back until tonight.'

Eleanor hid her disappointment. She was hoping she could get the matter sorted quickly and be home in a day or two. 'No problem. Has she been with you long?'

'Oh, over a year.'

'I see. Well, let's go back a step. You took your necklace off in your room, then placed it in the safe as usual—'

'No. Not in the safe.' Lady Chadwick fumbled with her sleeve. 'In my dressing-table drawer.'

Eleanor fought to keep a frown off her face again. 'But, surely it's a valuable piece of jewellery we're talking about?'

'Frightfully so! Which is why I locked the drawer. And made sure to hide the key in its usual place.'

'Which is?'

'Hanging under the skirt of the porcelain figurine on my bedside table.'

'I see. Well, actually, I don't,' Eleanor said, losing the battle to disguise her confusion. 'Why didn't you put it back in the safe, where I assume it usually lives?'

Lady Chadwick hesitated. 'It does. But my husband was away on business that night. And only he knows the combination. It's too much for me to be entrusted with, to his mind.' Her handkerchief balled in her hand. 'He treats me like a child!'

Ah, Ellie, now we're getting to why the necklace needs to be found before her husband returns home! Maybe he didn't even know about the soirée?

She smiled sympathetically, grateful for her own independence. 'I haven't the beginnings of an impression of him. But I'm sure I'll come across a photograph somewhere in—'

'You won't,' Lady Chadwick said emphatically. 'Reginald won't permit any of himself in the house.'

'Ah!' Before she could ask why, or how Lady Chadwick had got the necklace out of the safe without the combination, she jumped at the woman's cry.

'The children! They'll be home by now. Come, please.'

Eleanor took a deep breath and followed her into a wide corridor lined with tall, mirrored cabinets. As her hostess rounded the corner ahead, Eleanor paused at her reflection to tighten the lace net around her curls. Before she could catch Lady Chadwick up, she caught a flash of movement in one of the mirrors behind her. She ducked out of sight beside it as Withers, the butler, emerged from the room next to the drawing room. He silently closed the door, his eyes darting left and right, and hurried down the corridor to the staff stairs.

Well, well, Ellie! Eavesdropping, it would seem. But why would Withers be so interested in the appointment of a new governess?

11

'How perfectly lucky is that?' Eleanor enthused on reaching the top step.

The two small faces hanging glumly down between the spindles of the landing balustrade on the fourth floor exchanged a puzzled glance.

'Manners, children!' Lady Chadwick chided.

Pulling themselves up, the young boy and girl stood to attention. As their mother joined them, she tugged on the collar of her son's diminutive tweed jacket, then flapped at the buttoned cuffs of his matching knickerbockers.

'This is Hubert. He will be seven next month. He is going to be an eminent banker when he grows up. In the city's square mile and nowhere less!' She straightened the white satin bow framing her daughter's ringlets. 'And this is Octavia. She is ten months older than Hubert.' She gestured at Eleanor. 'Children, this is Miss Smith. Your new governess. Now, I expect to hear only excellent reports about you. Say hello, politely.'

'Good evening, Miss Smith,' they chorused mechanically.

Eleanor winced. The two of them had less bounce about having a new governess than a couple of deflated balloons.

'Good evening, Octavia and Hubert. I've been looking forward to meeting you enormously. Where shall we start in getting to know each other, I wonder?'

Lady Chadwick waved a finger at their brighter-eyed look. 'Now, now! What time is it when you return from your pianoforte lesson?'

'Bedtime, Mother,' Octavia said dolefully.

'No teatime first?' Eleanor let slip in horror.

Lady Chadwick tutted. 'Piano lessons are taken alternately. One plays while the other takes tea so they can listen and learn at the same time. And vice versa.' Her lips pursed. 'The previous governess had insufficient competence, among other things, hence private lessons were arranged. Opposite the conservatoire, you know.'

'Wonderful.' Eleanor thought even a novice tutor with a fumbled melody would have cheered up the over-formal atmosphere of this sombre house. 'Well, children, on the way to bedtime, perhaps you can treat me to a whistle-stop tour of your little province up here?'

'We're not allowed to whistle, miss,' Hubert said, glancing at his mother.

'And treats aren't allowed upstairs,' Octavia added.

'Naturally!' Lady Chadwick said. She stifled a yawn. 'Oh, excuse me, I feel the need to retire myself.'

Eleanor nodded, hoping she didn't look too keen. Lady Chadwick pointed along the run of plain blue rugs lining the wooden passageway. 'Your room is to the right of the school-room. The children's is to the left. Goodnight, everyone.'

'Goodnight, Mother,' the children chorused, wrapping their arms around Lady Chadwick's legs. She patted them both affectionately on the head. 'Sleep well. Because I expect to see everyone at their lesson-ready best at breakfast. Miss Smith, you must join us tomorrow, seeing as it will be your first morning in post.'

Eleanor was appalled. Working her way leisurely through the finest of breakfast salvers was her favourite pastime. Why wouldn't she join them every morning? Then it dawned. Of course, eating with the staff would give her extra opportunities to grill them on the necklace theft.

As Lady Chadwick's blonde updo bobbed away down the stairs, Eleanor turned to the children. 'Right, we've something important to do first. Then it's pyjamas ahoy!'

'Is brushing our teeth really so important, miss?' Hubert said.

'Yes. But that isn't what I meant.'

Octavia poked his arm. 'She means saying our prayers, silly.'

'Those are important, too,' Eleanor said. 'But, well, I shall need you to show me the schoolroom first, please.'

On stepping inside, her heart sank. A lectern-style desk and high-backed chair dominated the head of the room. On its nearest corner, a beige pot held pencils, rulers, mathematical compasses, protractors and their equally dull brass brethren. On the other, a large and stern-looking hourglass, its bottom half filled with rain-grey sand. A pivoting chalkboard on two steel wheels was scrawled with a confusion of sums in rigid, white-chalked strokes. Evidently the abacus hanging on a hook at its side was intended to be an aid to fathoming the answers, though the wishy-washy coloured beads mounted on its horizontal rods couldn't have been less engaging to curious, lively minds. Eleanor shook her head at the two miniature desks in front of the lectern with their chairs built into the base frames. Even sitting positions were dictated. No chairs there had ever been scraped back in glee when the end of school bell finally rang. A slate sat on each with a single finger of chalk and a small cloth.

The nearside wall held a framed sampler of The Lord's Prayer, and next to it a times table. On the opposite wall, a chalkboard was marked with a long line of errors under each of the children's names, Hubert's far longer than his sister's. The whole space felt too much like the austere classrooms she had been forever in trouble in at her hated boarding school. Even if she had been an experienced teacher, in this disenchanting bastion of instruction, how could she instil a single ounce of learning in a pair of impressionable young minds?

Her eyes fell hopefully on the bookcase in the corner.

That's the answer, Ellie!

She turned back to the children, both staring at her in lacklustre expectation.

'Ready, me shipmates?' she said in her best gnarly sailor's voice.

Hubert giggled, then his face fell. 'But we haven't got a ship, miss.'

'Only a tin toy one, in the trunk,' Octavia added.

'Ah, a games trunk, is it?' Eleanor said keenly, looking around.

'That's what our governesses have all called it. But there isn't much to play with in there,' Octavia said. 'It's behind the blackboard.'

'Right. Pencil and paper each, then, please.' Once they had scurried back from the cupboard with the items, she relayed a list to each of them. 'Just as many as you can find between you will be wonderful. Ready, steady, go!'

The two children dashed off and, after much toing and froing, breathlessly declared the job done. At Eleanor's feet lay a heap of items from each list, to which she added some extras she'd found.

'Miss, are we allowed to ask what all this is for?' The children's eager words tumbled over each other's.

'Wouldn't you rather guess?' Eleanor said.

Octavia's brow furrowed as she sank to her knees, tucking the skirt of her dress up under her as she concentrated on the pile. Hubert sprawled down beside her on his stomach, kicking his legs up behind him.

'I know,' he huffed. 'A lesson in how to tidy up the schoolroom!'

Eleanor had to hide her chuckle, as that was exactly what she would have grumbled as a child. She shook her head.

'A spelling test to name each of the things we've collected?' Octavia said with a disappointed sigh.

Again Eleanor shook her head.

Hubert rolled over onto his back to stare up at her, then jumped to his feet at his sister's anxious tug on his collar.

'Please tell us before we burst!' he pleaded.

'Yes, please, please,' Octavia breathed. 'We'll never sleep for wondering if you don't.'

'Alright. It's very simple,' Eleanor said. 'All of these things we shall need to build our schoolroom sailing boat.'

The two young jaws fell open. 'Schoolroom...'

'... sailing boat?' Hubert finished for his sister.

'Well, of course!' Eleanor said in mock surprise. 'How else are we going to sail to Zanzibar to find the treasure?' At their joint gasp, she nodded. 'That's why we need the atlas, cushions, rolls of paper, compass, flags, protractor and everything else you cleverly found. Plus this wheel to take turns at steering. We've got to plot our course through the oceans, keep calculating our distance, write our captain's log and work out the riddles on the treasure map itself. So there'll be plenty of maths, geography and English, but it'll be fun. And the best part is, we'll have unearthed the treasure at the end!' She left out plenty of sketching too for her, as she would have to stay up until the early hours to draw a map for the following day.

Hubert frowned as he picked up a large round tin containing a fishing game, one of the few fun diversions she'd found in the trunk. 'And the magnet fish, miss?'

'To hang our rods over the side and catch lunch so we can feed the other members of the crew, of course. Who I hope are

waiting on your bed with your pyjamas to hear part of which-
ever story you pick together first.'

*And then, Ellie, you'd better work out what the treasure's
going to be!*

12

In the children's shared bedroom, painted bright sky blue, Eleanor was relieved to see some leeway had been given to the age of its occupants. The pink bedspread on the left-side bed was set with a neat line of dolls in pretty dresses. And just a short gap away, the rucked-up blue one was scattered with several toy bears. In pride of place on the pillow was a droopy-eared rabbit.

Having hurled themselves into their pyjamas and under the covers, then out again at Eleanor's reminder that prayers and teeth really *were* important, the children jumped back into bed. She pulled over the white-painted rocking chair from the far corner and set it between the beds so they could both see the pictures in their chosen book. The space was so narrow it only just fitted, and they leaned their heads on her shoulders to see, which made her heart skip.

Oh gracious, Ellie. This side of all this pretence is actually rather... Her breath caught. 'Magical,' she murmured aloud.

Octavia smiled and slid her arm shyly through Eleanor's.

'Miss?' Hubert said. 'It isn't rude to ask what you meant by "lucky", is it? You know, at the top of the stairs you said it?'

She laughed. 'Not at all, shipmate. I meant isn't it lucky that three is the perfect number for friends as there are two of you plus one of me which makes...?'

'Three,' Hubert stammered. 'But—'

'But you're our governess!' Octavia said wide-eyed.

'Is there a written rule which says I can't be your governess *and* friend?'

They both shook their heads emphatically.

'Good,' Eleanor croaked, turning to the first page. 'Now, once upon a time...'

Ten minutes later, she tiptoed from the room and closed the door slowly, so as not to wake the sleeping babes from their slumbers.

Back in her bedroom, she sighed and looked over at her suitcase, which had clearly been poked into her room without ceremony. Likely on the end of Withers' shoe, she thought ruefully. Her mind wandered to her own butler.

'Well, Clifford, wherever you are,' she said as she undid the buckles, 'thank you for whatever you've instructed my wonderful housekeeper to pack for me. Ah!' She smiled as she lifted the lid. 'And for this addition you've painstakingly slipped in afterwards, I can tell, so as to avoid glimpsing my "under-frillies" as Polly calls them.' She picked up the little hard-backed book entitled *Hints for Governesses* and pulled out the meticulous handwritten note poking from the top.

> *I keep six honest serving-men. (They taught me all I knew);*
> *Their names are What and Why and When And How and*
> *Where and Who. – The Elephant's Child, Rudyard Kipling.*
> *Good luck!*

She looked back at her suitcase. Unpacking would be an

idea, but her nose wrinkled in disagreement. If she got started right away with the investigation, hopefully, she wouldn't be here long enough to make it worthwhile. Her heart skipped to the children, but she resolutely headed for the door.

With Lady Chadwick having retired, Ellie, the staff are likely all below stairs.

She crept out of her room and leaned over the balustrade, cocking her ear to check there were no voices or footsteps. The main stairs down to the third and second floors were carpeted, but the acres of marbled corridors in between could betray her. And it was the second floor she needed to start on. Or, more precisely, outside Lady Chadwick's bedroom. She slipped off her shoes and tucked them into the crook of her arm.

Tiptoeing along, she made a hasty mental map of the reception rooms that lay behind the five doors she peeped through. They all seemed to be indistinguishable from each other. Wishing Clifford were there with his elephant-like memory and wizard's knack of sketching the most complex layouts in a blink, she sidled back to the main staircase. She took solace that at least she knew door six led into Lady Chadwick's drawing room, the seventh to her bedroom suite.

The sound of a door closing below made her freeze. With a jolt she realised the main stairs would have been too conspicuous for the thief if they were a member of staff. If it had been her now, she'd have been as good as trapped if whoever that was had come up, rather than down!

She risked a peep over the banister, but could see and hear no one. That suggested they had taken the staff stairs. As the thief could have, her thoughts urged as she hurried down to the other end of the hallway. But as she inched the door to the staff stairs open, she discounted that possibility too. The theft had taken place during a party. The staff would have been racing up and down those very stairs to the first floor at least, to tend to Lady Chadwick and her guests' every need. And she'd experienced first-hand how exposed that narrow mustard stairwell was. Thankfully, now it was empty save for her. Turning around, her gaze followed the steps up.

Upstairs, Ellie! None of the staff would have been up there at that time. The thief could have snuck out of Lady Chadwick's suite with the necklace, and nipped up to... to what? To hide the stolen prize in the staff quarters? But surely that would have been the first place Lady Chadwick would have looked, given her belief one of the staff was responsible?

She crept up, but was so busy thinking the idea through, she inadvertently let her grip on her shoes lessen. One clattered back down the wooden boards with a heart-stopping noise.

Withers' frosty face appeared on the landing below. 'Footwear is an obvious requisite, Miss Smith,' he called up to her disdainfully. 'Something even the children have grasped.'

'Not surprising.' She stepped down to collect the shoe he'd left lying in front of him. 'They're delightfully bright.'

Without replying, he turned on his heel.

'Oh, Mr Withers?' He spun around impatiently as she finished slipping her shoes back on. 'Temporary I may be, but one of Lord and Lady Chadwick's household staff, I am. Thus, I would like to meet my colleagues, please.'

'Tomorrow. They are all busy with their duties until then. As am I.' He continued on his way.

She hurried down the stairs and out into the passageway after him. 'Gracious, that could never be in question. Your expert hand obviously runs a very tight ship.'

He opened a door into a small reading room and straddled the threshold. 'Which you needed to remove your footwear to find out, it appears. Good night,' he added firmly.

She pretended not to have heard as she watched him check the window was secure before pulling the cord to close the muted-grey checked curtains. 'Yes, you have my full admiration, Mr Withers. It can't be easy, even once you've learned a family's particular habits and requirements. How long have you been in service here?'

He looked her over as if she'd crawled out from the bottom of a garden pond. 'I have been the Chadwicks' butler for three years.'

'Well, how fortunate your master and mistress are.' She stepped further inside. 'As am I. Even a temporary position here feels a privilege already. Although, goodness!' She feigned a guilt-ridden look. 'I didn't mean to sound uncharitable about the previous governess losing her post. Why did she leave, Mr Withers?'

He flapped a hand towards the door. 'She was dismissed. By the master.'

She stayed put. 'Oh my! After her references would have been so thoroughly checked too, as mine were. It must have been just a minor slip the poor woman made?' He rolled his eyes. 'I only thought, Mr Withers, you might help me not make the same inadvertent mistake?'

He snorted. 'Miss Smith, I am too busy to stand and discuss my employer's actions with you!'

'Ah, yes, silly me.' She walked towards the door. 'Because of course you lost a good, what, fifteen minutes or more, taking an interest in my conversation with Lady Chadwick earlier?'

His stolid form caught her up so swiftly, it fluttered the lace net of her curls against her neck. And raised a rash of goosebumps.

'Are you insinuating I was listening clandestinely, young woman?' he barked in a low voice.

'No, no, of course not.' She cupped her hand and whispered, 'But in case you missed the last part, Lady Chadwick was confiding in me about her missing brooch.'

'She said her neckla—' He broke off. His scowl deepened momentarily but smoothed quickly, as if catching himself.

Aha, so he was listening, Ellie!

'Has anything been stolen from the house before?'

His tone dripped ice. 'Miss Smith, if you want to gossip, go find another of your kind! Good night.'

He stalked away down the corridor.

'That's exactly what I'll do, Mr Withers,' she muttered. 'First thing in the morning.'

13

Having made sure no one saw her, Eleanor slipped out of the house and set off at a brisk pace. The address she was walking to was unknown to her. All her years abroad meant she wasn't even on nodding terms with London's labyrinth of streets. However, her butler's meticulously inked map made sure her route took her only along respectable avenues graced with grand cream stone and red-brick mansions. He'd even highlighted Belvedere's chocolate shop as the halfway marker from Lady Chadwick's house. A clear suggestion that she pause to indulge, she thought. It was, of course, at that hour, closed, which seemed an uncharacteristic oversight on his part. Resolving to tease him thoroughly about it, she increased her pace to a brisk trot.

She arrived at the spot marked on her map, pink-cheeked and trying to hide her slight shortness of breath. But she forgot about that as she ran up the steps to the smart red double-front door and stopped.

It's not a restaurant or even a café that Clifford has arranged to meet in, Ellie. It looks like someone's house!

She groaned and raised the large brass knocker.

The door was opened by a grey-whiskered chap in a vivid burgundy and emerald striped waistcoat and wire-rimmed spectacles.

'Good evening.' She held out the card with the address on to him. 'I'm possibly in the wrong place. I'm Lady— I mean, Miss Smith.'

The man laughed and tapped his nose. 'Don't worry, m'lady. Your secret's safer than the Bank of England's vault with me. Now, welcome to Dionysus Mews. Mr Clifford is eagerly awaiting your arrival on the top floor.'

She thanked him and crossed the echoing oval hallway, glancing at the framed caricatures. They were mostly of men sporting, what looked to her, high fashions of the last century. The steps of the mahogany staircase were tiled in red and yellow, matching the wallpaper. They ended on the fourth floor in a sweeping right turn, which stopped at a glossy wine-red door. She knocked. Then spotted the bell and rang that too.

'Madam is particularly keen,' Clifford said as the door opened.

She hurried in. 'I'm sorry, but a certain chocolate shop was closed!'

His eyes twinkled. 'No matter. Please come this way, my lady.'

He led her past a small billiards room to a set of bold burgundy doors, which he opened. For a moment, she took in the room's eclectic range of comfortable claret settees and inviting leather wingbacks clustered around coffee tables. Then she was literally bowled over backwards.

'Gladstone. And Tomkins!' She buried her face in her bulldog's soft wrinkled jowls and her tomcat's velveteen ginger fur. 'Oh gracious, what a wonderful welcome. And surprise!' She winced as Gladstone put his front paws on her stomach and exuberantly thrust a soggy slipper at her. 'And your pussycat tail tickling my nose, too, Tomkins. Thank you, chaps, I've missed you both terribly.' She laughed at her butler's raised brow. 'Though I really can't think why. Now, Clifford, as you haven't so much as tutted that I'm inelegantly splayed in someone else's flat on my underfrillied ru—'

'Ahem! Yes, we are alone, my lady.'

'Good. Then you'll have to tell me who owns this place before I burst. Oh, unless discretion forbids, of course?'

'Not on this occasion. However, might I at least settle you in a more ladylike manner first?'

She scrambled up with the help of his proffered elbow and settled into the chair he pointed to. Tomkins promptly curled around her neck like a winter scarf, while Gladstone sprawled lovingly across her lap. With them both content, she examined the room properly. Bookcases filled two of the walls, each shelf sporting bookends in the shape of top hats or fiddles. The duck-egg blue curtains framing each of the rosette mullioned windows were printed with silhouettes of dancing couples, while the floor lamps all sported giant carved ostrich legs. In one corner, a statue of Atlas held a drinks globe on his shoulders.

Clifford returned bearing a tantalising tray of savoury nibbles wafting oven-fresh whispers of Stilton, sausage meat and honey-cured bacon. He set it down, then flinched as she pointed at a row of paintings.

'Hang on, those aren't dust covers hiding them, Clifford. They're tablecloths.'

His hand strayed to his tie. 'In the words of Rudyard Kipling, my lady, "And the first rude sketch that the world had seen was joy to his mighty heart, till the Devil whispered behind the leaves, 'It's pretty, but is it Art?'" Ahem.'

'I'll peep when you're not looking, then.' She smiled impishly. 'Since I imagine you covered them before I arrived because they are rude, as in "nude", perhaps?'

'Would that were all,' he muttered.

She laughed. 'Well, whoever our absent host is, I'd love to meet him.'

'Ah! Regrettably, that can never be,' he said quietly.

'Oh, gracious?'

He nodded as he handed her a sherry. 'The gentleman who owned this modestly sized but remarkable pied-à-terre was young Lord Bramforth. A lively spirited and dedicated patron of the musical arts, gentlemen's social reform clubs, and the capital's orphanages.'

'What a top egg! But you said, "young lord". What happened to the poor fellow?'

'Unfortunately, he was informed by his physician at the age of seventeen that he would not live beyond twenty-nine. And so it turned out. However, he lived his brief life with unrelenting gusto.'

She ran loving fingers over her bulldog's head. 'Goodness, what a sad way to grow up.'

'Perhaps, my lady. Or a blessing to never worry one whit for the future, should one choose to see it as he did,' he said gently. 'And plenty time enough to make provision for his heirless ancestral estate to be converted to a children's home. And to leave a dedication to the memory of the one who meant the most to him; his late father's valet, and his own constant companion.'

'Sounds familiar,' she said affectionately.

He bowed from the shoulders. 'Lord Bramforth bequeathed this, his favourite London bolthole, to the gentlemen's gentlemen's club, of which his valet had long been an honorary member.'

'Dashed useful as well, you being just around the corner from where I'm holed up in Chadwick House.' She smiled, but it faded quickly. 'Though, with our hands tied, we can't be our usually dynamic duo in relation to the murder.'

'Not yet,' he murmured.

She shot him a look. 'Clifford? You've had news?'

'No. If I might therefore suggest a distractingly inelegant amount of pastry devouring instead?'

Not wanting her frustration to spoil their time together, she settled for savouring two Stilton twists and then a sausage meat pinwheel. She tutted at his raised eyebrow as she then reached for a bacon and mushroom turnover.

'Purely in the name of appreciating the divine results of your thoughtful efforts in a pinny, Clifford.' She took a bite. 'Mmm. Actually, have you hidden Mrs Trotman in your bedroom because these are sublime.'

'Categorically not!' he said with a horrified look.

She stared around in surprise at the sound of a telephone bell jangling. As Clifford raised the lid of the drinks globe, she chuckled at the apparatus set between two bottles of brandy. He gestured for her to answer it. With a puzzled frown, she picked up the receiver.

14

'Hello?'

'Blast it! I mean, apologies,' a deep voice answered. 'Wrong number.'

'Wait! Hugh, it's me!' Gladstone leaped from the settee with a flurry of woofs on hearing the name of his favourite policeman.

'Eleanor?' Seldon's voice came back stronger than before. 'And did I hear Gladstone? What in blazes are you doing in whatever male boarding house Clifford's holed up in?'

'Trying to salvage the remaining tatters of my reputation. You'd be shocked if you could see where we are,' she teased.

His rich chuckle rolled out. 'No, thank you. However, your tormented butler is almost certainly the only reason you have any reputation left, tattered or otherwise, so I shan't ask. Besides, I need to be quick. Unfortunately, this isn't a social call. But an update... of sorts,' he ended earnestly.

'We're both listening.' She beckoned Clifford nearer.

'Excellent,' Seldon said. 'Now, I had a man quietly check the bullet you found. He'd got as far as confirming it was a thirty-eight, so it could have come from a number of handguns.

Unfortunately, that's as much as we're likely to find out. Foolishly, in hindsight, at that point I went to my superior with the news.'

'But Hugh! What about—'

'No time for questions, Eleanor. But don't worry, I didn't mention either of you two.'

'Go on,' she breathed.

'I wish I didn't have to.' His voice lowered. 'What I'm going to say is in the strictest confidence.' They craned closer to catch his words. 'My superior told me, in truth, the exhibition has been put on partly to try and help Britain's badly flagging economy, which is why it has to make a profit. And a good one, along with a strong increase in trade. The reality is, countries like Germany and America are taking our traditional markets. If the newspapers get wind of a murder, it will decimate attendance for sure.' He sighed. 'But that's the lesser of the two problems.'

She took a deep breath. *Stay calm, Ellie.*

'Hang the exhibition, Hugh! We're talking about cold-blooded murder here. Surely bringing a killer to justice is more important than pounds, shillings and pence?' She winced. 'I'm sorry. I know that's how you feel too.' She frowned. 'But you said it was put on partly because of Britain's unstable economy. What's the other reason?'

'Political unrest, Eleanor.' Seldon's tone was sombre. 'Within the Empire itself, that is. You see, the exhibition was conceived as a means of presenting the Empire as united happily under English rule and governance.'

'Really, Hugh? That wasn't quite the impression I formed when I was travelling through large parts of it.'

'I realise that, Eleanor. The reality may be, well, quite different. For certain nations anyway. And Whitehall are worried those nations are trying to use the exhibition to highlight this.'

'Of course! The unfinished pavilion at the murder scene!'

'Shrewd as ever! That's just one case recently. That country was supposed to be represented, but relations collapsed to the point where they basically pulled out, which can't become public knowledge. Reporting a murder there and holding an investigation would run the risk of being perceived as an attempt to embarrass that country. In retaliation for its no-show, as it were. And, of course, its surrounding countries are eager to make political mileage of the situation if they can. Which could fuel anti-Empire feeling elsewhere.'

Fearing she knew the answer, she asked tentatively, 'The bottom line then, Hugh?'

'Is that I've been officially warned there can be no further investigation, bullet or no bullet. I tried to argue with my boss, but he told me the edict came directly from Whitehall.' He groaned. 'Eleanor, I'm sorry, I have to let you down, but... blast it. Someone's coming. Got to go!'

The line went dead.

Dash it, Ellie! You didn't get the chance to tell him you didn't blame him.

Clifford swapped her half-finished sherry for a brandy. She pointed at another balloon glass. 'You'd better join me. Hugh's news was quite the bombshell.'

He adjusted his cuffs. 'My lady, the chief inspector has done everything he could. And more.'

She sighed deeply. 'I know. There's nothing more he *can* do.'

'Quite. Perhaps closing solace might be drawn that the bullet found at least proved a gun had been fired in earnest. And thus you are neither hysterical nor over-fanciful?'

'Honestly... no. Because a murderer will still walk free.'

Her bulldog let out a quiet whimper and pressed his wet nose against hers, which made her tomcat bat a soft paw at her forehead with a yowl.

Clifford whipped a box of Belvedere's chocolates from beneath the cloth on the tray and held it out to her. 'My lady, perhaps discussing your developments in the case of Lady Chadwick's necklace might be countenanced? To save your entire menagerie's concern that sleep will never feature for you otherwise? Since, regrettably, I have no way of decorously keeping the Chadwicks' governess out all night to trump her at chess.'

She nodded. 'Good call, Clifford. And thank you for these,' she said, forcing herself to accept the murder was out of her hands.

If only for the present, Ellie.

She selected an almond praline from the box. 'And thank you for being up here in London to support me trying to help a fellow female in need.'

'My heartfelt pleasure.'

The uncharacteristic demonstrativeness in his tone made her slap her forehead. 'How did I miss your wily ruse? You guessed it would come to this, didn't you? That we wouldn't be able to investigate the murder. And you thought investigating the theft of Lady Chadwick's necklace would keep me occupied, didn't you?'

He looked away. 'I couldn't say, my lady.'

'Well, you've no need to. I'm grateful you're so thoughtful, if infuriatingly determined you always know best. I'm also delighted' – she waved around the room – 'you've finally accepted some digs you deserve.'

His lips quirked. 'Which "digs"? The character assassinations? Or the pied-à-terre?'

She laughed, her good humour in some part restored. 'Both. But your ruse might fail this time, as I haven't anything to report so far. Except that the children are beyond delightful. Hmm, and the butler is anything but! He's the only one of the staff I've met up to now. He's *Mister* Withers. He has made that exceptionally clear.'

Clifford looked thoughtful. 'Mr Derek Withers?'

She shrugged. 'Possibly. Do you know him if he is?'

'No, my lady,' he said solemnly.

'Then why...?' She shook her head. 'Oh no, I'm not going to take your bait again! At the moment, I'd say he and Lady Chadwick's maid, Grace, are the prime suspects among the staff because Grace was in the room when Lady Chadwick removed her necklace and placed it in the drawer.'

'And Mr Withers because?'

'Because he was eavesdropping in the room next door when Lady Chadwick and I were talking about the theft.'

Clifford's lips pursed. 'Unforgivable. Particularly for a butler! So, if you have no more to report, shall we to an agreed course of action?'

Having taken a large bite of another pastry, which showered a delighted Gladstone in flaky crumbs, she mumbled agreement.

Clifford raised his eyebrows but said nothing. 'Has a time been arranged for the staff introductions?'

'Possibly. But don't worry, I've a plan to make sure it happens before or after breakfast.'

'An actual, thought-out-in-advance plan?' He arched a mischievous brow. 'A new departure for a certain lady, might one dare believe?'

'Very droll. But don't get your hopes up. It's actually just my determination not to be trumped by *Mister* Withers.'

He arched a brow.

She laughed. 'Don't ask! Anyway, tomorrow, I shall subtly grill each of the staff as quickly as the chance arises. And since you can't be at Chadwick House, for once you can relax with the terrible two here.'

'And there,' he added enigmatically.

'Where?' she whispered.

'At the gentlemen's gentlemen's club. Where I have an inkling I may find out more about Mister Withers.'

'Excellent!' Pointing at the tablecloths along the wall, she smiled innocently. 'Don't stay away from your naughty nudes too long, though, will you?'

15

As Eleanor rose to return to Chadwick House she spotted Clifford's favourite leather bookmark peeping from Rudyard Kipling's *Barrack-Room Ballads*. She picked up her bag. To leave him to indulge his love of reading was the least she could do for a man she knew loved solitude, but rarely found it. Besides, she daren't risk being away for too long on her first evening as governess.

He helped her into her coat in the entrance hall, arching a questioning brow.

'If you must know,' she said airily, 'to save you needing to constantly re-starch all your underthings in future, I'm skipping off to practise being ladylike.'

He tutted. 'Having fallen at the first hurdle. Titled ladies do not "skip". They glide.'

Her teasing reply was halted by an urgent knocking at the door. Clifford opened it to reveal a harassed-looking Seldon, running his hand through his chestnut curls.

'Oh, thank heavens you're still here, Eleanor.' He hurried in, glancing around the smart hallway in confusion. 'Wherever here actually is?'

'Somewhere my wonderful butler deserves to be. For once. But this is a surprise, and a treat, Hugh.'

'Do come through, Chief Inspector,' Clifford said.

Seldon waved his hand. 'Thank you, but I can't. I've a taxi waiting outside.'

Eleanor's heart skipped. 'Have you dashed all the way here just to bid me goodnight?'

He shook his head. 'No, sadly. Against my better judgement and every grain of gentlemanly decency, I'm here to ask you to come and do the unthinkable with me.' His expression fell grave. 'Look at a body.'

'Oh, gracious!' She shrugged in bafflement. 'But, yes, of course.'

Clifford peered sideways at her. 'I stand corrected. "Skipping" is entirely an acceptable pursuit for a lady. In comparison to observing the dead!'

'We need to be really quick. And very discreet,' Seldon said. 'We shouldn't be going at all.'

'To a mortuary. You don't say,' Eleanor caught Clifford mutter with a sniff as he collected his hat and coat.

As the taxi shot away with them barely settled in the back, she turned to her fiancé. 'What's this about, Hugh?'

'Me doing what I can,' he said soberly, 'to investigate what you saw from the balloon.'

Her jaw fell. 'But, you said—'

'I know. And that still stands. But just after I had to put the phone down on you, a fellow officer contacted me. A good man. And after talking to him, well, my conscience got too loud to let me hurl the information in the river. Especially when he called back with an extra snippet.'

'We're listening.'

'The colleague I mentioned, his area covers the east side of Wembley and beyond. And I'd let him know I was looking for a shooting victim, or missing person. When he learned a man's body had been brought into the mortuary on his patch with strict instructions it was to be kept hush-hush, he quietly contacted me.'

'Who brought the deceased gentleman in, Chief Inspector?' Clifford said.

'Government men, apparently. Luckily, the mortician there owes my colleague a favour, which he called in to let us view the body.'

'Top egg!' Eleanor said.

'Definitely. But I cannot stress enough it must be a lightning in and out. And it cannot extend to seeing the post-mortem report when there is one.'

Immensely grateful Hugh was going out on such a limb purely on what she'd seen, she was still confused. 'Is the hush-hush order the only detail that makes you think it might be our missing corpse?'

'That, combined with the body having been brought in on Friday, the day of the incident. And the victim was shot. The bullet passed straight through.'

Her eyes widened. 'So the bullet that shot our poor unfortunate corpse could be the same one I found in the hay bale!' She frowned, thinking back to Clifford dropping it into Seldon's palm that night. 'But hang on, Hugh. Before you take this risk, maybe we're wrong? After all, there was no blood or' – she swallowed – 'other "bits" on it.'

Seldon scanned her face, worry lines etched on his forehead. 'Eleanor, explaining that is not a conversation I ever want to have with you!'

Clifford nodded, but clearly knew she wouldn't let it rest. 'My lady, suffice to say, bullets are far from all the same. A smooth one such as we found can penetrate and exit without, ahem, collecting any matter en route.'

'Goodness. I see. So, what's the extra snippet of information you mentioned, Hugh?'

Seldon grimaced. 'The body is being moved out tonight. So it's now or never.'

From outside the mortuary, Eleanor wondered if the building could be any grimmer. Once inside, she knew the answer was yes. The austere grey-metal doors led into a room lined floor to ceiling with tiles that were, she assumed, once white. And not cracked. She looked around mournfully. Oddly, she'd expected the place to be more... well, sombre. Instead, it gave off an air of everyday matter-of-factness. After all, she admitted to herself, death was a daily occurrence. But not murder, fortunately.

A sinewy man in his late forties hurried through another door, anxiously picking at the stitching of his battered leather apron. Eleanor thought he was pallid enough to have been one of the actual bodies stored in the cold room. On seeing them, he strode over to Seldon.

'I'm the chief mortuary attendant. And I have to say I'm not comfortable about this at all.'

Seldon held out his hand. 'Chief Inspector Seldon.' With the briefest of hesitations, the other man shook it. 'And neither are we,' Seldon said firmly. 'But we're very grateful you agreed.'

The attendant was still hesitating.

'You might be the only person who can make sure a murderer doesn't walk free,' Eleanor said determinedly.

He took a deep breath. 'His effects are on the table on the other side of that swing door. His body's on the end gurney in the chiller just beyond. And we never met. Please be quick.' He hurried back the way he'd come.

They hastened to the examination room.

'Well, "effects" in the plural was rather generous,' Eleanor said as Seldon picked up a smart embossed wallet sitting alone in the middle of the dented metal tabletop.

He read the initials, 'J.C.', then flicked it open. He

rummaged inside. 'Nothing except a few pounds, and his name stitched in the silk lining; John Clemthorpe.'

'Does that mean anything to you?'

'No. But we need to hurry.' He scrutinised her face. 'If you're absolutely sure about seeing the body?'

'*Another* body,' Clifford muttered.

Seldon frowned at him. 'You think I'll ever forgive myself for asking her to do this?'

She nudged them both forwards. 'Chaps, stop it. I'm the only one who saw the man that was shot. And I am the one who insisted there had been foul play. So let's get on with it. We should probably have been gone already.'

Her eagerness to be quick for Seldon's sake fought with her own quiet horror at stepping into the macabre atmosphere of the cold room. She tried to hide her shiver as Seldon squeezed her hand before hurrying ahead to the last wheeled trolley in the line. Evidently, she'd failed.

'Ahem, "the chiller" being particularly apt on more than one level, perhaps, my lady?' Clifford whispered.

'It does feel a little discomfiting. Like confronting death oneself,' she admitted, sidling around the first gurney which bore a worn, off-white sheet draped over a mound that had once been a living, breathing human being. 'But I saw plenty of this in the war. And I'll never sleep if I don't see if it's him now.'

Seldon was looking under the sheet as she reached his side. He dropped it quickly. 'Bullet hole is just as I'd expect from what you described seeing. You need only see his face, of course, Eleanor.'

'Lift it, please, Hugh,' she said quietly. As the cotton peeled backwards, she swallowed hard at the square-headed, blue-white corpse staring at her with unseeing eyes. 'That's definitely the man I saw shot in the exhibition enclosure.' A wash of anger made her cheeks flush. 'And I'll never forget the other man's face, either!'

As Seldon let the sheet fall, her jaw clenched.

And if you ever lay eyes on the murderer again, Ellie, you'll go up against the might of Whitehall itself, if need be, to make sure he answers for his evil crime!

16

'I do not know where you went yesterday evening, Miss Smith, but I suggest you return at a more seemly hour in future!' It was the following morning and Withers was several steps below Eleanor on the staff stairs as he led her down to the basement. Which was just as well, as he was unable to see the face she pulled, only partly from tiredness, after having sat up into the small hours creating a treasure map for the children. Her features smoothed as they reached the bottom of the stairs, but a hint of a frown remained.

You'll have to be more careful in future, Ellie. You can't risk blowing your cover so early on.

She felt an uncomfortable prickle as she followed him into the vast chamber-like kitchen. Having just finished taking breakfast with Lady Chadwick and the children, it was time for her to be introduced to the staff. She shook her head to herself. Lady Chadwick really seemed to be struggling. She'd been short with the children and looked as if she had got even less sleep than Eleanor. However, she'd more pressing things to think about at the moment. Now she was in the kitchen, the staff were continuing about their duties as if she were invisible.

The furtive gazes flashed from every side, though, showed she was anything but.

Withers led her to the centre of the room and then abandoned her with a curt 'wait here'. He then taxed each staff member over a trifling detail while she stood there, the atmosphere growing ever more awkward. Eleanor, however, was not going to give the Chadwick butler the satisfaction of seeing her squirm.

Roll your shoulders back, Ellie. You're not here to make friends. But to help a friend, well, acquaintance, out of a difficult situation.

The image of Lady Chadwick's distressed face flew into her mind, fanning the flames of her indignation over the butler's manner toward her. He might have time for petty games, but she didn't. What exactly was his problem?

She looked around at the white cotton caps and pinafore aprons worn over smoke grey or black dresses. All hands, except Withers', seemed preoccupied with polishing, peeling, or paring, fetching, folding or fixing. Catching that all eyes, however, were still surreptitiously on her, she waved a cheery hand.

'Good morning, everyone. I'm—'

'Supposed to wait for me to introduce you!' Withers snapped.

'If only you had said so, Mr Withers. Or did I miss it?' she said innocently.

She caught a derisive snort behind her. The footman, she guessed, given that he was over six feet tall and in his late twenties.

Withers ignored her question. 'Staff. This is Miss Smith, the *temporary* governess.'

Two of the younger women smiled tentatively at her, while the footman gave her a jaunty tip of his head.

Withers nodded at a woman with stiff, malt-coloured hair in

her late fifties whose expression was as sour as his. 'Mrs Hawkins, Lord Chadwick's long-serving, and respected, housekeeper.'

Eleanor smiled at her. 'Lovely to meet you.'

'Likewise, I'm sure,' she said tartly.

Withers gestured curtly behind him. 'Tateham, the footman.' He then turned to the short, puddingish woman who surely needed no introduction. With scarlet-cheeks as pillowy as kneaded dough, Eleanor was certain she was the cook, even before spotting the rolling pin she held. 'Mrs Rudge. In charge of meals and the pantry.'

He wafted a weathered hand around the room at the four remaining staff. 'The maids in order. Grace, Lady Chadwick's maid.' To Eleanor's mind, the earnest-looking, caramel-haired young woman had all the hallmarks of a girl who'd cruelly lost her youth striving to provide for herself. The worry lines dogging her forehead should have had no place on such a pleasant face of barely twenty.

Conversely, the next maid to be presented seemed at ease with herself. And pleased with her strikingly dark features and thinly disguised curves as she had stepped forward without waiting for her name to be called.

'Hannah, head housemaid,' Withers said. 'And the between-stairs maid, Alice...' He peered around the room. 'Alice! Where are you, girl?'

'Right here, sir.' A sweet round face hidden by a strangled bush of bubbly blonde curls poked out from behind the footman. The dumpling-proportioned girl stepped forward hesitantly. She smiled up at Eleanor, but thought better of it at Withers' grunt. This left only the owl-eyed waif of a girl with red-raw hands who already seemed overawed by the whole scene.

'Molly, scullery maid. Now, Mrs Hawkins aside, double speed back to your duties, everyone!' Withers stepped up to

Eleanor. 'Introductions are over. The schoolroom is on the fourth floor, if you recall.'

'Quite so.' She nodded at the clock above the door. 'Oh, except that Lady Chadwick said at breakfast she needed to whisk my delightful charges off to the tailor for a fitting. For which she will require her carriage fifteen minutes from now.' Pretending to scour the kitchen, she added, 'Perhaps, on my way out, I can tell Mr Tateham to alert the coachman for you?'

'Just "Tateham",' Withers snorted. 'And no thank you.'

'Noted.' She stepped aside to let him hurry out ahead of her. He pulled the lady's maid with him by the arm. 'Grace, outerwear for your mistress and the children immediately, as I'm sure Mrs Hawkins must have informed you.' As he reached the door and the footman appeared with a loaded tray of silver, he barked, 'Put that down, you fool! And come show me how you missed such a thing being listed in the upstairs diary.'

As they left with Lady Chadwick's maid, the head house-maid, Hannah, joined Mrs Hawkins, who was standing between two giant wicker hampers ticking off a list. She scooped up an armful of smartly folded linen from the nearest with a pout. 'Well, that didn't help the beds get changed in time, I must say.'

'No. That only lost us valuable minutes,' the housekeeper agreed firmly. She marched over to the cook, who was remonstrating with the maid, Alice, over an array of vegetables and a confusion of knives spread across the long wooden preparation bench. 'Mrs Rudge, Hannah will need Alice to assist with the beds. Now.'

The cook's hands flew to her hips, her cheeks wobbling with the force of her irritation. 'And who's going to help me get lunch ready then, Mrs Hawkins?' she carped in a strong Irish accent. 'To say nothing of straining the cheese curds good and proper and lining each of the aspic moulds as they need to be filled? Who, I ask you?'

'You and your marvellous talents alone,' the housekeeper said, 'which you really need not remind me of so often.'

'Alice!' the cook huffed, pointing at the housekeeper. 'Her ladyship has issued a decree. Go on with Hannah, I suppose. But then straight back here.' As Alice scuttled over and through the door after the head housemaid, Mrs Rudge pointed a finger at her own chest for the housekeeper's benefit. 'Back here, I meant, to where the house is *really* run.'

It was only then that the two women seemed to notice Eleanor was still there. Their power dispute seemingly forgotten, they shared a suspicious look.

'Yes?' Mrs Hawkins said stiffly. 'Was there something you needed?'

'Actually' – she joined them at the table – 'there's something I needed to say.'

'Pff!' the cook scoffed. 'Enough hot air's blown through my kitchen in the last ten minutes already. I'll be getting on, if it's all the same.' She opened a drawer and heaved out a stack of heavy-looking ancient chopping boards.

'Of course. Although it concerns both of you. Equally,' Eleanor said smoothly. That had the desired effect as Mrs Rudge elbowed her way past the housekeeper. 'In that case, go on then, Miss Smith.'

'Thank you. That's all I wanted to say.'

Mrs Rudge's hands let fly a cloud of flour as she clapped them together and flustered back behind her preparation station. 'Well, that's a first. The governess troubling to haul her virtuous shoes all the way down to the end of the stairs to say that.' She frowned. 'Thank you for what, mind?'

'My very welcoming accommodation beside the schoolroom and my delicious breakfast this morning.'

'Of course it was delicious! You sat with the mistress and the children upstairs,' Mrs Hawkins said waspishly.

'And thank you for your compliment there, Mrs Hawkins. Finally,' the cook wheezed.

Eleanor mentally shook her head at their point scoring.

'Ladies, I'm sure you've both been here at Chadwick House for a while.' She hurried on before that could prompt another contest over who could claim the most number of years in service. 'I just wonder if you remember—'

'There's not a thing at all wrong with my memory,' the housekeeper said haughtily.

Mrs Rudge looked piqued. 'Likewise!' She turned back to Eleanor. 'Now, for the love of potted mackerel, what are you asking?'

'The reason the governess post became vacant?' Eleanor said. 'I want to know, because I want to make sure I don't make whatever mistake my predecessor made.'

The women's eyes lit up, clearly eager to trump each other. The housekeeper got there first.

'She was dismissed by the master for being too lax with the children.' Looking smug, she walked over to the laundry hampers.

The cook eyed her in annoyance. 'Maybe that's one reason. And one tale.' Her gaze darted to Eleanor as she leaned over the bench as though it were a back-garden fence. 'Another reason may be that the mistress wasn't too keen on her being so... familiar with the master!' She nodded at Eleanor's expression of horror. 'That's right. And fierce familiar she must have been too. Seeing as the mistress sent her packing. And it's the only time I can ever recall her standing up for herself to the master.'

Before Eleanor could respond, the housekeeper bustled back over with a written rota of the maids' duties for the week. Mrs Rudge huffed and seized a daunting-looking knife and a cauliflower that could have fed the entire street.

'I don't know why we're discussing the last governess. I'm

more concerned with these burglaries what the police haven't solved.'

Eleanor smiled between the two of them. 'Well, I hope neither of you has been too unsettled by them?'

Mrs Rudge turned to Eleanor. 'Actually, Miss Smith, it's sure got me flustered. I tried to tell Mr Withers. Extra security we need, I said. To save us all being murdered in our beds before the Lord planned to welcome us to heaven. But he wouldn't hear a word of it, of course. Said it was all a lot of fuss over nothing. Though my friend along the road knows otherwise. Seeing as the house she works in has been broken into as well!' She waved a large brown bowl of unshelled peas to emphasise her words.

The housekeeper's meagre lips set in an even thinner line. 'Mrs Rudge! Mr Withers is nothing short of exemplary in conducting his duties. And he was quite right in his response. There is no danger here, just because of some petty thieving from a couple of houses in the street.'

She stalked out the door.

The cook rolled her eyes. 'No need, she says! Like she'd ever say anything contrary to him.'

Eleanor shrugged sympathetically. 'Well, that's probably her duty as housekeeper. To support the butler of the house.'

The cook snorted. 'If that's the only reason she's always waving his flag, I've a head of cauliflower myself where my eyes and ears are supposed to be. 'Cos they know otherwise.'

'Really? Well, going back to the topic of burglary, single or plural, did Lady Chadwick mention anything specific to you, I wonder? About being upset over something precious she... maybe can't find?'

The cook shot her a sharp look. 'Just arrived and you've a nose for gossip keener than all of my knives put together.'

Easy, Ellie. You'll give yourself away if you're not careful.

The cook's face split into a sly grin. 'Which suits me, alright.

I get wind of all the downstairs shenanigans. And you, well, you'll be getting wind of them upstairs, won't you? We could share... things.'

Eleanor nodded conspiratorially.

'Well, you're right,' the cook said, looking over her shoulder and lowering her voice. 'The mistress was complaining about a pearl necklace she's missing, so she said. Terribly expensive. Reckons it was swiped by someone in the house. One of us downstairs, mind you.' She jerked her gaze to the door the housekeeper had just left through. 'If that's the case, and I'm not saying as it is, there's only one here as is brazen enough!'

17

The atmosphere in the schoolroom couldn't have been more opposite to the tense and antagonistic one below stairs. Or more welcome, Eleanor thought with a delighted smile, immediately caught up in the children's excited air as she stepped in.

'Aye aye, shipmates!' She saluted them theatrically.

Dressed in matching sailors' navy smock tops, Octavia and Hubert giggled under their paper hats adorned with wobbly writing across the headbands. 'Aye aye, miss!' they chorused, saluting back smartly.

'You both look the part!' she cheered, beckoning them towards her to praise their clearly zealous efforts. They raced forwards, hats held out proudly.

'We know we'll be swapping lots, but we did one each,' Octavia said.

Hubert looked fit to burst. 'I did this one!' he cried, waving it at her.

Eleanor's lips twitched in amusement at his wildly enthusiastic start to the word "CAPtain". The first three letters were so large, he had written the remaining four in tiny letters, so squashed together as to be almost illegible.

'It's positively wonderful,' she said. 'And Octavia, the quartermaster's hat is brilliant too!' She couldn't help smiling that the young girl had put the symbol for a quarter first and then the word 'master'. She'd also contrived to make sure the letters fitted on the hatband neatly, unlike her brother's. Either way, the pair couldn't have been keener as they bounced on their plimsolled toes.

Eleanor saluted again. 'Time to inspect our boat and crew!'

Set centrally in the schoolroom, several feet apart, the children's desks formed the fore and mid-section of their make-believe ship. The inkwells provided the perfect holders for the slim poles to which the nautical flags were attached. Additionally, Eleanor had ferreted out some string to keep the cloth emblems extended as if filled with exotic ocean winds.

The front desk's built-in seat was occupied with an impromptu ship's wheel, which promised endless adventures for unbridled imaginations. Next to it were the evidently no-longer daunting brass measuring compass and protractor, given how eagerly the children were running their fingers over them. On the desk itself was an atlas invitingly open at a large fold-out colour map of the world. Reading out loud the names of each of the oceans in the small hours had been enough to transport Eleanor back to her happiest memories as a child. Sailing the seas with her parents, the salty tang on the breeze accompanying her every breakfast. Always savoured in pyjamas, and on the front deck, weather and waves permitting.

On the second desk, she had arranged two new exercise books headed 'Ship's Log' and 'Ship's Supplies' above a sea of inked scrolling waves. The desk's seat was filled with the dolls and teddies from the bedroom, all sporting a miniature version of the children's hats. Eleanor had to smile at Hubert's beloved floppy-eared rabbit propped high on the shoulders of the others. Behind it, two blankets were stretched out, their knotted top and bottom hems giving a passable impression of hammocks.

The previously disappointing games trunk now held several improvised sailing and navigation aids and also formed the transom, or rear of the ship, as she explained to the bubbling pair.

'Well done! All shipshape and Bristol fashion, me hearties,' Eleanor said in her gnarly sailor's voice, which made the children giggle again.

Hubert's head shot up. 'What does that mean?'

'It means we're ready to start our voyage to Zanzibar!' she whispered.

'And find the treasure,' Octavia breathed, as wide-eyed as her brother.

'Yes. But that will take us more than today.'

'Hurrah!' Hubert sang. 'I want to spend all day, every day, on a sailing boat. Even' – he folded his arms firmly – 'when I'm a grown-up in long brown trousers working in the Bank of England.'

Eleanor couldn't keep in her chuckle, nor her hands reaching out to cup his flushed cheeks. 'My dear Hubert, in that case please reserve your very first investor's appointment for me.' She slid her arm around his sister. 'And Octavia, of course.'

A moment later, the three of them were looking down at the atlas. The children gasped as Eleanor unfurled her more elaborate than originally envisaged treasure map. Despite not having started until eleven the previous night, she'd become absorbed in tracing a selection of countries' outlines, plotting a course between them, and thinking up riddles to accompany each one. She smiled to herself, remembering the first summer she'd spent at Henley Hall after her parents had disappeared. Her uncle had been out of the country on business, and she'd felt lost and bewildered. Until Clifford had secreted a riddle in her doll's house which, with some artful steering where necessary from him, had led her to unearth a very treasured prize. One which still occupied pride of place on her bedside table at home over thirty years later. A rare picture of her as a baby with her parents and uncle. It was one of the few family photographs she had.

'This map looks very old,' Octavia breathed.

'Most treasure maps do,' Eleanor said airily, leaving out that it wasn't actually printed on ancient parchment, but a roll of paper she'd found yesterday, discoloured yellow with cold tea.

'First, you need to find Zanzibar on the atlas,' she said to her two eager charges. 'Then we can solve the riddles and work out which route to start out on.'

She produced the magnifying glass from the science cupboard, which led to much scouring of the page together. Octavia looked thoughtful.

'Miss, if you know the treasure is in Zanzibar, why don't we just sail the shortest way there?'

'Excellent question,' Eleanor said. 'Because we need to collect some things hidden along the way first which will help us when we arrive.'

'And the riddles will tell us where to find them!' Hubert chirped, still poring over the page. 'Ooh, Zin-bran-za. I've found it!' He tried again, managing to get his tongue around the name as Eleanor helped him spell out each letter.

Octavia's shoulders rose with glee as she read the first riddle from the treasure map. '*Stop at the country almost square. Christopher Columbus first sailed from there. Collect a numbers table and measure. To help you find where is your treasure.*'

The children 'oohed' at each other as they fell back to studying the atlas. The schoolroom rang with their enthusiastic discussion over the shape of each country.

'We think it might be Egypt or Spain,' Octavia finally said.

'But we need to know, who was Christopher Columbus?' Hubert urged Eleanor.

'A man who has inspired sailors to travel the oceans for

almost five hundred years.' She reverently pulled out an illustrated history book she'd found in the locked dresser.

Once the explorer's tale had been devoured by the children, Spain was declared their first port of call. Having agreed they couldn't need to carry an actual table on their trip, as mentioned in the riddle, their curiosity had them staring around the schoolroom.

'Numbers... a times table!' Hubert trumpeted, far more eagerly than Eleanor had expected, given the list of errors under his name on the wall.

'And a ruler!' Octavia cried.

'Amazing!' Eleanor cheered.

Next, they plotted the first leg of their course, calculating time and distance with the theoretical wind speed she'd conjured up. Then they were ready. She pointed to Hubert.

'Right, Captain, collect your ship's log and stand at the helm, or steering wheel, please. Quartermaster, from the stowage trunk, we need our hourglass to track our timing. Plus, to dangle over the side to confirm our speed, our other ship's log. Which looks a little like your skipping rope wound around the handle with some knots tied in it.'

Eleanor couldn't help joining in staggering and swaying as Hubert proclaimed they'd hit a choppy section part-way across the Bay of Biscuits.

'Is that right, miss?' Octavia looked doubtful.

Eleanor laughed. 'Almost. It's Biscay. But I like Hubert's version better.'

An hour of absorbing geography, maths and history later saw them pulling into an imaginary Spanish port to despatch their quartermaster to retrieve the items the first riddle had hinted at.

'Your go as captain.' Hubert swapped hats with his sister as she re-boarded. 'I'll read the next riddle.' He started in with gusto. '*The Africa dessert—*'

'Might it say desert, I wonder? A sandy place with little to no green growing?' Eleanor suggested, recognising her own self at that age forever hoping everything had to do with food. Not that she'd discernibly changed, her thoughts heard her mischievous butler quip.

'Ah!' Hubert read on slowly with Octavia's help. '*The Africa desert is dry. Where it's wet, stop by. Collect a donkey's suitcase. To keep your treasure safe.*' His eyes were bright with questions.

'This is such fun!' Octavia cooed, racing him to rifle through the pages of the atlas. Eleanor discreetly steered them towards the right place.

'Sa-ha-ra desert,' Hubert read aloud. 'Miss, what do you find in a desert?'

'Well, would you like to learn about which animals live in very dry places?'

'Yes, please!'

Before she could relate any fascinating details about snakes, lizards, or scorpions, the door opened and Lady Chadwick appeared.

'Mother!' Hubert cried. 'You can't come in! You need wellington boots. We're at sea!'

Octavia shook her head. 'Actually, we're in the desert, Mother, learning about the animals that live there.'

Given how much the children were enjoying and absorbing the lessons, Eleanor bit her lip, hoping her unorthodox teaching methods weren't about to be deemed improper.

Thankfully, it seemed her worries were unnecessary. Lady Chadwick beamed as she scanned through the ardently completed pages of the captain's log and the lengthy calculations in the supplies log.

'Well done, children. I can see you've been working hard.'

'They really have,' Eleanor said genuinely as Octavia sat with Hubert in the quartermaster's chair so they could catch magnetic fish over the pretend boat's side for the toy crew's rations.

'Goodness, what a gift you have.' Lady Chadwick stared at her animated children as if she couldn't quite believe they were hers. She frowned, as if remembering why she'd come. Then she blinked and lowered her voice.

'Sorry, I didn't want to interrupt, only I'm so desperate to hear you've made some progress about, you know... my missing necklace?' she ended in a whisper.

Eleanor fought a frown. As far as she knew, Lady Chadwick was still adamant it could only have been one of her staff, but Eleanor hadn't found any overwhelming evidence of that yet. She was unwilling to share what she'd learned so far for fear of repercussions against anyone she mentioned.

'I have made inroads,' she said quietly. 'Though nothing concrete enough to pass on at the moment.'

'But I need...' Lady Chadwick tailed off with an apologetic shrug. 'To let you get on with what you're clearly better at than I am.' She glanced at the children again. 'Or the previous governess was.'

Eleanor shook her head ruefully. 'Any skills at investigating I've acquired didn't come through choice.'

Lady Chadwick gestured at Octavia and Hubert. 'I meant inspiring my children.'

With a sad smile, she glided out the door and pulled it closed behind her.

Oh, Ellie, what a mess this household seems to be in!

For the sake of the children, she slapped on a hearty smile, only to find them staring at her as she turned back around.

'Well, me shipmates. What is it?'

The pair looked at each other and nodded.

'When we find the treasure, miss,' Octavia said haltingly. 'We want to give it to Mother.'

Eleanor's heart warmed. 'That's a lovely idea. But you're

the ones who will have earned it. It's always thoughtful to share, though.'

Octavia shook her head. 'Mother should have it all. She lost hers.'

'That's what you were talking about just now, wasn't it?' Hubert said quietly.

Eleanor hesitated, unsure how she could tread carefully enough. In truth, she didn't want to discuss anything except fun and games with them.

'We weren't listening. Honestly,' Octavia said. 'But Mother looked upset. Just like when we heard her asking the staff if anyone had seen it.'

'Seen what?' Eleanor said tentatively.

'Her necklace.' Hubert wrinkled his nose. 'I don't see what girls like about dangles and sparkles. But Mother liked that one very much.'

Octavia nodded. 'We think she must have dropped it somewhere. Maybe when she goes out at night when Father is away. But we can't say that to Mother because she doesn't know we know.'

Hubert nodded in turn. 'And we're not sure Father knows.'

Eleanor was torn. To question the children further went against her conscience, but... Hubert saved her the dilemma by letting out a long huff. 'It's silly. We have to keep pretending we don't know, but we do. Last time Mother said Octavia had just had a bad dream. But she hadn't! There was a thunderstorm, and we went down to Mother's room in the night because we were scared but she wasn't there.'

'Or anywhere else in the house,' Octavia said. 'We looked.'

'Gracious, storms can be very noisy, can't they?' Eleanor said quickly. 'But fortunately, there are none coming across the oceans today.' She pointed at their satchel bags. 'And I see you've cleverly worked out the donkey's suitcase puzzle. So, how about you read out the next riddle together?'

'*Leave good hope in your cape...*'

The rest Eleanor heard only as a blurred buzz of excited voices as her jumbled thoughts overtook her.

Now, where can Lady Chadwick be going late at night without her husband knowing, Ellie? And more importantly, has it anything to do with her missing necklace?

18

As Eleanor reached the second-floor landing, the sound of the door below opening jerked her to a stop.

'Dash it!'

Keeping up the convincing pretence of being a governess was challenging in itself. On top of that, tiptoeing around didn't come easily to her energetic, impulsive nature. She imagined Clifford's voice in her ear. 'Instead of a governess, what a pity the Chadwicks did not require a temporary rhinoceros, my lady!'

She hung over the railing to see who it was, flinching at the sight of Withers' sourpuss expression glaring up at her.

'You are required in the blue room, Miss Smith. Immediately.'

'How lovely.' She pointed one hand up the stairs and the other down. 'And where among all the rooms I haven't been introduced to is that?'

It was childish, she knew, but he'd really got her goat in the kitchen earlier.

Withers tugged on his jacket collar and said in a strained

tone, 'It's the police. They wish to speak to all members of staff. Separately.'

'The police?' She stepped slowly down the stairs, trying to hide her confusion. Lady Chadwick had been adamant they must be kept out of the affair. 'Why would they be here, Mr Withers?' she said airily.

He fumbled with his tie. 'There was another burglary. Further along Park Lane, apparently. The policeman in charge is currently with Lady Chadwick. He will call each staff member in turn shortly.'

She bit her tongue. 'Fine. In what order will we be called?'

He snorted. 'In hierarchical order, obviously!' Without a backward glance, or a helpful answer to her question of where to find the blue room she was to wait in, he marched away.

She hastened along the first-floor corridor, looking left and right while formulating a plan. The policeman might think he would be the one asking the questions, but she had other ideas. Whatever he knew about this other burglary could have a bearing on the necklace theft here, she reasoned.

She lurched to a stop beside a half-open door, her gaze caught by a narrow glass cabinet of Wedgwood blue china plates.

Ah! The blue room, I presume, Ellie.

She stepped in. It was furnished in the modern minimalist style, with just a few pieces of furniture in light oak set against silver and ivory damask wallpaper.

She started pacing the floor. How to put the policeman off his guard? Maybe play the outraged governess? *How dare you question me like that, young man?* She sighed and rolled her eyes. Playing the terrified female, seeking assurance for her safety, was guaranteed to be most effective, she knew. Even Seldon had admitted he would do almost anything to placate a hysterical woman.

'I think one of us is confused,' a voice said from behind.

She whipped around to see Grace, Lady Chadwick's maid, running a finger over the worry lines on her forehead.

'Thankfully for both of us,' Eleanor said in a sisterly tone, delighted the one person she'd really wanted to question yesterday afternoon was now here in front of her.

'I'm sorry, Miss Smith, I don't follow you,' Grace said. 'Mr Withers was very clear. We all have to wait separately. So, we'd better each be where he told us to be. And quickly.' This came out with more force than Eleanor had expected from the wilting young woman she'd seen in the kitchen. And all the more unexpected, as the maid hadn't moved, implying Eleanor should be the one to go, despite being above her on the staff hierarchy.

Mind you, Ellie. She's come a long way at a youngish age. That doesn't happen to trembling wallflowers.

She nodded. 'Yes, we had. To avoid a ticking off, maybe. But standing on your own fretting for goodness knows how long about what the police want to know is going to be hideous.'

The maid turned her back as if perusing the plates in the display cabinet. 'Why would you think I'd be fretting, Miss Smith?'

'Because Mr Withers said it's all in relation to a burglary. Much like the one Lady Chadwick has suffered, perhaps?'

Grace spun around, both hands clasped over her mouth. 'How can you know about that?' she stammered.

'Because Lady Chadwick confided in me. But she was adamant the police mustn't be told.'

The maid looked at her oddly. 'That's what the mistress told me, too. I've not even spoken to the other staff about it.'

'Hasn't that made for some difficult conversations?'

'Yes.' She folded her arms. 'But that's no different to most days. Some are always sniffing for titbits about life upstairs.' A haunted look passed over her face. 'When the mistress told everyone her pearl necklace was missing, honestly, I felt my heart sinking.'

'Because you'd be under their suspicion for being the one who took it?'

The maid jumped so hard her white cap rode backwards over her head. 'Me! Why would they think that? Just because I'm the only one of the staff supposed to be in the mistress' room! I've never... I wouldn't, I mean, and anyway, when I left her, she hadn't finished taking it off.'

Eleanor fought the frown that threatened at this stark contradiction to Lady Chadwick's version of events.

'As her lady's maid, you didn't wait for her to remove it and place it in her dresser drawer? She was rather distracted, I imagine, about abandoning her guests?'

'Yes. I mean, no.' Grace took a deep breath as if regaining her composure. 'Yes, the mistress was in a fearful fluster. But, no, I didn't stay to help her remove her necklace because she sent me out in a fit of cross words for choosing then to tidy up. I... I didn't even know she'd put it in her dresser drawer.'

Something about the way the maid said this last statement made Eleanor jump on it.

'Do you believe she never did?' she whispered.

Grace hesitated. 'Of course not!' she whispered back. 'The mistress would never tell a lie.'

'Look, Grace,' Eleanor said quickly, sensing the woman was becoming suspicious. 'I feel bad for adding to your worries. And we hadn't even got as far as "hello" before I did. If there's something you know, isn't it better to get it off your chest?'

The maid hesitated. 'I'm... I'm not sure. Not meaning to be rude, but you've only just started. I don't even know you.'

'True. And the police constable who wants to talk to us both has only just arrived. And you don't know *him*. But supposing he frightens Lady Chadwick into reporting that her necklace was stolen? Especially as her husband isn't here to intervene. You'll have to confess to him then.' She nodded at the maid's gasp. 'And Mr Withers suggested this constable fellow is rather fierce.' She shrugged. 'But if you're completely honest with him, you'll probably be alright.'

The maid took a step forward. 'I'd rather tell you.' She cast her eyes down. 'You're... you're not like the others downstairs. Or upstairs.'

Eleanor waited patiently on the outside, but not so on the inside.

Someone could come at any minute, Ellie.

Finally, the maid seemed to have screwed up enough courage. But instead of speaking, she glanced around furtively and slid her hand into her inner garments. Withdrawing it, she held out a small folded tissue.

'I... I found it on the floor of the mistress' bedroom the day she said the necklace had gone missing.'

Eleanor's eyes were transfixed on the object. 'Did you tell her you'd found this?'

Grace shook her head, her brow furrowed. 'No. Because it would mean I'd be accusing the mistress of lying and she'd have dismissed me on the spot.'

Eleanor winced. 'Very true. And you were right not to. In fact, I wouldn't mention it at all. Not even to the policeman.'

Grace nodded eagerly. 'I won't. You keep it. I don't want it.' She glanced around again. 'He probably wouldn't believe me anyway. Just as he also won't believe that I saw someone lurking outside the mistress' room when she threw me out that night.'

Eleanor's pulse quickened. 'Hmm, that depends on who you saw?'

Grace leaned forward. 'It was Tateham!'

'Tateham? He's the footman, isn't he?' Eleanor knew he was, but wanted a moment to gather her thoughts. At Grace's nod, she frowned. 'What would he be doing outside Lady Ch—'

'What is this?' Withers barked from the doorway.

Eleanor groaned quietly. 'Grace and I were simply getting acquainted.'

He strode up to her like a storm cloud. 'You have little need of even remembering her name!'

'Because I'm in post temporarily?' she said, annoyed at his brusque tone and words.

'Exactly! And because your duties should be confined largely to the fourth floor. Where the schoolroom is! Not the second, where the lady's maid is mostly occupied.'

'Noted,' she said. 'Most helpful, Mr Withers.'

'Unlike the need to waste time trying to find you, Miss Smith!'

She managed a contrite expression. 'But I was sure you told me to wait in the blue room?'

'I did. But as anyone with sense can see, this is the Wedgwood room. The blue room is at the end of the next hallway.'

'Ah!' Eleanor admitted to herself she might have wondered why the wallpaper had only silver and ivory in its stripe. 'This Wedgwood collection is all blue, though, isn't it? Do you know it comes in sea green and other colours as well?'

Withers' eyes narrowed. 'Follow me now! That policeman was expecting you some minutes ago.'

She smiled sweetly. 'How lucky you found me then while I can still be fashionably late. Otherwise, this officer would feel bound to caution me for wasting police time. Thank you, and lead on, Mr Withers.'

19

Eleanor mentally shook herself as she followed Withers along the corridor. She couldn't confirm what Grace had given her until she was alone, so she needed to concentrate for the moment on what she could learn about the nearby burglary.

At a walnut door, Withers knocked and then opened it without waiting for a reply.

'Miss Smith has finally been located. Shall I send her in?'

'Of course. Right away,' a familiar voice replied.

Over Withers' shoulder, a flurry of chestnut curls and broad shoulders in a charcoal-grey suit swam into Eleanor's view. Her breath caught.

What on earth, Ellie?

'You won't need long with this one,' Withers said sniffily. 'She's new as of yesterday, Chief Inspector.'

Her fiancé's tall frame cleared the chair and desk in two familiar efficient strides. 'Mr Withers, I shall be the one to—' He broke off, blinking slowly as he stared at Eleanor over the butler's shoulder. 'To... to be the judge of that, thank you.' There was a ruffle of a pen pot falling over as he reached back behind him to pick up his notebook. He held it up. 'In fact,

someone new in service here is the most likely to have noticed
something dismissed by others. So, I shall require an extra ten
minutes with Miss… umm?' He blinked again as she stepped
forward.

'Miss Smith. How do you do?' she managed matter-of-
factly.

'Better, usually,' he muttered. At normal volume, he said,
'Please take a seat. By the desk.' He nodded at the butler, still
hovering in the doorway. 'That's all, thank you, Mr Withers.'

Seldon waited until the butler had closed the door behind
him, then ran a hand around his neck. 'Governess? What the—'

'Careful,' she whispered. 'The walls here have ears.'

He retook his seat, shaking his head as he laid both hands in
silent question on the green baize blotter now festooned with
pens.

'Your wrist!' she hissed in concern, spotting a congealing
patch of blood. 'What have you done?'

'Jabbed myself with the letter opener to check I wasn't going
mad when I saw you, Eleanor,' he whispered back as he rubbed
a handkerchief over it briskly. Yanking his cuff down, he started
picking up the pens he'd knocked over while doing it. 'And I'm
still far from convinced I'm not!'

'There's a very simple explanation,' she said, trying not to
worry about the exhaustion still haunting his handsome face.

'I doubt that. "You" and "simple" rarely, if ever, seem to
meet.'

'Perhaps you're right, Hugh. Because I can't actually tell
you why I'm here.'

'Even though I'm your fiancé, blast it? And in charge of this
investigation?'

She nodded. 'Yes. And the finest senior policeman
anywhere. In fact, that's the problem. I swore I wouldn't involve
the police, you see?'

He closed his eyes and counted to three out loud. 'No, I

don't, Eleanor. Not at all.' He opened them and sighed. 'But then, that's nothing new, is it?' Her heart faltered. Then she caught his tender smile. 'And I probably wouldn't have it any other way,' he said softly.

She laughed. 'Only "probably"? That sort of leaves a girl a little in the dark.'

'Good.' His gaze softened. 'Because the moment this baffling charade is over, I shall somehow muster the courage to lay my deepest feelings for you under the spotlight.'

Her heart skipped. 'Feelings, Chief Inspector? You once told me most emphatically they have no place in a policeman.'

'And I was right,' he groaned, staring at her hands. 'Because this is torture. Especially, after all the agonising I've been through since leaving you last night...' He grimaced. 'I'm truly sorry about all of it.'

'Don't be, Hugh. You did all you could.' She cocked her head. 'And you really aren't here about that, but about a burglary in the street?'

'Yes, blast it!' he muttered into his notebook.

She winced. 'Oh, Hugh, please don't say you're no longer in charge at the Empire Exhibition because you went to your superior with the bullet Clifford found?'

He held up his hands. 'No point railing against the truth, Eleanor. Nor my pretending otherwise to you.'

Her insides clenched as she breathed, 'Hugh, I'm *so* sorry.'

He shrugged. 'At least they didn't find out I took you to see the body at the morgue!' He smiled at her. 'And no matter what's happened at work, you look no less beautiful, even in that stern matronly grey dress, by the way.'

'Thank you. But I didn't, and don't, want to get you into trouble. Now. Or ever again. But, this burglary thing, well... I was expecting just a beat policeman, not Scotland Yard's finest.' She paused, desperate to keep her promise to Lady Chadwick but hating herself for holding back from him.

He grimaced. 'It's too high profile for that. It needs to be kept discreet because the theft happened in one of the mansions further along Park Lane. Which, would you believe, is rented by a foreign dignitary from—'

'The Empire Exhibition?'

'Spot on! So yet more having to investigate on eggshells.' He pointed a teasing finger at her. 'Thank goodness we aren't working together, hmm?'

Her sharp hearing caught a creak outside, halting her retort. 'Hugh!' she hissed. 'Someone's out there.'

Like a streak of lightning, he was at the door, pulling it open. Closing it again quietly, he stepped back to his seat. 'A flash of black trousers disappearing around the corner?'

'The footman or, most likely, Withers.'

'*Mister* Withers,' Seldon said gruffly. 'He couldn't have hammered that home any harder if he'd had an anvil to swing. Bit surly for a butler, isn't he?'

'Only so as you'd notice.'

He chuckled. Sobering quickly, he picked up his pen. 'I'd better add something under the Chadwicks' governess for my report.'

She nodded. 'I heard the staff talking about burglaries in the kitchen. Tell me about the one you've come about, and I'll give you a plausible statement.'

'Which you won't be able to sign in your fake name, because that would be breaking the law!' He shook his head. 'But as for the burglary. The latest is one of three in the last six weeks. It took place five doors along. Which is about a mile away, given the size of these homes! No sign of a break-in. Estimated time of burglary, half-past three in the afternoon.'

'Gracious, not even under the cover of darkness?'

'The previous ones were. But it seems the thieves are watching the houses and know the staff routines now. No one saw anything or anyone out of place.'

'Or they're all inside jobs,' she murmured.

'Exactly. A member of staff could have been bribed to allow entry in each of the thefts.' He scanned her face, looking concerned. 'Eleanor, I won't ask why you're here because it's clear you feel you can't tell me. But I wish with all my heart you weren't.'

'So do I,' she said honestly. 'I'd rather be at Henley Hall, waiting for my fiancé to find enough time to dash down and at least eat a proper meal for once. You look shot through, Hugh.'

'No, I've only been shot once, remember? On a case you...' He tailed off. 'Listen. I just wish Clifford was here with you. Because in the burglary yesterday, one of the staff was knocked unconscious.' He shook his head at her horrified gasp. 'No, he's not too seriously hurt that he won't pull through soon enough. But I'm worried for you. This house could be targeted next. Which is why I would install Clifford here if I could. At least he might temper some of your wildest recklessness. And do what I can't. Look after you,' he ended glumly.

His words made the conflicting tales she'd heard about Lady Chadwick's husband and the previous governess flood into her mind. Lord Chadwick would be back on Friday, and she had no desire to be on the receiving end of his overeager libido! Not that she couldn't defend herself, but an ally on hand sounded good.

And Clifford could help with the necklace investigation, Ellie. If only you could work out how to get him into Chadwick House?

'That's a brilliant idea, Hugh.'

His expression suggested he would have fallen off his chair if he hadn't been resting his elbows on the desk. 'Just like that? No fuss. No arguing "I'm perfectly capable, thank you, Inspector!"'

She shook her head. 'Chief Inspector. And no argument.

But partly because I shall need someone to adjudicate when I step in the ring with Withers. Gloves off!'

Seldon rose. 'I'll have to let you go now, or Withers will become suspicious. But be sure to give him an extra especially hard biff from me when you do, won't you?'

Up in her room, she forced herself to tear her head, and fluttering heart, away from her fiancé and back on to the small tissue bundle Grace had given her. She carefully unwrapped it and placed the item on the dressing table. Reaching into her dress pocket, she drew out a small bag and placed the contents next to Grace's discovery and stood back, shaking her head in disbelief. The item Grace had found on Lady Chadwick's bedroom floor was part of a clasp. And it completed the broken one she'd found at the exhibition centre perfectly!

20

'Hello?' Eleanor called through the half-open double doors into the library. She frowned at the silence that came back. Withers had begrudgingly insisted if she needed to speak to Lady Chadwick, she might find her there.

She let out a low whistle as she stepped inside.

In the subdued lighting, she made out gold-leaf motifs adorning the bookcases and carved mouldings below the half-galleried landing, accessed by the narrow spiral staircase on the far side. She ventured further into the room and squinted at the books. Oddly, there seemed to be almost as many bookends as books themselves. There were also no cosy chairs beside the fireplace to curl up with one's favourite read like in her uncle's library. In fact, there was no fireplace. Instead, where the chimney breast should have been, there was a large mahogany panel inset with two rows of what looked like scientific brass instruments. An apparatus made from glass tubes along with a slowly rotating drum in a glass case stood on the central oval table. Overall, the space had hallmarks of a traditional library. But one more fitting in a scientist's art gallery than a reading room in a wealthy home. Even the expected smell of leather was barely discernible. The air felt cooler than in the rest of the house, too. Looking around, she had the oddest feeling she was standing in a mausoleum for books.

Having closed the door against prying eyes, she stepped across the rugless oak flooring and ran her eye along the titles.

'How deathly,' she murmured.

'Aren't they though?' She looked up to see Lady Chadwick on the mezzanine above her.

'Gracious, you surprised me.'

Her hostess drummed her fingers anxiously on the rail. 'As I hope you haven't me, by telling that policeman anything?'

'About your necklace? Not so much as a single hint.' Eleanor folded her arms indignantly. 'I do not go back on my word.'

'Thank goodness!' Lady Chadwick hurried down the spiral staircase. At the bottom she halted, suddenly awkward. 'Of course you wouldn't. Forgive me. I've just been so unnerved by that inspector.'

'I can't imagine he was anything but a perfect gentleman when he questioned you,' Eleanor said, trying not to sound defensive.

Lady Chadwick shuddered. 'That he was here at all is too much!' She pulled a lace-edge handkerchief from her cuff and dabbed at her nose.

Eleanor nodded sympathetically. 'That's why I settled Octavia and Hubert into their new reading corner we've made so I could pop down to check on you.'

Lady Chadwick reached out and patted Eleanor on the arm. 'Oh, you are a dear! But honestly, all the while he was talking to me, I just sat there terrified he would demand we look in the safe together to make sure nothing was missing.'

Eleanor felt a prick of confusion. 'What would have been

the problem, though? You said that only your husband has the combination?'

'He does,' Lady Chadwick said tautly.

Eleanor hesitated.

Maybe you should just move on for the moment, Ellie.

'Well, so far I've only managed a brief chat with Grace and an even briefer one with Withers. And played discreet arbitrator between Mrs Hawkins and Mrs Rudge in the kitchen.'

'Tell me you've learned something helpful?' Lady Chadwick said eagerly.

'It's a bit early to say, in all honesty. There's been some finger-pointing. At Mrs Hawkins and Tateham, actually.'

'I see. And what... what did Grace say?' Lady Chadwick said guardedly.

'She said she left your room *before*, not after, you put your necklace in your dresser drawer.' At her hostess' sharp intake of breath, she nodded. 'She insisted she didn't even know that was where you had put it until I told her. I find that interesting, don't you?'

Lady Chadwick tossed her coiffured updo. 'Are you accusing me of *lying*?'

Eleanor chose her next words carefully. 'Not at all. I merely wondered if you might... have remembered the sequence of events a little wrong, perhaps? Given the strain you've been under, after all?'

Lady Chadwick twisted her handkerchief into a knot. 'I have. It has been simply too awful.' She lifted her chin up. 'But no, I've... I've remembered that part perfectly.' She hesitated. 'I suppose Grace told you I'd had too much to drink as well?'

Eleanor's tone remained even. 'No, but had you?'

Lady Chadwick coloured. 'It's... it's something I never do when my husband is home. So I'll admit now, I had rather indulged.' She looked up pleadingly. 'I possibly shouldn't have kept that from you. I'm sorry.'

Eleanor smiled encouragingly. 'Don't worry about it. But what else haven't you told me because you feared I would judge you? Maybe the real reason you didn't put your necklace back in the safe?'

Lady Chadwick hung her head. 'You're even shrewder than I credited you for. Alright, yes, I was too embarrassed to admit it. I was a little too tipsy to remember the combination.'

Eleanor slapped the table in frustration. 'But you told me only a moment ago, your husband has never shared that with you.'

Her eyes lit up. 'That's true, I tell you! He hasn't. Reginald doesn't think I'm responsible enough to have it. He keeps the household money in there as well. Yet expects me to run the house like a proper wife in line with his mediaeval way of thinking. He's simply preposterous in his outlook!' She cast her eyes down and sighed. 'Deep down, I'm sure he... he loves me, but' – she glanced up at Eleanor, her eyes red-rimmed – 'communication is so hard, don't you think? Surely you find that, too? I know you're not married, but you must have a beau?'

Even though Eleanor felt for Lady Chadwick, she didn't want to be drawn into a conversation about her love life. Besides, she'd put herself out to help Lady Chadwick recover her necklace and so far it seemed she had returned the favour by lying to her.

'So how did you find out the combination, then?'

Lady Chadwick shrugged sadly. 'By spying on him. Just as Withers does on me!'

This pulled Eleanor up short. So Lady Chadwick was aware Withers was spying on her? She wandered a few steps to the next bookcase, trying to think where to take the conversation. Everything seemed so much more complicated than when she'd first agreed to help. She flinched on feeling Lady Chadwick's hand grip her arm.

'You aren't thinking of letting me down, are you?'

'By running away from the promise I made you?' Eleanor shook her head, leaving out that she wished now she hadn't promised in the first place. 'But I need to make quicker progress.'

'Much quicker! Reginald will be home in a few days.'

Eleanor gritted her teeth. If she'd been told the truth from the start... She turned around to face the other woman. 'If you're still insisting a member of your staff is responsible, I need a plausible way to spend more time with them below stairs. Which Withers is adamant a governess should not do. Especially a temporary one.' She smiled at the fun she'd already had with the children in the schoolroom. And at the delight she'd seen in each of them, as they'd mastered understanding something that had previously eluded them. 'And it's not fair on Octavia and Hubert for me to throw a half-baked lesson at them and then duck out to try and investigate. They've been nothing but diligent and wonderfully well-behaved.'

'I've got it!' Lady Chadwick said. 'I'll take the children away this very afternoon to visit a friend until Lord Chadwick's return on Friday, on the pretext of it being a reward for impressing their new governess with their studies.' She tapped Eleanor's arm with a manicured nail. 'Which will give you an excuse to spend more time below stairs because you will have no duties upstairs until I return except preparing lessons.'

Eleanor nodded. 'That sounds like an excellent idea.'

Although you'll miss the children, Ellie.

Her brow furrowed. She waved a hand around the library. 'If you find the books in here so deathly, why did you come here after feeling so rattled by the chief inspector?'

'Hmm, oh that. Well, it will sound quite the pathetic female, so I'd rather not say.'

Eleanor held her gaze until Lady Chadwick raised her hands in surrender. 'I know, I know.' She pointed at the shelves. 'You see, this is my husband's other real love.' She laughed bitterly. 'Perhaps his *only* real love, I sometimes think. Not his wife. Nor his children. Just these old books!'

Eleanor kept a frown off her face, remembering Lady Chadwick's insistence earlier that she believed her husband did still love her, despite his outward behaviour.

'He's a collector, you understand,' Lady Chadwick continued. 'Of first editions. And after my trauma with that inspector person, I came up here with a desperate idea. That Reginald might also be marginally less angry when he hears about my missing necklace, if I'd arranged for his oh-so-precious books to be indexed. Or catalogued, or whatever the term is. As a surprise, for his birthday next week, you see. But it's a hopeless thought. I've no clue where to find someone expert enough to undertake such a tedious task.'

Eleanor's eyes lit up.

Who better to play the part of a bookish expert than your own book-loving butler, Ellie?

'Hmm, I might have just the contact.' She tried to keep the eagerness out of her voice. 'I had, um, a very good chap do a fine job in the library at Henley Hall recently. However, he's very select about the engagements he will consider.'

'Excellent,' Lady Chadwick said quickly. 'Then he will be honoured to deal with my husband's books. Tell him I need him to start this very afternoon, as they must all be done before my husband returns.'

Eleanor nodded. 'I'll give him a call and see if he's free. If he is, please inform Withers before you leave with the children. He certainly wouldn't take my word you'd asked for the man to be engaged. Oh, and say the recommendation came from someone else.'

'Right away.' Lady Chadwick glided towards the door, calling back, 'Do remember to impress on this book person that my husband will be home on Friday. Everything must be perfect for him.'

'To find his children have a new governess,' Eleanor muttered to herself. She hurried to the door. 'Actually, I meant to ask, why did your last governess leave?'

Lady Chadwick bit her lip, then shrugged. 'I have no idea. Really. She, well, she just informed me one day that she would work her notice and go. No explanation. But that's staff for you!'

Eleanor bit her own lip as Lady Chadwick swept out of the library and down the main stairs.

So she's still hiding things from you, Ellie?

For a moment, she felt angry. Then she remembered Lady Chadwick's words. *By spying on him. Just as Withers does on me!* She frowned. Aspects of the absent husband's behaviour were beginning to bother her. He expected Lady Chadwick to run the household, but kept the money locked away. That suggested he made sure she never had much independence either. Not only that, but she had to wait until he was absent to have friends around, it seemed. And to ever relax. Was Withers spying on her on the orders of her husband? Eleanor shook her head. Was Lady Chadwick more unstable or incapable than she appeared? Or was Lord Chadwick just a blinkered traditionalist? Or was there another explanation?

A set of stealthy footsteps approaching out in the corridor caught her ear. She crept over to one of the bookcases, where she was hidden from view by the spiral stairs.

The floor creaked as the door closed silently behind someone.

She stepped out. 'Hello, Tateham.'

Rather than seem surprised, or concerned, at her presence, he smiled cheekily.

'Hello, Miss Smith. We haven't had a chance to say so much as howdeedoo, have we?'

'Is that why you're here?' she said, wondering if he'd been eavesdropping like the butler.

He laughed. 'What? And have Mr Withers chase my

gizzard all around the pantry for being so brazen? No, I was looking for... someone else.'

'Who?' she said, casually taking a book off the shelf and leafing through it.

He smiled again, but this time, it made her skin prickle. 'No one who's here. Because that's only you, isn't it?'

Thinking that a strange answer, she nodded. 'Yes. I was hoping to find something interesting for the children.'

'To take with them? Can't imagine they'll fancy reading when they've been let off lessons.' He grinned. 'I wouldn't have.'

'Where have they been let off to?' she said smoothly, now all the more sure he'd been listening at the door.

'No idea, Miss Smith. But I've been sent to pull their weekend bags from the luggage loft so Grace can pack them in double quick time.'

She fought the urge to ask why then he had come into the library and nodded instead. 'So efficient. Can I share something with you, Tateham? In confidence, though?'

'Absolutely.' He stepped so close she could feel his breath on her cheek.

'Well, with no disrespect at all to Mr Withers, but I've always thought it's really the footman who keeps the house ticking along perfectly. You're the ones at the heart of everything. In my experience, anyway.'

Tateham nodded vigorously. 'Too right! I could do a better job than old Withers, that's for sure!' He tugged on the hem of his jacket. 'And I could really do with the money. Badly. But that's my secret. Don't tell. All I need is the break, you see? The chance to show what I can do.'

Eleanor was nodding along, trying to think of a way to ask what he had been doing hanging around Lady Chadwick's bedroom just before her necklace was stolen, but he froze. 'That's Mr Withers' footsteps,' he hissed. 'I'll be for the high jump if I don't have those bags in my hands when he finds me.'

'I can't hear him,' Eleanor said.

His disconcerting smile returned. 'That's because you're listening for his footsteps to echo down the corridor. He's a slyer old fox than that. Take it from me, Miss Smith, he'll spy on you like he does the mistress. And then he'll learn your secrets and you'll be gone quicker than the last governess!'

21

Furthering her pretence of being a real governess, Eleanor busied herself in the schoolroom for two hours after her odd exchange with Tateham in the library. Truth be told, she was rather enjoying herself. With the children having left with Lady Chadwick, she was free to conjure up a few surprise treats for their lessons when they returned. She also needed the distraction to stop her impatience running wild. With the discovery of the two matching parts of the jewellery clasp, it seemed there might be a tenuous connection between events at the Empire Exhibition centre and Chadwick House. But how? Eating with the staff would be her next chance to really question any of them further. And she couldn't wait to revisit the library.

As the schoolroom clock struck the hour, she made the final adjustments to the red-and-white striped pillowcase acting as a curtain for her improvised puppet theatre. Her delightful charges could now act out their history lessons with their own beloved dolls and teddies. Chuckling at the image of King John's re-enactment of signing the Magna Carta being portrayed by a floppy eared-rabbit, she scooped up her exercise book and hurried down to the first floor.

Pressing her ear to the library door, she smiled at the familiar voice she could hear on the other side

'I can see no obstacle to the endeavour, Mr Withers. I shall commence immediately.'

'Good. You may arrive at ten sharp and leave at five,' Withers' haughty voice answered.

She knocked and stepped inside, pretending not to recognise the bespectacled chap wearing white cotton gloves with a brown velvet jacket and a looped ochre cravat. He glanced at her as she entered, but said nothing. As she strode over to the butler, the man returned to examining the brass instruments above the fireplace.

'Excuse me interrupting, Mr Withers, but Lady Chadwick suggested I introduce myself to this gentleman.' She pointed at Clifford. 'On account of the children.'

Withers frowned. 'There are no children's books in here, Miss Smith. And Mr—'

She waved a dismissive hand. 'Quite right too. Sticky fingers and jam everywhere otherwise.' She held up the exercise book. 'However, this gentleman might be kind enough to spare a few snippets about the history of printed books I can jot down. To help bring their reading lessons to life.' She turned to Clifford. 'I'm Miss Smith, the governess here.'

Looking every inch the bookish expert, Clifford offered a grandfatherly nod, his hands clasped behind his back. 'I am Mr Welch. And, Miss Smith, to a dedicated bibliognost like myself, or lifelong devotee of printed matter for clarity, engendering the love of books in any form is a privilege.' He held up a finger. 'Especially to children!'

She hid another smile. Even though Clifford was playing a part, it was a role that suited him to a T. His insatiable appetite for devouring the weightiest of ancient tomes she could only match with her insatiable appetite for devouring the flakiest of fresh pastries.

Withers was watching their exchange intently, she realised. Clifford caught her coded glance and gestured at the instruments on the central table. 'Perhaps I might also impart a few details regarding the intricacies of the hygrometer, barograph and thermograph, to pique scientific curiosity in the young minds under your charge? The gentleman of the house is indeed a true connoisseur of rare book collecting to have such items installed here.'

She walked up to the table. 'Which of the names you mentioned is this rotating drum with an ingenious inking needle making some sort of chart?'

'That is a barograph. It tracks eight days of continuous barometric pressure changes by means of this needle mounted on a moving arm. The graph paper is wound around the drum, you see. And the information it provides allows for the most precise adjustments necessary to the library's temperature, relative humidity, et cetera, to avoid the horrors of mildew.' He shuddered. 'Or worse!'

Withers cocked his chin. 'Within what ranges?' His eyes betrayed a hint of...

Suspicion, Ellie?

Clifford adjusted his spectacles. 'Temperature range from sixty-eight to seventy-two degrees Fahrenheit. Range of relative humidity from forty-three to fifty per cent, being slightly reduced in deference to the number of limp vellum and early Coptic bindings I have observed.' He nodded appreciatively. 'Most admirable to check your master's collection is in safe hands, Mr Withers. Perhaps I might relieve you of winding duty on the clockwork mechanism of respective instruments while your master is away? Likewise the storage and replenishment of the barograph record paper?'

At Withers' grateful nod, Clifford selected a box of graded pencils along with a bound set of folio papers from a brown leather briefcase. 'Please do not let me detain you further, Mr

Withers. You have been most helpful.' He turned to Eleanor. 'Now, Miss Smith, the calibrations on the hygrometer have evolved from the once groundbreaking machines whereby a human hair's expansion and contraction was—'

The door clicked shut. She tiptoed over and listened as the sound of the butler's footsteps receded.

'He's gone,' she whispered. 'Hello, my favourite fountain of all knowledge. You look no less dapper in your disguise, by the way. But honestly, how do you keep all that unnecessary twaddle in your head?'

Clifford eyed her in amusement. 'Perhaps by not filling it with the deplorable twaddle of penny dreadful novels instead?'

She laughed. 'Touché. Now, first things first, Withers is definitely the one to be extra careful around regarding our assumed personas.'

'And in other regards, my lady,' he muttered gravely, sliding the exercise book respectfully from her hand.

'Excellent! What have you found out?'

'The reports from the gentlemen's club which I mentioned at the pied-à-terre are far from favourable,' he said, not looking up from the diagram he was drawing on her page.

'Hang on.' She tugged his jacket sleeve, making his pencil scratch on the paper. 'The one you're an honorary member of, Clifford? We've messed up! Withers probably recognised you. I thought he sounded a touch suspicious!'

He shook his head. 'Extremely unlikely, if you will pardon the correction, my lady. We have never met at the club and it does not have portraits of honorary members, unlike the butlers' and valets' club.'

'Good thing too! Then go on.'

While talking, he added a magnifying glass to his cataloguing tools on the table. 'For brevity, and ahem, with regard to a lady's sensitivities, suffice to repeat only that Mr Withers is far from liked. Or welcome at the club anymore. There was even talk of expelling him after he did a fellow member a calculated disservice which lost his counterpart his position.'

'Oh my! What did he do?'

'I am sorry, my lady, but club rules forbid me to go into detail. The same rules that have stood since 1783 and state clearly that expulsion may only occur on production of irrevocable, written evidence by another member. Which, in this instance, could not be produced. The unanimous consensus, however, is that Mr Withers is the slipperiest eel ever to have disgraced a butler's uniform.'

She gestured around the library. 'Then how did he get such a prestigious position here at Chadwick House?'

He adjusted his cuffs. 'I really couldn't say, my lady.'

She snorted. 'Then I'll say it for you. Unless he is just the sort of slippery eel Lady Chadwick's husband wanted as a butler!'

Clifford nodded, but quickly turned back to the table and his tools as the door opened.

'No pens required, thank you, Miss Smith.' He picked up a pencil. 'Ink has no place within three miles of rare books!'

Mrs Hawkins rustled over in her stiff-collared black housekeeper's dress. 'Miss Smith, I understand from Mr Withers you will be taking meals with the rest of the staff in the children's absence. Food will be in fifteen minutes.'

'How kind to let me know,' Eleanor said genially. 'And perhaps Lady Chadwick's newly engaged biblio... book expert too?'

Mrs Hawkins glanced at Clifford, her hand sliding around to pat the back of her meringue-stiff hair as she looked him over. 'I've no instructions for you, sir. I'm sorry, you'll have to go elsewhere to eat. Or bring your own food.'

'Entirely as it should be, dear lady,' Clifford said smoothly, receiving the first hint of a smile Eleanor had seen from the frosty housekeeper.

As she disappeared, Eleanor laughed. 'Dash it! If you could just waft your inimitable charms beyond this library, the entire female contingent of staff would be singing like birds about anything they know concerning stolen necklaces or anything else!'

He tutted. 'Enjoy the extremely modest fare a governess would partake of, won't you?'

As she reached the bottom of the staff stairs, voices rang out from every open door along the stone passageway.

'Molly, where are my skimmer and potato ricer?' the cook's strident voice yelled from the kitchen.

'Comin', Mrs Rudge!' the scullery maid said tremulously as she shot across the passageway balancing a stack of mixing bowls.

Free to make her own way this time, rather than herding after Withers, Eleanor took her time. She walked slowly with her exercise book open, as if musing over the diagrams and notes Clifford had quietly added while she was in the library. In truth, she was keeping her ears alert. And trying to figure out if the thief had come downstairs the night of the party, where they could have hidden the necklace until the fuss died down.

Above her head was a long panel with a series of bells, each marked below with a number, presumably referring to a particular room upstairs. And below this, six thick black rubber stoppers set in the wall. Part of a previous internal communication system, she guessed. She removed a stopper and placed her ear near the tube. She could faintly hear voices at the other end.

I wonder if that's one way Withers snoops, Ellie? Or a handy temporary hidey-hole, perhaps?

She surreptitiously removed all six stoppers one by one, but the tubes were all empty.

She hastily shoved the last one back in place as the scullery maid struggled past with a huge pan of steaming water and nearly collided with Tateham. He was carrying two large corked glass bottles and a tall jar of amber coloured crystals.

'Tateham!' Withers barked from the doorway of the butler's pantry, waving a thick ledger. 'I clearly instructed you to make sure the polishing paste was finished before lunch.'

The footman stretched himself to his full height. 'That's why I'm rushing back to the hotplate in the pump room with this sulphuric acid and gum arabic. To do just that, Mr Withers. I'm not one to flout rules, you'll remember?'

Eleanor was surprised to see the butler hesitate. 'Well, now you're needed to wrestle with the dumb waiter instead,' he gruffed. 'Its electrics have stuck again.'

Tateham groaned. 'It would have been better if it were still manual. It's always getting stuck, wretched thing!'

'You'll have to hurry before the motor burns out. And then miss pudding to finish the polishing paste after,' Withers said with satisfaction.

Eleanor smiled between them. 'It's partly my fault for holding things up here. So sorry.'

With little grace, Withers nodded and waved her onwards after the footman before disappearing back into his pantry.

As Tateham put down his burden and set off again, Hannah, the head housemaid, blocked his way with her curvy figure.

'Oh, Tateham, I've left the ivory black by the hot plate to save you getting into more trouble.' She batted her long dark eyelashes. 'Only I forgot to do my turn of the water pumping for the upstairs bathroom tanks.'

He winked at her. 'Don't worry. I'll do it. It'll be my pleasure.'

Hannah turned and sashayed ahead of him towards the kitchen, both oblivious to Eleanor standing beside a pile of crates, trugs and baskets. Peeping inside the room opposite, she frowned at the long workbench with a motor running a belt at one end attached to what looked like a tall handled pump. An open wooden toolbox stood on the floor with a scattering of hammers and wrenches around it. On one wall, two deep utility sinks were each set below a low arched sash window. Buckets, pails and a rack of mops and brushes were lined up in the far corner. She sighed. The thief could have hidden any number of necklaces and no one would have found them. Not straight away, anyway.

Back in the corridor, three large hampers stamped with 'laundry' stood between the next two doors.

More hiding places, Ellie!

The first door obviously led into the cake and dessert pantry given the plethora of stands, moulds and muslin-tented dishes. The next, into the dairy room. Inside, Alice was bent over a triangular stand almost as tall as she was. She was wielding a short-handled, heavy-looking paddle to press white lumps, of what Eleanor was not sure, through a fine mesh hung over a large bucket. She reminded her of her own maid Polly as she had more on her apron than in the bucket.

'Looks tricky,' she whispered.

Alice spun around, her blonde curls bouncing. Before she could reply, the cook's stentorian rasp came from behind. 'No wonder, Alice, my girl! What in the world are you doing taking a butter paddle to my cheese curds?'

The maid's lips flapped. 'Only tryin' to be quicker 'n hot treacle like you said, Mrs Rudge.'

'Hopeless! Get off and help hurry up the table setting. And change your pinny for pity's sake before Mr Withers gets wind of the mess you're in.' She pushed Alice out ahead of her.

Eleanor followed behind but only as far as the next door. It was a thick oak-panelled affair with sliding circular vents. Inscribed on an enamel plaque were the words: *Meat Store. Mr Withers only!* Somehow she couldn't picture the thief hiding a piece of jewellery among the cuts of meat. The door was also locked, so she moved on.

At the end of the passageway Eleanor caught sight of the housekeeper lauding it over a blue-aproned tradesman on the back step. In a wide alcove opposite her, Tateham was leaning inside a deep inset cupboard, a trolley filled with polished glassware nearby.

Ah, Ellie! The dumb waiter.

The footman leaned further into the cupboard, muttering expletives. After a moment, he thumped a large button on the wall marked "Up". The dumb waiter shot upward half a foot with Tateham's head still inside before coming to an abrupt halt again.

The footman withdrew his head carefully and straightened up. He glanced at Eleanor and rolled his eyes.

'One day this dumb waiter will be the death of me!'

22

Entering the kitchen, Eleanor noticed three rows of gleaming copper pans hanging on the dresser at the far end. The remaining empty hooks were evidently usually home to the three large pans bubbling and simmering on one of the black iron ranges. Beside it, another dresser was filled with creaming bowls, colanders and casserole dishes. Against the right wall, a narrow ten-seater table was half-set with cutlery and enamel cups, a long backless bench tucked underneath. An open wooden cupboard further along was being emptied of plates and bowls by Alice and Molly. Eleanor stepped towards them, hoping to ask a few quiet questions about the stolen necklace. But as Hannah joined them, they crowded into a huddle. Mrs Rudge seemed occupied in one of the pantries, so Eleanor idled over to the nearby table in a windowed alcove and pretended to read a recipe book.

A moment later, Tateham sauntered in.

'Dumb waiter's fixed, ladies. Just needed the firm hand only a powerful set of muscles could give it!'

The three maids giggled and nudged each other as he whipped up his jacket tails and bent over the long bench to pull it out. Wiggling his hips cheekily, he straightened up and carried a stiff-back chair to the head of the table, then walked to the other end to drag another over.

'Told you! He can't get enough of me,' Eleanor heard Hannah crow to the other maids.

Alice's sweet, round face broke into a grin. 'And I told you, you'll get caught. Honestly! The way you trail him around the house like a dog after a bone'll get you both in the spittin' hot fat.'

'She's right!' young Molly gasped. 'Mr Withers'd string you up for the rats to eat.' Her face fell. 'Like he said he would me once when I was so sick I woke late.'

'I'm too clever for the likes of him,' Hannah scoffed. 'Anyways, I'm not scared of Withers! Neither's Tateham.' She nodded at the others' slack jaws. 'That's right, he's got that puffed up old goat whipped into a corner!'

'Tell us!' Alice begged.

'What's it worth?' Hannah hissed. Eleanor bent further over the recipe book. Hannah folded her arms. 'Agree to fill my coal scuttles for three days, then I'll tell.'

Molly shook her head, looking terrified, but Alice nodded. 'We'll both do it. Now tell.'

Hannah looked smug. 'Well, 'twas the night of the mistress' party what the master knows nothing about. Yet! The one, you know, where she says her pearl necklace was nicked by one of us!' She scoffed. 'Anyway, Mr Withers had a right go at Tateham, carping on 'bout how he had no right being in the mistress' bedroom.'

Eleanor's breath caught.

So Grace was telling the truth about seeing Tateham lurking outside Lady Chadwick's bedroom, Ellie.

She cocked her ear not to miss whatever else the maids might let slip.

'Mr Withers poked him in the chest,' Hannah continued to

her mesmerised audience. 'Said he was going to report him to the master before he'd even got his coat off. And that Tateham'd get kicked out.'

The other two gasped. 'No more Tateham!'

Hannah grinned smugly. 'Oh yes, there will be. And longer 'n Mr Withers himself if he so much as bothers him again! Tateham's so fearless he shot back that he'd end Withers. And that he'd tell the master exactly what Withers has been up to, which'd see him straight out on his pompous backside!'

Alice's curls shook with horror as she looped her arm through Molly's. 'But what's Mr Withers been doin' that's so wrong?'

Hannah lowered her voice further as the maids leaned in. 'Well, you know he and—'

'Girls!' Mrs Hawkins marched into the kitchen. 'Why is the table not ready? Disgraceful! And why,' she called pointedly towards the pantry, 'has Mrs Rudge not admonished you for it?'

Mrs Rudge appeared wielding a heavy, metal-tipped meat tenderiser with menace. 'Because I was more behind than all the cows' tails on account of losing Alice to help with the bed making, remember? Now the mutton collops are long ready. And don't be complaining the turnip mash is dried out. Nor the greens are like ghosts of themselves. You're all late. And this is my kitchen!'

As the maids finished setting the table, Eleanor quietly pitched in. A minute later, Withers strode in and sat at the head. He nodded to Mrs Hawkins as she sat at the opposite end. All eyes slid to Eleanor, who settled onto the centre of the bench, the better to hear everyone.

Unfortunately, she learned little from the shrouded jibes thrown around under the guise of civilised conversation. It severely soured the meal, which was actually rather tasty, especially the fried cabbage and potato patties.

Therefore, that night, she put her upset stomach down to

the bitterness of the words served up over the table, not to the food. Unable to sleep, she tossed and turned.

'Quarter past midnight,' she muttered, eyeing the mantelpiece clock as she dragged herself out of bed and into her dressing gown. Only it wasn't. The unfamiliar ankle-length grey dressing gown she'd found in her suitcase, like the rest of her clothes, had been picked out by her housekeeper and butler to suit those of a governess. Not a titled lady. And, despite being sure she'd put them there when she'd got into bed, she couldn't find her slippers anywhere.

She sighed. 'And no Clifford to magically appear, bearing his chess set and a stomach-soothing warmed milk.'

He had left at five to keep up appearances and she daren't go around to his pied-à-terre so soon after Withers' warning.

Now that she knew her way around, however, she decided to simply fix herself a comforting drink.

At the bottom of the staff stairs, she peered about in the gloom. The only light was from the moon, peeking in through the glass panel above the back door at the far end of the passageway.

Dash it, Ellie! Why didn't you find your slippers! And have the foresight to bring your bedside candle?

She froze. It seemed someone else had. A growing glow was coming from the meat store. As the door opened, she silently slid back around the corner and peeped out. The eerily lit face of Withers appeared below the lantern he held. He turned back to glance inside the store, holding the lantern up as if checking something, then nodded and closed the door. Placing the key carefully in his jacket pocket, he checked the door was locked, then walked cautiously towards the pump room. There was something in his manner that made Eleanor tiptoe after him, silent in her bed socks, now grateful for her lack of slippers.

A moment later, he slid through the open door of the pump room. She crept to the doorway and peered inside. Back turned,

Withers was reaching over the sink towards the second of the arched windows. She noticed with surprise the window was open. She coughed behind him.

'Good evening, Mr Withers. Or is it morning now?'

He jumped like a scalded cat. 'Miss Smith! What are you doing down here? And at this hour?'

'Looking for milk. And a pan. But without a light, foolishly. Which is why I followed yours into here.'

'Milk?'

'Upset stomach.' She held up a finger as her stomach let out a long growl in support of her story. 'You too, perhaps, Mr Withers? Although, there's no milk in here. So what are you doing?'

'Nothing! Merely... finishing my rounds. And I found this window open. So I came in to close it, naturally.'

Eleanor's thoughts flew back to the burglaries in the street.

Maybe Withers had opened the window earlier, Ellie?

'It's very late to be finishing your rounds, isn't it? Especially with the family not here?'

Withers turned the latch with a huff. 'The butler is always the last to retire. And as the milk is locked away, I shall thank you to return to your room!'

Back in her bed, she was more awake than ever, running over the possibility that Withers had been bribed by the gang that had burgled the other houses in Park Lane.

With that unsettling thought further upsetting her grumbling stomach, she finally drifted off into a fitful sleep.

23

The following morning at a quarter to nine, Eleanor trudged down the staff stairs. She was a lady who needed her sleep, and after only four unsettled hours in the land of dreams, she was not at her brightest. Certain she'd missed breakfast, she batted away the idea of nipping out to find sustenance on the pretext of running an errand for the children.

You're here to help Lady Chadwick, Ellie. And find out if there really is a connection between events at the Empire Exhibition and Chadwick House. So, you need all the minutes you can with the staff.

Her mind flashed back to the night before. At least there appeared to have been no burglary during the early hours. She'd heard nothing, and no one had roused her. Perhaps it had been a simple case of forgetfulness and Withers had been dutifully closing and locking the window? Or she'd interrupted him and put the wind up whoever he was leaving it open for?

She paused on the second to last step. The air seemed tense this morning, the bustle more frenetic. She shook her head. The family was away, so surely everyone's duties should have been lighter than usual? And yet...

Mrs Hawkins was stationed at the end of the passageway, delivering a near ceaseless flurry of orders.

'Alice! Don't dawdle, girl! Pick your feet up! Tateham! Finish polishing the master's boots and then you and I will collect the silver-rimmed glassware from the receiving room together.' She glanced at the clock. 'Then you will polish it in the kitchen under my watchful eye.'

The footman shook his head. 'Not meaning to be rude, Mrs Hawkins, but that's Mr Withers' job. Besides, he's the one with the key to the cabinet.'

'Don't worry about that,' the housekeeper said dismissively. 'Now, be on your way.'

Eleanor watched him stride off, shoulders set angrily. Had Withers enlisted the aid of Mrs Hawkins to put the footman in his place? she wondered. Was Tateham's threat that Hannah had overheard the last straw for the Chadwicks' butler? If so, if Tateham really had something incriminating on Withers, the butler was playing with fire. She had no doubt that if Tateham were forced to leave, he would take Withers with him.

Fixing a genial smile on her face, she walked up to the housekeeper, but received only a stiff, 'Morning, Miss Smith,' in reply.

She kept smiling. She needed to speak to Withers again about last night and also now, about his apparent running feud with Tateham.

'Good morning, Mrs Hawkins. I've a few additions required for the schoolroom, so I need to see Mr Withers. He said all expenses must go through him. In his butler's pantry, is he?'

'No!' Mrs Rudge grouched from further down the passageway. 'He's not. Nor is he in my kitchen where he should be.' With a disgruntled toss of her head, she disappeared back into her culinary kingdom.

Just then Alice bolted out of the dairy room, clutching a butter dish only to run into Hannah, juggling two glass bottles.

At the sound of smashing, a face poked out of every door, except the butler's pantry, Eleanor noticed. She stayed put to defuse any fireworks from Mrs Hawkins directed at either girl. However, the fumes of ammonia rising from the glass and pottery-littered floor made her eyes water so much she found it hard to concentrate.

'Oops-a-daisy!' She blinked rapidly. 'Easily done when you're all so busy.' She coughed as the fumes hit the back of her throat. 'What's... what's that saying about spilled milk?'

'Nonsense! That's what it is.' Mrs Rudge elbowed Tateham aside as she stomped into the forefront, throwing her apron over her mouth. 'Milk's a pretty penny. And half a pound of my butter wasted is a good sight more!'

The housekeeper went to reply, but coughed violently instead. Recovering, she glared at the cook. 'Nothing compared to the cost of two bottles of my spirits of hartshorn!' Her hands flew to her hips. 'How am I supposed to get grease marks out of the family's clothing now? I've no more budget for wasting!'

'Neither have I!' Mrs Rudge shot back. 'Then it'll have to come,' a fleeting unity passed between the housekeeper and the cook as they stared at the two maids, 'from your wages, girls!'

'That's how!' Mrs Hawkins added, with unnecessary relish to Eleanor's mind. 'Now clean that up.' She stalked off.

Eleanor was about to offer consoling words when Alice burst into tears.

'It's your fault!' Hannah hissed. 'You'll pay me back every penny! Before Christmas too.'

Tateham grimaced and slid away, revealing a wide-eyed Molly dripping soapy suds onto the mess. ''Twas already the most terrible mornin', too,' she muttered dolefully.

Eleanor pulled the three maids to one side. 'Alice and Hannah, you'd better clear up. And Molly and I will hurry to the kitchen to fill in for whatever you two would otherwise be doing.'

Hannah's mouth dropped. 'Really?'

'Oh, thank you,' Alice gushed over her shoulder, as the head housemaid dragged her towards the mops and brushes on the back pump room wall.

In the kitchen, the duties Eleanor was trying to fill in for seemed mostly to involve laying out the table for breakfast. Which was a wonderful surprise after she thought it was way past the hour the staff would likely take it. Until she remembered in most households the staff weren't allowed to eat until all the morning chores were finished and the family had breakfasted themselves.

'Porridge bowls, miss, if you're bein' so kind,' Molly stammered. 'And plates for toast and jam. I'll do the tin cups, knives and spoons.'

Eleanor looked across to the range, hoping to see skillets of browning bacon rubbing shoulders with glistening sausages. Golden eggs frying and poaching, along with kippers sizzling in a buttery pan to accompany the meagre offerings Molly had suggested. There wasn't. With a sigh, she turned back to setting the table, counting off the staff who needed a place on her fingers. She frowned.

'How many of us are there, Molly?'

The maid thought for a moment. 'Nine, miss.'

'Eight,' Mrs Hawkins said, poking her nose between them. 'Grace is away with the mistress, remember?'

'Seven!' trumpeted Mrs Rudge. 'Mr Withers hasn't bothered to come down yet. And it's thanks to that we're all rushing around like fire with its tail alight. So when he does arrive, he don't deserve no place!'

Mrs Hawkins rounded on the cook. 'Mrs Rudge! There will be no question of Mr Withers not eating with us! So bite your insolent Irish tongue. Mr Withers can only have gone on an important errand that it is none of your business.'

Note she said 'your', not 'our', business, Ellie.

She added a bowl and plate at each setting from the stack she was trying not to drop. Clearly Withers' errand was an unexpected one, if even the housekeeper didn't know about it. Or was she covering for him?

Something, perhaps, to do with the window you disturbed him at last night, Ellie?

Her breath caught. Maybe there had been a burglary? And Withers had done a runner with his bribe money? Or even with the gang themselves? With neither Lady Chadwick nor her husband due back until Friday, Withers might have been relying on any theft going unnoticed. After all, it would normally be the butler who would be the first to discover any irregularities in the family's absence!

'Where's Tateham?' Mrs Hawkins barked.

Mrs Rudge's voice came from a cloud of steam as she poured a giant black kettle into an elephantine enamel teapot. 'He had the common sense to run to the coachman to cancel the booking for the mistress this morning. Seeing as she up and left with no notice yesterday. And no one thought to do it. No one as in Mr Withers, that is!'

'Well, that's not good enough,' the housekeeper snapped. 'I need him. The dumb waiter is stuck up in the dining room again and it can't be left like that. It does something dreadful to the motor if it's not un-jammed.'

'I'll try,' Eleanor said. With an idea fermenting, she was keen to get away from the bickering. 'I saw Tateham fix it yesterday, so I've an idea what to do.'

'That's as maybe, but you shouldn't go,' Mrs Hawkins said quickly. 'It's a most costly piece of apparatus and all damages are taken directly—'

'From staff wages, I know,' Eleanor said, hiding her dismay at the maids losing even a farthing of the slavish pittance they were doubtlessly on. 'I'll take the risk.'

She hurried away up the staff stairs. On the first floor, she hesitated, trying to get her bearings.

'If the kitchen is almost at the end of the passageway below...' she murmured, imagining stepping across to the wide alcove where Tateham had been cursing the dumb waiter in the staff basement. 'Then the dining room must be... through those double doors.'

Throwing them open, she gasped.

Over at the dumb waiter, a man she didn't recognise seemed to be manhandling something into it.

Her heart faltered at the sight of a pair of butler suit tails.

'That's... that's Withers! Is... is he drunk?'

The man jerked around. Her hand flew to her mouth as she stared in horror at his pockmarked cheek... *The gunman from the Empire Exhibition, Ellie!*

24

Shock rooted her to the spot. Eleanor felt herself sway as if still in the runaway hot-air balloon, watching helplessly as a man took another's life in cold blood. The man now standing in front of her. There was no mistaking that deeply pitted cheek, not with the way the scarring ran down almost to the left corner of his lips.

'Who the hell are you?' the stranger demanded.

She swallowed hard.

He hasn't recognised you, Ellie.

Trying to keep the wobble from her voice, she spoke up. 'I'm Miss Smith. The Chadwicks' new governess. More to the point, who are *you?*'

'Me?' he spluttered. 'I'm Sir Reginald Chadwick. Master of this house!'

'What! But...' Her gaze darted back to the crumpled form of the butler. 'But then why... I mean, you're not supposed to be here until Friday.'

'I will return to my own house whenever I please, woman! But for heaven's sake, stop gawping hysterically and help me with Withers. The man's as stiff as a board. Been raiding the drinks cabinet while I've been away, I'll warrant!'

She shook her head. Something was wrong. 'Why are you trying to manhandle him into the dumb waiter?' she said guardedly, keeping her distance.

He stared at her in exasperation. 'Are you a complete simpleton? Why on earth would I be shoving my unconscious butler into the dumb waiter? My dinner arrives in that! I found him lying on the floor next to it and I was trying to get him to stand up, the old drunk!'

Even though she was shocked by his brusque attitude, something in his unexpected manner made her act. She darted forward to get a grip under the butler's shoulders. Lord Chadwick grabbed his legs and together they heaved Withers onto the side table next to the dumb waiter.

Instinctively reaching to press her finger to Withers' neck to check for a pulse, she realised Lord Chadwick was already doing so. Eyes closed as if summoning all his focus, he winced, then pressed harder. She watched him, perplexed. He was either an excellent actor, or—

He withdrew his fingers and shook his head. 'The damn fool's dead!'

Pacing the blue room was doing nothing to settle her thoughts. The sound of police boots passing outside in the corridor didn't help. Withers was dead. Not absent on a mysterious errand. Not drunk. Dead!

Her thoughts flew back to Lord Chadwick's baffling behaviour in those final moments in the dining room. A moment after pronouncing Withers dead, he'd declared he was calling the police. Not the action of a man she thought had been trying to hide the butler's body in the dumb waiter when she'd first entered.

Maybe he was, though, Ellie. Maybe he realised the game was up?

She shivered. She'd already seen him take a man's life in an instant. Had she just seen him switch plans in a split-second without faltering too? If so, he was a dangerous adversary. No. A deadly one.

She wished she could speak to Clifford, but it was too dangerous to be seen together at the moment. Even though she had no idea what was going on, she instinctively felt it was still better no one knew of their connection.

She felt for the envelope hidden in her inside pocket. While Lord Chadwick had left to telephone for the police, she'd quickly searched Withers' body. She was loath to do so, but the last man she'd seen Lord Chadwick kill had disappeared in moments and a monumental cover-up had taken place. If it was going to happen again, she was going to amass any evidence she could first.

Before searching the body, however, she'd quickly looked for the cause of death. She'd had time for no more than a cursory glance which had drawn a blank. Withers could have just dropped dead from a heart attack as far as appearances went. She'd briefly thought of doing a more thorough examination, but dismissed the idea. Lord Chadwick could return at any minute and who knew what his response might be if he'd found her intimately examining the man she was fairly sure he'd just killed.

Instead, with fumbling hands, she'd quickly checked his pockets.

A quiet rap on the door brought her back to the present. The constable she'd met half an hour earlier poked his head around the door. 'The chief wants to see you next, miss. He's done with Lord Chadwick.' As he turned to lead her out, her sharp hearing caught him mutter, 'Or more like Lord Chadwick's done with the chief!'

On entering the writing room, her heart leaped on seeing "the chief" was actually her fiancé.

'Ah, Miss Smith,' Seldon said, trying to hide that he was anxiously scanning her face. 'Please come straight in. And take all the time you need to tell me whatever you can.' Waving the constable away, he called after him, 'And see we are not disturbed, Jones.'

She tried to rally a reassuring smile as he closed the door. Then felt her heart flutter as he pulled her into his chest.

'Eleanor, my love,' he murmured, burying his face in her hair. 'How I stopped myself racing through the house to do this first, I'll never understand. Or forgive myself for.'

'I know why, Hugh. Because you're the most dedicated policeman ever. So you went immediately to the body as you had to, and should have. And there's nothing to forgive, silly. Besides, I heard Lord Chadwick reporting on the telephone that everyone in the house was fine except his butler.'

'Fine?' He gently led her to a chair he'd pulled around to his side of the desk. 'Thank goodness I was only at the far end of Park Lane, investigating the other burglaries, because Lord Chadwick reported a Miss Smith was in the room with him when he telephoned. You! And with a body. Again! How could that ever be fine?'

'You make it sound like I actively court these things.' She smiled as he wound his long, strong fingers around hers under the desk. 'But I should have realised it was you who'd been put in charge when that constable said he'd been sent to sit with me until his chief was free.'

'Honestly, I feared I might blow your cover when he came back, saying you'd refused. I've still absolutely no idea why you are posing as the governess, but I shan't ask. Though it's killing me not to. But I should have ordered the constable not to take no for an answer.' He shook his head. 'You really are impossible to look after.'

She batted his arm. 'No, really I'm not, Hugh. At least not always. Ask Clifford. But you are usually doing at least two people's work because of a lack of manpower, I know, so I wasn't going to waste the constable's time by being faint-hearted and feeble.'

He sighed. 'Can I say that, selfishly, I wish you would be precisely that? Sometimes, anyway. So my heart doesn't give out worrying about you whenever I'm not with you. Blast it!' He turned to the tea tray she hadn't noticed on the desk and poured a cup. 'No arguments. And plenty of sugar. Police orders.' He slid it across to her. 'And I know how you enjoy following those!'

She laughed. 'Thank you, Hugh.' She took a hasty sip, not wanting to let on that her teeth were threatening to chatter with delayed shock. She was also feeling somewhat light-headed.

He looked at her under his brow, but said nothing. Opening his notebook, he turned to a fresh page. 'Now, I'm aware your mystifying intuition will probably have given you a theory already about Withers' death, but could you recount everything you know as... plainly as possible? It's critical I stay objective.'

She nodded. 'Of course. Although' – her brows knitted – 'in all honesty, I'm rather confused, so here goes. At a quarter past midnight last night, I crept down to the kitchen—'

He chuckled. 'There's a surprise.'

She tutted. 'Not to raid the biscuit barrel or the cheese board, actually, you rotter! Anyway, I caught Withers opening... or closing a window in the pump room.'

Seldon frowned. 'Which was it?'

'I couldn't be sure.'

'Shame. Because if he was closing it, it could have been another member of staff that was bribed by the thieves to leave it open. Withers then discovered them and that got him killed.'

'Or,' she said, leaning forward, 'Withers was the one bribed. Then perhaps he succumbed to greed and threatened to turn them over to the police unless they gave him more? The footman, Tateham, thinks he has some damaging information on Withers. Maybe that's it?'

'A possibility.'

'And there's more.'

She passed him the envelope. Seldon took it and looked at her enquiringly.

'I found it on Withers.' She raised a hand as he went to speak. 'The last body I came across disappeared almost immediately, remember?'

He nodded and opened the envelope.

'Money, eh? Do you think Lord Chadwick spotted you taking this from the body?'

She shivered. 'I hope not!'

He leaned forward and cupped her chin. 'Eleanor, this can wait.'

'No, it can't, Hugh.'

'Ever the pursuer of justice. But we don't know what happened to Withers yet. It might just have been natural causes. I couldn't find any immediate indication that he'd died from anything sinister.'

She nodded. 'I know. I could only come up with heart attack as a likely cause. But' – she shook her head – 'it's too coincidental. And I'm almost sure Lord Chadwick was trying to hide Withers' body in the dumb waiter when I came in. *Almost* sure.'

He was staring at her with incredulity. 'Why would Lord Chadwick kill his own butler?'

'Because he killed Clemthorpe.'

Seldon leaned back slowly and rubbed his hands over his lean cheeks. 'Where's that letter opener to jab even harder into my wrist this time? You can't mean what I think you're saying?'

'I'm deadly serious, Hugh. I'm sure he's the same man I saw looking up at me after poor John Clemthorpe fell. That scarring disfigurement on his cheek. It's so particular. And it explains why there isn't a single photograph of him anywhere in the house. Lady Chadwick made me believe her husband was just rather vain, but he probably doesn't want to be constantly reminded of it. And I don't blame him.'

Seldon stared at his notebook. 'It's not that I doubt you, Eleanor, but—'

'Look, I've no idea how a murder at the Empire Exhibition could relate to the butler being killed here in this house. But it has to. Lord Chadwick was at the scene of both. That can't be purely coincidental?'

Seldon ran his hand around the back of his neck. 'Eleanor, please drink your tea.' He fiddled with his pen while she took a sip. 'You know I can only go on facts.' He opened and closed his mouth, then threw up his hands. 'I mean, what would someone like Lord Chadwick have even been *doing* at a half-finished pavilion enclosure at the Empire Exhibition in the first place?'

She was silent for a moment. 'I don't know. But I know he was the other man. I'd swear it under oath.'

Seldon exhaled slowly. 'Then I have to believe you, Eleanor. Only Lord Chadwick isn't someone that can be investigated with impunity. I'd need to have an exemplary case against him first. And permission from above.'

She groaned. 'I know. He works for the government. In Whitehall. Lady Chadwick mentioned it.'

She sat back, trying to replay exactly what she'd seen on opening those fatal dining room doors.

That's what's wrong, Ellie!

'Rigor mortis!' she breathed.

Seldon nodded. 'Yes. It had already set in when I examined the body. Withers had died some hours earlier.'

Of course, Ellie! Lord Chadwick said Withers was as stiff as a board. Rigor mortis doesn't set in until around two hours after death and can take up to eight hours to render a body completely stiff. Despite your wartime nurse's training, you were so busy concentrating on not letting your guard down with the living, you couldn't concentrate on the dead.

'Yes, but my point is, I caught Withers at the window at probably eighteen minutes past midnight, seeing as my bedside clock said a quarter past when I got up. And I climbed back into bed at twelve forty-two exactly. Which means I left Withers around twelve forty.'

He frowned. 'So?'

'So, Lord Chadwick could have killed Withers any time after I left him and stuffed him in the dumb waiter. Then pretended to find him in the morning.'

Seldon looked thoughtful. 'He could have. But why would he? It still seems more likely if Withers was murdered, it was by the gang of jewel burglars operating in the area. But until we know the cause of death...' He shook his head. 'Frankly, Eleanor, I don't like you being here.'

She shrugged. 'Neither do I, Hugh. For a variety of reasons, actually. But I gave my word to... to someone. And honestly, Lord Chadwick has no idea who I am or why I'm here. He certainly doesn't recognise me from the hot-air balloon.'

'In that governess get-up? I'm not at all surprised. If I hadn't dreamed of your beautiful face every night for three years before finally finding the courage to propose, I wouldn't either.'

She leaned over and scanned down his notes. 'Where's your list of people at Chadwick House to question?'

He flicked back a couple of pages. 'Here. Why?'

She tapped the last entry on the list. 'When you see who this is, you'll feel better about my being here. Only make sure that letter opener is nowhere within reach.'

He waved a resigned hand. 'More mystery, but alright.'

She drained her tea and dropped her cup back on its saucer

at a sudden realisation. 'Hugh! We've both been too fixated on the scene this morning to see the obvious. If he was killed because he caught the thieves in the act, then something would have been stolen. Unless they lost their nerve.'

He shook his head.

'Oh? You think they did and fled empty-handed?'

'No. I mean, something was stolen. Lord Chadwick said after he reported the murder, he found his safe was open. And a valuable pearl necklace missing.'

25

That evening, the clack of billiard balls echoing from the games room of Clifford's pied-à-terre made Eleanor beam as she stepped through the open front door.

'Finally, Clifford!' she called, undoing her coat buttons. 'I'm delighted you're actually relaxing for once. Hopefully, next time I'll find you attacking the drinks cabinet with your feet up on the settee.'

'As if, my lady!' Clifford called back from the opposite end of the entrance hall.

She pointed at him and then at the sound of more ivory balls rebounding off each other. 'If that isn't you playing, then who?'

'I wonder.'

She tiptoed over to the games room.

'Oh, gracious!' She gasped at the absurd spectacle. Her ginger tomcat was darting around the billiard table's green baize, batting the coloured balls off the cushioned sides and into the pockets. Each time one disappeared down the hole, her wildly panting bulldog would hurl himself under it, catch the ball, and run out of the room. A moment later, he'd return at full tilt to wait to grab the next. She followed him as he scrambled off with another ball, to find him piling them up in his bed by the kitchen range.

'Masters Gladstone and Tomkins. That is categorically not how one plays snooker,' Clifford said firmly as she returned.

She nodded in mock admonishment. 'Whatever adaptation of billiards that is, I'm sure you're supposed to sink the balls in a certain order.'

He lifted a wriggling Tomkins off the table and deposited him on the floor. 'And not while dancing on the baize!'

At a suspicious thud, she winced. 'Or by tugging on the string pockets until the ball falls out!' Clifford pinched the bridge of his nose while she tried to hide a smile. 'If only these monsters earned their board and lodgings, you could dock the cost from their wages rather than your precious household accounts.' She frowned, her expression falling serious. 'Like the staff at Chadwick House are made to do.'

He took her coat as she let it slip from her shoulders. 'My lady, the generosity and leniency you bestow upon your staff is far from common.' He shook his head. 'Luckily for Polly, who, with all her breakages, would otherwise have been in debtor's prison before the end of her first week in service. Now, please accept my sincere apologies for not meeting you at the door. Whilst I dish out suitable punishments to the terrible two in the kitchen, perhaps you would like to avail yourself of the treat which awaits in the sitting room?'

'Excellent. More chocolates?'

He arched a mischievous brow. 'It is far from my place to note the lady has oft described this particular treat as significantly more delicious.'

Thinking he meant a tiered stand of nibbles or similar, she barely held in her delight at the unexpected sight of her fiancé over by one of the covered paintings. She waited until he had lifted one of the cloths, before announcing her arrival.

'What a lovely surprise, Hugh!'

'Agh!' He dropped the cloth rapidly and spun around, his cheeks scarlet. 'Hello, Eleanor. These, er, paintings. I was just wondering, umm...'

'If we might get some for Henley Hall once we're married?' she teased.

His handsome face split into an embarrassed smile. 'Why they were covered, actually.'

'The work of my ever-chivalrous butler.' She pointed to the coffee table. 'Who has clearly poured us both a brandy and retired so we can be alone for a few minutes.'

'I wish it could be for a lifetime,' Seldon murmured, pulling her gently into his arms. After a gentlemanly kiss, he surprised her by following it up with a passionate one that made her heart leap.

'Blast it, I'm sorry, Eleanor,' he whispered into her fiery-red curls. 'That was unf—'

'Unforgettable. So don't wait long to do it again because I shan't have a single sensible thought until you do.'

She dragged him over to the two-seater settee. He sat down and sighed.

'Well, I need you to, I'm afraid. And this evening, if you can bear it. Shamefully, I'm here to pick your brain about Withers' death.'

'Good.' She passed him his drink.

'Hardly good.' He groaned. 'I can't believe that I'm going to sour another snatched half hour with you talking shop.'

'Don't worry. We've got a lifetime ahead to talk about respectable things.'

He rubbed his chin. 'Lady Swift and respectable? No, I'm pretty sure they've never met. Likewise, convention, decorum, etiquette or tact. But do correct me, Clifford?' he added as her butler cleared his throat, his back to them in the doorway.

'I believe you omitted "seemliness" and "sensibility", sir.'

She laughed. 'Rotters! The pair of you.' Her nose tingled as a delectable scent floated in. 'I say, Clifford, you haven't?'

He turned to bow from the shoulders. 'I have. Dinner is served.'

Seldon glanced at his watch. 'Very kind, Clifford, but I haven't really got the time.'

'If you insist, Chief Inspector,' Clifford said. 'Though, of course, the beauty of slow-roasted lamb in a mustard grain and rosemary crust is that it is quick to eat as it melts in the mouth.'

'Which will save you time having to scrummage up a crust of bread later, Hugh,' Eleanor said as her fiancé's eyes lit up. 'Clifford, thank you. You're a marvel.'

In the dining room, Clifford bowed and slid her familiar investigations notebook from his inside pocket. 'I shall take notes so you might both eat, my lady. But before that, to keep the terrible two from more thievery...'

He set two bowls down on a rubber mat beside him.

'Some punishment! You softie.' She chuckled over the flurry of ecstatic woofs and happy yowls.

The animals dealt with, Clifford served dinner.

'Sublime!' Eleanor murmured, savouring a mouthful of tender sweet lamb accompanied by creamed leeks, scalloped potatoes and a honeyed vegetable medley. 'And too good to rush. Yes, Hugh?'

Seldon nodded gratefully as he reopened his eyes after savouring his. 'Right, I feel a heel for ruining such a special meal, but I'd better launch in first, if that's alright?'

Eleanor waved her fork in assent.

He glanced at his notebook. 'So... the coroner's initial report on Withers.' He glanced up. 'At least I'll be allowed to view the full report for this death when it's done. That's a step up! Now, time of death. The coroner narrowed it down to between half past midnight and half-past two in the morning.'

Clifford made a note. 'Commensurate with her ladyship's last sighting of said person.'

Seldon looked across at him. '"Said person"? Not your usual way of referring to a fellow butler?'

Clifford sniffed. 'Mr Withers was the furthest from such one could be, sir.' He relayed what he'd learned from his club.

Seldon nodded. 'Ah, I see. Perhaps the money in the envelope you found on his body, Eleanor, is not so strange then. It could well be money paid to him by the gang of thieves robbing houses in Park Lane.'

She nodded slowly. 'Or was Withers blackmailing someone and that's what got him killed?'

'Mmm, possible,' Seldon said. 'But back to the coroner for the moment. He hasn't had time to do anything else yet, really. His very brief initial assessment was death due to unknown causes, blast it! He did agree it could have been a heart attack, but wouldn't commit himself until he's had time to do an autopsy.'

'Which will get priority, yes, Hugh?'

He winced. 'The problem, Eleanor, is that we have only one coroner, due to all the usual staff and budget cuts. And he's already got a body or two before Withers to do. So, if I try and make this one a priority, I need to have a seriously good reason.'

She smiled wryly. 'And you can't give the reason that you suspect Lord Chadwick of killing his butler. Nor that you're worried the body might disappear, as has happened before when Lord Chadwick murdered someone. Or at least that is what that mad woman from the closed enclosure at the Empire Exhibition incident told you.'

Seldon grimaced. 'If I did, it would definitely get reported to my superior, and then...'

She sighed. 'We'll just have to wait, I suppose.'

He nodded. 'Obviously there is also the possibility that Withers was poisoned. As we know that could explain why there were no immediate outward signs. And some poisons can mimic heart attacks. So the time of death may be right, but when the poison was planted could have been some time before. But, as I said, until we get the official verdict, we can only work with the facts we've got. Now, reports from my interviews at Chadwick House.' He groaned. 'In a nutshell, everyone has the same alibi.'

'All asleep in their quarters, Chief Inspector?'

'Spot on, Clifford. The only ones who were able to corroborate each other's statements were the maids, since they share a room. And if Withers was killed maliciously, it was done cleverly and I honestly can't imagine any of those maids having the knowledge or ability to carry it out. So I'd say they're eliminated as suspects for the moment. Agreed?'

'Agreed.' Eleanor took a sip of wine which had appeared by magic. 'Molly, the scullery maid, is just a waif, poor thing. Alice, the maid-of-all-tasks, doesn't even come up to Withers' shoulders. And Hannah, the head housemaid, is far too precious.'

Seldon paused with a forkful of glazed carrot batons. 'Precious? I've never heard that used as a defence in court, Eleanor.'

'We women have an intuition for such things. Which is why our blinkered legal system should allow us to become barristers,' she said vociferously.

Clifford coughed politely. 'Actually, my lady, two ladies were called to the bar but recently.'

'Ah!'

Seldon shared an amused look with him. 'Right. Gardeners next. Ruled out because they are only part-time, don't live on site and have no access to the house at night. They also live next door to each other and on the night in question, a neighbour's wife was having a difficult... time of things. So, they were round there giving moral support to the imminent father-to-be while their wives tackled... er, what needed to be tackled.' He looked down at his notebook hurriedly. 'Next, the coachman—'

Eleanor raised her knife. 'Hang on, Hugh. I haven't seen any gardeners. Withers didn't mention any.'

'Hardly surprising, my lady,' Clifford said. 'Staff hierarchy is strictly adhered to at Chadwick House as you know. Perhaps you might wish to do so back at Henley Hall in future?'

She laughed. 'Nice try, but no. My wonderful ladies might collectively melt the starch from your collar on a regular basis, but they're a team. And they think the world of you. If you could hear the backbiting up and down the ranks at Chadwick House, though, your underthings would actually disintegrate.'

Seldon's lips quirked at Clifford's horrified tut. He waved his notebook. 'Now, the coachman also has no access to the house, as he's not even directly employed. Also his alibi checked out, so—'

'A carriage hired singularly according to need?' Clifford shook his head at Seldon's nod. 'Most irregular for a household on Park Lane. As are part-time gardeners.'

'Thanks, Clifford. That might be something to follow up.' Seldon added a note to his page.

Eleanor finished another forkful of melt-in-the-mouth lamb with a moan of pleasure. 'So, the other staff. I think the house-keeper, cook and the footman all sleep alone. Really, any of them could have killed old Withers.'

'Yes.' Seldon consulted a previous page. 'Mrs Hawkins, Mrs Rudge and Mr Tateham.'

'Just "Tateham". Withers was very clear he was not to be called "mister".' Eleanor paused in spearing a new piece of lamb she'd just cut up. 'Remind me to tell you about their spat in a minute. When it's my turn.'

Seldon seemed to choke. 'Waiting your turn? That's new!'

Clifford nodded as he topped up Hugh's plate. 'Indeed, sir. Her ladyship has been trying out all sorts of new approaches lately. With, ahem, varied success.'

Seldon coughed into his hand at her mock huff. 'Moving on.

Lord Chadwick said he found Withers' body around nine. To repeat, the coroner confirmed time of death to be around twelve thirty to two thirty in the morning. Which is before Lord Chadwick arrived back home, according to him.' He shook his head. 'One thing I can't figure out yet, is why the body was found where it was. Either Withers died there, or he was taken there after his death. By his killer, I assume. But why?' He held up a hand. 'I know your theory, Eleanor, and maybe you're right. Maybe the body *was* hidden in the dumb waiter.'

Eleanor slapped the table. 'Which means Withers could have been killed in the servants' basement and then ferried up to the dining room!'

'Like a roast turkey,' Clifford said with a shudder.

'Excellent point.' Seldon jotted down a few words. 'Back to Lord Chadwick before I lose my train of thought. His office has yet to confirm if he was actually staying at the London hotel he mentioned in his statement.' He sighed. 'I daren't ask the hotel staff until they have.'

Her eyebrows rose. 'So you *are* checking on him?'

He nodded. 'Extremely cautiously, yes. And only because he volunteered the name of his superior for us to speak to. Again, odd if he *did* kill his butler. But he might just be a cool character. I'm obviously not mentioning the "m" word to him or anyone else he is connected to at the moment. However, he's being very cooperative.' He glanced across the table and muttered, 'Unlike some. In fact, I must say,' he paused as Clifford added more lamb to his plate, 'if it were not for this incredible spread, I might be placing you, Clifford, under arrest for not telling me what you two are doing masquerading at Chadwick House.'

'Most kind, Chief Inspector.' Clifford seesawed his head. 'Though on reflection, a stay at His Majesty's pleasure would be preferable to a single day more of Lord Chadwick's ire.'

'Oh, Clifford!' Eleanor said, feeling bad she'd involved him.

Seldon shrugged. 'You didn't say that when I interviewed you as the biblio... book person.'

'"Bibliognost", Chief Inspector. And that was because I had not met the gentleman at that time. But I did afterwards. And in far from the best of moods.'

'Well, he had just found his butler dead.'

'That was not the cause of his consternation, if I might humbly offer an opinion.' Clifford cleared the plates. 'The task for which I have been engaged by his lady wife is not one he is at all happy with.'

Seldon glanced at Eleanor, concern in his eyes. 'Don't tell me he threw you out, Clifford?'

'He did. But in almost the same breath, peculiarly, then retracted the command and told me to continue cataloguing his, admittedly remarkable, collection. With the proviso, however, that I stayed religiously within the library and did not touch his first editions.'

She frowned. 'Odd. Lady Chadwick sounded very sure he'd be over the moon at having his treasured books catalogued. She said sometimes she thought they were the only true love of his life. Not her. Nor the children, sadly.' She bit her lip, struggling with her conscience.

'Foolish man,' Seldon muttered into his vegetables. 'Then why did he change his mind so abruptly do you think, Clifford?'

'My only logical conclusion is that the gentleman thought it might look suspicious acting so immediately after his butler's body was discovered.'

'Agreed.' Seldon added another jotting to his page. 'Anyone object if I get back to Lord Chadwick's alibi?'

Eleanor nodded. 'We are all ears, Hugh!'

26

Seldon cleared his throat. 'Good. Firstly, the initial part of Lord Chadwick's alibi checked out. His office confirmed he was away on business. Although, frustratingly, Whitehall departments may sometimes confirm things that aren't true and withhold other information that is, depending on the nature of their specific remit.'

Eleanor cocked her head. 'Clifford? As my infallible expert on the English language, what's the official linguistic difference between "withhold" and "cover up", would you say?'

'All the letters except "o" and one additional syllable, my lady.' He threw Seldon an apologetic look. 'And the generous application of whitewash in the latter.'

Seldon groaned. 'Yes, alright. Now, on the night Withers was killed, Lord Chadwick got back late from his trip. So he went to a hotel as he had work to finish. The manager confirmed that he checked in just before midnight. He then telephoned reception at half past midnight asking for some sandwiches to be sent up but left outside his room. Because he was too busy with his work to be disturbed.'

'Rather convenient for an alibi, perhaps?' Eleanor said.

Seldon shrugged. 'I can't deny that. Particularly as the empty tray was collected by the porter at five o'clock the next morning. But that only makes it a possibility at most.'

'If you say so, Hugh,' she offered contritely, thinking otherwise. 'But the coroner placed Withers' time of death between twelve thirty and two thirty in the morning, so...'

'So yes, Eleanor, Lord Chadwick could have had time to sneak home to Park Lane, do the unthinkable to Withers and return to the hotel.' Seldon waved his notebook at her. 'Which is why I had the taxicab records serving the Park Lane area checked. There are no night buses on that route, and the underground trains had stopped the hour before for the night.'

'And?'

'No record of anyone of Lord Chadwick's description taking a taxi.'

'Hmm, he is rather recognisable with that unfortunate disfigurement to his cheek, I suppose,' she said.

Clifford cleared his throat. 'Though he could easily have paid "extra", shall we say, so as not to be remembered. Nor his journey.'

'True. Which means he isn't ruled out. But he isn't ruled in either,' Seldon said.

Eleanor frowned. 'What about him being back earlier from his trip than expected though?'

'He wasn't. Not according to his office. In fact, he was actually late arriving home. He was due back the night Withers was killed.'

She shared a puzzled look with Clifford.

But Lady Chadwick begged you to solve the necklace theft before he got home, Ellie. Maybe she misremembered his return date was in two days' time on Friday?

'Lady Chadwick could have deliberately lied to you, Eleanor,' Seldon said.

'I concur,' Clifford added.

She grimaced. 'I suppose so, although I can't think why she would. What about her alibi? Does it hold water?'

Seldon nodded. 'Seems to. She was away, staying at a friend's house with her children. That's been confirmed. She was still away when I arrived as you know, Eleanor. Lord Chadwick rang her after finding Withers and told her to stay put. He didn't want the children, or her, coming back until the body had been removed and the police gone. Though it's not far from Chadwick House. So she could have sneaked off home, dispatched Withers and returned easily in time. Although not unnoticed, as she would likely have needed someone to let her back in.'

'What about her maid, Grace?'

Seldon consulted his notebook. 'She was with her mistress at the friend's house. And at night shared the room with the other dressing room maid, or whatever their proper title is. She corroborated Grace's story. And in truth, seemed too daunted by me asking anything to have been lying with any conviction. I don't think she would have let Grace, or Lady Chadwick, back in and said otherwise.'

'Daunted, Hugh? Or more... flustered? Sort of pink-cheeked and slightly breathless?'

'The second one. Peculiarly perceptive though, even for you?'

She hid her smile, still amazed her fiancé had no idea of how handsome he was or the effect he had on most women. 'I think it's pretty safe to believe her.'

At Seldon's puzzled look, Clifford looked away. 'Perhaps chalk it up to the unfathomable intuition of the opposite gender, Chief Inspector.'

Seldon shook his head and continued. 'It also means it would have been extremely unlikely Grace could have let Lady Chadwick back in without the other maid, or someone else in the house, noticing, as the family who live there were also all there that night.'

Discussion paused as Clifford served dessert.

Eleanor's face lit up as she picked up her spoon. 'Jam roly-poly and custard! My favourite since I was a child...' Her face clouded. 'Actually, chaps' – she laid her spoon back down – 'I need to do something I've never done before. Even as a child.'

Seldon slowly sat back in his chair. 'I'm listening, Eleanor.'

She sighed. 'I've been wrestling with my conscience and... the short of it is, I need to break a promise. And not only because there's been a murder which changes matters, but also because I'm beginning to think the party I made the promise to has lied to me about pretty well everything.' She bit her lip. 'You see, Hugh, the reason Clifford and I have been "masquerading", as you put it, at Chadwick House, is because we're investigating Lady Chadwick's stolen necklace.'

Seldon's jaw fell. 'What! But the theft only occurred last night.'

Eleanor shook her head. 'Not according to Lady Chadwick. Last Saturday, she pleaded with me to help find out who'd stolen it before her husband got home. She was convinced it was one of the staff. Or so she says.'

Seldon stroked his chin. 'Mmm. Interesting. Tell me everything you can about the Chadwick household, Eleanor. It might just throw some light on what's really going on here and whether it's related to Withers' death or not.'

She nodded and gathered her thoughts. 'Well, apparently, Lady Chadwick's husband treats her like a feeble, weak-minded individual who cannot be trusted with anything responsible, such as the household monies or the combination to the safe.'

'Ahem, not uncommon among gentlemen of traditional values, my lady,' Clifford said.

Seldon pulled a face. 'Hmm, I'm definitely of Eleanor's

opinion that his wife doesn't feature much in his view. I had to respectfully insist that he telephone Lady Chadwick to come home, as she might know something helpful to the investigation.'

'Might he not have been protecting the lady from unpleasantness?' Clifford said.

'Possibly, but I rather formed the impression that he thought she would have nothing useful to say.'

'There's more,' Eleanor said. 'There's agreement among the staff that he and the previous governess were—'

'Acting inappropriately?' Clifford said quickly.

'I'd say him sliding under the sheets with her would qualify as that, yes.' She shook her head as the two men looked away, fiddling with whatever was at hand. 'But in his defence, it's only tittle-tattle. I've no evidence. But I can see why Lady Chadwick is so determined to claim some independence. Though she's trying to do so furtively.'

Seldon glanced up from his notebook. 'As in, she's terrible at hiding it?'

'No. More like she's going behind his back, but at the same time wants him to know. Take the supposedly "secret" party she held while he was away. Tateham told me Withers reports everything straight to him. So she must have known he'd find out.'

Seldon tapped his chin with his pen, then made a note. 'Mmm, nobody really knows what happens behind closed doors. Relationships can be complicated. Now, you mentioned before about Withers and Tateham being at odds?'

'Loggerheads, more like, Hugh. I think they each have enough incriminating information on the other to lose their jobs if it were to come to Lord Chadwick's ears.'

'Incriminating as in?'

'For starters, apparently Withers found Tateham in Lady Chadwick's bedroom the night she claims her necklace was stolen.'

Seldon whistled over Clifford's outraged tutting. 'And Withers?'

'I don't know yet. But Tateham confessed he wanted Withers' job. Badly. He resented him. And he needs the money desperately, for some reason.'

Seldon's pen flew across the page. 'Thank you, Eleanor. I appreciate you breaking your promise to tell me.' He stopped writing and read what he'd written. 'In summary, then, the top current suspect for Withers' murder, as we're calling it' – he glanced at Eleanor – 'looks to be Tateham, the footman. Then possibly, but very unlikely, Lady Chadwick if she had involved herself in something she didn't want Withers to report on her husband's return. And if her alibi is found wanting. Quite a few ifs! Finally, the housekeeper and cook also both had the opportunity, but no known motive as yet. And also Lord Chadwick on the basis solely at the moment that he was present at the previous death.'

Eleanor tried to keep her voice level. 'Not wanting to disagree, but Lord Chadwick is the top suspect to my mind, Hugh.'

'I'm sorry, but I don't agree, Eleanor,' Seldon said gently but firmly. 'And not just because he's a bigwig in Whitehall. Even if he was the killer at the exhibition enclosure, there's no link with Withers' death. He was absent from the house when the murder took place. At least until his alibi collapses or we find out a poison was administered to Withers earlier. And he has no known motive. He rang the police immediately on finding the body, remember? Even you thought he seemed genuine. There really is no evidence linking the two murders, let alone linking the two murders to one person.'

She tried to keep her frustration from her voice. 'But you're not seeing the link! Aside from Lord Chadwick, which is the most obvious one. The missing necklace! Lady Chadwick accosted me at the Empire Exhibition itself to ask for my help in recovering it.'

'The one her husband is adamant was stolen only last night?'

'Yes, but that's probably because he believes his wife doesn't know the combination to the safe. But she does. She spied on him to get it.'

'Not much of a marriage,' Seldon said to his jam roly-poly. 'There's obviously something fishy going on, I'll give you that. However, I spoke briefly to Lady Chadwick. She'd just arrived as I was leaving. She was rather... upset to talk to easily, if I'm honest. I did manage to ask if she knew how her missing necklace could be related to their butler's death.'

'And?'

'She said she'd have to speak to her husband as he was the keeper of the necklace. She was only "allowed" to wear it occasionally. I must say, she sounded rather bitter. However, there was no sign of the safe being broken into, as in the other burglaries in the street.'

'Which sounds like an inside job?'

'Yes. That, or the thieves had the skill to open the safe without the combination.' Seldon's gaze slid to Clifford. 'Quite a rare ability that, though?'

'Ahem.' Her butler drifted away to the serving table with the empty dessert dishes.

Eleanor flapped a hand at her fiancé. 'I'm telling you, the necklace is the link between the two murders, Hugh.'

Seldon held up his hands. 'I fail to see how, sorry.'

'That's because you haven't seen this.' She fumbled in her jacket pocket. 'It's a broken clasp from a piece of jewellery. Guess where I found part of it?'

He groaned. 'I daren't.'

'Inside the closed exhibition enclosure. Near where I saw poor Clemthorpe murdered. By Lord Chadwick.'

He reached out a hand for the two parts of the clasp. 'Leaving him out for objectivity, what makes you think this might be from Lady Chadwick's necklace?'

'Several reasons. She was at the exhibition when she accosted me. She told me she took the necklace off at the party because it was "scratching" her. Badly enough that she abandoned her guests for ten minutes.' She shrugged. 'Apparently, a hostess isn't supposed to do that.'

Clifford shuddered. 'It would be a dreadful faux pas, my lady.'

'And secondly, but most importantly, because Grace found the other half of that clasp on the floor in Lady Chadwick's bedroom! The pieces match.'

Seldon frowned. 'But, Eleanor, why would she lie about the clasp being broken? And how did it end up at a murder scene?'

'No idea. But I'll find out.'

He sighed. 'But that's still no good without the rest of the necklace to prove the clasp came from it.'

'Then I'll find that too,' she said determinedly.

He smiled ruefully. 'Infuriatingly, I have a horrible feeling you might.'

'Perhaps a brief action plan for all of us might be agreed upon, Chief Inspector?' Clifford said. 'Before the chance to enjoy coffee under the stars on the private rooftop terrace is lost?'

Eleanor jumped up. 'That sounds too romantic for words.' She didn't miss the eager expression on her fiancé's face. 'Right, I'll hurry us up. Hugh, I shall tackle Lady Chadwick about when her necklace actually went missing, the broken clasp, and anything else I can pump out of her.'

Seldon raised a finger. 'But not her husband! Just in case, by some twist of mad fate, he is the murderer. Now, Clifford, see what you can turn up in the library. And maybe Lord Chadwick's study when he's out at work?'

Clifford raised an eyebrow. 'That would be trespass in the case of the latter, sir. And my sincere pleasure to execute.'

Seldon chuckled. 'Good man. I'll check all staff backgrounds. Withers' particularly, after what you said earlier, Clifford. And I'll try and discreetly establish where each member of staff was when the exhibition killing took place.'

Eleanor frowned. 'I'm best placed to do that, Hugh.'

'Maybe, but you're not to, please. I can just about reconcile my conscience over you staying in the house after the events of this morning. But I've just had the horrible, if unlikely, idea that Lady Chadwick might only have taken the children away purely to have an alibi for Withers' murder. Now, where's this romantic roof terrace?'

27

'I'm busy!'

Eleanor frowned at the terse reply to her knock, the last of her hard-won patience evaporating.

'So am I,' she called equally tersely, opening the door, stepping in, and closing it behind her. 'Trying to help you!'

Over at the elegant writing bureau, Lady Chadwick flinched. 'Oh, it's you. My apologies. I thought it was Grace.' She fanned out the stack of envelopes. 'Back with more responsibilities I haven't the heart for at the moment.'

'I'm sure whatever they are, they can wait a while.'

'That would only make it worse.' Lady Chadwick sighed, waving at the desktop. 'Endless rounds of letter writing. So many invitations from every quarter. All requiring replies, of course. To say nothing of those one simply cannot fail to send out oneself. Organising the social calendar is a constant headache. Even in an ordinary week.'

'Which this one is far from. For both of us,' Eleanor said pointedly. She stood squarely in the other woman's eyeline. 'I rather expected you might have sought me out when you returned yesterday. Or at least this morning. What with the police having been here again.'

Lady Chadwick coloured. 'Yes, well, I probably should have. I'm so sorry. But a slice of normality was my only way of coping, do you see? And I'm already behind on learning to improve my game.' She knocked over a book on the mastery of bridge, fumbling to pick up a pretty blue glass jar. 'None of this is easy for me. My... my husband expects me to achieve so much. It's beastly.'

Eleanor was confused. The picture Lady Chadwick had painted of her husband was a man who thought his wife rather vacuous and too lacking in mental capacity for any serious responsibility. What exactly did he want her to achieve?

As if Lady Chadwick had read the confusion on Eleanor's face, she rose sharply and stared at her reflection in the gilded mirror above her writing bureau. 'I meant in terms of being the perfect picture wife. Hence, hours must be given over to my complexion through the application of cleansers, astringents, lotions, glycerine, creams, buttermilk, and powders. Then there are the oils for the scalp, others for the roots and more still for the tresses. Along with relaxants, tonics, shine enhancements, whitener for one's hands.' She seized the blue glass jar again. 'Liniments for one's nails. Balms for one's cuticles. And that is only in the morning. At night, it all begins again. My dressing table would keep any chemist in business for a year!'

'Isn't it any comfort he must still consider you beautiful?' Eleanor said quietly.

'It is a relief,' Lady Chadwick said stiffly. 'Although, to my husband and all men, in fact, the weather is only noticed because it dictates which overcoat to select. They have no care for the ageing effects of sun, wind, rain, heat and cold. Reginald will never understand.'

Eleanor remembered Hugh's remark about how complicated relationships could be. 'Be honest. Is it a struggle because

you want something more out of life? Like some independence?'

Lady Chadwick's expression hardened. 'What I want and
what I need are entirely different. Really, even you must understand that.'

'Even me?' Eleanor said, not hiding her irritation.

Lady Chadwick reached out both of her milk-white hands
placatingly. 'Oh, I didn't mean to sound churlish. Or uncharitable. It's just that... we society ladies are expected to conform to a
great many things. And yet you do not. Conform, I mean,' Lady
Chadwick added hurriedly as her eyes roved over Eleanor's
face, then glanced away. 'However, unorthodox becomes you
tremendously. Not only do you have no need of the alchemy
that fills my dressing table,' she said, waving her hand at her.
'You have no husband to work tirelessly on the shape of
even... even your ankles for, so he won't leave you for a more
youthful woman!' She held her handkerchief over her mouth,
taking a series of deep breaths.

Eleanor mentally shook her head. This conversation hadn't
gone as planned.

*How did you inadvertently wrench open the lid on so many
of Lady Chadwick's insecurities, Ellie?*

Eleanor thought this was definitely not the time to mention
that she was engaged. And to a man who held her in far higher
regard than that of a pretty clothes horse, so she bit her tongue.
It was imperative she gave no hint her fiancé was the detective
investigating Withers' death.

She tried to look at Lady Chadwick with fresh eyes. What
she saw was a lonely woman buried beneath the stress of her
husband's expectations, and her own follies. She realised with a
start that there was probably only a year or two between them.
But Lady Chadwick seemed so much older. In fact, she had a
seven-year-old daughter, Octavia.

Keep focused, Ellie. You can't afford to let sentiment cloud your judgement.

Forcing away the thought of what it would be like if one day she had a daughter, she brought her focus back to what she'd come to find out.

'Lady Chadwick,' she said more sternly than intended. It had the desired effect, however, as the other woman jerked to attention. 'I offered to help recover your necklace and now I find myself wondering why, exactly? You see, I had a long chat with the inspector after your husband reported Withers had been killed.'

Lady Chadwick's eyes widened in alarm. 'So I was right to fear asking you? You told that detective why you're really here when he interviewed you, didn't you?'

Eleanor shook her head, searching for the words without actually lying. 'No. When I was interviewed here I answered the inspector's questions. But that wasn't one of them. Besides, it would have made me look suspicious if I'd confessed to him then. And the theft of your necklace has nothing to do with Withers' death, does it?'

'Of course not!' Lady Chadwick cried, flopping back down into her chair. 'And thank heavens you didn't confess. I've been frantic with worry you had.'

Eleanor waved her hand. 'Don't thank me yet. Because I shall be forced to reverse my decision if you don't tell me the truth about what is going on.'

Lady Chadwick blinked. 'Whatever do you mean?'

'The inspector mentioned your husband reported your necklace was stolen. But from the safe. And only the night before last! Quite the contradiction to the tale you told me when asking for my help.'

Lady Chadwick narrowed her eyes for a brief moment. 'Oh, you heard that, I see? But I can explain. Only... only don't think the worst of me, will you?'

Eleanor folded her arms. 'I'm listening.'

'Well, firstly, you can't imagine how much my heart faltered when Reginald telephoned me at my friend's house to say I needed to return home.'

Eleanor nodded. 'Because Withers had been found dead?'

'No. Although that obviously came as... as a shock. I faltered because it meant I had to tell him about my necklace! He was furious. He fumed that the insurance company wouldn't pay at all if they found out it hadn't been kept in the safe. And because the theft wasn't reported to the police immediately.' Her tone turned defensive. 'I had no choice but to go along with his insistence that I lie. To back up his statement to the detective that the necklace was taken from the safe the night before last.' She looked at Eleanor sharply. 'You do understand, don't you? Any lov— Any wife would have done the same.'

Eleanor kept her expression neutral. 'I appreciate how difficult your position was. But your staff all knew it had been stolen earlier, didn't they?'

She shrugged. 'What of it?'

Eleanor was at a loss for a moment. 'Lady Chadwick, how long have your staff been with you?'

Lady Chadwick sighed. 'I really don't know. Most of them for a while. But you just can't get staff to be loyal these days. The only ones I can recall joining notably recently were the scullery maid, whatever her name is, who came about six months ago and that rather cheeky footman, Tateham. He joined a month or so ago, I think. Not that it matters. However long they've been in service here, they'll say exactly what my husband tells them to.'

No doubt because they would otherwise be dismissed on the spot, Ellie. And without a reference.

She forced herself to bite her tongue. Staff were people too. Only with no one and nowhere to turn to except the workhouse in such circumstances. Then again, she thought, she'd never heard Lady Chadwick mention any relatives. If she left, or was thrown out by her husband for refusing to support his lie, where would she go? How would she earn money? Ironically, probably the only course open to her would be to become a governess!

She frowned, remembering the children telling her about their mummy's repeated late-night disappearing act. She briefly thought about tackling Lady Chadwick about it, but decided it wasn't the time. She would almost certainly become defensive immediately and just deny it.

Adopting a more sympathetic tone, Eleanor stepped closer. 'One last question, and then I'll leave you in peace. When you removed your necklace the night of your soirée because the clasp had broken, you put—'

'Broken?' Lady Chadwick paused in sinking onto the cream chaise longue and looked up sharply. 'Why, that's not what I told you! I appreciate you trying to help, but if you aren't going to remember things correctly, I shall end up in even more fearful trouble. It was irritating me, that's all. Just as I said originally. Now, I really must get back to my letter writing. I'm sure you've plenty to do yourself?'

Eleanor did have plenty to do. Nevertheless, the rest of the day passed frustratingly slowly. With the police still around – although not Seldon himself – Eleanor had to be doubly cautious. This ruled out sneaking into the library to see Clifford. And with the staff at Lord Chadwick's every beck and call, she had no luck in advancing her enquiries by speaking to any of them again, either.

That evening, she lay in bed unable to sleep, watching the hands of the mantelpiece clock inch around the dial. As she'd visited Clifford's pied-à-terre the night before, it had been decided it was too risky to do so tonight, so that avenue of distraction was out of bounds.

At close to quarter past midnight again, she admitted to herself that sleep was not going to happen. Not without something to lift her mood. There was only one answer with the milk locked away; raid the biscuit tin in the pantry! Swinging her legs out from under the twisted covers, she made a mental note to chide her butler over his gross oversight of not including his lock picks in her suitcase.

Holding her bedside candle out in front to illuminate the stairs, she tiptoed carefully to the basement. As she started down the passageway, the flame flickered. She shivered, remembering the last time she'd done this was the last time she'd seen Withers alive.

Then the candle flickered again and almost went out.

Where's that draught coming from, Ellie?

She stole a few yards along the passageway to the doorway of the pump room and peered inside. The cause was obvious. The window was open. And Alice was balanced precariously on an upturned bottle crate reaching across the sink below.

'Alice, you'll fall!' she hissed, rushing forward and grabbing the maid's legs.

'Oh, miss! You as good as stopped my heart,' Alice whispered, her blonde frizz of curls bouncing as she spun around.

'Never mind that. Get down now.' As Eleanor helped her, she noticed the maid was holding a small lidded dish. 'And whatever you're doing, it can't be worth risking Mrs Hawkins' anger, surely?'

'Maybe not, Miss Smith. but I'm lucky to have even that! What have I to grumble 'bout even with Mrs Hawkins' tongue sharper than a serpent? There's still a roof over me head and supper in me belly.' Her face fell. 'Unless you tell, of course. Then he'll have no one to help 'im!'

Eleanor's brows furrowed. 'Have you done this before, then?'

Alice nodded meekly.

'Since when? And how often?'

'Every night. But only the last few days, miss.'

Eleanor looked up at the window.

So Withers was trying to shut it that night, Ellie.

She gingerly climbed up on the crate and closed the window, turning both catches so it was locked. Then she jumped nimbly back down.

'Now, Alice, tell me, who is that dish for?'

'Nobody, Miss Smith!' she mumbled, tears springing to her eyes. 'I didn't steal any of it. Honest.'

Eleanor lifted the lid and peered inside. 'Food scraps?'

Alice nodded. 'Every one of 'em is from me own supper plate. I swear.'

'So you're feeding what? A stray cat?'

Alice shook her head hesitatingly. 'No, miss. For... for 'im. As... as is hidin' in the garden.' Fat tears rolled down both cheeks. 'Only, if you tell on me, they'll drive him away and he's nowhere else to go. I has to leave the window open 'cos there's no ledge to put the dish on outside, so I leave it here.'

She pointed to a shelf that ran along the wall and stopped a few inches short of the window.

Eleanor took the dish and put it on the crate. Taking the girl by the shoulders, she forced her to look at her.

'Alice. You must promise me you won't leave this window open again. In exchange, I'll do something for your... friend that's hiding in the garden. Okay?'

Alice wiped her tears on her sleeve and nodded. 'Thank you, Miss Smith.'

'Now, don't mention this to anyone. And get back to bed before anyone notices you're gone.'

The maid nodded again and fled silently.

Eleanor turned to the window. Someone from outside could definitely reach through and grab the bowl. And, if they were nimble enough, climb in.

But who? And why?

28

Given the late hour, Eleanor rang the doorbell of Clifford's adopted pied-à-terre, rather than trying the handle as her impetuous nature wanted her to. Then she couldn't help herself from knocking as well. At the sound of the lock clicking open on the other side, she turned her back.

'I know you're probably in your sleeping underthings, Clifford, but—'

'Do step in, my lady,' her butler's measured tone floated out. 'There is nothing inappropriate about my attire. And the night porter is the soul of discretion. Although,' he continued with a sigh, 'I may have to put up with a certain amount of ribbing for receiving a lady at such an indecorous hour.'

She laughed. 'He did seem quite amused when he let me in. Now, there's no time for a telling-off. We need to make a telephone call. I couldn't risk someone overhearing me at Chadwick House. Which is why, so as not to appear in my unmentionables, I hurled myself into whatever was to hand, and hot-footed it over here.'

'Evidently,' he said drily, eyeing her bed socks tucked haphazardly into her boots below her misbuttoned coat.

She pointed at his impeccable suit tails. 'Tell me you haven't sat up in your butlering togs just on the off chance I'd dash around here in the small hours?'

'I have not, my lady. If only in the obviously forlorn hope you playing the part of a virtuous governess would have restrained such a shameful escapade. And because we agreed you would not come tonight.'

'Then why?' She cocked her head as she caught a noise along the passage.

'I am, ahem... entertaining,' Clifford said, one finger tapping the knot of his tie.

'Dash it, I'm so sorry!' she hissed. 'Finally, you've allowed yourself to entice a gorgeous girl into your lair and I've messed it up.'

'What gorgeous girl?' a deep voice rumbled in her ear.

'Hugh! I came here to try and telephone you!' she cried, unable to keep down the butterflies that erupted at the unusual sight of her fiancé out of his grey work suit. 'Nice, er, pyjama bottoms and jumper combination.'

He rolled his eyes. 'Thanks to Gladstone! He managed to tip coffee down my suit with his usual over-exuberant welcome. Clifford's kindly drying it out, so he lent me these. But what are you doing here?'

Before she could reply, Gladstone tottered out sleepily, his quilted blanket wrapped over his back, ferrying Tomkins still curled up on the trailing end of it.

As she bent to give them both a loving ear rub, she caught her butler's pursed lips.

'Yes, my lady. Chief Inspector Seldon is the visitor I was referring to. Not a "gorgeous girl". And if I might note, "lairs" and "enticing" are the singular province of spiders, not butlers.'

She straightened up. 'Well, I hope both are good at planning traps, because we need one. Tonight!'

Still standing in the entrance hall, Seldon and Clifford

listened intently as she relayed how she'd found the maid leaving food at the open window.

'Blast it!' Seldon muttered. 'You're right, Eleanor. This needs acting on without delay. But I can't haul in any other police officers because there's too much risk my superior will get wind of it.'

Her brows knitted. 'Even though you are officially investigating Withers' death? Albeit with your hands tied by Lord Chadwick's position in Whitehall?'

'Yes. Because my boss rose to where he is by being one of the best detectives in his day. I can't take the chance he'd work out you are the very same infuriating troublemaker from the Empire Exhibition enclosure.' He held his hands up quickly. 'His words, not mine. Though, that was a far politer version of what he actually said.'

She huffed. 'Well, the day I finally meet him, I'll put him straight. Don't worry.'

'Fair enough. But what I'm trying to say is he'll add two and two together and make five!'

'But that means it's up to us three.' At his look, she nodded. 'Yes, Hugh. The three of us. So let's work it out on the way. Grab your hats and coats. Clifford, your one with the extra pockets,' she added airily.

As Seldon shrugged into his coat, Clifford cleared his throat. 'And trousers, perhaps, Chief Inspector? Even damp ones might be better than pyjamas?'

'Blast it!'

With the three huddled into the back of a late-night taxicab, Seldon frowned. 'An intruder in the garden, eh? But if it's one of the burglary gang, why return? They've got Lady Chadwick's necklace, we assume. And with the police alerted, it would be too dangerous if the house were being watched. Which they can't be certain that it isn't.'

Eleanor nodded. 'True, Hugh. But Alice said whoever it is, is hiding in the garden. She's clearly been leaving food out for several days.'

'But why, if this person is the one who killed Withers, would the maid be harbouring him?'

'Simple, Hugh. You've met Alice. Bush of bouncy blonde curls as bubbly and sweet-faced as she is natured.'

'Ah! That one. Mmm. So you're fairly sure it could be a case of her being impressionable enough to be easily fooled into innocently helping this intruder?'

'Categorically so.'

Clifford nodded. 'On the admittedly few occasions I have come into contact with the young lady at Chadwick House, I have been reminded most sharply of her ladyship's maid, Polly. Brimming with good intentions, but naive in the extreme.'

'I see,' Seldon said. 'I do think it unlikely to be the thief or Withers' killer that she's been feeding, though. I can't imagine that he wouldn't have long fled the area.'

'Another conjecture strikes, Chief Inspector. It could be a vagrant. One who has taken advantage of Alice's impression-ability.'

'The absolute wretch! I'll break his neck,' Seldon growled.

'No, not taking advantage like that, Hugh,' Eleanor said quickly. 'Clifford means she probably thinks he's just after the supper scraps she's been leaving in the dish on the shelf. But he could actually have taken advantage of the open window to climb in and burgle the house.'

'And kill Withers when he was caught?' Seldon scratched his chin. 'He may not even have intended to kill him, I suppose?'

'Possibly,' Eleanor said. 'But we can't take the chance. We need to act fast. Now as the gardeners left hours ago, and hopefully all the staff are still asleep, here's what I suggest we do when we get there...'

Chadwick House was in total darkness as the taxicab carried on past Park Lane to drop them at the next street corner in the shadows of the gas lamp opposite.

'The side garden gate comes out just along there,' Eleanor whispered as they reached the back of the Park Lane mansion. 'The dratted latch dropped down behind me though when I came out earlier, so we'll have to shimmy over.'

Seldon and Clifford both stepped in her way as she gestured they make a brace for her.

'Eleanor, for Pete's sake, can't you just wait until one of us has dealt with the gate?' Seldon gruffed.

'And then opened it so a more ladylike entrance might at least be made?' Clifford added, indicating to Seldon he'd go over the top.

'Alright, my chivalrous knights,' she whispered. 'Only you'd better hurry up. We're hoping he saw Alice closing the window, thinking she was disturbed and that she'll return. So we need to be in position when he does. I'll slink through the garden with you both keeping an eye out for me, and then make my way to the pump room and open the window as agreed.'

'Wait, Eleanor,' Seldon whispered, once they were all inside the gate. 'How are you going to get back inside the house? I thought only a butler would have been given a key. And you surely didn't leave it unlatched after all that's happened?'

'You're right. On both counts. But don't worry, I'll use a trick a nameless scallywag might have been teaching me.' She patted her pocket.

Seldon's gaze shot to Clifford to be met with an impassive look. He groaned quietly. 'Just don't ever tell me the worst of what you two have got up to!'

Eleanor crept towards the house, the garden feeling eerily quiet as she hurried along the neatly bordered path which followed the line of the ivy-covered wall. The earth smelt damp as if it had been recently watered.

Concentrate, Ellie.

Even having a good grounding in Bartitsu, a form of martial arts used by the Suffragettes among others, she still felt jumpier than she wanted to. She was relying on their quarry spotting her and assuming she was one of the staff who'd overstayed their curfew. The one weak point in the plan was she'd need to pick the back-door lock. Hopefully, it would just look as if she were fumbling with the key in the dark.

The wind rustled through the trembling bamboo and the grandiose lines of swaying poplar trees leading to the ornamental pond in the centre of the garden. She wondered if a pair of eyes was watching her from the elaborate summerhouse or the far less elaborate gardeners' tool shed. Either way, her catching their quarry's attention would leave Seldon and Clifford free to pincer around to either side of the pump room window unobserved, using the bank of rhododendron bushes as cover.

Having reached the staff entrance, it took a long minute faffing with Clifford's pick locks before she finally heard the lock turn and she was in.

Flattening herself against the nearest wall, she listened carefully. Wanting the intruder to see her was one thing. If anyone in the house did, however, their plan would be in tatters. The lights streaming out across the garden would send the intruder to ground in a blink. And likely throw Seldon or Clifford into a very unwanted spotlight.

Fingers crossed, he's still out there, Ellie.

Pleased she'd thought to leave her bedside candle and several matches hidden behind the pile of wicker trug baskets, she lit the wick and started towards the pump room. Then it struck her. The three of them had overlooked something major. If Alice had disobeyed her and crept back down to put the scraps out while she'd been gone, the intruder could be in the house already! She shook her head, calming her breathing. Seldon and Clifford would have realised that on getting into position and found a way to warn her if the window was already open. To be doubly certain, she watched her candle flame intently along the passageway, relieved it didn't flicker.

Just before the doorway of the pump room, she paused, straining her ears. Nothing. She hurried past the door to the laundry room and swapped her coat and scarf for a maid's cap and apron from the linen hamper. Then darted back. Fumbling under the apron, she pulled out a small cloth bag and emptied the extra tantalising food scraps Clifford had given her into the dish.

Now looking like Alice, the maid, to anyone staring in from the garden, she climbed up onto the crate, making sure her silhouette was illuminated by the candle. Placing the dish on the shelf, she opened the window and hissed into the darkness. ''Tis a bit more tonight. Seein' as 'tis so late. 'Tis summat special from supper on account of less of us 'ere now.'

Carefully climbing down, she left the pump room, changed back into her coat and scarf, and swiftly returned to the staff entrance.

Once there, she listened, ear to the door. Only the wind seemed to stir on the other side. The torch Clifford had given her in her hand, she crept out and slunk slowly up the steps.

Wherever Seldon and Clifford had hidden themselves was perfect, she thought, as she scoured the darkness for any sign of them. She just had time to think that not charging into action on her own without a plan was progress, as Seldon always bemoaned her reckless streak, when she caught it. The barest flash of movement behind one of the dustbins near the pump room window. She waited, fearing she'd imagined it. Then caught it again. A small shadowy figure darting towards the open window like a starving wolf. She broke cover as Seldon erupted from the bushes opposite. The figure switched direction with amazing speed and headed towards the giant rhododendron beds.

We're going to lose him, Ellie.

Then a tall figure stepped out of the shadows into the middle of the path. The smaller figure had no warning and ploughed straight into it.

'One intruder apprehended,' Clifford whispered as Eleanor and Seldon reached him, the shadowy figure firmly held in his grasp.

'It's three against one,' Seldon barked sotto voce. 'And two of us are armed, so don't do anything foolish.'

The shadow nodded frantically as Seldon leaned forward and pulled the hood off the diminutive, cloaked figure.

Not daring to turn on her torch lest it be seen from the house, she still had no difficulty in recognising the intruder in the moonlight.

'You!' she gasped.

29

In the gleaming blue and yellow tiled kitchen of Clifford's pied-à-terre, Eleanor shook her head at Seldon as she thrust a bowl of hard-boiled eggs at him.

'Hugh, please stop fussing and shell these instead.' She looked over at the young ebony-skinned boy kneeling on the floor, delighting in Gladstone's wrinkled jowls and Tomkins' velveteen ginger fur. She lowered her voice. 'I feel terrible I had us all trap him like a criminal. All the more so as I should have helped him days ago.'

'*We* should have,' Clifford said sombrely, stirring several saucepans on the white enamel stove beside her. 'It was far from your responsibility alone, my lady.'

'Blast it, these are piping hot.' Seldon frowned at the eggs as he shook the heat from his fingers. 'But helped him, how? And when? Neither of you have explained a thing. All I know is in the middle of the night we trapped a young foreign boy in a Park Lane mansion garden and then whisked him away to here.'

Clifford nodded. 'Indeed, we did, Chief Inspector.'

'And thank goodness,' Eleanor added, sharing a relieved look with her butler.

Seldon groaned. 'Will one of you please tell me what on earth is going on?'

Clifford nodded. 'With apologies, that will be rectified the moment this hasty stew is ready and served.'

'Clifford, I need answers, not a midnight supper!' Seldon hissed.

'It's not for us, Hugh,' Eleanor said. 'And it's your turn to dig out some patience for a change. Because police protocol, procedure and the law and every court in the land can go hang until we've got something warming and nutritious into that poor little chap.'

'I still don't see—'

Eleanor pulled him to one side. 'Hugh! Am I or am I not up to my neck in domesticity? Has my usually sniffy butler uttered a single chiding remark about it being inappropriate for a titled lady to be stirring vegetables or straining rice and beans?'

Seldon shook his head, distractedly retying the strings of her apron around her waist. 'I know. That's the oddest part of it all, actually.'

'No, it isn't,' she said softly. 'Because the boy is thousands of miles from home, with no one he feels safe to turn to, and hungrier than any child should ever be. And it is breaking Clifford's heart. As much as it is mine. But please don't ask why.'

The truth was that the scenario was too close to the mark for her butler. He had confided to her a similar snippet of his long-troubled upbringing one night when they'd found themselves in dire straits. He'd been orphaned and sent to a guardian at the age of eight. And from the age of twelve, lived on his wits on the streets.

Seldon nodded contritely. 'Understood. Eggs done. What can I do next, my beautiful, aproned boss?'

With all Clifford's culinary wizardry and Eleanor and Seldon's additional efforts, it was only a few minutes later that a simple but hot and tasty feast was ready. Clifford stepped back into the kitchen with the boy now swathed in a thick grey jumper which hung from his slim shoulders to way below his coloured robe. A pair of matching socks flapped past the end of his toes.

'Thank you all for this great kindness,' he said solemnly.

Clifford smiled. 'You're very welcome, young friend.'

Eleanor smiled through a hot prick of tears, barely resisting the urge to scoop the boy into her arms and hug him.

The lad's bright dark eyes shone as he held his left hand behind his back, offering his right one out to her. 'My name is Kofi Oppong.'

'And you're starving, so please sit and eat. That is Mr Seldon and I'm Eleanor. But my butler, Mr Clifford, there,' she mock whispered, 'will be quietly horrified I didn't say "Lady Swift".'

'Or "Miss Smith". The pretend governess,' Kofi said with a grin.

Seldon stared at her, but all she could do was shrug.

'Master Kofi, please eat whatever you wish.' Clifford pulled out a chair for the young boy and glanced at Seldon. 'Perhaps questions might wait until at least a goodly plate has been devoured, Chief Inspector?'

Seldon nodded. 'Of course.'

'I can give answers between eating, sir,' Kofi said while spooning several helpings of vegetable stew onto the generous portion of rice and beans he'd taken. 'I think to begin, you want to know that I am from the Gold Coast. And I am eleven years old.'

'And you speak very good English,' Seldon said in a puzzled tone.

'A basic mastery of the language is not so uncommon, Chief Inspector,' Clifford said. 'The British have exerted their influence there since 1821. Though young Kofi appears particularly well-educated.'

'I miss school lessons,' the boy said with a frown. 'My parents always taught me it is noble to learn.' Eleanor smiled as Clifford nodded in agreement. 'But' – Kofi gestured with his fork – 'I have much to learn to become the man to help my country.'

Eleanor folded the nearest cuff of his oversized jumper back several turns to keep it out of the stew. 'A very admirable aim as well. Right now, though, what you need to do is eat.'

He smiled and held out his other wrist. 'Thank you. And for the time before at the exhibition. You saved me much trouble then.'

Seldon's mouth flew open, but he quickly clamped a hand over it.

Eleanor threw him a grateful look. 'Kofi, is that why you were hiding in the garden where we found you? Because of that angry man I stopped from chasing you?'

'Yes. His name is Jafaru.'

Eleanor shot Seldon a look. 'The man from the Gold Coast Pavilion next door is the one who got you into trouble with the ambassador, Hugh.'

Kofi nodded. 'Always he is angry. And never does he teach me anything. Yet, I am the one who should be angry! Jafaru took money for me to become his apprentice. But never has he taught me anything. Only he has treated me as his possession. I have to do everything he commands or he beats me. Like come to England with him when he got the job at the exhibition. I did not like to play pretend that I cannot speak English and that I live in a hut back home. It is a lie. Before my parents died, I lived in a house. Most people in my city do.'

'Who paid him to take you?' Seldon coaxed gently.

'My uncle, sir. He was forced to accept me to his house when my mother died. My father had also died some years before and I had no other relatives. But my uncle did not want me. When I reached nine years old, he paid Jafaru to take me for his apprentice because Jafaru was a successful businessman and owned several shops in our town.'

Eleanor didn't miss Clifford's pained look as he spun around to busy himself at the stove. Nor Seldon spooning another egg and more hot stew onto the boy's plate while shaking his head sadly.

Once the lump in Eleanor's throat had receded, she said, 'Kofi, why were you hiding in that garden particularly?'

'Because of you,' he said brightly. 'After you help me by knocking into Jafaru when he was chasing me, I did not know where to hide. Then the night after the next, I saw you creep into the enclosure at the exhibition with these two gentlemen. And I followed you.'

Seldon stiffened.

'It is no trouble, sir. I do not tell anyone.' Kofi turned back to Eleanor. 'And after, I followed you back to the big house by hiding in the box of the...' He tapped his forehead.

'Carriage?' Clifford said.

'With the horse to pull it? Yes.'

'But Kofi,' Eleanor gasped, 'I didn't go to Chadwick House until the next morning.'

He shrugged and took a large forkful of egg. 'It felt safe in the box. I was quite comfortable, but I did have some hunger. And thirst.'

'Thank heavens Alice spotted you,' she murmured. She looked between Seldon and Clifford. 'So we weren't as stealthy as we thought that night. You know what that means?' She pointed discreetly at Kofi and lowered her voice. 'He might have seen something.'

Clifford added the juice of an orange to the boy's glass of water. 'Master Kofi, do you know why the three of us visited that enclosure at the exhibition that night?'

'I know you were looking for something, Mr Clifford. Or someone. Mr Seldon is a policeman, yes?'

'Yes,' Eleanor said gently. 'Unfortunately though, Kofi, we went because I saw someone hurt somebody there. Badly, in fact.'

'People are strange and unkind that way,' he said in a tone of wisdom beyond his years. 'But I think you mean maybe the person is dead? You do not need to be careful to say so with me. I have seen the dead, and I read many history books, and it is the same now as always. Like the butler in the big house. He is dead by the hand of another, perhaps? I hear the gardeners talk of this when I am hiding.'

Seldon shifted in his seat, still looking very uncomfortable. 'Can I ask where on earth you were hiding in the garden, young fellow? Because my men searched it carefully, but they had no idea you were there.'

The boy grinned. 'Yes, they searched most thoroughly, sir. But you must tell them to also look in the tall trees another time. At the very top! I watched them all the morning from up there.'

'Ah! In one of the poplars, I imagine, Chief Inspector,' Clifford said.

Seldon groaned. 'Not only do I have too few officers to be effective, now I need ones who can climb blasted trees!'

Eleanor laughed, but when she spoke, her tone was serious. 'Kofi, I don't like to ask you to keep a secret, but—'

He raised his hand and said solemnly, 'I promise not to tell anyone you went to the exhibition in the night-time.' He lowered his hand. 'But is it because of Jafaru you keep this secret?'

Eleanor grimaced. 'Sort of. Let's just say he's part of the reason no one must know that Mr Seldon is... interested in what happened there.'

The boy turned to Seldon. 'Then I wish to help, sir. What can I answer for you?'

Seldon ran his hand around the back of his neck. 'Well, did you see or hear anything about a man being... hurt in that enclosure? With a gun? Or a... a person being moved from there?'

'No, sir. Especially not a dead person. Neither did I hear that someone was shot. Of the closed enclosure, I know only that Jafaru goes there each evening to have the goats from our display eat straw that is not his. The food given for ours he sells when no one is looking and puts the money in his pocket.' He grinned at his laden forkful of beans. 'And he gets the reward of hurting his back for his trouble with the heavy gates he has to open and close. I think this is just. Like when the biggest goat bite his bottom through his robe. He could not sit down for two days!'

Eleanor couldn't help laughing with him, Seldon joining in as Clifford added pithily, 'Most discerning creatures, goats.'

Kofi looked at Seldon over his orange water. 'But I am most sorry. I have not helped you, sir.'

'No matter,' Seldon said, quietly drumming his fingers on the table. 'There's something I need to discuss with Lady Swift for a moment anyway.'

Eleanor stared at him, then at Clifford, who stared back with his ever-inscrutable expression. 'You rotters! You two know something I don't.'

Seldon held up a placating hand. 'Clifford has no more idea than you do. I was thwarted from telling him what I've learned so he could relay it quietly to you at Chadwick House. Thwarted, first, I might add, by this clumsy bulldog hurling coffee all over me.' He ruffled Gladstone's ears where the dog's heavy head lay adoringly in his lap. 'And then by a vision in governess grey rhinoceros-ing her way in here with the demand we lay a trap, despite it being the small hours.'

'And you in your pyjamas,' she teased. 'Yes, I did do that, didn't I?'

Kofi looked confused. 'This rhinoceros word is not correct English, I think, Mr Clifford?'

'Only where her ladyship is concerned, young friend,' her butler said mischievously as he mimed a charging beast with a horn.

The boy's chuckle was drowned out by Seldon's. He shook himself and led Eleanor and Clifford away from the boy, who was heartily tucking in to his food.

'Listen. I discreetly enquired about the movements of the staff on the day, and at the time, of the man's murder at the exhibition. And also of everyone's whereabouts the day Withers was killed, after you told me you believed there was a link between the two.'

Eleanor's jaw fell. 'Should you have done that?'

He shook his head ruefully. 'Absolutely not. There is still no evidence that there is a link to the murder at the exhibition. Except that is, for the shrewdest, most intelligent and possibly, most reckless woman ever born believing there is. So therefore.' He sighed. 'I do.'

'Thank you,' she breathed. 'That means so much.'

He nodded. 'However, that statement is no longer true.'

Her breath caught. 'You mean you no longer believe—'

He held up a hand. 'No, I mean that there was no evidence to link Withers' death with the exhibition murder. But there is now.'

Eleanor's mouth dropped. 'The post-mortem report—'

'Isn't in yet. What I mean is, I went ahead behind the scenes and asked a good, very discreet, friend at the office to search for anyone called "John Clemthorpe", the name in the wallet of the body at the morgue. Well, there were quite a few as you might imagine. The problem being, that normally you'd narrow it down to anyone of that name who had been recently reported missing or dead. But, as you know, in this case, Clemthorpe's disappearance, and death, seems to have been covered up.'

She nodded. 'Go on.'

'Well, my friend narrowed it down to the most likely

suspects. Three John Clemthorpes live within fifty miles of the exhibition site. The first one I spoke to today and he's alive and well. The third I never got to speak to because I never spoke to the second.'

She frowned. 'Why because you never spoke to the second did it mean you never spoke to the third one on your list?'

'Because the person I spoke to told me that the second John Clemthorpe is on extended leave from his office.'

She shrugged. 'But that could be true.'

Seldon took a deep breath. 'It could be. But it's the same office a certain Lord Chadwick works in!'

30

Eleanor gasped.

'That's the missing link between the murders, Hugh! The first victim, Clemthorpe, worked *with* Lord Chadwick, and the second victim, Withers, worked *for* Lord Chadwick!'

Seldon grimaced. 'True. You may, however, hate me for this, Eleanor, but it doesn't prove that Lord Chadwick killed either man. There may be a further hidden connection that we've yet to uncover.'

She nodded slowly, catching Clifford was too.

Possibly the missing necklace, Ellie.

She bit her tongue, not wanting to say anything until she'd spoken to Lady Chadwick.

'What does the coroner's report...' She shrugged apologetically at his look. 'Sorry. I know he has other, equally pressing post-mortems to do first. So what can we do now, Hugh?'

He shrugged. 'I've already asked people I trust to do things that could get them into serious trouble. I really feel I've pushed this to the limit.'

'I agree, Hugh. We shouldn't involve anyone else in this. We've had a breakthrough. Perhaps for the moment, we should go back to your news about the whereabouts of the staff at the time of Clemthorpe's death? Maybe this further "hidden connection", if there is one, might concern one of them?'

He nodded. 'Good idea.'

'So what did you find out?'

'To start with, all of them have alibis for the time of Clemthorpe's death except one.'

She nodded eagerly. 'Which one?'

'Tateham, the footman. He'd been granted leave to go to a medical appointment. But the cook remembered Withers tearing him off a strip for returning late.'

'How late?'

'She couldn't remember exactly. But I checked and Tateham never had an appointment booked! Now, normally it would be impossible to get from Chadwick House to Wembley and back in under two hours without a taxi, which would be prohibitively expensive for a footman. And it would be a fare a driver would notice as highly unusual. Unless Tateham also changed his clothes, which is adding more time to an already tight schedule. More likely, he could have used the new underground services laid on especially to encourage visitors to the Empire Exhibition. That's pure theory, though. I need to examine a timetable.'

'I have one in the adjacent room,' Clifford said.

Eleanor held up a finger. 'That's interesting, Hugh. Lady Chadwick told me all the staff have been in service at Chadwick House for a while. Except two. The scullery maid who was taken on six months ago. And... the footman, who was taken on only a month ago!'

'Which explains a lot,' Clifford sniffed. 'He strikes me as being entirely new to the responsibilities of his role.' He swung around. 'Are you full, Master Kofi?'

The boy trotted up to them and nodded. 'Yes, thank you, Mr Clifford. Very.'

Clifford's ever-impassive expression relaxed, giving away his relief. He turned back to Eleanor and Seldon.

'Might I be so bold as to suggest decamping to the comfort of the sitting room with liquid refreshments? I can prepare them with Master Kofi's assistance.'

Seldon nodded. 'Good idea, Clifford.'

A few snatched minutes alone with Seldon in the apartment's cosy sitting room couldn't come soon enough for Eleanor. He wrapped her gently in his arms, making her breath catch. And when he nuzzled her cheek, she wished time would stop forever.

'Thank you, Hugh,' she breathed as he reluctantly released her.

He laughed. 'Rather formal, my love? Especially from you.'

She batted his arm. 'I meant for still relentlessly pursuing Clemthorpe's murderer despite the possible consequences, you daft thing.'

'Pity,' he said more soberly. 'Stuck talking about blasted murder yet again with you. When all I can think of is...' He tailed off as he rubbed his hands over his lean cheeks with a long sigh.

'Is what, Hugh?'

He ran his thumb tenderly down her chin. 'Is sweeping you over my shoulder and leaping onto a white charger to gallop you away to a castle, so you shan't suffer being involved in anything unpleasant ever again.'

'That sounds too wonderful for words, Sir Galahad. Though I'm not actually a damsel in distress.'

'For once.' He ran a frustrated hand through his chestnut curls. 'But I know how things usually pan out when I try and do the romantic thing. I'd probably more likely than not crack your head on a door frame on the way out and then discover my noble steed was a wretched donkey.'

She laughed. 'Definitely go for a bicycle with a basket on

the front instead, Hugh. Clifford and I ended up being reliant on a very single-minded donkey in Ireland for our transport once. It was hilarious, but absolutely hopeless.'

He shook his head. 'Well, let's get this next bit of business under way. It's going to be a long night otherwise.'

'Morning, sir.' Kofi's lively brown eyes peeped around the door. 'It is already morning, I believe.' His close-cropped black hair disappeared again.

'Gracious, he's starting to talk like Clifford already!' she whispered, settling onto the nearest settee.

A streak of ginger tomcat and a lumbering bulldog bundled into the room, followed, more sedately, by Clifford bearing a silver tray. He tutted.

'The strain of not stealing Master Kofi's supper has proven too much for your two over-indulged menaces, my lady. If I might, therefore, recommend taking extra care with these cobble stones as a necessary precaution.'

He set the tray down on the coffee table and laid out cups and saucers with side plates.

'Cobble stones?' Seldon looked hungrily at the pyramid of golden-brown savoury scones.

'An impromptu recipe adaptable to whatever one can, ahem, scrummage to hand at this hour, Chief Inspector.' His tone softened. 'Renamed by Master Kofi while assisting most efficiently.'

With cups of delectable rich roast coffee poured for Eleanor and Seldon, and a long glass of something chocolatey for Kofi, Clifford turned to Gladstone and Tomkins.

'Gentlemen, it is way past your bedtime. And in the inimitable parlance of her ladyship, hideously long until breakfast.'

This prompted Gladstone to hurl his top half up onto the tartan rug spread out on the settee beside Kofi. The tomcat leaped up onto the bulldog's back and pranced along it to claim the prize spot against Kofi's curled up legs.

'Share and share alike, you rascal.' Eleanor lifted Gladstone's back half onto the settee to join them. She stifled a yawn. 'I think it might be way past all our bedtimes. It's been a tough few days.'

Seldon nodded. 'Well, I've only a small amount left to impart.'

'We are all ears, Chief Inspector,' Clifford said.

Kofi flapped his hands on either side of his head like an elephant, making Seldon chuckle.

'In essence, there's not much to tell, blast it! I'm still checking into the backgrounds of all the staff, but nothing to report so far. What about you two, anything new on the missing necklace? Or from Lady Chadwick?'

Eleanor pursed her lips. 'Only that she is happy to lie. Although I sort of knew that already. What I hadn't realised is that she is a little too good at it. She admitted she backed up her husband's story to you about the necklace theft because he told her to.'

'Not surprising. A wife will usually do as her husband commands.'

Clifford peeped mischievously at her. 'Shall I make a special note of that, my lady? For the future, as it were?'

'No!' she said emphatically. 'She said Lord Chadwick told her the insurance company wouldn't pay, otherwise. But she was adamant her original story of the necklace being stolen the night of her soirée was the actual truth.' She took a sip of coffee and a bite of one of the scones. 'Delicious. And, Hugh? You asked the staff at the time, didn't you, about when the necklace was stolen?'

'Yes. And to a man, they swore they'd first heard of it after learning of Withers' demise.'

She sighed. 'Which is what Lady Chadwick said they would say if her husband told them to.'

Clifford topped up her coffee as Eleanor shuffled into a thoughtful, cross-legged position.

'Wensleydale cheese and walnut or Double Gloucester and chutney, Chief Inspector?' He gestured at the plate with a pair of silver tongs.

'One of each,' she answered for him. 'Make it two, in fact, as he won't eat again until you entice him back up here, Clifford.'

Kofi contentedly rubbed his own tummy and Gladstone's at the same time. He looked up at Seldon.

'Catching bad people cannot be easy, I think, sir?'

Seldon shook his head wearily. 'No, smart fellow, it really isn't.' He leaned forward and whispered, 'Don't let on to her ladyship, but maybe that's partly why I am grateful to have her help on occasion.'

The young boy stretched his legs out for Gladstone to sprawl more comfortably across and grinned. 'And because she is so very pretty.'

'Ah! Doubly smart fellow.'

She laughed. 'Flatterers! Now, let's finish up this lovely food and coffee. My pyjamas are calling me!'

31

The following morning, outside the closed door of Chadwick House's boot room, Eleanor paused, surreptitiously listening for sounds within.

'Sickening for something?' a cocksure voice whispered in her ear.

She spun around. 'Tateham! I thought you were polishing the silver?'

He held up two pairs of gleaming boots. 'These first. Master's home, isn't he? And don't we know it? Crikey, I wish he'd bang his head hard enough to forget where he lives. The maids are running about like headless chickens, Mrs Rudge lunges at you with her scariest kitchen knife if you go near her, and Mrs Hawkins looks like she's rubbed her eyes raw over summat.'

More like tear-tired eyes, Eleanor thought from briefly seeing the woman earlier. Either way, he'd inadvertently thrown her the perfect conversation opener.

'You know, yes. I believe I am,' she said in a convincingly weak voice.

Tateham cocked his head. 'You are what, Miss Smith?'

Clearing her throat, she held her hand to her forehead. 'Also sickening for something. Can you give me a recommendation? For a doctor.'

'Me? Doctor? Nah, don't have one. Too strong and vigorous to ever need mollycoddling like the women do.'

She frowned. 'See, now that can't be right. I heard you got the most fearful telling-off from Mr Withers for coming back late from your doctor's appointment the Friday before I started.'

He stared at the boots, avoiding her eye. 'Heard that, did you? Blummin' maids can't keep their tongues stiller than dogs' tails on hunting day.'

'But you were fibbing about having an appointment, weren't you?'

Tateham's head jerked up, his eyes blazing. 'Says who?'

She laughed. 'You, silly. You've just told me you were too strong and vigorous to go to the doctor.'

For a moment he didn't reply, then his face broke into a grin. 'Yeah, alright, you got me there.' He lowered his voice. 'Don't tell any of this lot, but I pretended I was sick with chest pains. Anything less and Mrs Hawkins would have marched me into that witch's cupboard of hers and forced me to drink some foul home remedy from those creepy bottles of hers.'

'So where did you go if not to the doctor?'

His grin widened. 'I went to see my sweetheart if you really must know, Miss Nosey.'

'Does Hannah know?'

Tateham glanced over his shoulder and put his finger to his mouth. 'Shh! That girl's got an unsettling knack for overhearing things!' He looked at her oddly. 'Like you.'

She stiffened.

Does he suspect you're not who you say you are, Ellie?

She forced herself to relax. 'Of course I do. All us women

can eavesdrop from a mile away. And tell what you're thinking without you telling us.'

He shuddered. 'I hope not! Anyhow, Hannah doesn't know. And I don't want her to either.'

Eleanor held her hands up. 'She won't hear it from me. So who's your sweetheart?'

'Nobody here,' he said dismissively. 'And I'm not saying any more than that.'

'Good for you. We girls are supposed to have an air of mystique, I've heard.'

His gaze roved suggestively over her face. 'You've got one going for you, alright. And I've heard governesses were always the stiff, frigid types.'

She didn't miss that he didn't say that had been his experience while in service. Maybe Clifford was right, and this was Tateham's first job as a footman?

'Well, I hope seeing your sweetheart was worth Mr Withers' fury.'

'He didn't rattle me!' Tateham said arrogantly.

'I heard you stood up to him and what was it? Oh yes, threatened to "end him".' She grimaced at his shocked expression. 'Bit of an unfortunate turn of phrase now he's dead, isn't it?'

'I didn't mean I was going to kill him! Those wretched maids gossiping again, I bet. I meant "end" his career here. And I only threatened him 'cos he threatened me. I told him I'd spill the beans to Lord Chadwick about him taking backhanders to keep his mouth shut about—' He froze. 'Why on earth am I telling you of all people? Has Mrs Hawkins given you one of her witch's potions that makes a man's tongue looser than all the pretty maids put together?'

'It's alright, Tateham,' she said hurriedly, putting a hand on his arm.

He shrugged her off. 'I've told you way too much already. Keep those amazing looks of yours upstairs, will you, before I get myself into more trouble?'

She groaned as he hurried away.

Backhanders for what, dash it, Ellie? Could that explain the money in the envelope on Withers' body?

She shook her head and tried to refocus. Tateham had mentioned Mrs Hawkins and her "witch's cupboard". That had to be her next port of call.

Having located the room, she breezed in with a cheery, 'Good morning!'

'If it seems that way to you, I suppose, Miss Smith,' Mrs Hawkins said coolly, taking a small blue glass bottle from the wall cabinet in front of her.

Eleanor stepped across the tiled floor to the woman's side.

'That might have sounded a little insensitive of me. My apologies. I find offering condolences hard. Maybe I can start again by saying how sorry I am about Mr Withers?'

Mrs Hawkins still didn't meet her gaze. 'I shouldn't bother. Thank you. We were just colleagues. And I'm... extremely busy. As always.'

'All the more so now, until a new butler is appointed in his place.'

It went against Eleanor's nature to be harsh, but she had to know the truth. She peeped around the housekeeper's shoulder. Despite the reading spectacles she'd never seen the woman wear before, there was no missing the red rims of her eyes again.

'Mrs Hawkins, none of us can help having emotions. Even if we need to hide them.'

'Emotions? Nonsense! I'm a professional housekeeper. I've no idea what you are thinking, but don't care to find out, frankly.'

'If you insist,' Eleanor said. 'Though with you being so busy, you can't hole up in here all day, I imagine. I shan't be the only one to realise you've been crying.'

She blanched as Mrs Hawkins turned to face her, causing the unstoppered blue bottle to thrust uncomfortably close to her. 'Oh goodness, those fumes are fiercely pungent!' She pushed it away, her sleeve pressed over her nose.

'And irritating to the eyes, Miss Smith,' Mrs Hawkins said caustically. 'Which is all that has caused any reddening to mine.'

Feeling her own stinging already, Eleanor couldn't deny that might be the reason. She took a few steps back. Partly to put a little distance between the astringent contents of the bottle and the equally astringent housekeeper. She also needed a moment to think of another way to try to draw something useful from this stony-faced woman.

She looked along the long narrow bench, filled with empty bottles, saucers, bowls and vases of all shapes and sizes. A selection of dried flower arrangements stood among them, beside a glass atomiser containing an amber-coloured liquid. Around its base were several crystals. At the end of the bench, a metal sink on wheels with a bucket below was hung with a long cotton bag stained with green, vibrant yellow, and pink streaks. An empty jug was balanced on each corner. A run of lockable drawers that wouldn't have been out of place in an apothecary's shop dominated the opposite wall. She ran her eye along the handwritten labels slotted into the brass holder on each drawer; *camphor, alum, pumice, lye, spirits of lavender, linseed paste, gum tragacanth crystals, blacking, plate powder, emery paper, ivory-black, lamp wicks,* and particularly the intriguingly named *rottenstone powder.*

At one end, hanging on a metal rack, was every conceivable paring and trimming knife. She shivered.

Relax, Ellie. Withers wasn't stabbed. He was... what?

She stared again at the array of glass bottles and drawers,

wondering if any contained poison. Obviously Seldon's team were checking.

She jumped as Mrs Hawkins plonked the blue bottle back into the cabinet and slammed the door closed. Pulling out a ring of keys on a long chain from her dress pocket, she locked it, then spun around.

'Don't let me keep you, Miss Smith.' Her lip curled. 'I'm sure your lesson planning must be calling you.'

Eleanor stepped over and picked up the simple glass rose bowl she'd spotted the housekeeper shielding from her view. Set with a posy of yellow umbrella flowers, lilac globes and cream bunny tail tipped grasses, it was really rather lovely.

'Of course, Mrs Hawkins. Now, that's amber resin in that atomiser, isn't it? To preserve this posy. The one Mr Withers gave you, I imagine?'

'No!' Mrs Hawkins snatched it back.

Eleanor shook her head. 'I've already done my lesson planning, you know. With the children being away still, I'm not in a hurry.'

Mrs Hawkins hesitated, then shrugged. 'Alright. Mr Withers picked the flowers for me. What's wrong with that?'

'Absolutely nothing. Every girl loves a floral gift. Most especially from her… beau.'

Mrs Hawkins shot her a malevolent look. 'No doubt you've been gossiping with the maids rather than getting on with your duties!'

'Not exclusively. But I don't think it is gossip. I believe you loved Mr Withers.'

For a while, the housekeeper said nothing. Then she muttered, 'Once. Maybe. Before…' Her voice wavered. 'Before he let me down.'

'Ah! By refusing to tell Lord Chadwick that he wanted to marry you, perhaps?'

'No!' Mrs Hawkins shook her head sadly. 'He would have. Only he didn't get the chance.'

Eleanor frowned. 'Then how did he let you down? I promise I won't tell any of the other staff. Sometimes it helps to get these things off your chest.'

Mrs Hawkins stifled a sob. 'It doesn't matter now. And anyhow, he'd have only gone and got us both into trouble for... for taking it, silly fool!'

Eleanor's eyes widened. 'He stole Lady Chadwick's pearl necklace?'

'No!' Mrs Hawkins said defensively. Mr Withers is...' – she pressed a handkerchief to her mouth – '*was* a long-serving and loyal employee here.'

'Loyal staff don't steal from their employers?'

'But you don't understand!' Mrs Hawkins wrung her hands. 'We only planned he would take the necklace and I would hide it for a while. Then, when the master was at his wits' end as it were, Mr Withers was going to go to him, saying he'd found it hidden somewhere.'

'To curry favour with Lord Chadwick so he would agree to you both marrying and staying under his roof?'

Mrs Hawkins nodded. 'Yes. But Mr Withers let me down. He was all talk and no do! So I had to try and stea— Take it.'

'On the night of Lady Chadwick's soirée? You saw her go upstairs and then come down without it?'

Mrs Hawkins nodded. 'Mr Withers found Tateham in the mistress' bedroom having a to-do with one of the guests who had drunk too much. While Tateham was getting rid of the guest, Withers whispered to me that the necklace was on the floor in the mistress' bedroom. But when I got there and searched the room, it wasn't there.' Her eyes darkened. 'None of this is your business!' she hissed. 'You should never have come here!'

She sprayed the posy with the atomiser again. Eleanor's nose wrinkled.

That's not resin, Ellie. That's alcohol.

Mrs Hawkins snatched up a match, struck it and tossed it into the glass bowl.

Eleanor gasped as the posy burst into flames.

Mrs Hawkins laughed bitterly. 'That man made a fool out of me. But he's the one crying now!'

32

In the taxicab, the atmosphere was tense as it trundled through the late-night traffic.

The determined set of Seldon's jaw didn't flinch at Eleanor's repeated pleas.

'Eleanor, I'm not letting you and Clifford into that exhibition enclosure alone again. Blast it, I'm still grasping for a way to stop you coming with me. If either of you are caught there, you'll be charged with trespass, disturbing the peace, inciting unrest, and probably a dozen other charges! My superior made that very clear.'

'As clear as his threat about your career if you go back there?' she said, catching Clifford's concerned nod in the opposite seat.

'Yes, that clear. But that's his job because I'm a policeman. Though for a shameful moment, I almost lost sight of why I became one all those years ago.' He let out a long breath. 'I can just about swallow my guilt at walking away from a murder for the good of my country. Especially as it seems the man killed was working for the government, so the government deals with its own, as it were. But Withers was a civilian. And I intend to find out how he died! Not wearing a uniform any more hasn't changed why I do this every day.'

Eleanor's thoughts flew back to the framed photograph which hung in his house. She'd seen it the first time he'd allowed her a glimpse into his private world. A fresh-faced uniformed version of the now senior detective beside her. The one who selflessly accepted the gritty life his career mired him in. But also the one who somehow hadn't let it harden his heart.

'I can't betray my conscience either, Hugh. So it's a stalemate.'

Clifford cleared his throat quietly.

Eleanor groaned. 'Say your piece. Which is you are respectfully siding with Hugh, no doubt?'

'Actually, my lady, I was minded of something Master Kofi noted while we were putting out the flames of his breakfast toast this morning. "Two men in a burning house must not stop to argue." An ancient Gold Coast proverb, apparently.'

She and Seldon glanced at each other, a smile playing around both their lips.

'Truce, Hugh?'

He held up his hands. 'Yes. Since I've been defeated by an eleven-year-old, again. Even though he's not here. How's the young fellow been, by the way, Clifford?'

'In fine spirits, Chief Inspector. And in even finer appetite for devouring both comestibles and anything he can learn in the small library of our impromptu accommodation. All the while delighting in the company of an already devoted bulldog and tomcat.'

'That's wonderful to hear.'

Eleanor beamed at her butler. 'Speaking of libraries, Clifford. You haven't had a chance to tell Hugh yet.'

Seldon leaned forward. 'News from Chadwick House?'

'Indeed, Chief Inspector. In short, in Lord Chadwick's library, I found two first editions expertly hidden inside false books. Though the outer concealments themselves must have been costly enough as they were remarkable copies.'

'We already knew he collected first editions, though?'

'Quite. But these two are extremely rare. Both being a *florilegium*, or treatise on plants, with exquisitely detailed plates of every botanical specimen therein. The author is the celebrated Bavarian apothecary, Basilius Besler.'

Seldon shrugged. 'That means nothing to me.'

'Suffice to say, the gentleman was considered the greatest authority in his time when he died in 1629.'

Seldon let out a low whistle. 'That old, I see. So we're talking very expensive?'

Eleanor nodded. 'Eye-wateringly so, Clifford said. Which got us thinking.'

'About Lady Chadwick's necklace?' Seldon said. 'A hobby that pricey would overstretch anyone's finances if it got out of hand. I've heard of collectors becoming obsessed and having to win an auctioned item at any cost.'

'Even at the cost of bankruptcy,' Clifford said. 'Bibliomania has been long recognised. Notably so after being immortalised in Charles Nodier's satire of 1832 in which his character Theodore instantly falls into the gravest of maladies one afternoon on finding a copy of a valuable book. One which is one third of a line larger than the one he owns! By midnight, his anguish over such has claimed his life.'

Eleanor and Seldon shook their heads in disbelief.

'There is more. And a confession. My discovery of the hidden editions occurred a while ago. However, I felt it best to check my theory before wasting your limited time, Chief Inspector. So, I asked a few of my counterparts at my club to enquire of the most likely suppliers to Chadwick House. It transpires that Lord Chadwick's name is well known, mostly due to outstanding debts owed to a great many merchants.'

Eleanor snapped her fingers. 'Which tallies with his wife

only having minimal jewellery, Hugh. And the carriage hired only according to need. Plus the gardeners being part-time. And, I think, the staff not staying long. I imagine they are not paid particularly well, even for staff!'

Seldon looked thoughtful. 'Excellent, both of you. Sounds like biblio… a book obsession then for Lord Chadwick. Which could explain why he lied about when the necklace was stolen, to ensure the insurance company paid up. To buy more editions or save himself from bankruptcy?'

'The shame of which would kill him like that Theodore chap, I'd go so far as to say,' Eleanor said, catching Clifford nodding. 'It strikes me that everything about his life is for show.'

'Including his wife,' Clifford tutted.

'Foolish man!' Seldon muttered. Then he thumped the seat. 'The envelope you found on Wither's body, Eleanor!'

She nodded, her eyes widening. 'Of course. Maybe Withers found out what Lord Chadwick had done and tried to blackmail him. I'm pretty sure Withers spied on everyone, above as well as below stairs.'

'But he underestimated Lord Chadwick. Who promptly silenced him.'

'It fits,' Eleanor breathed. She shook her head, frowning. 'Although, to be fair, I have to tell you I had a conversation with Mrs Hawkins, the housekeeper. She confessed to being in love with Withers and to planning to steal Lady Chadwick's necklace with him. But he let her down. Badly!'

'I see. So a strong motive, perhaps, to have killed Withers?'

She nodded. 'And I'm sure you know, but she has a witch's cupboard full of—'

'Who knows what! Yes, my men took a sample of all of them and we're having them tested right now. It'll take some time, but I honestly don't expect to find anything. If she *did* poison Withers, I'd imagine she'd have disposed of any poison left over pretty thoroughly by now.'

Eleanor pursed her lips. 'So, Mrs Hawkins aside, all we need is some solid evidence, as you would say, that Lord Chadwick is a double murderer, Hugh, and case closed!'

Seldon pointed through the window at the Empire Exhibition entrance they were pulling up a little distance from. 'Fingers crossed, we're about to find it.'

Her jaw set firm. 'Having the three of us to re-enact the scene will be the key this time, I'm sure.'

Their cautious route through the labyrinth of the exhibition grounds felt even more fraught than on their last visit. And hideously slow, repeatedly needing to duck into the shadows as an army of overalled workers cleared up and restocked for the hordes due in the next day. Likewise, pairs of security guards appeared with heart-stopping regularity. Even the sporadic trumpeting of the elephants made her jump.

As her ears tuned into the sound of loud whirring, she grabbed Seldon and Clifford's arms. 'Something's coming.'

'It is merely the Never-Stop Railway, my lady,' Clifford murmured. 'Behind the Burma Pavilion.'

She sighed in relief. 'Gracious, it really never stops then. Even when the exhibition is closed at night.'

Seldon's lips tickled her ear as he whispered, 'It's used to ferry workers, stock replacements and take away the rubbish.'

She froze. 'And recently, one dead body, perhaps?'

Seldon nodded grimly as they hurried on past the tall gates of the unfinished enclosure and around to the low wooden one on the far side.

In a blink, Clifford had picked the lock.

'Here goes everything,' Eleanor caught Seldon muttering as he led the way in. He nodded as Clifford relocked the gate behind them. 'Security is set to check the pavilions every hour.' He turned to Eleanor. 'You've both searched here before. Our only hope is that you can remember something extra you saw from the hot-air balloon. If—'

'Hide!' Clifford hissed. 'Someone is unlocking the gate.'

'An over-zealous security guard!' Seldon groaned. 'They're only supposed to check the doors are locked.'

As fast as the wind, the three of them hid. Eleanor ducked down behind a barrel, Seldon and Clifford's longer legs propelling them to the stack of hay bales opposite.

But neither of the two men who slipped in through the gate were security guards...

33

Behind the barrel, Eleanor's breath caught as she risked a peep. One man was wearing a dark suit, the other a colourful robe.

Jafaru and that hard-nosed Englishman, Ellie.

The two men hurried up the steps of the porch and disappeared inside the partially finished building. A moment later, they re-emerged, each burdened with a sack and a stack of crates in their arms. They paused at the bottom of the steps, seemingly deep in an animated discussion. The hiss of their voices reached her ears, but she couldn't make out the words. Until they both put down their loads and the hard-nosed man's voice became more heated.

'Why have you stopped?'

'I do not trust you,' Jafaru said coolly. 'So pay me tonight or I will tell.'

The hard-nosed man took a step forward. 'Not if I make sure you can't!' he growled.

A cruel smile lit Jafaru's face. 'You English are so amusing. You really do want to hang, don't you?'

Even in the shadowy light, Eleanor could see the anger on the other man's face as he reached inside his jacket. Jafaru stiff-

ened, then relaxed as the man pulled out a small wad of
banknotes. He counted some into Jafaru's hand with bad grace.

'Eight, nine, ten. Now move!'

'We agreed on fifteen.'

'I changed my mind.'

Jafaru looked at him mockingly. 'And who will you find to
do as good as I have for you?'

The Englishman slapped another five notes in Jafaru's
palm, picked up his load and strode off. Jafaru, with a smug
smile, picked up his and followed leisurely.

As the gate swung closed behind them, she heard the lock
turn. Hurrying over to the hay bales, she felt her heart skip as
Seldon's arms reached out and pulled her in beside him.

'Eleanor, where did you disappear to? I was worried you'd
followed them inside the building.'

She tutted. 'I was only over there, behind that barrel. But I
wish I had followed them in. I only heard the end of what they
were saying. But more to the point, you do know who they
were?'

Clifford looked thoughtful. 'Young Master Kofi's wretch of
a guardian, Jafaru, yes. And the other man I think we saw with
him elsewhere at the exhibition, my lady?'

She nodded. 'I don't know his name, though.'

Seldon frowned. 'Let me guess. They were arguing about
payment?'

'Yes. For moving whatever was in those crates and sacks.
What could it have been, though?'

Seldon shook his head grimly. 'Whatever they've stolen
from the display pavilions. It's been a big problem, partly
because security have been hired from anywhere they could.
The entire issue has been hushed up, though, of course. To
avoid adverse publicity.'

Eleanor didn't miss the extra strain now dogging his expression. 'Poor Hugh, this exhibition has been one hideous headache for you, hasn't it?'

He shrugged. 'I never expected being a policeman would be easy. But I can't arrest either of those two, even carrying stolen goods, because I'm not supposed to be here, blast it!'

She patted his arm. 'Good. Because catching a murderer is more important than catching a thief. So, let's do what we came here for.'

Clifford led them back to the spot the two of them had scoured before.

'Why do I suddenly feel despondent?' she whispered to him.

'Because this matters to you more than your heart wishes to acknowledge, my lady,' he said gently. 'A double injustice occurred on this very spot. A man's life was taken. And the career of the most diligent policeman ever has been besmirched.' He clicked on a torch, beam pointing down, and handed it to her.

Seldon stepped up next to Clifford. 'You two have proved the best team at this. I'll just follow your lead.'

Eleanor shook her head. 'Actually no, Hugh. You need to play a lead role. Clemthorpe's body.'

'Marvellous!'

'Her ladyship has a point, Chief Inspector,' Clifford said. 'Now there are three of us, you and I can re-enact the scene while her ladyship observes, rather than her needing to stand in the gunman's shoes as last time.'

'Alright.'

'Clifford, you're Lord Chadwick.' Eleanor steered him into position. 'And, Hugh, you're Clemthorpe. That's it.' She stepped backwards a few yards. Then one yard to the left to face them at more of the angle that her memory whispered to her. Closing her eyes, she thought back to the creak of the balloon's basket, the feel of the wicker under her fingers as she gripped the side. The cold of the wind against her—

'No, it's not the wind that's cold. It's the shackle of the drag rope against my forehead,' she murmured.

The feel of two muscular arms holding her made her eyes flick open.

'Blast it, Eleanor. I should never have let you come,' Seldon said.

She shook her head, smiling. 'This isn't the time for that sort of thing! My butler's watching, you know. And you're supposed to be over there, waiting to get shot.'

'And just stand there while you faint! You were swaying, my love.'

'Faint? Oh, Hugh, I was just calling up the feel of being in the balloon.'

Seldon slapped his forehead. 'Which is why your butler didn't rush over with me.' He sighed. 'Clifford's always one wretched step ahead of me when it comes to knowing what you're doing or thinking.'

'If he is, it's only because the poor fellow is lumbered with me all day, every day. That'll be your treat after we're married. Now, hurry back before anything else halts what we're doing.'

With Seldon on his spot again opposite Clifford, she hissed across to them. 'I'm looking down the rope. Down, down. And I see you both standing... no... squaring up aggressively. Then... there's a glint. A gun barrel raised high in Lord Chadwick's hand. I realise I can't see Clemthorpe's hands. Maybe he has a gun too?' She shook her head. 'Then, one of Clemthorpe's arms is raised. No, wait.' She rubbed her forehead. 'Something's wrong? Yes, Clemthorpe's arm was raised before Lord Chadwick raised his gun. But that can't matter, can it? And there's something in it, but what, I can't see. It's too small and I'm too far away. And... and too horrified! Because now Clemthorpe's falling backwards, away from the hay bale. And I can't help him,' she ended in a croak, the horror she'd felt on witnessing the murder intensified by the far too convincing death fall Seldon had acted out. Unable to stop her legs, she was kneeling at his side in a heartbeat.

He opened his eyes and smiled. 'I thought you said this wasn't the time for that sort of thing?'

'That was too real... too much like in Scotland when you got shot.'

Seldon jumped up. 'Well then, tell me it was worthwhile me putting you through that awful memory because it helped?'

'It most assuredly did,' Clifford said, glove poised to dust off Seldon's coat.

'How?' she breathed.

'My lady, your prophecy was spot on. Three of us were the key this time. You see—'

'The gate!' she hissed. 'It's opening again. They're coming back.'

The three of them dived behind the nearest hay bale.

From their hiding place, she could see—

'Clifford. It's Jafaru and, oh no!' Her hand flew to her mouth.

'Police officers,' Seldon muttered with a grimace.

Her jaw clenched. 'Jafaru must have spotted us.'

He nodded. 'And realised if he got in there first, he might have a chance to turn the tables!'

A man in a trilby and overcoat strode into the centre of the enclosure, brandishing a pistol.

'Come out! My men have surrounded the outer compound as well and are armed.'

Next to her, Seldon blanched. 'Both of you stay here,' he hissed. 'And don't come out under any circumstances.'

She gasped. 'What about you?'

He shook his head wearily. 'It's over, Eleanor. It's Hendricks, the man who took over from me as chief of security here. He's smart, but he hasn't got enough men or had enough time to surround this whole enclosure yet. I'll divert his and his men's attention while you and Clifford get out any way you can. Don't argue. There's no time.'

'But, Hugh...'

Seldon stepped out, his hands up. The man in the overcoat turned and raised his gun, then lowered it slowly. 'What the devil!'

She went to show herself, too, but Clifford tugged her back down by the wrist.

'My lady, you will only make it worse for him.'

'But Hugh...'

The rest of her words were lost as her butler propelled her like lightning to the next stack of hay bales. There, he paused.

'I'm sorry, my lady. But us being found here as well will do Chief Inspector Seldon no favours.' Waiting until the policemen had surrounded Seldon, he tapped her arm. 'Now!'

As they ran for the next shred of cover, she sent a prayer heavenward for her fiancé.

34

Eleanor had kept up appearances by staying in the Chadwick schoolroom for most of the next day. But planning none of the lessons the staff assumed she was preparing in the children's extended absence. She'd even forgone lunch as her stomach was churning with worry for Seldon. Her and Clifford's escape through the exhibition site had been a hair-raising race against the odds. Those same odds were now stacked against her fiancé whom she'd unwillingly left behind to face the music.

Knowing that Clifford had been keeping up his pretence in the library had been no consolation either, as Lord Chadwick had not moved from his study next door, giving her no opportunity to talk to her butler. At three o'clock, she'd given up. Evidently, leaving the house at all was not on Lord Chadwick's agenda.

Lady Chadwick hadn't yet surfaced from her room, having dispatched Grace first thing to tell Eleanor the doctor had prescribed a sleeping draught for her shattered nerves and she wasn't to be disturbed.

So what to do? There was no sense in questioning the maids any further over the theft of the necklace. Or of Withers' death.

She was as sure of that, as Seldon had been at their last discussion. And Mrs Hawkins was avoiding her like the plague, as was Tateham. Even Mrs Rudge was still in a foul temper, which meant Eleanor would have next to no chance getting anything out of her.

Had it not been for Clifford's plea on seeing her safely to the Chadwicks' back gate well after midnight, she would have thrown in her governess dress there and then. And left Lady Chadwick a note telling her the theft of her necklace was her own problem. She had far bigger ones. But Clifford had been right. To leave now wouldn't help Seldon. Nor would it get justice for Clemthorpe. Or Withers. Besides, she still believed the theft of the necklace was somehow the key to the whole affair.

Striking out alone was all she could do. But to do what? Without hearing why Clifford had thought their murder re-enactment had been enlightening, there was every chance she'd only make things worse. In truth, all her frustration had achieved was for her to feel more despondent. And filled the schoolroom with a tense atmosphere as gloomy as the blustery rain lashing the windows outside.

As an imaginary school bell pealed the end of her governess duties, she threw on her coat and ran to the staff stairs, inadvertently ramming her hatpin into her hand as she did.

'I've too many errands to be back for supper, Mrs Rudge,' she called, sucking on her palm.

Leaving the cook grumbling, she flew out of the house, down the garden and onto the street.

Racing to Clifford's pied-à-terre proved a battle with the elements as the wind battered her, and the rain soaked her. As she arrived at the fourth floor, Clifford was opening the front door, clutching a handful of bags and looking far more composed than her in his smart overcoat. Having let her in, he shook his head at her bedraggled appearance.

'Would it really have taken so many extra seconds to have pinned your hat before your clearly unladylike dash through London's smartest streets, my lady?'

'I meant to.' She shook herself like a wet cat. 'Only I pinned my hand by mistake.'

'And made a gift of your hat to the wind.' Kofi appeared with a Clifford-worthy tut at her sodden red curls. He held out a towel to her. 'It will be the lucky day for the lady that finds it.'

As the boy skipped off to the kitchen with the shopping bags, she turned to her butler.

'Surely you could be teaching the young chap something more useful than how to join forces with you in admonishing your mistress, Clifford?'

'It is rather more a case of vice versa, my lady. He is quite incorrigible.'

'Fibber! But I appreciate you're trying to take my mind off the hideous mess I've let Hugh get into.'

Clifford held his hands out for her coat. 'My lady, your betrothed would not agree the difficulties he is facing are any of your making. Ahem, any more than your butler would, were it his place to say so.'

She managed a wan smile. 'Hugh's a grown man and made his own decision, I know. But he made it to save me. Well, us, I suppose.' She sighed, fearing she knew the answer already. 'Please tell me he has telephoned?'

'Would that I could relay any news of the gentleman, my lady. Master Kofi was primed to take any message throughout my hours away at Chadwick House, but to no avail.' He waved her forwards. 'If I might suggest not holding out hope that the telephone will ring this evening?'

'Dash it, Clifford! I don't want to hear that level of honesty.'

She slid into a chair in the kitchen, grateful for her eager bulldog and tomcat's cuddles as they assaulted her lap in turns.

A cup of tea appeared in front of her via Kofi. And then an added splash of brandy fortification from Clifford.

'Thank you, both.'

She watched them unpack the shopping together with the same care and precision. With everything lined up along the table facing the stove, they nodded to each other as they donned matching aprons. Kofi's wrapped around his slender frame twice and swished at his ankles. Even their heart-warming ease with each other couldn't raise her spirits enough to think of eating.

'I shan't manage a thing, chaps, I'm afraid.'

'If you say so, my lady.' Clifford shared a wince with his young helper. 'Indeed, it is worse than we feared, Master Kofi.'

She buried her face in Gladstone's wrinkled forehead, trying to rally herself to be better company. Tomkins curled around her neck, offering soft purrs of solace. When she looked up, the kitchen was awash with steam and the sound of sizzling, but no butler or young boy. Instead, a vision of handsomeness in a soaked dark-grey suit was stepping in through the door.

'Hugh!' she cried, hindered from leaping up by her bulldog lunging off her lap to greet the new arrival. Tomkins skipped across to the edge of the table to stretch up Seldon's shoulder as Gladstone scrabbled at his trouser legs.

Seldon smiled, but it didn't wash away the strain in his exhausted face. He scooped Tomkins under one arm and then bent to catch Gladstone's wiggling portly form under the other. 'How come I get a better welcome from the terrible two than my fiancée?'

'Because she's trying to do the ladylike thing and cling to a bit of composure at the most unexpected but wonderful sight in the world.' She beckoned him over eagerly with both hands.

'Ladylike? Then I've another case to solve because someone's stolen the woman of my dreams.' He bent to press his lips tenderly over hers, the romance of which was rather ruined by Gladstone's licky exuberance getting between them first.

'Yuk, old thing!' Seldon groaned as he set both her pets down on the floor gently. 'Blast it, Eleanor, why does nothing I try with you work out?'

'Except saving me from being the one to get arrested, you mean? Hugh, I can't believe you did that.' Her breath caught. 'But hang on, your quip about having another case to solve...?'

He nodded. 'Yes, I'm still part of the police force.' He held up a hand. 'For now. The disciplinary hearing is set for Monday. And then, my superior made it clear, I won't be. Nevertheless, you won't convince me I shouldn't have done it.' He wound his fingers into hers and pointed at the stove. 'Should whatever is in that pan be doing that?'

'No! Clifford! Kofi!' she shouted. 'It's kind of you to give us a minute alone, but help!'

With the aproned pair back at their post and Seldon furnished with a fortified tea too, she shifted her chair up against his. 'So what exactly are you being accused of?'

He sighed. 'Organising the wholesale thieving that has been going on at the Empire Exhibition. Or, minimum, being aware of it and turning a blind eye.'

'That's preposterous!' she cried, catching the back of Clifford's head nodding vehemently.

'Only to us, Eleanor,' Seldon said. 'And, I must admit, to my superior. However, he made it very clear that I have tied his hands. As, at this point, I'm unable to arrest the actual culprits, the powers-that-be are happy to accept a scapegoat instead. And as my superior curtly pointed out, and I couldn't deny, like a fool, I put myself in the perfect spot for that to be me.'

'By returning to the exhibition at night and being in that enclosure when Jafaru reported you?' The name of Kofi's guardian flew from her tongue before she could stop it.

The boy came to Seldon's side looking pained. 'I am very sorry he has made trouble for you, sir.'

'Thank you, but it's not for you to think about, young fellow.' Seldon put a hand to the boy's shoulder. 'I was just in the wrong place at the wrong time. And I'd already sealed my fate by continuing to investigate Clemthorpe's murder despite the ambassador and my superior warning me off.'

Eleanor patted his arm. 'Hugh, it doesn't make it all go away, but you did what you could. And what you thought was the right thing.'

'Which *was* the right thing, Eleanor,' Seldon said firmly. 'And there's one small silver lining. My superior's a good man. His job is way more political than mine, and sometimes he's just got to toe the Whitehall line. But underneath, he's an honest policeman at heart. He told me that he's leaving me on active duty until the hearing on Monday and he'll take any fallout. Which means, in reality, he's giving me time to clear my name.' He gestured at the table. 'So, if it won't ruin whatever you three are going to eat, can we get down to business? I've got my work cut out to get through everything. The only hope of saving my career is to gather enough irrefutable evidence against the thieves. And quickly. While continuing with the other matters.' He frowned at Eleanor's sharp intake of breath. 'Yes, of course I'm going to carry on investigating the exhibition murder as well.'

'Even unsanctioned to do so?'

He nodded. 'It can't ruin me any more after Monday's meeting. Although, to be blunt, I've no idea what I can do. I daren't ask for help from colleagues for their sakes, and I'll be watched like a hawk. I'm also no longer in charge of Withers' death, which means I can't go near Chadwick House or the Chadwicks themselves. And...' He held a hand out.

She groaned. 'You won't be shown the coroner's report!'

He nodded resignedly.

Eleanor's eyes blazed. 'We don't need it! The three of us have solved cases like this before without any outside help. And we're going to do it again. Now...' She turned at a soft tap on her arm. Kofi looked up at her with polite dissent in his eyes. She smiled. 'Sorry, Kofi. The three of us *have* solved cases like this before without help, but there's a fourth musketeer now. So game on!' She pointed at Clifford. 'Come on then, my infallible wizard, tell us what our re-enactment last night revealed?'

35

Clifford's eyes lit up. He placed her investigation notebook beside her. 'Due to playing the victim, Mr Clemthorpe, so admirably, the chief inspector was distracted from the unforeseen conclusions the re-enactment threw up. First, however, if I might check? My lady, in my role as Lord Chadwick, I raised my hand as if I were raising a gun? Was that correct?'

She closed her eyes and replayed the scene, looking down from the hot-air balloon. 'Yes, I'm sure.'

'Very good. And would you say, in the role of Mr Clemthorpe, the way and position in which the chief inspector fell was a passable likeness for what you witnessed from above?'

She shuddered. 'It was horribly too close, actually.'

'Better still,' Clifford said. 'And before the chief inspector fell, the stance you asked him to adopt was also as your memory served?'

Seldon raised his hand.

'Yes. Just like that. As if he were holding something.'

'Hmm, that is the only confusion,' Clifford muttered. 'But everything else is clear.'

Seldon's eyes widened. 'Yes, I think I get it.' He took her by the shoulders gently. 'Eleanor, are you absolutely sure the way I fell while playing Clemthorpe was correct? *Away* from the hay bales?'

She nodded emphatically. 'Yes again. And I wouldn't doubt it if you both spent the rest of the evening asking me over and over.'

Seldon tapped the table. 'Excellent!'

She frowned. 'Dash it, now I feel like the bluntest brick ever!'

'Let me explain. When you and Clifford tried to re-enact Clemthorpe's murder, you had only a few minutes and only the two of you, so neither of you could take it all in.' He spun around. 'The bullet you found embedded in the hay bale before, Clifford. You realised last night the angle was completely wrong if it had come from Lord Chadwick's gun, right?'

He nodded. 'Indeed, Chief Inspector. I believe it was fired by *another* gun. From another place where a third person was concealed. Such as where her ladyship hid when Jafaru and the Englishman entered the enclosure last night.'

Seldon winced. 'I was so concerned I thought you had gone into the pavilion after them, Eleanor, I didn't understand the significance at the time.'

She gaped. 'You mean because you couldn't see me from where I'd hid? But I could see you?'

'Exactly! That means there was almost certainly a third man at the scene, as Clifford just said. One neither Clemthorpe nor Lord Chadwick were necessarily aware of.'

Eleanor stared at her half-drunk tea. 'So a third man might actually have shot Clemthorpe, we're thinking? Or was he trying to save him by shooting Lord Chadwick?'

'And hit Mr Clemthorpe instead?' Clifford sniffed. 'With respect, my lady, the latter would have made him a particularly lousy shot.'

Seldon tapped the table. 'Unless he was distracted by an

out-of-control, low-flying, hot-air balloon as he pulled the trigger!'

Clifford raised an eyebrow. 'I had not thought of that, Chief Inspector.'

Eleanor frowned. 'But I only saw two people from the balloon.'

'My lady. You told the chief inspector and myself that the first thing you noticed were two men squaring up to each other. And then a split-second later, one of them drawing a gun. You would not have taken your eyes off them. And the balloon can only have been over the enclosure for a matter of seconds.'

She groaned. 'You're right. So how on earth are we going to find out who the third man could have been?'

Seldon sighed. 'Unfortunately, I can't even see the coroner's report to confirm the calibre of bullet that killed Clemthorpe and passed through him, so I can't even be sure it's the same bullet you found. If I did try and get hold of the report, not even my superior could keep me out of jail then!'

'In which case, let's start with the most obvious.' Eleanor scrabbled for her notebook. 'Oh, but of course, that would be...' She tailed off.

Kofi picked her pen up where she'd dropped it and put it back in her hand.

'Thank you for the kindness, but it will not be upsetting for me to hear you say Jafaru's name.'

'If Jafaru was the third man,' Seldon said quietly, 'or the Englishman he hangs around with, what reason would either of them have had to kill Clemthorpe?'

'To cover up their thievery, I suppose?'

Seldon looked doubtful. 'That's all I came up with, too. But I keep coming back to why Clemthorpe was there in the first place? Let alone Lord Chadwick? There's no reason at all for the government department they both worked for being inter-ested in stolen goods from the exhibition. That's the police's job.

Mine now again, unofficially, in fact. And fast!' he ended ruefully.

'*Our* job, Hugh,' she said firmly. 'But you're right. And why would one shoot the other?'

'Perhaps,' Clifford said, 'one of them was "on the take", as the parlance is?'

Seldon shook his head. 'I can't see people like Lord Chadwick taking backhanders from men like Jafaru or his accomplice.' He sighed, rubbing his hands over his face. 'All of this is academic, if I'm brutally honest. There's no way I... any of us can come within a mile of Jafaru, or the Empire Exhibition! Hendricks will be looking out for all three of us. We may get in if we're lucky, but it'll end the same way as last night! Only this time, all three of us will be marched to jail. To stay there!'

Clifford coughed. 'If you will forgive the significant overstepping, it strikes me that in your most unjust position, Chief Inspector, bringing the true Empire Exhibition thieves to book is imperative. As is unmasking the third man at Mr Clemthorpe's murder.'

Seldon shrugged. 'Absolutely. But that doesn't change the facts.'

'If you insist, Chief Inspector.'

'Clifford?' Eleanor breathed, feeling a tingle of hope. 'What are you trying to say?'

For a moment, he said nothing. Then he cleared his throat. 'That I am experiencing a most vexing mantle of guilt, my lady. I feel responsible for the chief inspector's plight.' He held up a respectful hand at their chorused protestations. 'It is true. Had I not allowed my old fears to stop me, I would have joined you in the hot-air balloon. And thus would have witnessed Mr Clemthorpe's murder, too.'

'It wouldn't have altered what either of us saw, though, Clifford. You mustn't feel bad.'

'I shan't, my lady. If, perhaps, we can squeeze the good from the bad as it were.' He looked heavenwards fleetingly. 'My lady, you often ask for a tale from your late uncle's adventures.'

'Yes, but I understand discretion forbids and all that.'

'Not on this occasion, given the dire circumstances. I am sure his lordship would agree most wholeheartedly.'

'I can leave?' Seldon said, eyeing Clifford with a puzzled frown.

Clifford bowed. 'Thank you, Chief Inspector, but no.'

'I too, Mr Clifford,' Kofi said.

Clifford smiled at the boy and patted him on the shoulder. 'I think we can trust you and the chief inspector to be the souls of discretion?'

At Kofi's nod, he took a deep breath. 'Then the tale begins many years ago with the very last time his lordship and I stepped into a hot-air balloon...'

36

Eleanor was thankful to be in something other than her governess gown. But she was bewildered by Clifford's uncharacteristic insistence that she needed to pull off more the high-class showgirl image than the titled lady. She fluffed out the silvery skirt of her mid-calf-length dress as she felt the discreetly curtained taxicab he had ordered slow to a stop.

'You really think he'll see me?' she said doubtfully. 'I take it he's someone frightfully important.'

Clifford nodded. 'However, he will see you, you have my word. Whether he will agree to help, I cannot promise.'

'Given that I can't even know his name, it doesn't sound very hopeful. Especially as he would never have heard of me before you somehow wangled this meeting.'

'This "brief conversation", my lady, if you will forgive the correction. There will be no "meeting" between you.'

'Whatever you say, Clifford! Let's go.'

'Ahem, this is most definitely an occasion I cannot accompany you, my lady. Even to the door, with apologies.'

All the more mystified, she watched as he slid his gloved

hand up behind the curtain on her side and tapped twice on the glass.

'Good luck,' he whispered.

The carriage door opened to reveal a liveried porter. She gripped her organza stole and stepped out into what seemed to be the rear entrance of a hotel. The door in front of her had no name, just the words "MEMBERS ONLY".

Ah! A gentleman's club, perhaps, Ellie. That's why Clifford insisted you needed to look like a showgirl!

She turned back to the porter. 'I have an appointment. In the, umm, Hogarth room.'

'Naturally. This way please, madam.'

She followed him through a frosted door and along a thickly carpeted passageway peppered with several sets of curving staircases. They took the last one. The porter opened the door at the top and waved a grey-gloved hand.

'The Hogarth room, madam.'

The door closed behind her.

She blinked in the dim lighting of the windowless room. It was lined with bookcases filled with gold-lettered tomes and ivory busts of evidently eminent men. Across the thick dark-green carpet, patterned with bold Tudor roses, was a single chair. The deep-buttoned, high-backed leather wingback with an octagonal side table in darkest mahogany matched the very masculine wall panelling perfectly. On the table was a soda syphon, a small bottle of gin, a highball glass and a gold-rimmed dish of lime slices. A shaded lamp cast a soft crimson glow. Next to the chair was a high wooden screen with a carved oak crest.

She sat down and waited, intrigued to see who was going to walk through the door to join her.

It must have been a full minute later that her nose tingled. Was that a curl of smoke rising on the other side of the screen? As if in answer to her unspoken question, the oak crest panel opened inwards a few inches. She shuffled forward, only then able to make out another wingback chair on the other side. The velvet cuff of a midnight-silk smoking jacket raised to offer an imperious wave. 'There you are, young woman,' a rich madeira-wine voice said.

'Yes. It's good of you to see me. Lord X, I presume?'

'Your presumption is correct. And it is good to see you. Being Henley's niece, I knew of your exploits years ago, of course. Bold, daring and peculiarly adventuresome for a lone female, but not entirely unsurprising, given your remarkable heritage. Still, you have my admiration. And my interest.'

'Thank you. I imagine then you're wondering why I'm here?'

'I am in the dark as to the reason for the request. But curious.' The glow of the cigar end intensified, followed by a plume of pearl-grey smoke being exhaled. 'All the more so after receiving a missive from Henley's man. Given the colourful life he led as Henley's unwavering loyal aide for the most eventful decades of his master's career, I assumed he was long dead.'

Eleanor blanched at the unthinkable notion of losing Clifford, her rock. And her last and only link with her beloved late uncle.

Lord X's voice became more serious. 'Henley, if he were alive today, would be the first to tell you, young woman, that I always return a debt. Even a long overdue one like my debt to your uncle. Like an elephant, I never forget.' The clink of ice swirling against a glass sounded the other side of the screen. 'How much did Henley's man tell you?'

'Honestly, only that you might be kind enough to listen. And to help, if you saw fit. And that somehow a... hot-air balloon journey some decades ago now has a bearing on why you might?'

A long sigh floated through to her. 'Ah! I see now. Dark days. Dark days indeed! But they could have been so much darker. Have a drink, young woman. I shall have another, only a stiff double this time.'

She mixed herself a small glass and sat patiently, though she was aching to know what was coming next.

'At the time you just mentioned, I was but a paltry junior minister,' Lord X started in. 'But eager, ambitious, and determined. And then a once-in-a-lifetime opportunity cannoned through my office door one otherwise paperwork-filled afternoon. A most unexpected promotion. Overseas. Suffice to say, I left that night.'

'Very dedicated,' she said.

'As were all my efforts, young woman. But no amount of zeal can make up for a marked lack of experience. Something I learned the hardest of ways in only my second month. The mass uprising in the area I was now responsible for hit like a torpedo. Alas, I had not recognised the warning signs. In no time, the situation blew up in my face. The inevitability of a military crisis unless immediate steps were taken finally became evident, even to me.'

She sipped her drink, surprised this clearly now powerful man was so openly admitting his past blunders. 'So you acted, I'm sure?'

Lord X sighed again. 'Yes. But from foolhardy ignorance. And pride. In an effort to redeem my position, I issued a... bold order without waiting to consult up the chain of command. But, I admit, not only to try to contain the crisis as quickly as possible but also, and maybe largely, to my shame, to be the hero of the hour. To propel my career upwards!' There was a pause as he took a long sip of his drink. 'However, it soon became clear that I had played directly into the enemy's hands. I thought I was finished. But more, that I was responsible for the downfall of the very thing I had been entrusted to guard!'

The sound of the chair arm being thumped made her wince for the shame that clearly still haunted this man. He took another sip of his drink, then cleared his throat. 'Then word came that one unit had not carried out my orders. The officer in charge had the temerity to tell his superior that they were clearly the orders of an apprentice boot boy who should learn what a brush was before he wielded it! Rather than deal with this insubordination, his superior informed me he had given the man, along with his batman, permission to undertake a mission to reverse these calamitous events. A mission from which the superior, and the men themselves, were in little doubt they would never return.'

Eleanor's chest constricted. 'The hot-air balloon,' she breathed.

'Quite, young woman. However, fate did not know it was dealing with Henley and his man! They proved that impossible odds can be defeated, no matter how toweringly they are stacked against one.' His tone held a hint of reverence. 'But for the actions of your uncle, I would have spent my subsequent days in some ghastly back office, exiled to the furthest corner of the Empire. Or more likely in jail, taking the rap, not undeservedly, for the political fallout of my own actions.'

In her chair, Eleanor's emotions were racing at learning a snippet of her beloved uncle's secret life, and how much he clearly meant to the man in front of her.

And of Clifford's, Ellie! No wonder the poor fellow excused himself from joining you for the balloon ride.

'Lord X, thank you. Especially for your honesty. I can't tell you how much it means to hear that tale. I knew only a small part of it.'

'Of course. His man is unquestionably beyond reproach in divulging such matters.'

'Indeed. Perhaps, then, if you can help me now, I can call your debt to Uncle Byron repaid in his absence?'

A puff of smoke wafted above the screen. 'I will listen to what you have to say. With no further promise other than I will assist if I see fit.' His tone hardened. 'But if anything goes awry, I shall deny this conversation ever took place.'

'As will I.'

'I expected nothing less from Henley's niece. Now, tell what has brought you here.'

In as few words as she could, she relayed the events of the past week, leaving out only names and places. 'So,' she finished, 'the man I saw at the murder scene was a... Whitehall man, thus he's... above investigation. And, perhaps, justice?' She winced, sure she would be thrown out on her ear as Lord X was clearly also a Whitehall man.

But much higher up than Lord Chadwick, Ellie.

'Not entirely so,' he replied to her surprise. 'In Henley's debt, I will impart something you cannot possibly know. And then, if, and only *if*, you can return with incontrovertible evidence regarding whomever is responsible, I promise a fair trial will follow. Although, maybe not a public one. That is all I shall give my word on.'

'Which is far more than you should in your position,' she said gratefully. 'I fully understand.'

'Good. Then I will say only that the Whitehall man you suspect is currently central to a classified investigation. It relates to leaks in the department he works in. That is all I can reveal.'

Eleanor muffled her gasp.

So, Lord Chadwick is under investigation by his own department for internal leaks, Ellie?

Lord X continued. 'There is, however, another Whitehall man, who is also currently central to another classified investigation.'

'More leaks?'

'No. He was found dead at the closed pavilion in the Empire Exhibition. Death due to a bullet passing through his heart.'

Clemthorpe, Ellie.

'Then who arranged for the body to disappear?' she said before she could retract it.

For a moment, there was no reply. Then Lord X's voice came again. 'As I thought, young woman, we are on the same page. So, I will tell you. It appears the chap in charge of the Gold Coast village next door used his head for the good of the exhibition and the Empire.'

'Jafaru hid the body,' she murmured. 'That explains that.' She grimaced at the thought that Kofi's guardian had ingratiated himself with the authorities. 'He hid it in a barrel, didn't he, Lord X?'

'Hmm, even shrewder than I imagined. Yes, in a barrel. Then raked over any signs of the killing before the police arrived.'

'And secreted away the murder weapon?'

'No. Of that, there is no trace. One additional element to the affair is that found in the dead man's house were photographs of another man's wife. The man who is being investigated in the other classified investigation.'

Clemthorpe had photos of Lady Chadwick, Ellie!

'So, young lady,' Lord X continued, 'I am entrusting you with this information because I owe Henley that debt. And also because of your reputation for solving such matters. And I appreciate that you are also concerned for your fiancé's career.'

She blinked, amazed he'd also heard about that side of her life and knew about her engagement. 'Yes, Hugh, I mean Chief Inspector Seld—'

'Is a fine man, I'm sure. However, I will only intervene in police matters if I have irrefutable evidence. And then, only if I see fit. Are we clear, young lady?'

The sound of shuffling made her reach for her bag and stand up. 'Absolutely, Lord X, I'm so grateful for your time. And offer of help. Conditional, I fully understand. I don't know how I, personally, can ever repay you.'

Lord X chuckled richly. 'By mentioning to your man that his insubordinate joke, in Henley's spirit, of sending you in here in the guise of a showgirl was...' – he chuckled again – 'not entirely unappreciated. Only sit back down. There is one more pertinent fact that you should be aware of before you leave concerning the Chadwicks' footman...'

37

Eleanor fixed her butler with a determined look in the back of the curtained taxicab as it rumbled out onto the street away from Lord X's club. 'Stop fussing. No one can see in. Just close your eyes or turn around.'

He blanched. 'Categorically too indecorous a suggestion, my lady, even from the one who is the pinnacle of such.'

She flapped the hem of her silvery dress. 'Clifford, I'm only stuck in this unhelpful garb because of you, you terror! Though the stiff talking-to I shall give you relating to that matter, I shall save for later. Likewise, news of what I've just learned. Because right now, I am going straight to Chadwick House to follow up on something. And I can't arrive like this.'

'Neither can you change in the back of a taxicab!'

'Oh, can't I? Well, just watch and learn otherwise.'

'My lady! I respectfully tender two weeks' notice if you carry out your threat.' At her horrified gasp, he nodded point-edly and called out of the window to the driver. 'A brief devia-tion to Brown's Hotel, my good man.'

Ten minutes later, she'd changed out of her silvery silk attire into stiff grey cotton in the hotel facilities and was back in her persona of an upright governess. Under a smart black umbrella, Clifford was deep in discussion with the carriage driver up front. He gestured for her to retake her seat and came around to her door.

'If I might be excused, my lady? I need to check on Master Kofi.'

'Of course, you kind-hearted softie. I have to do this alone, anyway. If we're seen together, that's the end of it.'

With a plea that she be careful, he tipped his bowler hat and strode away into the gloom of the rain-shrouded streetlights.

A few minutes later, the carriage came to a halt. She looked out of the curtains as shouts came from up front. A coal cart had backed into a parked Fortnum and Mason delivery wagon, spilling its load over the wicker hampers of champagne and exotic delicacies. An irate lady, evidently now without her dinner party menu, was berating the driver. The fact the poor fellow was probably only trying to deliver her coal so her guests would be warm and snug on such a miserable day, seemingly counting for nothing.

Eleanor groaned. The road was blocked, and it looked as if it would take a while to clear it. The arrival of a police constable made up her mind. She recognised the street they'd stopped in. It wasn't too far from Park Lane. She stepped out and cast around for her driver among the excited crowd.

He spotted her and tugged on his soaked cap, pulling his equally drenched worsted jacket tighter around him. 'You're alright to go, darlin'. All paid up right off the slips, you were, by the gent in the titfer.'

Grasping only that she had nothing to pay, she noticed him looking her over while scratching his head. 'Only you're no darlin' now, are ya? Changed your fancy frock for that get-up? What d'ya do? Get religion in the back o' me cab?'

'It's complicated,' she said over her shoulder as she hurried away.

After only a few wrong turns, she saw the side garden gate of Chadwick House. Her feet slowed as she realised the shadows of the gas lamp just ahead of her weren't playing tricks. The gate was slowly opening. She ducked behind the ornate railings of the grandiose house she was passing. Intrigued which of the staff might be taking advantage of Withers' watchful eye being no more, she waited. A slender female form, swathed in a dark cloak, emerged. Eleanor couldn't place any of the four maids in the figure now tugging her hood further over her face.

Ah! Tateham's sweetheart, perhaps, Ellie? Leaving after a clandestine, intimate embrace in the summerhouse? He's cocky enough to believe he'd talk his way out of it if caught.

She shook her head as the woman started off. Something about her wasn't entirely unfamiliar. She decided whoever it was, finding out might give her some leverage in questioning Tateham again later about Withers' apparent backhanders. Now grateful for the rain and the dark, she slunk out from the railings in unobtrusive pursuit.

Given her quarry repeatedly glanced over her shoulder as she hurried along the rain-soaked streets, it seemed she was afraid of something. Or someone? Even more determined to find out her identity, Eleanor darted into every dark archway and behind every pillar box as she followed the woman's many twists and turns through the all-but-deserted roads.

And then, without warning, the streetlights ended as she turned into a narrow alleyway. Now well away from the smart roads of Mayfair, wash houses, pawnbrokers and menders of every conceivable kind proliferated. Grand homes gave way to run-down boarding houses, prices in the sooty shop windows advertised in farthings, pennies, and shillings, not pounds. There were no luxuries for sale here.

Eleanor realised now why Clifford had originally drawn her

such a detailed map to reach his pied-à-terre. She'd had no idea London's high society lived a life of extravagant indulgence only minutes from those living a life of frugal necessity.

The woman turned into another side street, skirting stacks of crates cluttering up the side entrance of what looked like a public house. Under the flickering gas lamp above the door, the wind whipped her hood off. She swiftly pulled it back on, but not swiftly enough.

It's Lady Chadwick, Ellie!

The sounds of raucous laughter and an out of tune piano increased as the woman pulled open the door and disappeared inside.

What on earth could such a society hostess be doing in this neighbourhood? Especially alone. And most particularly in a drinking den! The Chadwicks clearly strove to achieve an image of unassailable upper-class respectability.

'The Flask and Firkin. Snug bar,' she murmured, looking up at the faded sign swinging from one rusted hinge above the door.

Frustrated she couldn't follow inside for fear of Lady Chadwick recognising her, she spotted a glow from further along. At the soot-filmed window, she risked a peep. Nothing but the sort of rough-and-ready types who understood the meaning of endless hard work and make-do. Hunching down to shuffle under the sill to the other side, she crossed her fingers, hoping she hadn't let her quarry somehow slip away out through the front entrance.

Perhaps she saw you following her, Ellie?

But that would have meant her going through the main bar, forbidden to women. And as she'd heard no jeering cries or wolf whistles, it seemed unlikely Lady Chadwick had escaped by that route. She slid upright beside the nearest of the three rather pungent metal bins and peered through the glass again from the other angle.

At a small round table, Lady Chadwick was sitting opposite a man facing away from the window. His tired brown jacket and battered black trilby suggested he was more at home there than Lady Chadwick, who seemed to be pleading with him as he swigged back a beer. But the angry set of his shoulders and forceful tapping of his tankard on the table suggested he was unmoved. Eleanor risked clearing a tiny arc of soot from the glass to see better. Lady Chadwick's distress seemed to increase as she leaned forward, wringing her hands. Eleanor blinked. Was she wrong, or did the woman's companion have a hint of familiarity about him? Agitated that she couldn't slip inside to hear their conversation, she watched intently.

Suddenly, the tension between the two of them seemed to ignite. Lady Chadwick slapped the table, shaking her head vehemently. The man leaped up so aggressively, his chair slammed backwards on the floor. He leaned forward as if to strike her.

Eleanor jumped back. Whatever was going on between them, that was unacceptable. About to dart for the door, she realised the man was striding towards it, his hat brim pulled low over his face. She ducked back around the bins and crouched behind the last one, holding her sleeve over her nose. The man stormed out of the door, muttering angrily. He stopped under the lamp to fumble inside his jacket. Striking a match against the pitted brick wall, he lit the cigarette stuck to his drooping bottom lip.

Eleanor froze.

As the man walked away, she briefly thought of following him, but he hailed the only visible cab and was soon gone. Emerging from her hiding place, she slowly walked back the way she'd come, musing to herself.

Why had Lady Chadwick come to a place like this to meet Jafaru's partner in crime, the hard-nosed Englishman? How would a woman like her know a man like that? And why would she be meeting him in such a disreputable place? No answers came. But she was sure when they did, she'd be one step closer to solving the mystery of the missing necklace. And, possibly, Clemthorpe's murder.

38

The following morning, Eleanor was desperate to buttonhole Lord Chadwick in his study. But he'd disappeared before breakfast to deal with whatever governmental matters couldn't wait until Monday. She wondered if he even saw his children most days.

Sheltering from the permanent drizzle with her butler in the lee of London's landmark Westminster Abbey, she stared impatiently across the road.

'What a historic view,' Clifford said. 'The Palace of Westminster, seat of Parliament, with a façade of almost one thousand feet of sandy limestone. An exquisite building, wouldn't you say, my lady?'

'Probably,' she said distractedly, trying to peer through the rain at the building opposite.

He arched a brow. 'Which strikes you most, I wonder? The trefoil Gothic arches? The oculi gracing the mullioned windows? Or the myriad embellishments along the roofline?'

She frowned. 'Clifford. It's very good of you to stand out here risking pneumonia with me, but we're not doing so to play "what's your favourite architectural feature?", for heaven's sake!'

'Spoilsport.' He gave a mock pout. 'Just when it was my turn, too.'

She laughed and took another mint humbug from the disintegrating bag he was holding out to her. 'I promise you can witter my ears off later about the Houses of Parliament's tremendous... fingle-fangles and whorley-whatnots.'

'I'll have trouble,' he said drily.

'Dash it! What's keeping him in there so long?' she huffed.

'Nothing. Now.' He pointed along the pavement. 'One Lord Chadwick of Chadwick House emerging as we speak. Bound for the limited serviced taxi rank, I'd say.'

'Right! He won't escape me this time.'

'Take care,' Clifford hissed, holding his umbrella at an angle to obscure her face and pressing a handkerchief into her hand to dispose of her humbug. 'I shall follow in the taxicab currently waiting behind.'

She left the shelter of the abbey and, hunching down, slid around the opposite side of the taxi pulling up next to Lord Chadwick. As he barked 'Chadwick House, Park Lane' to the driver, she waited until he opened the door and stepped in, then did so too on the opposite side.

'Well, that was handy,' she said airily, settling into the seat facing him.

'Driver wait!' Lord Chadwick's disfigured cheek flinched as he glared at her. 'Madam, I got here first so get— Oh, it's you! The temporary governess my wife irrationally arranged.' He frowned. 'Miss... whatever it is, this is my taxi. You need to find another.'

'It's Miss Smith. And it's raining, so sharing this one with you will be perfect, thank you.'

'No. It absolutely will not. Rain, sleet, snow or biblical flood, I would never ride around the capital with a member of my staff. The very idea!' he gruffed.

Eleanor fought a frown off her face. He certainly wasn't

acting like the lecherous master of Chadwick House who had seduced the previous governess. Perhaps it was just all malicious downstairs gossip?

'Quite. Well, don't worry, because I'm not.' She made a show of settling herself in her seat.

'Not getting out? After I expressly ordered you to?' he thundered.

'Actually, I'm not getting out, Lord Chadwick. But I meant, I'm not a member of your staff. Not even a temporary one.'

He sank into the opposite seat, brow furrowed. 'What aberration is this? Pff! The female intellect is clearly no match for a little rain, I see. Water on the brain, I fear!'

'The committee don't think so,' she said, pleased her quickly thought up answer wasn't a direct lie. After all, with her, Seldon and Clifford, plus Lord X's conditional support, they made three and a half. Plenty enough to be called a 'committee'. Its ambiguity had also clearly hit the mark in intimating she was referring to an official body within Whitehall.

Lord Chadwick swallowed hard as his eyes darted back and forth between hers. 'What committee?' he said slowly.

Leaning out of the window, she hailed the driver. 'We're ready. A tour of the sights, if you will.'

Lord Chadwick held her gaze as she sat back against the seat, but his fingers drummed on his knees. 'Well, what committee?'

'The one investigating "the incident" at one of the Empire Exhibition enclosures. In the Africa area.' She didn't miss him twitch.

'I've no idea to what you are referring,' he said stiffly, rallying his composure.

'Ah! But I know that you do. And we can spend the entire day touring London until you realise how serious I am.' She leaned closer. 'But it might help if you understand I was at the very end of the line when patience was given out. And that I was placed in your household to gather information on you, Lord Chadwick.' She leaned back. 'And rather damning information I have uncovered.'

His face paled. 'Alright, curse it! I might know there is some sort of internal investigation under way. Something to do with... with the Empire Exhibition. But over what exactly, no one in my department has been told.'

'Then let me tell you. Though most of it you already know, I'm sure. A man was murdered last Friday in an unfinished enclosure there. The one next to the Gold Coast Pavilion and village. A close colleague of yours, actually. A Mr Clemthorpe. And you, Lord Chadwick, have been placed at the murder scene itself. At the very moment the deed was done, in fact. Which to my committee makes you the chief, and currently only, suspect.'

The colour drained from his face. 'I... me? No, stop! Think about what you're saying. I am Lord Chadwick!'

'Yes. And your colleague Clemthorpe is still dead. But you knew that days ago.'

His mouth opened, then shut. He shook his head.

She shrugged. 'Maybe it will make it easier for you to tell the truth if I tell you the committee knows you watched him die.'

'Oh good grief!' he murmured. His face crumpled. For a moment he was silent. Then he looked up. He seemed strangely calm. 'I didn't mean to fire. It... it was self-defence. Believe me, I only went because Clemthorpe said he had to meet me there. Told me he had information concerning the leaks in the department, but couldn't trust anyone. Except me. It was his set-up, not mine. But before we'd many words, he pulled a gun on me. So, in self-defence I pulled out mine. Managed to get a shot off first.'

She tutted. 'Not very responsible for a Whitehall man to go

around killing one of his colleagues. Or for you not to report the episode.'

'Report it! There was too much chance I'd be charged with murder.'

'Now there's even more,' she said curtly. She let him stew with his head in his hands for a moment. 'Especially as you disliked Clemthorpe intensely, didn't you? Intensely enough to want him dead.'

He looked up slowly. 'You and your committee can't know that. I've never shown any ill-feeling towards him.'

She folded her hands in her lap. 'If that's true, then this conversation is about to take a very awkward turn.' She wrinkled her nose. 'I shall ask you frankly; did you know Clemthorpe was madly in love with your wife?'

He blinked repeatedly as he jerked his gaze away. 'No. No, I did not.'

Utterly unconvinced, she had another question burning on her tongue. 'At the time of Clemthorpe's murder, who was the third man in that exhibition enclosure?'

He turned back to face her, his expression seemingly of genuine shock. 'What "third man"? I mean who?'

Is he bluffing, Ellie? Like pretending he didn't know Clemthorpe was in love with his wife? Or is he genuine?

'As to who, good question, Lord Chadwick. Now, it would be in your best interests not to mention this conversation to anyone at all.' She leaned out of the window. 'Driver, halt! Thank you, we are quite done.' She stared back at Lord Chadwick. 'For the moment. But rest assured, I shall be in touch. Enjoy the remainder of your day.'

.

39

Dash it, Ellie, it's going to be too late unless...

Hurling propriety to the pavement, she grabbed her skirts and ran the last stretch along St James's Park. If she didn't hurry, she would miss the next person she needed to grill over the truth. The final truth.

Whatever that may be, Ellie. For how do you ever know if something is the final, final, truth?

The tea room doorbell dinged genteelly as she entered. The establishment was half empty, but scouring the chintz-clothed tables produced no result.

'Is Lady Chadwick still here?' she asked the nearest neatly aproned waitress.

'Why yes, madam. But she has finished her tea.'

Eleanor followed the young woman's gaze to the pink curtain obscuring the door through to the ladies' powder room.

'Ah! I see. Then that little tucked away table for two just on the right there will be perfect, thank you. And a pot of deliciously strong coffee with whatever you recommend to accompany it.'

Sitting on the chair that gave the best view of the curtain, she waited impatiently. After some minutes, it was pulled aside. She rose quickly and intercepted her objective.

'Why there you are, Lady Chadwick!' She noticed the careful application of kohl hadn't quite hidden the red line rimming the woman's eyes.

Lady Chadwick flinched. 'Oh, hello. Yes, but do excuse me, I'm just leaving.'

She turned to continue on her way.

'Not quite, you aren't.' Eleanor gestured firmly towards her table, where the waitress was busy unloading a tray.

Lady Chadwick looked at her nervously. 'But... I've taken tea already.'

'I know. That's why I've ordered coffee.' Eleanor pointed at the opposite seat, then tipped her head to the waitress. 'We'll pour ourselves, thank you. You see, we have a great deal to talk about.'

Once alone together, Lady Chadwick leaned forward. 'Even though I am thankful, Lady Swift, for your efforts to root out the thief among my staff, I do not appreciate being waylaid like this.'

'I'm sure you don't,' Eleanor said coolly. 'But maybe less than I appreciate being lied to. Again. And again.'

Lady Chadwick coloured. 'Whatever can you mean?'

'Exactly what I said.' Eleanor's tone was blunt. 'You've had me running around in false guises, and on false pretences, no less. Yet, for some inexplicable reason, I'm still trying to help you. Or at least, trying to save your husband.' Ignoring Lady Chadwick's gasp, she busied herself pouring two cups of coffee, then took her time selecting from among the hot toasted teacakes and crumpets.

Lady Chadwick's eyes darted to Eleanor's face and then away. 'Why... why did you say Reginald needed... saving?' She took a hasty sip of coffee.

Eleanor took a long sip of her own coffee. 'Because he is in the most dire trouble. And I'm probably the only one who can help him out of it. I'm certainly the only one trying to.' She shot Lady Chadwick a sharp glance. 'But my continuing to do so depends on you telling me the truth. And I mean the real truth this time.' She spread her teacake with butter. 'Or frankly, he will be arrested shortly for a crime he may, or may not, have committed. Either way' – she took a bite of the teacake – 'his fate is in the balance.'

While Eleanor had been speaking, the colour had drained from Lady Chadwick's features, leaving her ghostly pale. She kept her eyes down, turning her cup slowly on its saucer. 'Assuming I haven't told you quite everything, what do you want to know?'

'Who was the man you met in the Flask and Firkin public house last night?'

Lady Chadwick's head shot up. 'Goodness, you saw?' She hesitated, then sighed deeply. 'He's... my brother. My no-good, troublesome wretch of a brother.'

'I'm listening,' Eleanor said more gently as a tear dropped into her companion's coffee.

'He's a... he's a bully. And one who regularly consorts with... criminal types. There's really no more supportive or sisterly way to dress it up. He's always penniless and has badgered me for money so many times, I've lost count.'

Thinking those criminal types currently included Jafaru, Eleanor's tone softened further. 'What does your husband think of him?'

Lady Chadwick shuddered. 'He thinks he's beyond the pale. Reginald banned him from the house long ago. Though he doesn't know the worst of my brother's beastliness toward me, thankfully.' Lady Chadwick dabbed at her eyes with a handkerchief. 'The first time he bullied me into giving him money, I managed to scrimp a little together from where I could without

Reginald knowing. He doesn't let me have money of my own, you see, although sometimes I wonder...' She shook her head. 'Since I'm telling you all our shame, I might as well mention we never seem to have much money anyway, despite my husband's position.'

'Haven't you any idea why?' Eleanor said tentatively.

'No. He doesn't share the account books with me. He's always insisted it's a husband's role.'

Eleanor thought this probably wasn't the time to suggest it was more likely a case of all their household money being spent on rare editions. She put a crumpet on a plate and slid it across the table. 'You said "the first time" you gave your brother money, suggesting there was more than one occasion. How did you get money the second time?'

'By... by pilfering it. It was in an envelope to pay some tradesmen. But that sneak Withers caught me at it. He seemed furious and told my husband. Reginald dragged it out of me why I had done it and forbade me from ever helping my brother again.'

Eleanor frowned, something nudged her thoughts, but she dismissed it.

You've got to get her to start opening up, Ellie. Don't let her off the hook.

'Which, I'm sure, wasn't as simple as he saw it to be?' Eleanor said.

Lady Chadwick nodded. 'Reginald warned me if his office found out about my brother's shady acquaintances, or behaviour, it might compromise his position. He is terrified of even a hint of scandal.'

Eleanor frowned. 'Lady Chadwick, you seem to know your brother very well. Do you believe he has anything to do with these other burglaries in Park Lane?'

Lady Chadwick laughed bitterly. 'Absolutely not. From

what that inspector was saying when he came around, they were all very professional jobs involving a gang. My brother has never done anything professional in his life, legal or illegal. And never managed to cooperate with more than one other person. And even then, not for long!'

Eleanor winced, feeling a touch more sympathetic. 'It sounds as though you've been caught between two hard places.'

Lady Chadwick shrugged. 'Reginald isn't a terrible man. He's just... controlling. It's all he understands from his own childhood, I think. But the first time he went away on a lengthier business trip, I found the courage to rebel. I disguised myself and slipped out to enjoy just one evening's freedom with a little money I'd managed to conceal from him and Withers.'

Ah, Ellie! So the children were telling the truth about Mummy slipping out at night when Daddy was away.

'And how did that go?' Eleanor feared she already knew the answer.

Lady Chadwick blanched. 'Terribly. I went to a... a gambling club. I soon lost the little money I had, but then a nice man offered to buy me a drink. And then he let me gamble with his money.'

Eleanor winced. Lady Chadwick nodded dejectedly. 'I know. I was so naive. And tipsy. Of course, the man worked for the club. At the end of the evening, he accused me of refusing to pay him back. Said he'd agreed only to lend me the money. I was taken to the owner of the gambling club, who told me I either paid him in full or he'd come around to my house and' – she gripped the table, her knuckles white – 'get the money from my husband.'

Eleanor waited for her to go on.

'I begged him not to. So, finally he agreed I'd bring him a piece of jewellery, my necklace, in fact, and he'd take the pearls as payment and replace them with imitations. Good ones, he said, so my husband would never know.' She cupped her face in her hands. 'But that was when my real troubles started. It was my husband, you see? He watches the markets or whatever they're called. And just before he went off on that last trip of his, he announced he was going to have my necklace revalued on his return. For the insurance, because pearls had risen in value.' Her shoulders stiffened. 'But I couldn't let that happen. They would have been spotted as fake immediately by an expert, and then the whole miserable story would have come out.'

She patted Lady Chadwick's arm. 'So, once more. Has your necklace *actually* been stolen? Or have you just hidden it away somewhere so your husband can't get it revalued?'

Lady Chadwick looked her in the eye. 'No! I swear, I haven't. It was stolen at the soirée, as I told you.' She cast her eyes down. 'But I believe I know who has it.' She grimaced. 'My brother.'

'You invited him to the soirée?' Eleanor said incredulously.

'Goodness, no! He turned up unexpectedly. I was scared he'd make a scene, so I let him in.'

'Then your husband must know that? Even if you didn't tell him, Withers would have, surely?'

Lady Chadwick shook her head. 'My reprobate brother apparently has some unsavoury information on Withers. From when Withers was in service elsewhere. My brother would never tell me what it was.'

That fits with what Clifford found out, Ellie. Withers really was a rogue.

'We got as far as your brother turning up the night of your soirée?' Eleanor coaxed.

Lady Chadwick nodded. 'Yes. To demand money, as ever. Well, that night, I'd had a little too much to drink, as I said, and felt a tingle of boldness from it. I told him I didn't have any money. And that he had to stop coming. But he became incensed. Said he was more desperate than ever. He threatened to pull me by my hair to the safe and make me open it. Thank goodness he eventually believed me that Reginald had taken every ounce of money with him. Because it was true.'

Ah! Another rare edition auction to bid for while away on supposed business, perhaps, Ellie?

'So then, what happened?'

'My brother said he'd take the necklace I was wearing instead and that I could tell my husband it was stolen. Do you know, that's when something snapped in me. Or more likely, it was the drink. I slapped his face and refused.'

'Rather rash, in hindsight? Given that if your necklace had been stolen, it would have solved your problem, wouldn't it?'

'Yes. Maybe. But not by him! I was too afraid that the sort of criminal types he knows would recognise fakes from real pearls. Then he would have the most unthinkable hold over me like the gambling club owner.'

'Did he overpower you then and grab it?' Eleanor's jaw tightened at the thought.

'No. He left. But in the morning, when I awoke, my necklace was gone. He must have returned and snatched it from my drawer whilst I was asleep.' She held her fingertips to her bottom eyelids as if holding in more tears. 'Because I was too tipsy to wake up.'

Eleanor filed all that away to sift through later. Something else was bothering her. 'What were you doing at the Empire Exhibition when you bumped into me?'

'I was trying to find my brother to get him to give me the necklace back.'

'Bit of a long shot he'd be there just because thousands of people visit every day, surely?'

'Not at all. He has a job there, temporarily. But he never

said what it was exactly or which part of the exhibition he works in.'

I bet I can guess, Ellie.

Lady Chadwick sighed. 'I trailed around all the blessed countries' pavilions, trying to find him, but never did.'

Eleanor finished her coffee. 'I still cannot fathom why you asked me to investigate.'

Lady Chadwick looked sheepish. 'I'd seen you earlier in the day at the exhibition. And well, when I couldn't find my brother, I was desperate and not thinking straight. Then by chance I spotted you again and remembered your peculiar reputation for solving such matters. So I pretended to bump into you.'

'I still don't understand,' Eleanor said, feeling genuinely lost.

'I had to, don't you see? Because of Reginald. The first place he'd have gone on getting home was the safe. He'd have demanded where my necklace was and I'd have to admit it was stolen. I... I'm not very good at lying to him. So my plan was to deflect some of his ire by telling him that instead of risking scandal by calling the police, I'd called in you, instead.'

Eleanor shook her irritation away again. 'But what would have been the problem in telling him you believe your brother stole it?'

'My husband's temper! Honestly, I feared what Reginald would do to him! And, stupid though it is, after all the bullying he's put me through, he is still my brother. At least in here.' She placed her hand over her heart.

Eleanor's thoughts flew back to the conversation she'd had not long ago with Lord Chadwick. 'I don't believe you did tell your husband I'm not really a governess, did you?'

She shook her head. 'No. I didn't have the heart. I mean, the guts.' She reached for Eleanor's arm. 'None of this has been my finest hour. You can't think very well of me, I'm sure.'

Eleanor collected her bag and rose. 'I think you have been put in a horrible situation that was mostly not of your own doing. However, that is no excuse for lying to me and wasting my time. And just so you're clear, I never set out to uncover which of your staff stole your necklace. My goal was to find out who stole it, whether they were staff, guests, or *you, yourself*! Good day.'

40

Eleanor groaned as she left the tea rooms. Why was London so wretchedly sprawling and confusing! Taxis helped, but still took an age to get anywhere with the weight of traffic. If there was even one to hail. Which right now, there wasn't.

Dash it, Ellie, Hugh's tribunal is tomorrow! And Clifford's pied-à-terre must be miles away.

The sound of brisk footsteps close behind interrupted her thoughts.

'The lady's carriage awaits. Apparently,' a deep voice intoned.

She jerked around. 'Cliff— Hugh, it's you! What fantastic luck.'

Her fiancé's exhausted face managed a tender smile as he pulled her into an embrace. 'No, not luck. Your butler. Who is one step ahead of us both again, it seems. And for some reason, he's waiting at Westminster Pier, only two minutes away.' He whipped out a note in Clifford's meticulous copperplate writing. 'This was pinned to the front door of his fancy flat.'

On reaching the pier, she sighed in relief. Her bowler-hatted butler was waving from the cabin of a small tugboat moored to a gnarled wooden post. Next to him was a smart, wool-capped Kofi.

As she walked down the wobbling gangplank with practised ease, she caught Seldon's quiet moan.

'A boat? Really?'

She laughed. 'You won't get seasick on the river, Hugh.'

'Not with the assistance of this, Chief Inspector.' Clifford pressed a small tin of crystallised ginger into Seldon's hand as he hopped clumsily off the end of the gangplank. 'And welcome aboard, my lady.'

He turned to a weather-beaten man in overalls, who appeared from nowhere.

'Pilot. Await my order to cast off, please. Where to, I don't yet know.'

'Whatever ya say, guv.'

With the cabin door closed, the three of them crowded into the bench seats with Kofi.

She rapped the table. 'Brilliant you've got us all together, Clifford. But what have you learned that means we require a boat?'

'Nothing, my lady, regrettably. However, whilst the roads are numerous, I'm afraid on a Sunday taxis are not. And even greater in dearth are bridges crossing the Thames for an expedient route to wherever we have need to venture next.' He cleared his throat quietly. 'And time is, perhaps, not ours to squander.'

Seldon's already harried expression deepened. 'Because of my disciplinary hearing being less than twenty-four hours away, you mean? In which case then, even sea or river sickness will be much appreciated, Clifford.' He took a piece of ginger. 'Eleanor, please tell me you learned something significant from your likely over-forthright grilling of Lord Chadwick?'

'I did. And the most unexpected thing too. Likewise from Lady Chadwick afterwards. And, thanks to Clifford, from Lord

X also.' She sighed. 'But I'm sorry, Hugh, I've no idea where we need to have the pilot race us off to.'

'Yet,' Clifford said.

Seldon nodded. 'That's why there's three of us, Eleanor.'

'Four, sir.' Kofi pointed at his new, black woollen-coated chest.

'I stand corrected. Four, of course, young fellow. Ticked off by an eleven-year-old again,' Seldon murmured into his notebook.

'Right then.' Eleanor relayed her conversation with Lord X, then with Lord Chadwick, including his surprise confession. 'But I didn't believe his insistence he had no animosity towards Clemthorpe. Nor that he didn't know the man had—'

'Ahem! Designs upon his wife,' Clifford said.

'If that's what you call keeping photographs of Lady Chadwick in his dressing-table drawer.'

Seldon frowned in disgust. 'That would drive any decent man to do the unthinkable! Hence Lord Chadwick's confession to firing first. But, Eleanor, I have a feeling you doubt his version of events is true? Which means I do too.'

Delighted by his confidence in her, she nodded. 'I do. Obviously, we can believe Lord X, so I'm in no doubt about the photographs. However, you and Clifford both deduced that Clemthorpe's killer was almost certainly our "third man". Now, I couldn't say with any certainty whether Lord Chadwick was lying or not when he denied knowing of the existence of a third person at the enclosure that day. But either way, why he admitted to killing someone it seems on the weight of current evidence he didn't, I can't fathom.'

'I can,' Seldon said. 'You made him believe his fate rested entirely with the powers that be. That is your "committee", who had a reliable report he was seen with Clemthorpe at the time he died. That would have been enough to convince him a murder charge would stick like hot glue.'

Clifford nodded. 'When the stakes are your liberty or life, my lady, pleading guilty, but in self-defence, might at least take away the threat of the er...' He discreetly mimed a noose around his neck.

'And, being a Whitehall man, there's a chance he might get off altogether on that plea,' Seldon said a touch bitterly. 'We still can't rule out that he did kill Clemthorpe, and we're wrong about the third man.'

Eleanor shook her head. 'A lesser detective would have fallen on Lord Chadwick's confession and delighted in signing off the case, Hugh.'

'I signed up all those years ago for justice, not feathers in my cap. Though I desperately need some to wear to my tribunal tomorrow, blast it!'

'Then listen to what I learned from Lady Chadwick.'

The tension in the tiny cabin grew as the others listened intently.

Seldon interrupted before she'd quite finished. 'Her brother sounds a nasty piece of work. But sponging from his sister isn't a crime. Even with her using the term "bullying". It's not blackmail or actual extortion.'

'Though it seems he may have stolen Lady Chadwick's pearl necklace,' Clifford said.

She raised a finger. 'You haven't heard the last part, chaps. Her brother works at the exhibition and is also Jafaru's partner in crime!'

'No!' Seldon breathed, as Eleanor patted Kofi's hand in apology. 'The man we saw stealing those crates with Jafaru?'

'The very same. And, perhaps, the "third man"?'

Seldon leaned back in his seat, drumming his fingers on the table. 'We've been here before. Why would he want to kill Clemthorpe?'

She shrugged. 'She was adamant there's absolutely no love

lost between her husband and her brother. Maybe he was trying to kill him and hit the wrong person – Clemthorpe.'

'Distracted by your runaway hot-air balloon?' Seldon said thoughtfully.

Clifford coughed. 'Or to be even-handed, he may have shot Mr Clemthorpe to save Lord Chadwick's life.'

Eleanor grimaced. 'So his sister would still be worth tapping for money, the louse!'

'A less even-handed assessment, my lady, but possibly.'

'Hmm, but even knowing he works at the exhibition, I have no authority now to have him arrested,' Seldon said ruefully. 'And none of us can safely go near the exhibition to find him.'

Eleanor sighed. 'And to make it worse, Lady Chadwick told me she had no idea where he lived.'

Kofi frowned. 'What does he look like?'

As Eleanor finished describing him, the young boy nodded. 'I know this man. I have seen him with Jafaru as well. But I do not know where he works at the exhibition.'

Seldon smiled at him. 'No matter. We couldn't let you go back to there, anyway.'

'We could lose you to Jafaru for good.' Eleanor caught Clifford's horrified murmur.

Kofi smiled between them. 'I do not know where the man works. That is true. But I know where he lives!'

41

As the boat pulled away from the pier, Seldon spun back to Kofi. 'Rotten Row, yes?'

The young boy nodded.

'Make for St Katharine Docks, Pilot!' Clifford called from the cabin. 'And full steam!'

He turned to Seldon. 'It's the nearest we can get by water. And faster than any road route.'

Seldon nodded. 'Right, then, this boat is perfect. Along the Thames to the docks it is.'

Eleanor hesitated. 'Kofi, can you tell us why you were taken there?'

The young boy smiled. 'I was sent. Not taken. And I was not harmed, so please do not worry.'

Relieved, Eleanor perched on the edge of her seat to hear his tale as the boat picked up speed.

'One afternoon,' Kofi continued, 'some men in smart uniforms came to see Jafaru. There was a problem. I think now because he was stealing.'

Seldon nodded. 'As I said, pilfering was rife at the exhibition. And probably still is. I didn't have the manpower to do more than send a couple of men around each time to ask questions after each incident.'

Kofi nodded back. 'Jafaru talked to these men. And then he gave me a note to take urgently to an address. Thirteen, Rotten Row, I remember this. There I was to find the Englishman and to tell him to come immediately. There is trouble.' Kofi spread his hands. 'So, I did. And he came and spoke to the two men and they went away. Afterwards, Jafaru and the Englishman had a big argument.'

'What about?' Eleanor said.

'The Englishman said the two uniformed men only came because Jafaru was greedy and took too much too quickly. And the next time they come, they would not believe the boxes were not stolen, but only moved to a temporary place while some repairs were being made.'

Seldon snapped his fingers. 'Which fits exactly. We know now the two of them are running a racket out of that closed-up enclosure.'

'How did you get to the man's house?' Clifford said quietly.

'In a taxi carriage.' Kofi grinned. 'This word I learn from you.'

Eleanor caught Clifford's angry headshake. 'I know. Clearly dispatched with sufficient money so the driver would accept an unaccompanied minor without questions.'

'The driver could still have abandoned him anywhere and taken the money, anyway,' Seldon said sadly.

Kofi held up a hand. 'I think this too, sir. So I sit up on the outside with the driver and talk, talk, talk all the way, making pretend I know London and that my guardian is an important man.'

'Bravo, Master Kofi,' Clifford said. 'Most resourceful of you.'

The district where the boat docked made the downtrodden area around the Flask and Firkin tavern seem positively prosperous in comparison. The rank-smelling docks seemed a haven for nothing but back-breaking manual labour. While the factories looked little more than poorly disguised workhouses, pouring out smoke and cloying half-burned ash over the multitude of dilapidated boarding houses. Eleanor's heart ached for those who lived and worked there.

A life of polluted drudgery for what, Ellie? Probably not even enough for a square meal a day.

'I wish you weren't here to see all this,' Seldon said, keeping a tight grip on her arm as they turned down yet another rubbish-strewn alley.

'I don't, Hugh. It will only make me all the surer I can put the privileges Uncle Byron generously bequeathed me to better use.'

'It is the perfect place for shipping out stolen goods, mind,' Clifford said.

Seldon looked at him pointedly. 'And all manner of other dubious activities, no doubt. I shan't ask why you're familiar with this area, Clifford.'

The door they stopped at had the faint impression that it might have been painted once. Now, it was all but bare, with a hole the size of a fist in the dead centre. Eleanor had no wish to know how it got there.

Clifford tucked Kofi in behind him. There being no bell or knocker, Seldon shrugged and called through the hole. 'Hello? Landlady, please?'

'She ain't talkin',' came the disembodied wheeze of a middle-aged woman, whose daily breakfast was obviously smoked rather than eaten. 'Not to the likes a' you!'

They looked up as a flurry of floor sweepings scattered down.

'This is important, madam,' Seldon called up to the scowling woman.

'Madam! Do I look like a madam to you?' the landlady spat.

'Let Clifford try, Hugh,' Eleanor whispered.

Her butler removed his bowler hat and held up a coin. 'S'only a quickie, dear lady,' he called in a rough accent.

'Right down I'll be!' The window slammed closed.

Eleanor shook her head. 'Your inimitable charm works every time, Clifford.'

'Even if I had charm, I couldn't use it. Nor bribery. I'm a policeman,' Seldon grumbled. 'If only until Monday!'

Desperate to counter that he had too much charm for most women but didn't realise it, she jumped back at the sound of hurrying slippered feet.

The door opened and the landlady leered out at Clifford.

'What can I do you for, sir?'

He wiggled his eyebrows. 'A great many things, likely. But today,' he paused at her girlish titter, 'just let this 'ere lady and gent in for a quick parley with a lodger a' yours.'

She looked Eleanor and Seldon over scornfully. 'None of my lodgers'd take kindly to their sort.'

Clifford rolled the coin down his arm and into her house-coat pocket. 'Still, what'd'ya say?'

'Alright. You can keep me company while they's getting' a mouthful,' the woman wheezed. 'Who they lookin' for?'

Kofi peeped around Clifford. 'I came before in a taxi carriage with a note for him.'

The landlady peered closer at him. 'So ya did, little mite. But that's Droopy you're after. He ain't 'ere.' She folded her arms. 'He ain't gonna be neither.'

'Moved out, missus?' Clifford said.

'Slung out, more like! Waster of the worst kind he was. Always behind with his rent was one thing. But the company he kept would'a made your toes curl.' She looked him up and down with a sly grin. 'There's other things as will do that too, ya know?'

Clifford shot a pleading glance at Eleanor.

'Please tell us the address he moved to?' she said, hiding a smile.

'Even though you ain't our sort, I would if I 'ad it. But I ain't, 'n don't care to neither.' She beckoned Eleanor closer with a yellow-stained finger. 'Tell ya where ya could try, mind.'

'Go on.'

'In the filthy ooze, bottom 'a the river, where he belongs!'

Her wheezy cackle sounded behind the closed door.

Seldon turned away. 'Blast it! Good effort, Kofi and Clifford. But now we've got no idea where to look.'

'Perhaps,' Clifford said thoughtfully. 'He's clearly shorter than ever on funds. Where could he sleep for free without being thrown out?'

'Or discovered?' Eleanor said, slowly. Her eyes widened. She hesitated, then turned to Seldon. 'You know, it'll be the biggest risk. You up for that, Hugh?'

'Of course, but where...' He blinked. 'Eleanor! You wonderful, brilliant creature. You've worked out where he is, yes?'

She nodded. 'Fingers crossed. To the boat!'

Seldon took a deep breath. 'And fast. I might as well be hung for a sheep as a lamb!'

42

Eleanor shivered. The cloying darkness felt horribly like the perfect cover for evil. But not for good. Their every furtive step seemed to echo along the wall of the Gold Coast enclosure, betraying their presence despite the night.

Just as she could hold her breath no more, the archway she'd been praying would arrive, did. She went to peer around it for any sign of life, but was stopped by Seldon's strong fingers holding her back.

Stretching up to cup his ear, she murmured, 'What is it?'

'You said you believed Lady Chadwick's brother would be hiding out in the closed enclosure,' he hissed.

'Yes. Because it's basically been abandoned. And it's completely free to camp in which suits his empty wallet. Plus, he works somewhere here at the exhibition, so knows his way about. So?'

'That enclosure is the next one along.'

'I know. But it dawned en route that we need to avert a potential problem first. Twice bitten and all that.'

Clifford stepped closer. 'Agreed, my lady. This is no time for unwelcome interference.'

'From who?' Seldon hissed.

'Jafaru.'

'Oh, him!' Seldon growled under his breath. 'Then I'm definitely going first.'

Ducking inside the open-air Gold Coast Pavilion, the three of them pressed themselves flat against the high wall, Eleanor in the middle. A chink of light showed in front of them. She could just make out an oil lantern toppled over on the compact dirt near the huddled straw huts.

She frowned. Anyone who occupied those huts during the exhibition wouldn't have left that lamp on its side. It was a fire hazard, just waiting to ignite an inferno that would engulf the huts in a trice.

Beside her, Clifford tapped her wrist in agreement, clearly having read her thoughts. Seldon, too, was scanning the area through squinted eyes and shaking his head to himself.

She nudged them. 'No time to explain now,' she whispered. 'But I have a feeling someone beat us here. Whatever unwelcome surprise we're going to find, it's in one of those huts.'

Approaching the huts from the rear, having quietly righted the lamp, they fanned out, one at each of the first three curtained doors of the five huts. Seldon raised his unlit torch as the signal. As a man, they each clicked theirs on, standing back as they shone them fleetingly through the curtain and then snapped them off again.

From inside Eleanor's hut, she caught a muffled moan. At her urgent beckon, the others were beside her in a single stride. She jerked her thumb at the curtain.

'On three,' Seldon mouthed.

He and Clifford gripped their revolvers. Her heart faltered as the two men who meant the world to her raced inside together. A moment later, she followed them.

'Oh, gracious!' she exclaimed at the unexpected sight of their quarry hunched on his side on the floor, tightly bound hand and foot. A gag around his mouth left just enough room for him to breathe through his nose. As she stepped nearer, he looked up, his amber eyes furious as he struggled against his bindings.

'Good evening, Jafaru,' she said sweetly.

He stiffened at his name.

She nodded. 'Yes. We know who you are.'

'And what you're responsible for,' Seldon said firmly. 'The thefts from this exhibition site.'

Jafaru tried to shake his head, which wasn't very easy given how comprehensively he'd been trussed up.

Eleanor pointed at his gag. 'We have a few questions for you. For which, that will need to be removed.' She sank down to look into his amber-eyed gaze. 'But before that, I'll let you in on a little secret.' She could tell from the way the muscle twitched below his eye, she had his attention. 'The chief inspector here, being a policeman, won't actually shoot you if you make a noise. But my butler,' – she grimaced as Clifford strode back in from checking the last two huts – 'he's just itching to. With or without you trying to give the game away. So, ready to play nice?'

Jafaru nodded.

Once his gag was pulled down, he took several deep breaths.

Eleanor tapped her foot. 'A falling-out between thieves, was it? Your partner double-crossed you and left you trussed up here to be arrested for his crimes and yours?'

Silence was his only reply.

'Or was it someone else?'

Again, silence.

'You're not helping yourself.' Seldon shrugged. 'Not that I care, you understand. I saw you moving stolen goods myself. Gag him again, please, Clifford.'

As Clifford moved to do so, Jafaru's eyes blazed. 'I will not say who did this to me. But I swear they will pay!'

Seldon shook his head. 'No. You will be the only one to pay. You can't escape justice now.'

'Justice!' Jafaru spat. 'You talk to me of stealing and justice! Then I will talk to you of wholesale plundering and centuries of injustice! Who is the true thief? The man who steals another man's food and leaves his family to starve or the one who tries to take back a bone that he and his family might eat?'

Seldon held his gaze. 'And the relevance of that?'

Jafaru's eyes narrowed. 'For hundreds of years, men from countries like yours have stolen everything from mine and left nothing in its place except despair! I never asked to come here. I was sent, without my choice even heard. So I decide I make the best of this and take back as much of the wealth stolen from my country as I can. But it will be pitifully small, for I would need a dozen lifetimes and a thousand of your Empire Exhibitions to even start to even the balance!'

Eleanor shuffled her feet at how uncomfortable she felt. She couldn't refute what he said. For centuries the powers that be had pillaged countries like his.

'Tell us why you hid John Clemthorpe's body,' she said. Whether or not she found herself unexpectedly sympathising with Jafaru, there was still a murderer to catch.

'Who is he?' Jafaru said with unconvincing innocence.

'Alright, we've heard enough,' Seldon growled.

'I agree, Chief Inspector,' Clifford said nonchalantly. 'If he wants to be tried for murder as well as theft, what can you do?'

'I did not kill this Clemthorpe!' Jafaru blurted out.

Eleanor cocked her head. 'Then why did you stuff his body in a barrel?'

Jafaru shrugged as best he could. 'Because a dead man found there would ruin my plan.'

'To return home with what you had stolen, you admit?' Seldon said.

Jafaru shook his head. 'Taken back. By right!' He glared at Eleanor. 'I had the body in the barrel and the footprints in the dirt gone when you come making trouble by shouting about murder!'

'That is something of her ladyship's speciality,' Clifford said drily.

Jafaru laughed curtly and turned his attention back to Eleanor. 'This I learn. Because of you, this policeman is called also.' His eyes flashed to Seldon. 'So again, I think quickly. I go straight to the ambassador and tell him I hid the body to stop the English authorities making more discredit to his country.'

'Thank you for your confession. All of which has been noted and may be used against you in a court of law,' Seldon said matter-of-factly. 'I shan't ask you to incriminate yourself further until you have legal representation. But there's still the outstanding question.'

Eleanor nodded. 'Want to tell us now who left you here completely helpless to take all the blame?'

Jafaru gave only a grunt in response. But she caught his gaze flicking again in the direction of the closed enclosure.

'Back in a jiffy,' Clifford said, deftly re-gagging Jafaru and checking his bindings. 'Don't go anywhere, will you?'

The enclosure where she'd witnessed the murder felt eerier than ever as she slipped in through the rear gate behind Seldon. That it had been unlocked made the three of them nod to each other. She forced herself to focus, shaking off the wish she had time to explain everything she'd worked out to the others. For a long minute, she scanned the inky hulk of the unfinished pavilion, sure of what she was looking for.

At Seldon's questioning tap to her hand, she frowned. He was right. Nothing on the ground floor. Nor the second. She peered harder and swept her gaze over the glassless carcass of the building again. And then she caught it. The faint glow of a lit cigarette.

She pressed her finger to her lips, then beckoned Seldon and Clifford to follow her. Clearing the porch without making a sound was the first hurdle. Even over the wind whistling around the nearest hay bales, each loose plank threatened to creak maliciously.

As she reached the gaping hole where the grandiose front door should have been, she mimed the three of them pouncing like tigers. Then pointed into the darkness in the direction of the glowing cigarette end.

She stepped gingerly over the threshold to pause at what seemed to be the beginnings of a grand entrance hall, given the double-width staircase. Glancing upwards made her gape. The building was even less finished than she'd realised. There was no roof, only a skeleton of wood batons open to the sky.

Ducking out of view from the upper landings in case she was wrong about where the owner of the cigarette was now, she waited for Seldon and Clifford to follow. Before she could move on, she froze as something wet splashed onto her cheek. Visions of the macabre flashed through her mind.

Was that blood, Ellie?

She clapped her hand over her mouth to halt her scream. Then took a deep breath.

It's just the rain-soaked roof beams dripping. Get a grip, Ellie!

As she crept forward, she dared not turn on her torch, which made progress painfully slow. The passageway was too dark to see more than a few feet ahead and the ground was littered with a multitude of building materials. As if tools had been downed and the workers walked out in sudden protest. That, however, told her she was right. The person smoking that cigarette had been here long, or often, enough to move about relatively easily despite the darkness and obstacles.

Further inside the building than felt at all comfortable, she paused for a second, feeling momentarily light-headed from holding her breath. Seldon squeezed her shoulder gently and gestured more insistently that he and Clifford should go first.

Before she could reluctantly nod, her sharp hearing caught it. The fleeting sound of a match striking a flint strip. But not at the furthest end of the building as she had expected, but only yards away. The hint of a blue-green sulphurous flame flared up ahead and died just as quickly. She pointed urgently to where it came from.

Torches held ready but still off, the three of them crept forward in a line.

'Took your time, Jafaru, you lazy cur!'

She froze. The man inside had obviously heard her approaching and thought it his partner.

Which means he definitely hasn't heard Hugh or Clifford, Ellie

Footsteps approached. 'I'm talking to you! And this time—'

As the man stepped into the corridor, Seldon and Clifford grabbed him and slammed him against the wall, winding him.

'And this time,' Eleanor said, shining her torch squarely in his hard-nosed face, 'your partner in crime is indisposed. So we've come in his place.'

Seldon quickly established Lady Chadwick's brother was unarmed. As she opened her mouth to question him, she caught the crunch of rubble as someone else entered the building behind them. She gestured fiercely for them to dart back into the room, hauling their captive with them.

As Seldon handcuffed him, she whispered, 'I'd stay quiet if I were you. That's not Jafaru down there, but someone who wants very much to meet you. And I'm pretty sure you won't want to meet him!'

43

The wind whistled eerily through the abandoned husk of the unfinished exhibition pavilion, making the hairs on Eleanor's neck prickle like thorns. Back pressed to the rough brick wall, she peered through the gloom at the rubble-strewn staircase. Whoever had just entered was now on the next floor.

Let's hope it's who you think it is, Ellie.

'Up there,' she mouthed to Clifford.

With only the faint glow of lights from around the exhibition site filtering through the tile-less roof, she crept up the banisterless staircase, avoiding the missing planks. They glanced at each other at the sound of brick dust crunching underfoot further along the second-floor landing.

Clifford tapped her wrist and mimed going first. She shook her head, gesturing at his service revolver. He leaned in as she cupped his ear. 'We agreed. It must seem the ball isn't in our court. This will all be for nothing unless we get the truth.'

He hesitated, then nodded.

As she reached the top of the stairs, the carcass of the unfinished second floor stretched in front of her; incomplete walls, missing doors and floorboards, with heaps of building materials abandoned along the gloomy corridor.

She strained her eyes in the half-light. Up ahead a shadowy form slipped from one room to another across the hallway. She turned to Clifford and nodded in its direction. He nodded back.

He saw it too, Ellie.

She crept forward, Clifford close behind with his service revolver in his hand. Reaching the opening of the room, she risked a glance inside. A silent silhouette stood a few feet away. She waved Clifford to a halt and walked in alone.

'Not very cosy, is it?'

The figure jerked around, gun raised.

She tutted. 'Don't you think that's caused enough trouble?'

She held her breath. The figure stayed mute. Unmoving. Then, slowly, the gun lowered.

She let out a silent sigh of relief.

Step one, successfully completed.

'Thank you, Lord Chadwick. I'm glad you've finally decided to cooperate.'

He shrugged. 'I confessed to you that I killed Clemthorpe in self-defence in that blasted taxi. Why in the blazes has your committee sent you here to hound me?'

'To stop you making another terrible mistake. You're here looking for your wife's brother. And you've come armed.'

He turned his gun in his hand. 'I'm not after that wretch.'

'We know better.'

'We?'

She jerked her head as Clifford stepped out of the shadows where he'd been covering her.

Lord Chadwick stared at him. 'You too? What the deuce is going on?'

Eleanor held up a finger. 'Let me explain. I'm not a governess, nor a committee spy from Whitehall. And he isn't a book professional. We've come here tonight to further the course of justice. And stop another murder being committed.'

Clifford, whose gun was concealed behind his back, held his hand out for Lord Chadwick's. 'Really, sir, most ungentlemanly of you to waste the lady's time. En route to this enclosure, we paused at the one next door. We were, you see, disturbed by a particularly bothersome person on a previous occasion. A Mr Jafaru.'

Lord Chadwick's face remained impassive, but Eleanor saw a hint of surprise flash across his eyes.

'We found the person,' Clifford continued. 'Tied up like an oven-ready turkey. Really, quite a professional job, if I may say so.'

She nodded. 'We also find him somewhat irksome, so we re-gagged him and left him as he was. For the time being.'

Lord Chadwick's eyes darted between them. For a moment, she thought they were going to have a full dance on their hands. Then the fight went out of him. He let his gun fall into Clifford's outstretched palm.

'Alright. I thought that Jafaru fellow might have seen me shoot Clemthorpe. In self-defence.'

Eleanor noted his fists clench as he said his colleague's name.

She folded her arms. 'Then what are you doing here?'

He flung his hand out. 'Jafaru told me his partner, my wife's reprobate brother, might also have seen what happened. And he was hiding out here.'

'Really? Well, let's ask him then, shall we?'

Lady Chadwick's brother stumbled into the room, gripped tightly by Seldon. Lord Chadwick's mouth fell open.

'Chief Inspector Seldon. Or are you not who you seem to be either?'

Seldon held up his wrist, showing that his captive was handcuffed to him. 'Oh, no, Lord Chadwick. I'm very much who I say I am.'

'You see,' Eleanor said, 'we actually captured this wretch before you arrived. So, go ahead and ask him whatever you want.'

Lord Chadwick shook his head again. 'I've nothing to say to the cur.'

Eleanor's tone hardened. 'I see. Very well, Lord Chadwick, I'll say it for you. You are not here because of what Jafaru said. Or saw. But because of what he *took*. Your wife's necklace. Not from her dressing-table drawer, but from Clemthorpe's dead hand!'

Lord Chadwick swallowed hard. 'You're wrong. I told you I killed Clemthorpe. What more do you want?'

'The truth!'

'Then I'll tell you the truth.' From the far doorway, a woman emerged. 'I killed Clemthorpe!'

For a moment, there was complete silence. Then Lord Chadwick let out a strangled cry.

'Philomena! What are you doing here? Go home. Now! I order you!'

Instead of obeying him, Lady Chadwick walked further into the room.

'I shan't, Reginald. Because there's no point denying the truth anymore.'

'Shut up, woman!' he cried, staring at his wife in horror. 'You don't know what you're saying. Leave now!'

She shook her head calmly. 'It's no good, Reginald. I know precisely what I'm doing. For once, I'm telling the truth. The *real* truth. Because I won't let you be punished for my crime.'

Lord Chadwick spun around to Seldon. 'Listen to me. My wife is not of sound mind!'

Eleanor shook her head. 'She is of perfectly sound mind. As

well you know. If you were a killer, why didn't you kill Jafaru, rather than tie him up? Or me when I appeared in this room unarmed? Or even Clifford, when he appeared apparently equally unarmed? Why did you give up your gun? You're no more a killer than I am.'

Lord Chadwick struck the wall next to him with his fist. 'You're wrong! I wanted to kill Clemthorpe! I came here that day to kill him, the dog!'

The rage in his voice made her recoil. Then she jumped as Seldon barked, 'Enough, Lord Chadwick! Clifford, would you?'

Eleanor's butler cleared the gap in a single stride and grasped Lord Chadwick's arm.

She pointed outside. 'Lord Chadwick, our reconstruction out there in that very enclosure where Clemthorpe died showed that the bullet which killed him could only have come from a *third* gun. And the only reason you would lie and take the blame was because you were protecting the person who pulled the trigger.' She turned and pointed at Lady Chadwick. 'I guessed your wife. And her confession a moment ago proved me right. Your wife whom you still obviously love more than liberty, or life itself, despite outward appearances.'

Tears rolled down Lady Chadwick's cheeks. 'And I still love you too, Reginald. I always have. That's... that's why I killed Clemthorpe.'

Eleanor took the handkerchief Clifford held out and passed it to Lady Chadwick. 'This is your one chance to tell the final, final truth.'

She nodded. Eleanor held up her hand. 'But I need someone to witness what you are saying for Chief Inspector Seldon's benefit. And mine.' She turned to the door once more. 'You can come in now.'

'Tateham!' Lord Chadwick and his wife exclaimed as the tall footman strode in and stood between Seldon and Clifford, the three of them cutting a formidable trio.

'What the blazes is my footman doing here?' Lord Chadwick demanded.

'He's not,' Eleanor said, 'your footman.'

Lord Chadwick snorted. 'More deceits! There can't be any more left in this charade, can there?'

'Only that we are the "committee" I mentioned.' She gestured between herself, Clifford, and Seldon.

'Good grief! Then who is Tateham? Really?'

'National Security Office,' Tateham said in a clipped Eton tone. 'And I'd rather not reveal my real name in front of everyone here, so you can carry on calling me Tateham. Some time ago, certain evidence was discovered that pointed to you, Lord Chadwick, as the source of long-running leaks in the department. I was planted as a mole in Chadwick House to spy on you.'

'How the devil did you know he was a spy?' Lord Chadwick asked Eleanor incredulously.

'That is on a need-to-know basis only,' she said, having no intention of divulging that it had been Lord X's final snippet of information to her.

And Clifford's observation, Ellie, that Tateham really didn't know how to be a footman.

Lord Chadwick stared at his wife, then at Tateham. 'Clemthorpe was actually the source of those leaks. He falsified the evidence so I appeared the guilty party. I know, because he told me so, just before he planned to shoot me in the enclosure.' His face reddened. 'He was trying to destroy me so he could have... my wife. He was obsessed with her. The swine strove to discredit me first. Then planned to kill me and claim I lured him there on the pretext that I had information on who was responsible for those blasted leaks.'

'And then also claim that he'd shot you in self-defence,' Eleanor added.

He nodded. 'But I played into his despicable hands.'

'Lord Chadwick,' she said sharply. 'You need to confess why you lured Clemthorpe into that fatal enclosure. You still haven't admitted the whole truth. And time's running out to convince Chief Inspector Seldon. He's your only hope.'

Lord Chadwick looked pleadingly at his wife. She smiled lovingly back. 'Tell them, Reginald. The truth. And nothing but. It's all we have left.'

44

Lord Chadwick slowly turned to Eleanor and Seldon. He swallowed hard. 'That despicable fiend, Clemthorpe, tried to... to force himself on my wife!' He gazed at her. 'You can't imagine how sick I felt when Withers telephoned to tell me. How fretful I was for you, darling.' He swallowed hard again. 'I called Clemthorpe and told him he either met me or I'd hunt him down. He said he'd meet me at the closed enclosure at the Empire Exhibition. I went home and collected my gun.' He shook his head. 'I was in too much blind rage to think straight. All I knew was that no one was going to get away with forcing themselves on my wife!'

'Good man!' Seldon blurted out. Clifford nodded vigorously.

Lady Chadwick stepped forward. 'But that's why I followed you, Reginald!'

Eleanor held up a hand. 'Go back a step, Lady Chadwick. To the evening of your ill-fated soirée. And this time, the truth of what really happened. It's your last chance, too, because I know so much more than you imagine.'

She nodded. Taking a deep breath, she spoke quietly.

'While Reginald was away on his business trip I arranged that fateful get-together and Clemthorpe showed up uninvited, not my brother. I didn't want to turn Clemthorpe away because I feared he'd make a scene. So I let him stay.' She laughed nervously. 'The only true part of the whole sorry tale I told you, Lady Swift, is that the clasp of my necklace *was* scratching my neck. I went to my room to take it off. Only Clemthorpe followed me there without my realising. He'd been drinking heavily. As my husband said, he was obsessed with... having me whether I wanted his advances or not! Then... then he grabbed me from behind and tried to... to' – she buried her face in her hands – 'to avail himself of me.'

Eleanor's stomach twisted at the sickening thought.

Lord Chadwick groaned. 'I'm so sorry I wasn't there, darling. I'll never forgive myself.'

She looked up and smiled through her tears. 'None of this was your doing. I fought back. As best I could. In the tussle, I felt the necklace clasp break and the necklace fall to the floor.'

So the broken part of the clasp Grace found in the room was from the pearl necklace, Ellie. Just as the part I found in the exhibition centre was.

'And then,' Lady Chadwick continued, swallowing hard, 'Tateham charged through the door and grappled Clemthorpe out. Thank heavens!'

Tateham nodded to Eleanor and Seldon. 'I can vouch for that. And that Withers then rang Lord Chadwick. In fact, I overheard him telling Lord Chadwick *he* threw Clemthorpe out!'

'Thank you,' Seldon said. 'Now, Lady Chadwick, take us back to the necklace, please.'

Eleanor raised her hand. 'Lady Chadwick. You told me Grace had lied about not seeing you place the necklace in your dresser drawer? Did you place it there or not?'

Lady Chadwick shook her head. 'No. Grace was telling

the truth. As I was trying to look presentable, and composed enough to face my guests downstairs, I noticed the necklace wasn't on the floor where it must have fallen. Somehow, in the scuffle of Tateham throwing him out, Clemthorpe must have taken it. Well, next morning I found Reginald in his study when he was supposed to still be away on business. When I asked him what he was doing there, he just slammed his desk drawer shut and stormed out. So, I went into breakfast and thanked Tateham for rescuing me the night before. That's when he told me Withers had called my husband and reported not just the soirée, but th... that awful incident in my room.'

Tateham nodded. 'I felt sorry for her. We're not entirely heartless in National Security.'

'Thank goodness!' Lady Chadwick said fervently. 'Because that made me realise why Reginald had come home. I broke into his desk and found his gun was missing. I ran to Tateham and asked if he knew where my husband had gone.'

Tateham nodded. 'And I did, having popped out to ask the driver to keep a handle on Lord Chadwick's movements, while he was still in his study. He'd gone to the Empire Exhibition.'

'So,' Lady Chadwick continued, 'I raced up to my room and slipped my own gun into my handbag. Th—'

'No!' Lord Chadwick shouted. He turned to Seldon. 'I've already confessed to killing Clemthorpe. You've an open and shut case. You have no reason to listen to the ramblings of a hysterical woman!'

Seldon ignored him. 'Where did you obtain a gun, Lady Chadwick? And why?'

'I bought it in a pawn shop, on the spur of the moment. When my husband was away on business, I used to steal out of the house late in the evening and I was nervous.' She stared at Eleanor. 'I told you the truth about what happened then as well, to my shame.'

Eleanor nodded to Seldon. 'I think Lord Chadwick deserves to hear that from his wife without an audience.'

Seldon shrugged. 'Very well. So, Lady Chadwick, you were saying?'

'I was terrified. All I could think of was finding my husband before...' She wrung her hands. 'I searched everywhere at the exhibition, and ironically, only saw you, Lady Swift. But I hurried on before you saw me. Then, when I'd given up all hope, I spotted Reginald and followed him.'

Lord Chadwick gave his wife a pleading look, but she smiled at him lovingly and shook her head. 'He entered one of the pavilion areas. It had a sign saying it was closed to the public for some reason. I stole around the fence until I found a small gate which was unlocked. I crept in and then spotted Reginald and Clemthorpe. I didn't know what to do, so I hid. Behind a barrel.'

Seldon glanced at Eleanor and Clifford. 'That tallies with our information. Go on.'

Lady Chadwick hesitated. 'Clemthorpe... had a gun pointing at Reginald. He was holding something in his other hand. I recognised it as my necklace. He was taunting him, telling him he was going to have me over... over Reginald's dead body!'

Eleanor couldn't contain herself any longer. 'Lady Chadwick, as you seem finally to be telling us the whole story, perhaps you could enlighten me? If you knew Clemthorpe had taken your necklace and your husband knew it too, why, truly, did you tell me one of your servants had taken it and ask me to recover it?'

Lady Chadwick held out her hands. 'I panicked. I didn't know Reginald had seen me in the enclosure. What I *did* know was that he'd seen Clemthorpe with my necklace. I... I was afraid he'd think I gave it to him and the... the incident in my bedroom wasn't what it looked like.'

Seldon held up his hand as Lord Chadwick opened his mouth. 'Let her finish!'

She turned back to Eleanor. 'I had to think of a reason why Clemthorpe would have it, if Reginald confronted me. And all I could think of was to say I noticed it missing and believed one of the servants had taken it. A few items have disappeared before. And now it was clear that the servant must have been paid by Clemthorpe to take the necklace. When I saw you at the exhibition again, I thought it would make my story so much more believable to Reginald if I had asked you, Lady Swift, to help recover the necklace quietly, without involving the police.'

Eleanor nodded. 'That kind of makes sense.'

Seldon nodded sombrely. 'Except, like others before you, Lady Chadwick, you underestimated Lady Swift. But back to your account, please. Clemthorpe had a gun pointing at Lord Chadwick and was taunting him, yes?'

Lady Chadwick shivered. 'Yes. I saw Clemthorpe raise his gun, so I fired.' Her hand flew to her mouth. 'But I didn't mean to kill him. Just scare him so Reginald would have time to escape. I couldn't have hit him if I'd wanted to. I've never fired a gun before. Only a hot-air balloon flew over as I pulled the trigger, mere feet off the top of the building. And... Clemthorpe fell like a sack of stones.' She broke off into sobs.

Lord Chadwick hung his head. 'I can't save my wife from a lecherous fiend, nor from the innocent crime of her trying to save me. What kind of a failed husband am I?'

'One with his side of the story to finish telling truthfully. Now,' Seldon said firmly.

Lord Chadwick exhaled deeply. 'Alright. Clemthorpe pulled his gun first, yes. The snake told me he was going to have my wife and that she already loved him.' Lord Chadwick's eyes blazed. 'He even held up her necklace and taunted me that she forgot it last time she... she stayed over in his house while I was away on business.'

Lady Chadwick's eyes flared. 'I never went near his place! Or encouraged him in any way! He took it the night of my party so he could further his plan to drive us apart so I... I could be his.'

'I know that, now,' Lord Chadwick said ardently. 'And I never doubted he was lying then. But I must finish my part of the story, my darling.' He turned back to Seldon. 'Just after Clemthorpe pulled his gun, I reached for mine, but there was an almighty roar above. Instinctively I looked up to see, as Philomena said, a runaway hot-air balloon of all things! As I spun back to Clemthorpe, he collapsed before I could shoot.'

'And then?' Seldon said.

'I ran. All I knew was that someone had shot him. And were likely after me, too.'

'He did run. I watched him,' Lady Chadwick confirmed. 'I stumbled over to Clemthorpe... to his body to grab the necklace. But then an African man dashed in through the back gate, so I raced to escape out of the front.'

'Which is when Lord Chadwick saw you?' Eleanor said.

Lord Chadwick shook his head. 'Not quite. It hit me before I was a hundred yards out of the gates that the necklace would link the murder back to me. But as I turned to return, someone ran out and disappeared.'

'Your wife?' Seldon said.

He sighed. 'Yes. To my horror. I realised in that hideous moment who had shot Clemthorpe. Which made getting the necklace all the more imperative. Now it would lead back to my wife being there! So I returned to the enclosure. But the gates had already been locked. It took me a little while, but I found another way in. By then, however, that bounder from Africa was already stuffing Clemthorpe's body in a barrel, and the necklace was nowhere to be seen.'

'Jafaru? The one you've bound and gagged?' Clifford said.

'Yes. Him. He must have locked the gates, too. Then I heard someone scrambling up the outside wall and I ran.'

'Ah,' Eleanor said. 'That was probably me. And what was your plan? You didn't have the necklace. It could still be traced to your wife?'

Lord Chadwick swallowed hard. 'I hurried back to my business trip before my absence was noticed. But that was all I could think of, day and night. I couldn't ask anyone at my office to trace that Jafaru person. And it was too dangerous to do it myself. Then, after I'd returned home and found Withers dead, I realised I was running out of time. Or my beautiful wife was! So, I bribed a few exhibition staff this morning. Later I found Jafaru and loosened his tongue. He told me he gave you' – he pointed to Lady Chadwick's brother – 'the necklace to fence because you two are colleagues in crime.'

Lady Chadwick's brother opened his mouth for the first time. 'Business partners, Reggie old man,' he said mockingly. 'A man like me is always in demand, you see. Unlike your sort. Sitting in a government office all day, doing nothing but judging everyone except yourself! You're in a bigger mess here than I ever have been.'

Lord Chadwick's fists clenched and then unclenched. He sighed. 'What do I care? I did it all for my wife.' He looked at Seldon. 'You know it all now, Chief Inspector. But I have something to say to Philomena.'

Seldon caught Eleanor's look and nodded. Clifford released Lord Chadwick's arm. They ran to each other, and he cupped her face. 'Darling, can you find it in you to forgive the way I behaved? The... controlling behaviour? My temper flares? Having Withers spy on you? I just... feared I'd lose you. From the day we married. You're so beautiful. And perfect. And I'm nothing but a' – he slapped his disfigured cheek – 'ugly, scarred fool who didn't know how to tell you I love you. You're the only person who has ever made me feel whole. Which is why I've forever lived in dread of you leaving me.'

'I would never leave you!' Lady Chadwick breathed. 'I love you.' She kissed his pitted cheek tenderly. 'Darling, I don't know how this is going to end. But just know, I would do it all again.'

Seldon cleared his throat. 'Lady Chadwick.' He looked her in the eye. 'I am arresting you for the murder of John Clemthorpe. And' – he swung his gaze to her husband – 'Lord Chadwick, I am arresting you for attempting to pervert the course of justice.'

They both turned to Eleanor.

She took a deep breath. 'I'm sorry. But how this ends is out of my hands.'

45

A coil of pearly white smoke spiralled up from behind the wooden screen.

'What's done is done,' Lord X's luxuriant voice filtered over to Eleanor.

She nodded as she sank slowly into the wingback chair. 'Yes, it's over. That's one thing, at least.'

Even though she had done all she could, she'd been filled with a sense of unease since stepping into the Hogarth room.

The carved oak panel in the screen opened an inch more.

'Young woman, the part you played in solving the matter was nothing short of remarkable. Though I expected nothing less from Henley's niece.'

Her heart swelled. 'Thank you, Lord X. But I can't accept all the credit. The two most brave and dedicated men alive played an equal part.'

'So I understand. Which takes us neatly to business. I made you a promise, young woman, that if you proved incontrovertibly who killed Clemthorpe, I would see they stood trial and justice would be served.'

She ran her hands down her arms. 'Yes, you did. But, frankly, I'm almost wishing you hadn't.'

A quiet chuckle followed a plume of cigar smoke through the opening in the screen. 'Never one to mince words, I see. But I think you have jumped the gun. Before I can send the accused, both of them, to trial and have sentence passed, there is one thing that puzzles me. Chief Inspector Seldon arrested Lady Chadwick for the murder of Clemthorpe. And her husband, Lord Chadwick, for perverting the course of justice. But which of them killed the butler, Withers?'

'Neither of them.'

'Then who did?'

'He did, Lord X.'

'Who the deuce is "he" when he's at home?'

'Withers.'

A snort emanated from behind the screen. 'You're telling me Withers killed himself?'

She nodded. 'In essence, yes. You see, he reported Lady Chadwick to her husband when she took an envelope of household money intended for a tradesman. She mentioned to me how furious Withers was at the time, which seemed a trifle odd, as it wasn't his money. Then I found a similar envelope on Withers' body. At first I thought it was money for taking backhanders, as Tateham suggested. Then I believed Withers was blackmailing Clemthorpe's killer, who in turn killed him.'

'In which case,' Lord X interjected impatiently, 'Lady Chadwick killed Withers!'

'Except she didn't. I finally realised the reason Withers had been so angry when Lady Chadwick took that first envelope was because he'd planned for it to be *his* money. For some time, he had been taking household money intended for tradesmen and then doing the jobs himself. Or pretending they'd been done. Fixing the faulty electrics on the dumb waiter was one such job. Pocketing the money, he crept down in the early hours the day his body was found to try and fix it. Only, instead, he electrocuted himself. Which is why there were no easily visible marks on the body and it seemed as if he'd had a heart attack. The coroner later found two small burn marks that both he and I had missed on our cursory examinations.'

Lord X chuckled. 'Then you are quite right, young lady. The fool literally did kill himself and justice has been dispensed in this instance!' There was silence for a moment. Then he spoke again. 'The trial of Lady Chadwick has taken place.'

'Gracious! Already?' she said falteringly.

'Yes. Just now. I am the only judge and jury here. And this old bulldog hasn't completely forgotten what true loyalty and love stand for. From the report it is clear. Lady Chadwick acted purely to save her husband's life. Nothing more. She also never intended to kill Clemthorpe. Only to distract him sufficiently so her husband could escape. To my mind, there can never be a crime in that. Turns out Clemthorpe was the worst kind of wretch, a despicable disgrace to Whitehall and mankind.'

'You mean—'

'Yes. She is acquitted. But best hear the rest, young woman. Lord Chadwick also needs to be tried. He went to that enclosure with the intention of shooting Clemthorpe in honour and defence of his wife.' The sound of his chair arm being slapped was followed by an exclamation. 'Good man!'

She smiled. 'That's exactly what my fiancé said.'

'Also,' Lord X continued, 'as you proved, he didn't shoot anyone. So there is no crime to answer for there. However, he did not follow departmental procedure and report his actions to his superiors. Which is categorically not how Whitehall works! They would have dealt with it according to protocol and limited any damage. Thus, whilst he has been cleared of any suspicion of leaking classified information, he cannot go undisciplined.'

She grimaced. 'I can see that. Am I allowed to ask his fate?'

'Yes. He will be assigned to a significantly junior post to his present one. In a less cosmopolitan part of the country, let's say. Just as soon as he can clear his domestic affairs here in London.'

She breathed a sigh of relief for both the Chadwicks. 'I think that's fair.'

Lord X chuckled. 'I'm glad you approve. Which leaves the matter of your fiancé. One Chief Inspector Seldon.'

Her stomach clenched. 'And?'

The silence stretched out. Finally Lord X chuckled again. 'I'm sorry, but I couldn't resist a little of the theatrical. Don't worry. He will be exonerated. And unreservedly so. With a well-deserved commendation for dedication to duty.'

She let out the breath she'd been holding. 'I can't thank you enough, Lord X.'

'No need. Just paying off an old debt. Now, let's see, who's left?'

'Lady Chadwick's brother?'

He snorted loudly. 'Repellent toad, by all accounts. He has been charged with organising thefts from the exhibition. It won't be a long jail sentence, unfortunately, as his crime sheet is as pathetic as the man he must be to bully his sister for money!'

She cleared her throat, trying to keep her voice level. 'And Jafaru. What of him?'

'He is being sent home to the Gold Coast. But with no charges pressed, for diplomatic reasons.'

She felt her heart sinking. 'But he had a ward here, Kofi. What's going to happen to him?'

'Exactly what must. He has to stay with his guardian.'

'No!' She leaped up.

'Young woman, sit!' Lord X said smoothly. 'One of my colleagues had a... frank discussion with this Jafaru character who made it clear he had no desire to continue to be the boy's guardian. Therefore his guardianship was removed from him without question by the ambassador.'

'But... oh gracious, then Kofi's going where?'

'That, you will have to ask his new guardian, who the ambassador appointed.' Lord X chuckled. 'But only once the boy had agreed too. Even at his young age, he has a mind of his own! Anyway, you'd best hurry. He is signing the papers through that door over there.'

She rushed to the door and opened it to find a room which held a desk with just two sheafs of printed paper set neatly side by side. And her butler.

'Tell me we aren't too late?' she pleaded.

'We are not, my lady.' Clifford took his favourite fountain pen from his pocket. 'There is a matter of permission to be asked first, however.'

She frowned. 'Whose?'

'Yours.' He held up one of the sheets of paper.

Her eyes filled with tears at the name printed at the bottom. 'Clifford! You? You're going to be Kofi's guardian?'

'With your permission, my lady, yes. The ambassador and Lord X interviewed Master Kofi while you were with the chief inspector this morning. He, very politely but firmly, put them right on a number of matters. The upshot being *his* decision won out. He will finish his schooling here in England. Hence, he needs a guardian in this country.'

'And you couldn't step forward fast enough. Oh, you daftie,' she croaked. 'You don't need my permission. I couldn't...' She thought her chest would burst. 'I couldn't be happier for him. Or you.' She tapped his pen. 'Sign it.' She turned to let him do so in peace.

He whipped a handkerchief from his pocket. 'Say you'll stay while I do, my lady,' he whispered, his eyes swimming. 'Please?'

46

The sun was shining over the Empire Exhibition as though everything was right in the world. It certainly was in Eleanor's. And clearly Kofi and Clifford's as they enthused together in the Palace of Engineering over the intricacies of some incomprehensible contraption. Gladstone was in his element, eagerly catching the drips of ice cream from passing children. While Tomkins, snug in his kitty kit bag held securely over Clifford's shoulder, shot his paw out to biff every passing fur stole.

At the sound of raucous giggling, Clifford turned and arched a suspicious brow. 'The ladies? They are supposed to be at Henley Hall, my lady.'

Eleanor smiled impishly. 'Ah! You see, I've been too busy to squabble properly with you with all this unpleasantness going on. So I intend to make up for lost time. For which I shall need some adjudicators. I telephoned yesterday to ask them to catch the train back up.'

His eyes twinkled. 'I see. Then let the games begin!' He turned to his new charge. 'Master Kofi, if I might apologise in advance for the disgraceful pantomime which is about to ensue.'

Kofi grinned and joined him and Eleanor as they crept up

behind the four women. They were standing around a stocky blond man who was holding up a variety of rubber machine belts.

'That big thick one would give one the fearful spanking of a lifetime if it came loose, I imagine?' Mrs Trotman said cheekily.

'Sure would, madam,' the man replied in a broad Australian accent. 'But you'd have to be sure to loosen all the tensioning bolts to get the best of it.'

The four women fell into a fit of giggles. Then jumped in horror at Clifford's firm cough. Quickly forming a smart line, they curtseyed to Eleanor.

''Tis the biggest surprise you wanted to see us aprons afore you needed to, m'lady,' Mrs Trotman said.

Clifford's lips twitched. 'Quite incomprehensible, one might say.'

Eleanor tutted. 'Not at all! In truth, I've missed you all dreadfully. Clifford tried to fill in for your absence, but fell short in one very important area.'

He rolled his eyes. 'My sincere apologies, my lady. However, this afternoon alone I'm sure the ladies will more than make up for my failing to devour mounds of cake and other sundry baked goods.'

Mrs Butters beamed at Kofi. 'And this delightful young man must be the one we've been dying to meet since we heard the wonderful news.'

Eleanor caught Clifford's chest swell. 'Yes, ladies. This is Master Kofi. Although I am not sure he could quite match her ladyship in the cake-consuming stakes.'

She watched with affection as the people who had quietly become her surrogate family welcomed their latest addition into their fold with open arms.

'And her ladyship told me all about your recipes, young man,' Eleanor's cook said. 'Too tasty for words, I hear. You must teach me.'

Kofi nodded. 'I would love to, Mrs Trotman. But I will only be able to in the holidays.' He turned to Clifford and hugged his jacket sleeve. 'I am grateful for your great kindness. Now I can work hard at my lessons in boarding school!' He clapped his hands. 'Always I have dreamed of this since leaving my home.'

She smiled and then held up a finger. 'Excuse me, ladies, but I just need one moment with Clifford.'

Having taken her butler to one side, she looked pleadingly at him. 'Please don't fight me on this, Clifford.'

'On what, my lady?'

'The money from the annuity Uncle Byron left for improvements to Henley Hall.'

He cocked his head. 'We have already agreed on the upgrades and purchases it is to be used for. And there is still plenty remaining.'

She nodded. 'I know. And I know sending Kofi to boarding school will eat up all your savings and your few shrewd investments. Please let me use the rest of the money to help fund the young boy's education?'

He frowned. 'My lady, that was never my intention.'

'I know that, categorically. But I also know you never got to go to school, which is perhaps why you have such an appetite for learning now. So, I understand how much you wish to help Kofi have what you never did. And Uncle Byron would have done exactly the same and you can't deny it.'

He bowed. 'I, and Master Kofi, will be eternally in your debt.'

She shook her head with an affectionate smile. 'I don't think so. You've already saved my life on more than one occasion. We're a team, remember?'

'Would I had chance to forget.' He winked.

This reminded her of something else she needed to bring up.

'On a side note, Clifford. I've been meaning to take you to

task for hoodwinking me into scoring an extremely belated point for Uncle Byron. By – don't deny it – getting me to visit one of the most powerful men in England, dressed as a showgirl?'

'Tell me she didn't!' a rich, deep voice said behind her.

She spun around. 'Hugh!'

Clifford held his hands up. 'I can explain, Chief Inspector.' He hesitated. 'Actually, no I can't. It was disgraceful behaviour on my part. But not quite as disgraceful as her ladyship disrobing in an enclosed taxi carriage with her butler present.'

'It's not true, Hugh,' she said. 'I didn't. But not through lack of trying.'

Seldon threw his head back and roared with laughter.

She slipped her arm through his. 'Now, enough nonsense. Congratulations on being in charge once again at the Empire Exhibition. And for your commendation. But I thought you'd be far too busy now to be hobnobbing with the likes of us?'

'I am. But I had a tip-off that handcuffs were going to be needed here very soon for an unorthodox titled lady. However, I thought you might prefer this sort of wrist cuff. Made to order in the Chinese pavilion.' He slid a pretty patterned box into her hand. As she opened it, he tugged awkwardly on his chestnut curls. 'It's only—'

'Perfect!' she breathed, running her finger over the delicate bracelet made of miniature jade hearts. 'Oh, Hugh, thank you.'

As he gently did up the clasp, she kissed him on the cheek.

'Miss Smith, Miss Smith!' two excited youthful voices called as they bounced over on their toes to jump up and down in front of her.

'Octavia and Hubert!' She knelt down and gave them a hug. 'What a wonderful treat to see you. I'd like you to meet my other fabulous new friend, Kofi.'

She straightened up to find Lord Chadwick standing there with his arm around his wife's waist. 'Good morning, Lady

Swift, if I may call you that now? I, we, owe you our sincerest gratitude.'

'We're going to live in the countryside!' Hubert cried, dragging his sister and Kofi back over with him. 'With a real garden. For building a den. And playing ball.'

Octavia tucked her dress up under her as she knelt to cuddle Gladstone. 'And we're going to have a dog. And go to school. With other children!'

Lord Chadwick nodded. 'Yes. The house in Park Lane is for sale. We're leaving and taking the remaining staff with us. I was... genuinely moved when they agreed to come. We'll see if we can make their duties a little easier in the new place. But I'm glad we're going. Truly.'

'We are all glad.' Lady Chadwick slid her arm tighter into his.

Lord Chadwick coloured. 'The, you know, demotion is well deserved, I admit. But I'm delighted. A less pressurised post means I can spend more time with my true love.'

'Ah, your books,' Eleanor said.

'No. I'm making arrangements to sell the entire collection. I meant my wife. And my children.'

Lady Chadwick cupped Eleanor's hands. 'How can we ever repay you?'

'Actually' – Eleanor's gaze slid to Clifford, who nodded, his eyes bright – 'you could let my butler finish cataloguing your books before they are sold?'

Lord Chadwick turned to him. 'With your very evident expert knowledge, I would be honoured if you wish to. However, please know, it is not with any ulterior motive that it will help me sell them.'

'Now, my only regret,' Eleanor said, holding out a hand out to each of the Chadwick children, 'is I didn't have the chance to find our buried treasure.'

'That's alright,' they chorused.

'Because it's here somewhere!' Hubert shouted, spinning in excitement.

'And we're halfway through solving the riddles to find it with Mother and Father,' Octavia added.

Eleanor looked up in confusion.

Lady Chadwick blushed. 'We found your schoolroom notebook. And sat up all night to, you know...'

Lord Chadwick pulled out a hand-drawn map of the exhibition site. On either side, it had a series of riddles. He rubbed his temple. 'Probably the most taxing challenge I've ever faced!'

'Happy treasure hunting. All of you,' Eleanor said, delighting in the children's farewell hug.

'And happy ever after they go,' Clifford murmured as they walked away.

Eleanor nodded. 'Enough case-solving forever, I say. Lady-like pursuits only from now on. So, Clifford, Hugh, ladies, Kofi, how about the finest lunch on offer here? Surely you're famished like me?'

A scream split the air.

'The elephants! They're rampaging again!'

'Oh stuff and such,' she said above a peal of trumpeting and general panic. 'They're just letting off a little steam again.'

'Steaming's the word! Right through the cafeteria any minute now, lady!' a worsted-capped man shouted as he ran past.

'The cafeteria? But what about lunch!' Eleanor cried. 'This is serious! I need to stop them immediately!' She broke into a run.

'What happened to ladylike?' Seldon said with a wry smile.

Clifford snapped his pocket watch closed as he broke into a longer stride beside Seldon as they chased after her, his other hand taken by Kofi's. 'It lasted a full half minute, Chief Inspector. I believe we can chalk that up as a record!'

A LETTER FROM VERITY

Dear reader,

I want to say a huge thank you for choosing to read *Murder in Mayfair*. If you did enjoy it, and want to keep up to date with all my latest releases, just sign up at the following link. Your email address will never be shared and you can unsubscribe at any time.

www.bookouture.com/verity-bright

I hope you loved *Murder in Mayfair* and if you did I would be very grateful if you could write a review. I'd love to hear what you think, and it makes such a difference helping new readers to discover one of my books for the first time.

I love hearing from my readers – you can get in touch on my Facebook page, through Twitter, Goodreads or my website.

Thanks to the wonderful team at Bookouture whose enthusiasm to make sure each and every book in the Lady Swift series is as good as it can be has not flagged, even though this is book eighteen!

Verity

facebook.com/veritybrightauthor

x.com/BrightVerity

HISTORICAL NOTES

BRITISH EMPIRE EXHIBITION

The British Empire Exhibition was the most ambitious event of its kind since the Great Exhibition of 1851. Set in Wembley over a massive 216 acres, it was opened by King George V and Queen Mary in April 1924, attracting over twenty-five million visitors. Held when the British Empire was at its peak, fifty-six of the fifty-eight territories attended. Seldon was correct when he said at the time Britain was challenged at home by America and Europe undermining its pre-eminent trade position. And abroad, by anti-colonialism in the territories themselves. And Eleanor's criticism of the way some countries were portrayed was also a hot topic of debate at the time.

BUTTER SCULPTURE

Eleanor's ladies weren't telling lies. There really was a full-sized diorama of Prince Edward, Prince of Wales made entirely of butter. And not just of him. It also included his horse, outbuildings, trees and a chicken coop, replete with chickens.

ELEPHANTS

There were actually several elephants at the Empire Exhibition. Three of them had an altercation in the main lake. One, called Simla, took particular umbrage at another elephant called Saucy. Neither could be restrained and eventually they left the lake of their own accord and munched their way through the exhibition's floral displays. Neither actually made it to the numerous eating places, so Eleanor's panic would have been unfounded in reality.

NEVER-STOP RAILWAY

This amazing attraction really did live up to its name. Travelling around part of the vast exhibition site, it slowed at stations as Clifford rightly said, but never stopped. Originally, it was invented to be used widely in London's underground train system, but unfortunately never caught on.

THE GOLD COAST

Since 1956, the West African territory formerly known as the Gold Coast has been known as Ghana. Before it finally managed to gain independence in that year (the first British African colony to do so), it was run by the British from 1874, and before that the Dutch and Danes also had a stake. The Portuguese had been there since the fifteenth century, originally naming it 'Mina', meaning 'mine', due to the amount of gold found there. Vast amounts were removed from the country over time. Jafaru was right about that.

HOT-AIR BALLOON RIDES

This is one of the few details I made up. Hot-air balloons were sometimes at these types of events, but I couldn't find any records of them at the Empire Exhibition. However, I needed an interesting way for Eleanor to witness a murder that she had never done before. The hot-air balloon allowed her to witness a murder from above. Maybe in the next book, I could find a way for her to witness a murder from below?

ELECTRIC CARRIAGES

The carriage that Lady Chadwick lends to Eleanor (and Kofi stows away in) is only rented due to the Chadwicks' straitened circumstances. Most upper-class families would have owned their own which would have been kept in the stable block. Unlike the Chadwicks, they would also have employed a full-time driver. Those who couldn't afford to own or rent had to rely on London's increasing number of taxicabs. An interesting historical fact about turn of the century taxicabs in London is that there was actually a fleet of electric cabs run by the Bersey company. The first electric vehicle was invented around 1835 and an electric vehicle held the world speed record at the turn of the century as well.

FIRST EDITIONS

Collecting books has been a hobby since books existed. But no one did it quite like the Victorians and Edwardians, who were obsessive collectors of almost anything. John Ferriar, a physician, used the phrase 'bibliomania' in a poem to a friend he claimed was bitten by this obsession. As Clifford mentions, Charles Nodier also published a book on the subject in 1832, while Thomas Frognall Dibdin, a Victorian cleric, published a book in 1842 entitled *Bibliomania, or Book Madness: A Bibliographical Romance*. Dibdin, who considered it a medical condition, broke the obsession into different categories, one being first editions. A pity Lord Chadwick never read it.

ACKNOWLEDGEMENTS

Thanks to our editor Kelsie for her stellar editing and support and to the rest of the Bookouture Team for their part in making *Murder in Mayfair* so much fun to work on.

PUBLISHING TEAM

Turning a manuscript into a book requires the efforts of many people. The publishing team at Bookouture would like to acknowledge everyone who contributed to this publication.

Audio
Alba Proko
Sinead O'Connor
Melissa Tran

Commercial
Lauren Morrissette
Hannah Richmond
Imogen Allport

Cover design
Tash Webber

Data and analysis
Mark Alder
Mohamed Bussuri

Editorial
Kelsie Marsden
Sinead O'Connor

Printed in Great Britain
by Amazon

47519093R00199